The Water Babes

The Water Babes

Norman Whitney

Copyright © 2016 Norman Whitney

The moral right of the author has been asserted.

Apart from any fair dealing for the purposes of research or private study, or criticism or review, as permitted under the Copyright, Designs and Patents Act 1988, this publication may only be reproduced, stored or transmitted, in any form or by any means, with the prior permission in writing of the publishers, or in the case of reprographic reproduction in accordance with the terms of licences issued by the Copyright Licensing Agency. Enquiries concerning reproduction outside those terms should be sent to the publishers.

This is a work of fiction. Names, characters, businesses, places, events and incidents are either the products of the author's imagination or used in a fictitious manner. Any resemblance to actual persons, living or dead, or actual events is purely coincidental.

Matador
9 Priory Business Park,
Wistow Road, Kibworth Beauchamp,
Leicestershire. LE8 0RX
Tel: 0116 279 2299
Email: books@troubador.co.uk
Web: www.troubador.co.uk/matador
Twitter: @matadorbooks

ISBN 978 1785890 925

British Library Cataloguing in Publication Data.
A catalogue record for this book is available from the British Library.

Printed and bound in the UK by TJ International, Padstow, Cornwall
Typeset in 11pt Aldine401 BT by Troubador Publishing Ltd, Leicester, UK

Matador is an imprint of Troubador Publishing Ltd

For Nigel West,
simply the best!

Prologue

DIANA

I arrived in London from Melbourne in 2004. That was six years ago. I was already twenty-eight by then. No husband, no partner, no children. Not good, at least as far as my parents were concerned.

My main ambition when I came to the UK was to try and get a reasonable job. I was naive about the bureaucracy that such ambition involved.

Also, I wanted to prove to myself – and to my parents – that I was as capable of leading as successful a life as my younger brother. I felt, or rather *knew*, that Mark was their favourite.

I'm of average intelligence. At school, I was only mildly successful at the academic subjects such as English, maths, the sciences, history, geography and the rest. But I was always very good at sport, especially swimming. I was destined to study for an 'easy' degree in sports administration, at a local college in Melbourne. Actually I did quite well. Better than expected, if I may say so.

My brother, Mark, on the other hand is highly intelligent. He was brilliant in every subject at school, though unlike me, not very sporty; OK, but nothing special. While I went to an unknown small college, he went to a posh, private university in Melbourne. Apparently it's known all over the world. Mark did spectacularly well. His degree was in politics and economics. He was clearly destined for what our dad proudly called 'big things'.

Dad was dead right. In 2003, the year before I arrived in London, Mark got a job as an international representative for various Australian tourist boards. I never understood exactly what he did, but it was important, and well paid. His first posting was in London. He was only twenty-five, and on some fast-track programme or other. In other words, Mark was two years younger than me, but already making waves. I was just the swimmer in the family, splashing around.

My parents never believed that before Mark's posting I had already started thinking of coming to London myself. But it's quite true (I'm good at keeping secrets, but I don't tell lies!). Job adverts had just started appearing on the Internet. Before I knew it, I had applied for the post of assistant manager of a health club in London. It was ideal for me. They replied, saying that they would love to employ me, but had I checked about work permits, residence requirements and all that sort of stuff?

Of course I hadn't. But I knew a man who could. Mark! For me, the timing of his arrival in London was perfect because he knew all about permits, visas and so on. And he had friends in our diplomatic service here.

Despite both of us knowing that he was the favourite child, we have always got on well with each other. No problem. Well, perhaps a bit of rivalry now and then, but nothing too drastic. Anyway, he helped me with all the boring paperwork: visas, work permits and all that. Soon, it was all sorted. How I would have coped without Mark's help, I'm not sure. It turned out that the job I had originally applied for in London was mine, if I still wanted it. Did I ever!

Mark met me at Heathrow, and even found me a room in a shared flat. It was in Earls Court, where all young Aussies seem to congregate. In those first few days, Mark showed me some of the sights, taught me how to use the underground, and generally looked after me brilliantly.

But I didn't like my room, or the flat. Or my flatmates. Their lives seemed to revolve around little more than beer and rugby (the boys), or beer and sex (the girls). I call them boys and girls, because although some were in the earlier twenties, they treated me almost as if I were from another planet. Not only did they begin to treat me as a sort of mother confessor, they also began to rely on me to wash the dishes, tidy up, and clean the place. Bugger that! So after about a month I told Mark that if he didn't mind, I'd rather live somewhere else. Eventually he found me a large but rather expensive bedsit in NW6, West Hampstead, not far from his place.

The first two years were fine. Before I came, I assumed that people in London might be rather formal and the city itself well ordered, tidy and clean. I was wrong on all counts. Everyone I met was informal, casual. People started calling me 'Di' rather than Diana. To be honest, I prefer Diana. And although the centre of London with all the famous buildings is well kept, large parts of it are a bit dirty and scruffy. Not like Melbourne, anyway.

I soon made one or two friends, largely through my job. I even met one or two through a singles' club. I did all the usual tourist things, especially the ones that were free. I also went to some shows and restaurants; but not many, because evenings out in London can be unbelievably expensive.

I found it increasingly difficult to establish and maintain any sort of social network here. I went to one or two of Mark's parties, but the people there were never really my type. Anyway, in 2007 he was posted to Thailand. As I've said, I preferred not to associate too much with the Australian crowd in London. Apart from the fact that they seemed to get younger and younger, they were constantly on the move, forever coming and going.

As for boyfriends, I began to think that all the good-looking, available men, especially English men, were either married or gay, or in some cases, both. So no matter how hard I tried, Mr Right (or even Mr Not-Quite-Right-But-Would-Do-For-Now) never came along.

I even began to doubt that I was attractive. I know that at five-foot eleven, that's one-metre eighty in metric, I'm too tall for a lot of men. So I stopped wearing heels. But I've got good legs, am not overweight, and have a reasonable figure. I admit that my swimmer's shoulders are a bit broad. But my brown eyes and long auburn hair had often done the trick back home in Melbourne. But not here in London.

I think that most men here consider that Aussie women are just sporty, and not much else. They think of us as no more than fair game – loose even! Endless boring, dirty jokes about going 'down under' really get me down. Ha ha bloody ha. I've heard them all so many times before. Why do so many British men want to keep their relationships with women on a jokey, matey level, with no thought of any sort of commitment?

I suppose that in my more romantic moments, I secretly want something more. The problem is, I've never really known what 'something more' might mean. For me, I don't think that women's lib, or feminism, are particularly helpful. But good luck to those women who do think that. It's true that when I was in college, the idea of being liberated from men, I mean sexually, emotionally, even financially (especially the last), all sounded fine. In theory. But you try that in London. On a low wage like mine. It doesn't get you very far at all. No siree.

Two years ago, in 2008, my mind began to clear. It was on my thirty-second birthday. I was out with some friends, acquaintances really, and I suppose I got a little drunk. I found myself announcing what I really wanted. I told everyone that what I really needed from a man was first of all, a decent sex life. Well, in the early days anyway. Everyone applauded. But I told them that at the same time, what I *really* wanted from a man was financial security. And why not? This was met with raucous sarcasm, mostly from the men, and howls of derision, mostly from the women. I didn't care what other people felt. It was simply the truth. At least as I saw it.

In my dreams. The reality was that most of the people I knew, male and female, had relatively ordinary jobs which were not well paid. We were all trying to make a living in a city where the cost of travel and accommodation is high, and where the cost of decent accommodation is beyond the reach of people like me. Flat sharing with other women and even men is all very well. But sharing with people who are practically strangers was never, and never will be, my first choice. I'm over thirty for God's sake.

In London, a lot of couples I know and meet get together and part not just for emotional reasons. Often, even couples sharing expenses simply cannot *afford* to live together! That's the plain unvarnished truth. That's what happened to my longest London relationship. We met in June last year, 2009. I really liked the guy. I thought we could make a go of it. But given that he was a freelance editor and proofreader, and an aspiring but unpublished novelist, I was well aware that he was not likely to come into any decent money any time soon. But together, we tried hard to survive, pooling our resources (I have to admit that he was great sex).

However, after ten months of living with me, he suddenly announced that his best option would be to return to Manchester and live with his parents, thus saving more of what little money he had. I had to accept that the relationship was going nowhere. I was beginning to panic. So much for my original ambition to prove to myself and to my parents that I could be like my brother!

Then earlier this year I met another bloke. On the rebound I suppose. He really was tall, dark and handsome. A bit younger than me (who isn't these days?) and gainfully employed, or so he said; apparently some sort of junior hospital doctor. That certainly explained his odd working hours.

I was so bloody stupid. I'm still so angry that I can hardly bear to think about what happened. I got home one Friday after work, about two months ago, fully expecting to go out to dinner with him. But the bastard had gone! Just like that. Without warning. No texts, no phone calls, nothing. It was as if he'd never existed. His mobile was dead. The two local hospitals had never heard of him. I was devastated.

So devastated in fact that for three days I didn't realise that he had also stolen my credit card, some cash, and some diamond earrings my dad gave me for my eighteenth. They were not particularly valuable, but I loved those diamonds. Of course I reported everything to the police. But nothing much happened. I got a crime reference number from them, but never heard anything more.

In the three months that we were together, Mr Tall-Dark-and-Handsome regularly went with me to the local cash machine. Using the excuse of wanting to protect me, he must have taken note of my pin number. The bank refunded me the five-hundred pounds he took from my account. But I was furious. Not simply with him, but also with myself. Apparently it's quite common for people to blame themselves for someone else's crime. I was embarrassed, ashamed, even though I had done nothing wrong; except to be so gullible, so incredibly *naive*. 'Well, Diana,' I said to myself, 'never again'.

After more or less marking time for five or six years in London, I had to do something fairly drastic. I was not completely broke, but nearly. I couldn't afford my own place, and didn't fancy sharing.

I'm already thirty-four. But I'm certainly not ready to go back to Melbourne just yet. They'll think I'm a failure. I couldn't bear that.

I never expected my luck to turn. But it did. Three weeks ago. I'll never forget it. It was the first day of June 2010. Someone told me about this job. It sounded just great. It had my name written all over it!

1. The day ahead

07:30
ONE FRIDAY IN MAY, 2014.

Diana, or Di as she is generally known, first saw the advert almost exactly four years ago. It was for a job at the Greenhill Community Sports Centre, in a resort on England's south coast. The post held three major attractions for her. First, it was out of London, which meant she could live more cheaply. Second, it involved promotion, which meant an increase in salary. And third – miracle of miracles – it came with a free flat, which meant she could save on rent! A wealthy benefactor had specified that the local authority could sell the flat at any time of its choosing, so long as any funds were for the benefit of community sports activities. Until that time, the flat was specifically to be used by a person 'devoted to encouraging sport in the local community'. It was not difficult for Di to persuade the interviewing committee that she was just the person they were looking for.

Her first impressions of the town were largely favourable. One area was said to contain the third or fourth most expensive real estate in the world. Di found that hard to believe, but apparently it was true. But her 'clients' as her employers insisted they be called, were not likely to come from there, where most residents presumably had their own private pools.

She knew that the town was renowned principally for its

large, relatively well off retired population. Hence the many expensive houses and impressive blocks of flats. Di learned that there was also a sizable Jewish community here, larger but not dissimilar from the one back home in Melbourne.

She also saw that there were lots of hotels, B&B places, and residential homes for the elderly. A university and several colleges helped give a bit of balance to the age profile of the citizens, as did the many English language schools for foreign students. When she arrived, the only crass note was a large concrete structure, a hugely unpopular building housing an IMAX cinema, which hardly anybody went to. It was a monstrosity, plonked down almost on the beach, in front of the pier. It completely blocked a great view of the sea.

Given the large student population, there was no shortage of clubs and bars, especially in the centre of the town. But, particularly on weekends, the town centre was no place for the faint-hearted. Not even for a confident woman who was more than capable of taking care of herself. Being rather older than most students, she felt somewhat out of place in the clubs.

This suited Di well. Especially because, in her new environment, she immediately decided to live in what she called a 'man-free zone'. No boyfriends. No time wasters. And definitely no money time wasters.

She was popular and sociable, though not exactly gregarious. She contented herself with a small circle of friends, with whom there had been the occasional dinner party, restaurant meal, excursion to local landmarks, beauty spots, and so on. There were no really close, intimate friends, but that was just fine.

Di's contract did not prevent her from giving private lessons. She was constantly surprised at how much money yummy mummies would pay for their daughters and sons to have private swimming lessons or tennis lessons. And she gave private keep -it lessons to men and women who were too shy or embarrassed to attend public classes. So from the start, Di's financial situation improved dramatically.

She threw herself into her job. One of her first decisions was to appoint an assistant, Luke. They got on well, at least in the beginning. He was a great asset, and loved working with kids. She was well aware that he was gay, which he did not hide. But she had no fears: he was no pederast, certainly. As he explained, he had had more checks than the Bank of England, and more screenings and tests than Joan Crawford! He was co-operative and conscientious.

But Luke could be difficult sometimes. And he had a wicked tongue. He had been especially hard to handle in the last two or three months, after it became general knowledge that she intended to leave England. She imagined that Luke hoped to replace her. But everyone knew that her post had not been advertised. Privately, she also thought that he was not really qualified for the post.

Luke helped Di to start a mums and toddlers swimming group, hockey matches, girls' football teams, keep-fit for seniors, and in the last two years, courses in aquarobics. The latest aquarobics group called themselves 'The Water Babes'. When their course began, it included two men. But perhaps overwhelmed by the majority of females, the men soon stopped coming.

The women in the class were fun, but Di wished they would try harder. Di felt that they were not really interested in keeping fit. It was just a morning out for them. She sympathised: she knew many of the adults who attended the centre were lonely and isolated, and just needed a bit of company. But she began to yearn for the dedication and stamina that many Australians, of all shapes and sizes, brought to their exercise regimes.

It was about a year ago, in the middle of 2013, that Di began to feel bored with her job.

'I think I've done all I can here,' she confided in a friend.

'The dreaded cuts don't help. I used to have a reasonable budget, but not now. The endless routine of attempting to save money, scheduling, planning meetings, doing interviews, and filling out those awful time sheets is beginning to wear me down. Suppose all good things must end some time.'

Indeed, Di knew every nook and cranny of the centre. She had worked every committee time and time again. She had exhausted all the administrative twists and turns that sports management could throw up. She had savoured the little triumphs and survived the greatest disasters that the work could deliver.

'You've done a great job here Di. Perhaps it's time to move on?,' said her friend.

'Yes. And it isn't as if I want to live here forever!'

It was that thought that eventually nudged Di forward. There was nothing wrong with the town itself. But Di began to feel that the resort was an uncomfortable mixture of quite different communities. She rather liked the buzz that a genuinely multicultural population could create. But here, the population was by no means a mixture of equals.

Di was never an expert on social class, or injustice. But she was humane enough to realise that the town had a largely white community serviced by other, largely non-white communities. The hospitality and catering trades in particular had attracted small groups of ethnic minorities, mostly Chinese, Italian, Indian, Thai, Filipino, Greek, Vietnamese, Turkish, and recently, Polish.

But Di began to feel that other than providing a variety of exotic eating places, food shops, massage parlours, nail salons, hospital staff and the like, these service communities seemed hardly to exist as real people. Their purpose was clearly to feed and to sustain the town's main industries, leisure and tourism. And of course the National Health Service. No matter how hard Di might have tried, she could not attach herself to any of these communities. And since there were hardly any Australians here, she began to feel that she was in a minority community of one.

She could admit that the town was better than most in the UK. Also – a real improvement – the IMAX horror on the seafront had been pulled down at last, only a few years after it was built. No one missed it. Di liked the new open space. There was a great sea view now. 'But don't be stupid Diana,' she said to herself. 'A sea view isn't enough to keep me here forever!'

She learned that like most places in the UK, the town had its underbelly. Beyond the train station, adjacent to the main resort, she was shocked to find so much visible deprivation, drunkenness and drug addiction. She hardly ever ventured there, and then only with friends, and always in the daylight hours.

Over the last few months, things began to fall into place, like a jigsaw putting itself together.

After Mark had spent some years travelling the world and being promoted several times, he was again posted to London. By now he had a beautiful Thai wife and two children whom everyone, including Di, adored. She knew that she might never have the career success or perhaps the offspring to compare with those of her younger brother. But, she consoled herself. You never know! Two months ago, a plan began to form in her mind.

She last emailed her best friend in Melbourne about six weeks ago. The original intention of her email was to tell her friend about a local scandal which affected Di's own job prospects. But even as she was writing the email, another large piece of the jigsaw – what she called her 'big decision' – suddenly dropped into place.

Dear B!

Have made the big decision! Have decided to come home. Pls don't say anything to Mum and Dad. I want it to be a surprise.

The last straw was the surf reef fiasco. I told you some time ago that the council was building an artificial reef here. Built, as it happens, by some outfit in NZ. The council's idea was to attract a younger crowd etc to the resort. Would have been an ideal opportunity for me to use my surfing experience, or even get a job managing a surf shop. I could even have started my own business of some kind. But it's all come to nothing. The reef is a big fat flop, and the firm that built it has gone bust I think. What a waste! Am really disappointed. Pissed off actually. So are a lot of other people here. What a bummer.

But my time here (4 years!) has not been wasted. Far from it. Have got some money together. Hooray. Have enjoyed the job, and gained a lot of experience. But can't see myself living here forever…no prospects. M'bourne is calling me!

Love, Diana x

PS. Guess what! The boyfriend situation has picked up! More later. When I see you?!?!

Her email was a little disingenuous. Diana had always been careful not to give away too many details about her private life. She usually kept most of the important details of her private life secret, even from her best friend B, who was a dreadful gossip. So she had only alluded to the most important factor in her decision to go home: the boyfriend. For the past few months, she had finally felt confident enough to relax her rule about living in a man-free zone. She had only known her new partner for about six months. But after she had established that he was not after her savings (by now quite considerable), their affair had developed well.

At last, she felt she could return to Melbourne with a modest display of wealth. Her parents should be pleased, especially with the news about her new man. Yes, she was now ready to leave England. All she had to do now was to get through the day ahead, her final working day at the Greenhill Community Sports Centre.

07:45
A TUMBLE.

Although the flight home was only two days away, Di still had a fair amount of packing to do. At the moment, she was searching for her album of photos she had taken during her time in London. These days, all her photos were digital. But until four years ago she had carefully stuck earlier photos in the red album. She had looked everywhere for it. It was not at home, in the flat. It was here somewhere. She clearly remembered bringing the album to her office, to show her colleagues.

'Where the hell has it got to?' she said to herself. 'Perhaps up there, on the shelf above my filing cabinet?' The shelf was stuffed with boxes of files about old committee meetings, notes on job applications, endless time sheets and so on. She decided to take a look.

This was not as easy as it might sound. First, she had to position the rickety office stool carefully on her desk. Then she had to climb on to the desk. Finally, she mounted the stool. She steadied herself. She held on to the wall with her left hand, and began searching through the messily arranged dusty boxes and papers with her right hand. She could just about see. And there it was! She reached awkwardly for it, and managed to grasp it with her right hand.

But before she could begin her descent, someone burst into the office through the door behind her. Di felt herself jump out of her skin. She turned round suddenly as a leg of the stool finally gave way. She tumbled awkwardly off her perch, her left shoulder hitting the desk. She tried to break her fall by holding on to her desk with her left hand. But her hand slipped further down to her chair, which just seemed to roll away from her. She finally landed on the floor, on her backside. But still clutching her album of London memories in her right hand.

It was not a graceful movement, to say the least. Humiliation and embarrassment – fortunately greater than any actual physical injury – seeped through her. Irritated with herself, she looked up. A large Mickey Mouse mask was leering down at her.

07:55
The face behind the mask.

'Dear, oh dear' said the face behind the mask. 'Now that wasn't very ladylike, was it! Are you OK down there?'

'Hell, you could have killed me! You could at least have knocked before you came in.' Di was struggling to regain her composure, while Mickey Mouse continued with his fatuous grin.

'Well, what do you think?' said the voice behind the mask, having first established that no physical harm had come to Di. He ignored the comment about having entered the office without knocking. He did not usually knock on the door. So why should he have knocked today? After all, it was his office as well as hers.

'What do I think of what?'

'Of my new outfit of course! The latest addition to Auntie Lucy's wardrobe of costumes for her glittering career as the star of the kiddie pool. And soon to be in charge of children's entertainment. Specialisms, playing the guitar, singing cute kiddie songs, and dressing up in stupid costumes.'

'Well you're right there. That one's a bit dated. A lot of kids today don't have a clue about Mickey Mouse. It doesn't mean anything to them. You need to be Spiderman or Batman.'

Luke removed the mask. 'Thank you, dearest Diana. You are always so supportive and encouraging. What would I do without you?' He walked over to his small desk. He was not in the least put out.

Luke busied himself by carefully storing his Mickey Mouse mask under his tidy desk. Di, her dignity fully restored, continued clearing the mess around her own.

There followed an abbreviated version of their now customary spat about the office being for two of them, and not just for one. Luke had grown tired of complaining about his manager's untidiness and disorder. He accused her of colonizing the space for herself, littered as it usually was with her newspapers, unread magazines, partially eaten sandwiches, old keys, files, outstanding parking fines, and an ancient cassette player, formerly used as the pool's very poor sound system. All this was not counting the detritus from several handbags and purses, including various pills and potions that Luke imagined had to do with feminine hygiene. Some of the items made him shudder with distaste.

Needless to say, Luke's portion of the office was by comparison not only rather smaller, but also a model of order and efficiency. He in his turn was accused of being somewhat obsessive about his surroundings.

'This office is still just full of your crap. Even on your last day! I hope you're going to clear things up a bit before you finally leave.'

Di threw her arm mock theatrically around the small office, as if to encompass a massive space. She attempted to mimic what she called Lucy-speak. 'Never mind, Lucy. From tomorrow, all this crap as you call it, will be yours, just yours. You will be king, or rather queen of all you survey.'

Di's attempt at emulating Luke's camp streak misfired. 'Can't wait,' he replied, in all seriousness. 'I shall be bringing in all the cleaning materials and special defumigating equipment known to man. Meanwhile, I'll go and collect today's time sheets.' He then duly swept out of the office.

They had not always been so severe with each other. The first notes of tension between Di and Luke had appeared about a year ago. This coincided with the start of Di's feeling that the sheer routine of a job well done was getting her down.

Luke had started work at the pool soon after Di had arrived on the south coast. Indeed, he was her chosen candidate for the post of assistant and lifeguard. She had encouraged him to climb what they both called the watery ladder of success. At first, they got on very well. They were both cheerful, outgoing, and conscientious. In Di's first two years, they had socialised now and again, and enjoyed each other's company and that of some mutual friends.

But from Luke's point of view, Di had recently developed a tendency to be overly officious towards all and sundry. Nerves probably, he thought. She had not always been so. On the contrary, she had been a good boss. In the past few months, however, she had been a stranger to the virtues of civility and good humour, believing that her rank alone would be sufficient to carry the day in any discussion, argument or decision making process, especially those of involving the lower ranks of the pool's pecking order. She had lost her grip on how to understand and to capitalise on what Luke melodramatically called "the ever shifting waves of pool politics".

Luke soon spotted the signs of her fading enthusiasm for her work. He concluded that not just her career but also her life prospects in this town were, notwithstanding her talents, limited.

He was well aware that her imminent departure could mean promotion for himself. He suspected that Di considered him unqualified for her more senior post. *But Di doesn't know everything, does she!* he thought.

08:05
DISCUSSING THE EVENING AHEAD.

Luke duly returned to the office with the day's time sheets. He saw that Di's desk was a little clearer and tidier. He also noticed an iPad, something that he had not seen Di use before.

'So what's the iPad for?'

'Oh, they take great photos.'

'Don't tell me. You're going to take some final sentimental souvenir photos!'

'Yes, I'm going to take one or two of my last Water Babes class. It'll be great to look at them later, when I get home.'

Luke was slightly taken aback by Di's sudden fondness for the people in her class. Recently, she had begun to be less and less enthusiastic about her work, and her dedication to her job had waned. In that time, the air around her had crackled with tension. The process of deciding what to do with her life and when to do it was clearly taking its toll. She became uncharacteristically irritable. Clients, especially those in adult classes, sensed her anxiety.

'By the way, I hope you remember that you're lifeguarding for me this morning?'

'Of course. For your swan song. Wouldn't miss it for the world, sweetie.'

Luke spotted next to the iPad an invitation card which he recognised. He decided to tease Di about it. Without a shred of embarrassment, he walked over to her desk and picked it up.

'Oh? A *billet doux,* methinks!'

'Hey, give me that. It's personal!'

'But Diana, darling. Of course it's personal. That's what makes it so interesting!' He read aloud:

'Farewell party for Di
And last day of the 'Water Babes'.
Friday 7.30pm.
Mrs C's house. 4, Glendale Avenue.'

Luke was at his most infuriating. 'Aha. We have a mystery. I wonder who Mrs C is?' he said, knowingly. 'Your secret lesbian lover? From Bonnie Scotland? From Liverpool? Or from some romantic Welsh valley?' He gave a poor, unfunny attempt at the appropriate accents. 'And Glendale Avenue? Such a smart address! My, my. We are going up in the world.'

'You know damn well who she is. It's that nice Pakistani lady. She and her daughter have invited me and the group to their house. And just stop it with the lesbian stuff. It's boring.'

'Oh, fear not, Diana. Your secret is safe with me. My lips, for once, are sealed. Lucy's mouth is well and truly closed.'

Di tried her best to reply in kind. She tried to use her Lucy-speak. 'Only until the next cock comes along.'

'Jealousy will get you nowhere, my dear. So. There's to be an aquatic hen party this evening. All girls together!' From the wall above Di's desk, Luke took down an old picture of The Studlanders, a group of local bodybuilders who hired themselves out for such occasions. 'I wonder if Mrs C has booked this lot of freaks for your entertainment?'

His suggestion was duly rubbished.

Unwilling to let go, he continued. 'Anyway. I'm sorry to be the bearer of bad news. But I happen to know that there will be at least one cock at the hen party this evening.'

'What on earth does that mean?'

'Because, my dear,' announced Luke expansively, ' *moi* is invited too! So the only floor show this evening will be me. Yours truly, Lucy!' He threw his arms into the air, as if posing for a fashion photoshoot.

'Oh. Hell, that's all we need. If you're the only cock there, then we girls have very *little* indeed to worry about, and with very *little* to amuse us.' She tried to make the most of that word 'little'. 'And even if you're really stupid and turn up in drag, none of us would find you at all funny.'

As it happened, drag of any kind held no attraction for Luke. At six feet one inch, broad shouldered and with a lean, muscled swimmer's build, he could pass for an alpha male whenever he wanted, especially if he deepened his voice. It was only when he chose to turn on the campery and lighten his voice that he became in any sense obvious.

Luke removed his wedding ring and put it into a small box. 'Time to prepare for the morning show, sweetie. Off with your jewellery. You know the rules.'

'You know very well I don't wear jewellery. I've only got my whistle.'

'Well, lucky you. And I've heard that you certainly know how to blow.'

'Ha bloody ha. Now bugger off. Open the gym and get ready for the class.'

'Yes, sir! But before I go, a word to the wise. It's about the party this evening.'

'What about it?'

'Mrs C. I agree that she's a very nice person. But she isn't from Pakistan. She's from India. Mumbai I think.'

'So?'

'Sooooooo, before anyone starts making any off-colour remarks about there being no pork chops or whatever tonight, they should think twice. In fact, Mrs C and her family may not even be Muslim. They may be Sikhs. Or Hindus. In which case there'll probably be no beef on the menu either. Just think Diana. If they are Hindu, the only cow there this evening could be you.'

'Well, since I'm not in the habit of making rude remarks in anyone's house, we should be ok. Sometimes you'll say anything for the sake of a cheap joke.'

Unprepared for Luke's patronising little lecture about religious and dietary etiquette, however ill or well informed, Di was secretly glad of the information. She began to feel that she should have known this evening's host Mrs C a little better.

'As you say, time to get on,' said Luke. 'Actually, we're not exactly flooded out with customers for the gym this morning. Jane, that spotty-faced girl who lives round the corner is waiting. And of course the muscle Mary from Macedonia, or Bosnia, or wherever he's from is here too. When I arrived, he was already outside, sitting astride his big new Harley, looking *tho* butch in hith leatherth.' Luke did his best impression of a lisping Balkan bodybuilder on a motorbike. 'He'll be champing at the bit I expect.' Luke switched his impression to that of a snorting horse.

'Don't be ridiculous. Anyway, some might think that a body builder would be just your type.'

Luke grimaced. He found the overly muscled type particularly unattractive, and Di knew it. 'But then I suppose he's not long enough in the tooth for you I would imagine.'

Di delivered her last remark with as much calculated venom as she could muster. It was difficult for her, because she was not naturally a spiteful person. On top of which, she had no particular prejudices about the age gap between Luke and his older civil partner Ted. But she was thoroughly fed up with Luke's gratuitous insults, teasing, and lame jokes. Her remark aimed to wound, or at least to put a temporary stop to his incessant bitchery. In this she had succeeded. Luke could have responded with any number of Luke-isms. But caught on the backfoot a little, he held his fire, and said nothing.

'Anyway, about the party,' he said. 'I'm hoping for tears all round tonight. *Mucho mucho lachrymoso.*'

They both knew that Di's final day would be an occasion for only modified grief. After all, the current Water Babes had known Di for only a few weeks. They had not seen her at her best. The group respected Di and liked her. But unlike previous groups, who knew Di in her less anxious days, they did not fawn over her. The people at the party would be polite, and would say that they were sorry to see her go. But as Luke well knew, tears would not be flowing, except perhaps in one or two cases. In fact, Luke suspected that it was only because the last day of this Water Babes course coincided with the last final days of Di's time in the UK, that there would have been a farewell party at all.

As instructed, Luke set off to open the gym. He opened the office door quietly. He then closed it even more nosily than he had intended.

08:15
SQUALLS AND STORMS.

The spats between Luke and Di were mere squalls. He had weathered far bigger storms.

Like the storm created by his mother some fifteen years ago when , accidentally, she discovered his cache of love letters in the back bedroom of their little terraced house. To her horror, the letters were from a man. There was a photo. It was a man Luke's father vaguely knew. Luke was cornered. So in a sense, he did not so much come out. He was forced out.

At one level of course, Luke's mother was right to storm. In 2000 her son was then just fifteen. Well below the then legal age of consent, which was eighteen, and still below the age of consent when later that year it was lowered to sixteen.

His mum's concern for his situation was nothing compared to her concern for her own. Where had she gone wrong? Was it her fault? Had her husband spent too much time away from home, in the army? What would the neighbours say, if they knew? These questions and the imagined answers were her main preoccupation, rather than any feelings her son might be experiencing.

Luke's father, who now worked for the local refuse department, was not so distressed as his wife. For, unlike her, to whom the revelation had allegedly come as a complete surprise, he had worked out that his son was probably gay. He was disappointed, but neither shocked nor disgusted. He loved his son deeply, and his only wish was to protect him from public exposure.

As Luke remembered it, and explained to his partner Ted: 'Dad was certainly angry. But he was pissed off not so much with me, but with the other guy. He worked for the council, like Dad. He was married. With three kids, can you believe! I think that what really shocked my Dad was that this other bloke was just a year older than him.

'Not that Dad actually blamed only the man for what had happened. Bless. I think for some time he must have suspected that he had sired a queer. He's always fancied himself as a man of the world. Said he knew the signs. I don't really know what happened. But I think that Dad made sure the bloke left town. Thank God there was no public fuss. Dad would have hated that. I still love him to bits. Am so relieved that you get on well with him, even if Mum's distant.'

Luke withstood the storm well. He was not going to be cowed by his mother, who even suggested he went to a psychiatrist "to be cured". He disabused her of any desire he might want to change into a "normal" person. He knew in his bones that such a change was anyway impossible. He brushed off his mother's concerns and tantrums as selfish, outdated, self-serving, and self-deceiving. He couldn't believe that she had been so stupid as not to notice anything. To his father, on the other hand, Luke was forever grateful.

Not academically successful at school, Luke excelled in sport, particularly in local junior swimming competitions. Somewhat mistakenly, he thought that his burgeoning physique, his good looks and his engaging personality were more than adequate compensation for a fist full of poor school leaving results, except in English language.

Luke and his classmates benefitted from the English lessons taught by a nearly retired teacher, Mr Jagger. Inevitably, Mr Jagger's nickname was Mick. His was an unfashionable approach. He believed in correct spelling, the parts of speech, well-turned sentences, thoughtfully constructed paragraphs, and essay planning. And in reading Shakespeare, Austen, and Dickens as well as Harper Lee. He encouraged creativity, but not at any cost.

His younger colleagues, themselves poor spellers and devotees of new-think spontaneity, were perplexed by Mick's charm and by his popularity with generations of pupils. They adored him. Many, including Luke, lived to be grateful for his practical guidance on the construction of well-honed letters of application. Luke's facility with written English was to stand him in good stead some years later.

Even at the age of thirteen, Luke had already developed a thick skin and an inner pride. These allowed him not to feel guilty of any moral weakness, or to feel in any way ashamed of his nature. He had known that he was different since he was eight years old! 'This is after all the start of the twenty-first century!' he told his mother when the storm exploded. She was not consoled.

He already knew that the great British public had long accepted that there were comedians, TV fashion gurus, and TV stars who were gay. Some of them achieved almost National Treasure status. And he realised too that the public harboured, sheltered and even respected gay ladies' hairdressers, gay middle-aged bachelors devoted to their mothers, and amusing gay men generally said to be light on their feet.

But neither homosexual national treasures nor homosexual stereotypes were part of Luke's teenage world. On the contrary, his was a secretive world of furtive meetings with his parents' plumber, a farmer who came to town once a month, a well-thought-of local solicitor, an unemployed drifter, a junior hospital doctor, a Baptist minister, and a local Tory councillor (a weekly arrangement, that one). The list was long and varied.

Not for such men the free and easy world of gay clubs, pubs and discos. These men were not pederasts or abusers. They met where they could: for example in the fast dwindling numbers of gents' toilets, and in the well-known cruising areas around town. Those who met Luke invariably liked him, and got caught up in his web. They were temporarily excited by his youthfulness, his athleticism, and his eagerness to please.

'The worst thing was school,' Luke explained to Ted. 'Especially the boys. A few real morons. Some of them had their suspicions of course. They were jealous of my popularity with the girls. And with all my successes in sport, especially swimming. They mocked me, calling me all the usual names like faggot, queer, cock sucker, bum boy.'

But Luke did not care what anyone said. Or at least he claimed not to care. But deep down, he minded, a lot. On many a night he cried himself to sleep.

But for the world at large, he developed coping strategies. Even at that early age he began to develop the art of the witty, even cruel put down. In later years he called this his "bitchometer". He learned to turn it on and off at the flick of a switch. One minute he was a perfectly normal person, and the next (with the help of a higher pitch to his voice) a raging queen. It was as useful a defence mechanism as any.

'God, it wasn't as if any of the boys at school had anything to fear! If only they knew. Never the slightest bit interested in boys of my own age. Always preferred the company of men in their thirties and forties. Or older even. Odd how that upsets some people. Even the queens around here. I have learned the hard way that even gays have their own prejudices. Fuck them. So what if I have a daddy complex! Get over it.'

So much for days past. Luke sailed on, weathering whatever squalls and storms came his way. Right now, he needed to get on with the day ahead.

2. Preparing for the Last Lesson

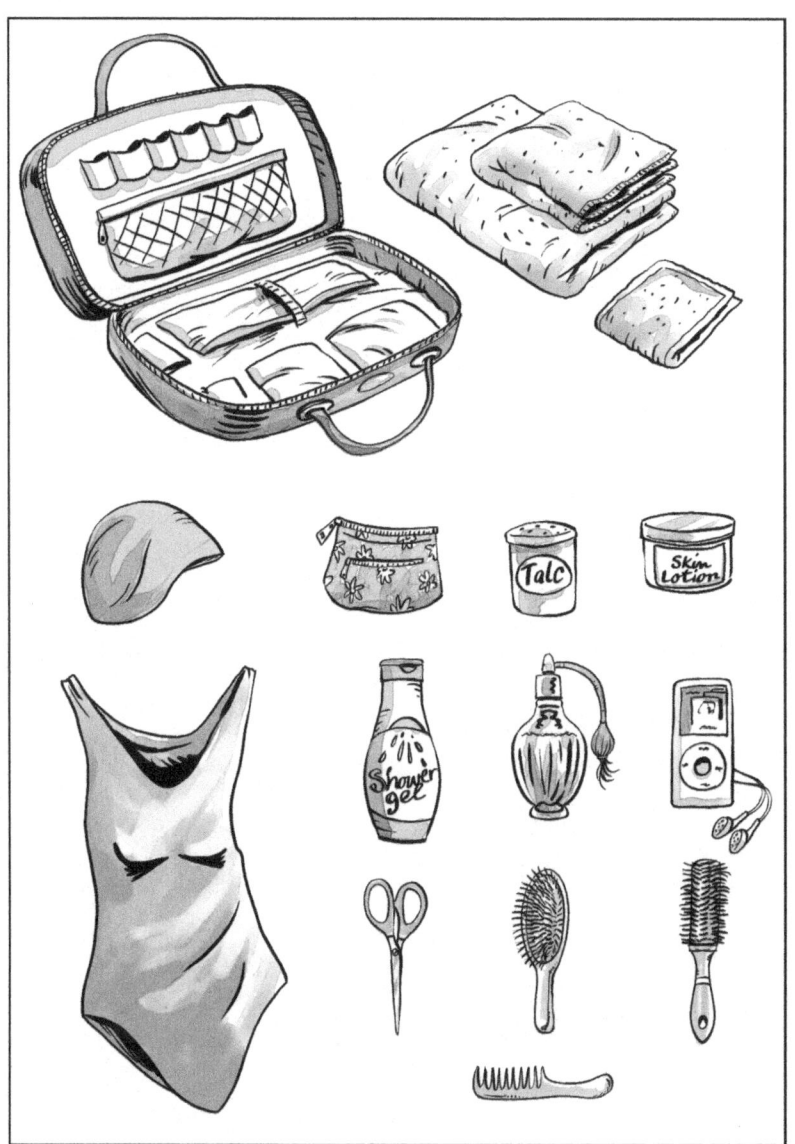

08.20
LYNNE SETS OFF

'Mum, tell Jason to hurry up.'

'Don't be so impatient, Gemma.' Lynne was attempting to leave the house, but her son was dawdling as usual and was still upstairs in his room.

'Come on, Jason. We haven't got all day you know. And it's Friday remember. So don't forget your footie things.'

'Coming,' Jason called down, as if he had all the time in the world.

Gemma, Lynne's thirteen-year-old daughter, was already at the car, with her tennis gear, waiting to be driven to school. A martyr to puberty if ever there was one, Gemma these days could, within the space of a minute, be impatient, angelic, ill-disciplined, considerate, quarrelsome, ultra polite, snobbish and breathtakingly priggish. She hated being seen in the street wearing her school uniform. She stood sulking near the car, waiting for her young brother to make an appearance.

Jason at last began his slow, ponderous descent from his bedroom to the front hallway. At least, Lynne noted with relief, he had remembered his footie things. 'Oh come on, I've never known a nine-year-old move so slowly. You should be full of energy at your age.' The admonishment clearly made no impression on the boy. In his own good time, he strolled past his mother, through the hallway, and sauntered off to the car.

Before leaving the house, Lynne bent down and picked up her post: one card and one letter. She checked who they were from. She had her holdall in one hand and all her keys in the other. So she stuck the post between her teeth. Once outside, she put her holdall down, locked the front door, and ran to the car, throwing her holdall on the back seat next to Jason. Gemma huffily got in the front passenger seat next to her mother, and began tut-tutting with disapproval. 'Honestly, Mother. You should tell Jason to–'

Lynne finally removed the post from her mouth and put it on the dashboard. 'I'll tell him what I want to tell him and when I want to tell him, thank you very much, young lady.'

'But Mother,' Gemma protested.

'But mother nothing. I've told you before. Mam was good enough for me when I was a child. It should be good enough for you. Or mum if you must,' she conceded. 'And stop pouting like a spoilt madam. It'll ruin your complexion. Seat belts both of you. Now.'

The three of them buckled their seat belts, and Lynne drove off. Fortunately the children's schools were both on the same site, which meant that Lynne did not have too much running around to do, but enough. Lynne turned on the car radio and heard the forecast: something about a beautiful morning but turning stormy later. Gemma reached over and switched channels. 'How many times have I told you not to do that, Gemma?' Gemma shrugged back into her seat.

'Anyway, what's in the post?' Gemma demanded.

'Oh, just a lecky bill.' Gemma winced as her mother used the word "lecky". 'And a postcard. For me.' Lynne reached for the postcard on the dashboard and handed it to Gemma. 'Here, make yourself useful. It must be from Sue next door. Read it out to us.'

Gemma held the postcard between two fingers. 'Ugh, but it's been in your mouth. It's disgusting. Sometimes Mother, you're so common.' Mildly embarrassed both with herself for holding the post in her mouth, but most of all with her uppity daughter, Lynne said nothing.

'Read the card. Read the card!' cried Jason, bouncing up and down on the back seat. Gemma ostentatiously wiped the card on the sleeve of her hated school uniform and reluctantly started to read aloud. The card was from Thailand.

'Dear L. Hotel fantastic. Food terrific. Beaches amazing. Lots of sun, sea, sand and ...' Gemma paused, and unamused, resumed with *'dot dot dot. Bet you wish you were here, Love Sue.'* Gemma's tone as she read the card was prissy, shocked and dismissive.

'You bet I wish I was there,' said Lynne, to no one in particular.

'Let me see the card,' said Jason. Gemma reached back and gave him the card. She rolled her eyes and tutted with distaste.

'Just a picture of some beach. Nothing about me and Jason I notice. It's all about you,' she said testily.

'Well, my girl, the card was addressed to me. She's my new bezzie.' Gemma winced again. 'And not everything in the world is about you and Jason, you know.' She added carefully, 'I've got a life of my own.' For once, Gemma made no comment. Lynne turned off the car radio.

Lynne knew that her remark was rather selfish. But it was how she felt. A few years ago, she had begun to realise that she had married too early. Finding herself pregnant at aged twenty, and being good Liverpool Catholics, she and her boyfriend had done the expected thing and celebrated their shotgun wedding in style.

Soon after Gemma's birth, she and her new husband, a jobbing builder, left Liverpool and came south. They had heard that jobs were more plentiful and better paid than in Merseyside. They found that though the streets on the south coast were not exactly paved with gold, and that the price of houses was considerably higher than in the north, work prospects were indeed much brighter. They were even able to afford to put down a deposit on a small semi on one of the town's estates.

As so called Scousers, marked out by their accent, their pride in everything Liverpudlian, and their sense of humour (which they considered unique to Liverpool), they, at first, set themselves apart from most of their neighbours. And with their northern directness, they suffered some initial suspicion and hostility. But gradually, they won people over, and the couple got on well with most people they met.

But by the time that Jason was born some four years after Gemma, the marriage was in trouble. Her husband, always a happy-go-lucky sort, had, it seemed, been rather too happy-go-lucky with at least two other women. Both of them were married, and one of them was a close friend of Lynne's. She saw no point in continuing the marriage. Despite her husband's protestations ('I can change, honestly, luv,' and so on), they were eventually divorced.

After eight years of bringing up the two kids more or less on her own, Lynne had begun to feel that she was disappearing as a separate person. She was no longer an individual. For years, she had been locked into a routine of child-rearing, chasing maintenance payments, cleaning other people's houses, and paying bills that she could hardly afford to pay. She made sure that she received all the welfare benefits to which she was entitled. But even then, she just managed to get by. She had main custody of the kids, and fortunately had been awarded her ex-husband's share of the house. Still, she was all but exhausted with the strain of it all.

Money was a constant problem. But she was careful with what she had and could get, and unlike many people in similar situations, she did not have credit card debts. And she was wise enough (and tough enough) not to have given in to her daughter's demands for a mobile phone and the various other electronic accessories which most parents seemed able to afford, and to which teenagers these days felt entitled. Lynne was well aware that the money she earned from cleaning jobs was undeclared income that could jeopardise the various state benefits she claimed. But she felt that her and her children's need to survive was greater than the state's need to collect taxes from her. She slept with an easy conscience.

However, a few months ago, Lynne started to sleep badly, getting up two or three times in the middle of the night, often to eat a sandwich or chocolate, thus ruining her normal appetite and digestion, and in the process putting on weight. Though she did not know it, Lynne also began to have mild anxiety attacks, apparently for no reason.

She confided in a friend, who told her to seek help from her doctor. Lynne reluctantly agreed. She came from that northern, working-class tradition that "didn't want to bother the doctor" every time she did not feel well.

Fortunately for Lynne, her doctor was not the type who prescribed sleeping pills and Prozac to every woman in her mid-thirties who presented with mild anxiety and depression. 'Perhaps what you need to do,' said the doctor, 'is to break your routine a little, if you can. I know it's hard for working mums. I'm one myself. But you need to find a little more time for yourself: some "Me Time".' To Lynne, that had sounded like good advice.

Lynne broke the silence in the car. 'And speaking of a life of my own, I've got something to tell you; something about this evening. And I don't want any nonsense from either of you. It's all arranged.'

'Oh, what now?' sighed Gemma.

'You listening, Jason?'

'Yes Mum.'

'Well, when I pick you up this afternoon at five, after your sports clubs, I'll take you home. But I won't be staying at home myself this evening. Uncle Ted will be coming round.' Lynne was careful to avoid any reference to babysitting.

The news predictably provoked opposite reactions in the two children. Gemma resented the mere thought that she needed any sort of looking after at all. Her mother did not actually need to say the dreaded "b" word for Gemma to know what Uncle Ted's visit signified. Babysitting. She also resented the fact that her mother could not trust her thirteen-year-old daughter to look after her young brother. But for his part, Jason was thrilled. He enthusiastically chanted, 'Uncle Ted's coming to babysit. Uncle Ted's coming to babysit.' *So much for my attempt not to use the 'b' word*, thought Lynne.

'But why can't you leave us on our own?' asked Gemma, querulously. 'I'm thirteen; old enough to look after us both. All the kids in my class do it. Why can't I?'

'Because I don't trust you two not to quarrel and fight while I'm out. Uncle Ted will keep the peace.'

'Keep the peace! Keep the peace!' Jason chorused.

'Anyway, where are you going this evening? You never go anywhere.'

'I know I don't. That's the whole point. That's why I'm going out.' Lynne took a deep breath. 'I'm going to a party!' She could hardly contain a note of triumph in her voice.

'A party? You?' said Gemma, disbelievingly. It was as if her mother had announced that she was about to go to the moon.

'Yes, a party, for the first time in a very long time. After all, I let you two go to parties now and again. Now it's your turn to let me go to one.' The natural justice implied by Lynne's remark impressed even Gemma.

Lynne was pleased that she had argued her case for going to the party reasonably well. Her daughter had tended to resent any time that Lynne spent doing her own thing, as though mothers had no right to enjoy themselves. No right to have any "Me Time".

Since going out on her own was a rarity, Lynne wanted this evening to be a treat. She had dyed her hair ash blonde for the occasion, to hide the grey streaks that were appearing here and there. She had bought herself a rather bright red lipstick, and even some perfume; not expensive, but not the cheapest either, she noted with some pride. She now regretted having had that butterfly tattooed on her right shoulder. Not one of her ex-husband's brightest ideas. But what was done was done, and it cost too much to have it removed.

'So who's giving this party?'

'Oh, just one of the ladies at the pool I go to every Friday. I'm going to the sports centre after I drop you at school. Today's the last day of our course and we're having a party. It's also a sort of farewell party. Di, the instructor, is leaving and going home to Oz.'

Gemma had heard her mother talk about the aquarobics class. Apparently when the course started about three months ago, the group consisted of two men and about a dozen women. But the men had soon stopped coming, and so had some of the women.

The women who remained decided to give themselves a name. They asked Luke for his suggestions. He came up with The Water Babes. The name delighted most of the women. It made them feel special, attractive, and young. They also knew that the name was gloriously inappropriate, and this made them laugh.

Gemma knew that her mother and Luke were friends, and that Luke lived with Uncle Ted, this evening's babysitter. So knowing something of The Water Babes' background, she immediately felt satisfied that the party would be boring, and therefore not worth going to. 'So I suppose it will all be just old women then, like–'

'Like me, you mean? Well, as a matter of fact, I'm not the oldest one in the group. Not by a long chalk. There's a woman with a really posh voice who must be in her seventies. I think she's the oldest. Even so, she seems to have more energy than the rest of us put together. Then there's a nice Asian lady who's about sixty. She's the one giving the party. Plus two sisters older than me and a really sour-faced, middle-aged woman called Jean. And–'

'Boring.'

'And by the way, I'm only thirty-four. I'm not an old woman. I'm not even middle-aged.'

Gemma did some calculations. 'So you're the youngest?' she said, not disguising her incredulity that so many older women could be in the same place at once, having a party.

'No, I'm not the youngest if you must know. There are two younger than me. One's a very beautiful black girl, late twenties I should think. She's a social worker or carer or something. She brings a Scots girl along, who's very fat, tattooed all over, and a bit of a nutcase.'

'In what way?'

'Oh, I don't know. Something missing up here, I think.' Lynne pointed to her head. 'Nothing very obvious, just something. I think she's what they call backward.'

'Oh, you mustn't use that word in public,' protested Gemma. She spoke with as much self-righteousness as she could muster.

'Sorry, luv. I know I shouldn't. Anyway, she's a very strange girl, and I expect she'll also be there at the party.'

'At school they call it learning difficulties.' Gemma was more than satisfied. This was definitely not a party that she would ever want to go to. 'So, where is it, this party?'

'In Glendale Avenue, chuck!' Lynne gave the street name special emphasis, and smiled. It was, after all, one of the two or three most desirable addresses in town. She knew that she had, at a stroke, impressed Gemma; and annoyed her too, by calling her "chuck". Lynne had got her daughter's undivided attention, even admiration.

'Wow. They must be really, really rich. Is that where the posh older woman lives?'

'No. I just told you. The party is at the Asian lady's house. She's dead sweet. Her daughter's a solicitor or something, and drives her mam to and from the leisure centre. The daughter just observes the class.'

'Glendale Avenue!' said Gemma. 'Fantastic! They must be millionaires. You'll have to wear something really special, to go with that hairdo.'

Lynne was not a vain woman, and anyway could not afford to give any thought to buying a new dress for the occasion. 'Oh, I expect I'll wear the green dress. Again,' she sighed.

'But you can't. You just can't. You got it from a charity shop. And you've worn it so many times before. And it shows your tattoo. They'll think you're poor or something – or a chav. Or common, which is even worse. Like your accent!'

This question of accent was a particularly sore point with Gemma. She once heard a less than sympathetic neighbour say that living near Lynne was like living near one of the Beatles: 'Fun for a day or two, but a bit wearing after a while.'

Her mother had never lost the characteristics of Liverpool speech. There was the sing-song intonation, and the short, flat "a" in words like *bath* and *laugh*. Lynne's pronunciation of *work* sounded like "w-air-k", while *there* sounded like "th-err". Not to mention the northern tendency to render all the 'u' sounds in, *'The butcher cut it up and put it under the good plum pudding'*, with the same "u" sound as in southern English *book*. Just the sort of speech mannerisms that many people in the south associated with a distinctly downmarket Liverpool accent.

Furthermore, Lynne never even tried to distinguish between the northern and southern pronunciations of such words. She was loyal to her vocalic roots, so to speak. So never once did she succumb to any of those pretentious northern posh sounds which mangled the vowels in *put* and *good* into sounds that sounded halfway between northern and southern English, but were in fact neither.

Gemma and Jason on the other hand had no difficulty in distinguishing between the "u" sounds in *butcher* and *cut*. Nor would they ever learn to use words like *bezzie* for best friend or *ozzie* for hospital. In those and other respects their speech was much closer to the more socially acceptable received pronunciation of southern English.

Thus began a gradual separation between the two children and their own mother. It was a separation – built on nothing more than accent – that was all too characteristic of parts of English society, even within families. And it was a separation that already upset and embarrassed Gemma, to whom accent-ism came naturally.

Lynne was dismayed by her daughter's rank snobbishness, and by her failure to appreciate the family's financial situation. She did not have to pay Ted for the babysitting. But finding the cash even for a family visit to the cinema had never been easy.

'They won't think anything of the sort. Not everybody thinks like you do, Gemma. They might be richer than me, but they're not snobs. Apart perhaps from that Jean, who seems to think she's better than the rest of us. Anyway, I'll tart the dress up with a new scarf and my black shoes or something. It's just an evening at a friend's house. Well, she's an acquaintance really. It isn't a sodding royal garden party.'

Gemma relented, and leant back in her seat, happy in the knowledge that at least she would not be at the party herself. So she would be spared the double humiliation of seeing her mother in the secondhand green dress and of hearing her mother's Liverpool vowels.

'Uncle Ted will order you both an Indian takeaway, like the one you had a few weeks ago,' said Lynne loudly. She wanted to change the subject, and to draw attention away from Gemma.

Right on cue, Jason chanted, 'Poppadoms, poppadoms, I want poppadoms,' as he once again bounced up and down in the back seat.

But Gemma's attempts to rile her mother were not over yet. Just as her mother was negotiating a difficult junction, she tried another tack. 'Anyway,' she said. 'I don't know why we have to call him *Uncle* Ted. He isn't our real uncle at all.' She pouted.

This was true. Three years ago, Lynne had seen a small advert in a local newsagent: *Couple, two men, seek help with housework and ironing.* The address was about two miles away. It turned out to be a very nice bungalow in a good part of town. One of the men was Ted, a big, bearded man about ten years older than Lynne, and inclined to be rather serious. The other man was Luke, about twenty-five or six at the time, who, on the surface at least, was anything but serious. Ted worked at the local further education college, which Luke called the local "college o' knowledge". Luke worked at the nearby sports centre.

The cleaning job was easy, and well paid. Lynne went in with her eyes wide open. She took to the couple immediately, since which time they had all become good friends. In fact, it had been at Luke's suggestion that she started aquarobics, a decision which, had she known it, gave Lynne the "Me Time" she needed. Doing the aquarobics course probably saved her from a lifetime of valium dependency and antidepressants. The class had certainly helped her start to think more positively about life. She began to look after herself more carefully. After all, she thought, she was not a lost cause. She was still an attractive woman. Standing five-foot seven in her best shoes, with her best clothes on, and now losing weight, she had not yet given up hope of finding a steady man-friend.

'And,' said Gemma, staring straight ahead at the road, and clearly revving up for a particularly pointed remark, 'apart from not being our real uncle, he's a pervert. That's what my new best friend Emma-Louise says, anyway. And that boyfriend of his, Luke, certainly is. He's so obvious at times.'

Gemma's remarks came out of the blue. They were not provoked by any particular dislike of Ted and Luke. On the contrary, Gemma got on well with them. But for some reason that even Gemma herself did not fully understand, she was hell-bent on annoying her mother. That was why she deliberately chose the offensive term "pervert". Lynne was taken aback. *Why is Gemma being so awful today,* she wondered. *Is she jealous about me going to a party?*

Whatever her reasoning, Gemma's timing was good, and she knew it. She had caught her mother off guard. She calculated correctly that Lynne would not want a row right now; especially a row about a gay couple, with Jason within hearing distance.

Lynne was furious. 'Just shut up, Gemma. For a start, Ted and Luke are not just boyfriends. They're civil partners. That's like being married. Not that it's any of our business. And as for your new stuck-up best friend, Emma-Louise, you can just tell her to mind her own bloody business and shut her big gob. I've a good mind to report you both.'

They had reached the schools. Lynne switched off the car engine angrily. She turned to face her daughter. 'And you can stop using horrible words like pervert, or there'll be trouble. I've a good mind to report Emma-Louise and you. Ted and Luke have been very good to me, and to you and Jason. More than you'll ever know. So don't you forget it. Ever.' She was trembling with rage.

Gemma was finally satisfied with the degree to which she had upset and rattled her mother. She got out of the car, saying nothing, and giving a sort of victory pout. She saw some girls she knew, and was gone. Lynne turned to the back seat. 'We're here, Jason. Out.'

In no particular hurry, Jason gathered his things together. Before he too left the car he said, 'Mum, can I ask you something?' His voice was hardly audible.

'Oh Jason, luv, can't it wait until later? I'm running late. And why are you whispering like that?'

'Don't want Gemma to hear.'

'She can't hear you. She's gone. What is it?'

The boy looked round him, as if to check that no one was listening. He spoke carefully. 'What's a pervert?'

Lynne was temporarily floored by her son's question. She realised that at this moment, in this place, any answer would probably be inappropriate, unsatisfactory, or even damaging in some way. She reached out and held Jason's hand. 'Sweetheart, it's nothing to worry about. Gemma was just being silly. Take no notice. It's just that – can I tell you tomorrow?'

Lynne was horribly aware of the inadequacy of her reply. Jason, however, felt reassured by Lynne's touch and her answer. He took his hand away from his mother's, got out of the car, and disappeared into the school grounds.

Lynne set off for the leisure centre, fully aware that the answer to Jason's question could not remain unfinished business for too long. She might try to talk to him tomorrow. But she secretly hoped that by that time, Jason would have found out the answer for himself, in the way that children often do. She suddenly felt insecure and inadequate. Right at this moment, she felt more comfortable and safer as a Water Babe than she did as a mother.

08.25
Luke Prepares

Once out of the office, Luke felt better. No longer face to face with Di, he could now relax. He knew as well as anyone that his wit had strict limitations. He realised that his so-called jokes were not to everyone's taste. It was just that some people and some circumstances brought out the campness and the bitchiness in him. He was aware that his intentions to amuse were often greater than their effect. And worst of all, he realised that he could often be a bore, even to himself.

Normally a reasonably tolerant, friendly and affable person, Luke's uncharacteristically hostile reaction to some people puzzled him. Turning on his bitchometer to nearly its full pitch was simply his way of coping with his irrational, instinctive and even guarded feeling towards Di. It was a feeling he could hardly describe, let alone explain or justify. It was just there.

Feeling lighter and unburdened from his little arguments with Di, he strolled over to the gym door at the far end of the pool from the office. Muscles, as the Bosnian bodybuilder was generally known, followed Luke. He was so muscle-bound that his walk was more of a lumber or a waddle – a gift for someone with Luke's talent for mimicry. Muscles was not tall, about four inches shorter than Luke. Even so, Luke's physical imitation of the Bosnian's gait was painfully and hilariously accurate.

Muscles spoke first, in his odd, light voice. 'Hello Luthie,' he lisped.

'The name's Luke.'

'Oh, thorry,' said Muscles, smirking and dismissing Luke's crisp reply. 'It'th a nithe morning, ithn't it?'

'Yeth, it ith,' snapped Luke. Muscles seemed wholly unaware of Luke's mockery. It was as though he knew – probably correctly – that his well-developed body carried more weight with the real world than his slight speech impediment. Almost to the point of cruelty, Luke pressed on: 'But the forecatht ith for rain later thith evening,' he replied. Muscles ignored him, or simply had not understood what Luke had said.

After unlocking the gym door, Luke shooed Muscles into the gym, whence the sounds of warming-up exercises and weights soon started up.

Luke started getting ready for the class by undertaking his circuit of various technical checks. Members of the public were generally unaware of these, except perhaps for his checking of the temperature of the water. Chemicals, filtration, the circulation of water in the pool, air temperature, water purity, air conditioning and so on all had to be double-checked and recorded.

This was a series of jobs which Luke had as it were inherited as part of daily routine, but which he now understood in some detail, thanks to his nearly completed part-time degree course, Sports Management in the Community, at the local university. He had started the course nearly five years ago, even before Di had appointed him as her assistant.

While he was busy with his preparations, Luke reflected on his studies. *At last, the coursework is now finished. Just the final dissertation to go. Then I will be fully qualified for a managerial post. Just in time for when Di leaves.* The words "final dissertation" had terrified him. But he soon learned that this was a rather overblown term favoured by the newer British universities. It was used simply to describe an essay of not much more than 5,000 words. With the next step of his career in mind, Luke had chosen for the title of his dissertation: *How to Organise Successful Community-based Aquarobics Classes (With Illustrations).*

Luke's degree-course leader, who was also his personal tutor, had no practical experience at all of working in the local or any other community. This, despite the title of the degree course she was leading. She was secretly relieved that here was a student who gave her some access into the real world of sports management in the community. Luke's work lent her academic pretensions a sort of vicarious credibility.

Following yet another internal restructuring at the university, Luke's final dissertation had been renamed a 'final research project'. His was nearly 10,000 words long. It contained not only illustrations, but also various ethnographical tropes such as tape recordings, transcriptions, and even two videos. Although he had sought permission from Di and the authorities to make recordings at the sports centre, he kept her and them largely in the dark about his progress. For her part, Di expressed little interest in his studies.

As an unlooked-for bonus, Luke's course leader was mightily relieved to discover that his final research project was also fairly literate. So many student efforts these days were frankly below par. Luke had blossomed during his course. He fared much better than his poor academic record at school (except for English) might have predicted. Notwithstanding the arguments about the expansion of tertiary education leading to useless degrees and to the general lowering of academic standards, his was a classic case of the benefits of higher education to students formerly considered unworthy of it.

Luke was rightly proud of his achievements, and thrilled to have all but completed the degree successfully. He would graduate next month. His success had been achieved with the help and support of the course leader, his partner Ted, and especially his proud father. *God knows how I managed to keep most of the work secret from Di*, he thought. But he did. Recently, she had been too wrapped up in her own problems to notice anything that Luke was doing in his spare time.

Luke carried on with his preparation routine. He was on his knees, his back to the pool, checking a floor-level air conditioning unit. He heard the unmistakable sound of high-heeled shoes clatter past him. The wearer was on the way to the small tier of bleachers behind him, at the far end of the pool. The shoes, he knew, were expensive. Very.

'Salma! Darling! You know you shouldn't wear those heels inside the pool,' said Luke still with his back to the water and to the heels. 'It's dangerous. It's too early in the day for me to be heroic and save lives, even yours.' In a pretend act of admonishment, Luke turned round and wagged his finger at Salma.

'Oh, I know, I know,' said Salma, smiling disarmingly, showing her full set of dazzlingly white, perfect teeth. 'But we came a bit early today because I have to get on with quite a lot of work during the lesson. I need to concentrate and the sooner the better.'

She sat down on the bleacher. In her smart black Jaeger outfit she was as elegant as any thirty-something Asian lady solicitor could possibly be. Salma was professional, graceful, competent and immaculately groomed. Her maquillage was perfectly applied, and her dark eyes shone. She extracted some documents from her briefcase and waved them in the air. 'I've told Mum that I need to get these reports signed off this morning and have asked her not to interrupt me.' She sighed and raised her eyes to the ceiling, acknowledging the unlikelihood of her being able to read and sign off the reports without interruption.

Luke's final research project contained a chapter about how aquarobics could be sold to – or in marketing parlance, how the sport could be "delivered to" – ethnic minorities. His empathetic nature alone appreciated the sheer effort required by Mrs C, Salma's middle-aged mother, even to turn up at a swimming pool, let alone attend one of its classes. His research also allowed him to understand the need for Mrs C to have as it were a chaperone, even if the chaperone did wear high heels in the pool area.

'Will your mum be OK on her own in the changing rooms?'

'Oh yes, she's absolutely fine. She was chatting quite happily to Jane when I left her.'

'Jane?'

'You know. The girl with…' And here Salma cupped her hand round her mouth, and whispered conspiratorially, '… the girl who uses the gym. Mum and she are quite pally.' Salma looked up suddenly, towards the changing rooms. 'Oh, hello Jane,' she said rather loudly and cheerfully.

Jane walked alongside the pool, past Luke, up to the gym door. She was shy, self-conscious, slightly overweight, her eyes more or less permanently averted from the world. Her hair was untidy and she wore no make-up, which merely accentuated her spotty face. She waved at Salma. Once inside the gym, a sort of grim determination took over her, and she immediately got down to her exercise routine.

Once or twice, Luke had tried to engage Jane in conversation. But it was impossible. *She's beyond my reach*, he had thought. *Beyond everyone else's reach too. I think she's a true loner, a genuine outsider.*

He was surprised but very glad to hear that Salma's mum, Mrs C, and Jane were friends. 'Oh, I didn't realise that your mum and Jane knew each other,' he said to Salma. 'That's really nice.'

So, he thought. *Our girl with the spots is not a total loner. Thank God for Mrs C. She's an angel.*

08.30
Jean Sets Off.

Jean began to assemble her things for the final class. She had recently become a little obsessive about her preparations. This was partly because she had little else to do, so she needed to fill out the time. But it was largely because she was by nature a tidy, well-organised person, verging, it had to be said, on the borders of some variant of obsessive compulsive disorder. Not that she would have admitted to suffering from any disorder at all. *Nothing wrong with me. No. Nothing at all*, she told herself again and again.

She placed her sports bag on the kitchen table, carefully positioning it so that it was exactly in the middle of the scrupulously clean surface. Throughout her married life, and even when her two sons were growing up, Jean had prided herself on her tidiness and especially her cleanliness. *No one could ever say that every room in this house is anything but spotless; especially my kitchen. Tidiness, cleanliness, godliness; that's my motto!* While she was cleaning, she often sang the childhood hymn 'Jesus Wants Me For A Sunbeam, To Shine For Him Each Day'. And shine for Him she certainly did, though not always in the sense that Jesus might have intended. Thanks to endless applications of a long list of cleaning products, beeswax, silver polish, and dishwasher liquid, her furniture, cutlery, crockery and glassware shone more brightly than any sunbeam could hope to. If, as Jean firmly believed, cleanliness really was next to godliness, then she was indeed a saint. Every room in her large, four-bedroomed detached house guaranteed her a place in heaven.

When she was a teenager, heaven was very much on Jean's mind. She was brought up to uphold a particular nonconformist version of morality. Her sense of what was right was based on a direct relationship between each sinning individual and an all-seeing God. She took this all very personally, as she was taught, and had maintained her views until now, in her mid-fifties.

Once, as a school prefect, she did the bible reading at school assembly. She began (somewhat too loudly), 'The Lord is MY shepherd.' Her headmistress cringed inwardly, wanting to declare publicly, 'Well, Miss Watkins, he isn't just YOUR shepherd. Isn't he everybody's? Isn't that rather the point?'

Attendance at chapel, at least twice on Sundays, was the foundation of Jean's personal credo. Her favourite rousing hymn was still 'Blessed Assurance, Jesus is Mine' which she always sang with the emphasis on *mine*. The hymn also spoke of *delight* and *rapture*. Words which she sang with dutiful gusto, but which, deep inside, she had never really understood. Or ever felt.

Her reward for all that pious hymn singing in her teenage years was the feeling she was "saved". In her own mind, she interpreted being saved as also being somewhat naturally superior to other people. She had always frowned easily. She was suspicious of pleasure, which in her adult years, she still considered something of a sin. A joyless tendency to be both snobbish and self-righteous had never really left her. It was this tendency that made her disapprove of everything from litter, short skirts, and loud music, to almost all things foreign.

Naturally, sex was always high on her prig list. She had considered it her Christian duty to hold on to her virginity until she was well and truly married. She clung on to it like a child cherishes its favourite cuddly toy.

She had inherited her parents' abhorrence of two vices. The first vice was homosexuality. Although she shared the great British public's tolerance of some show-business gays, she balked at the idea of knowing any gay people personally;

with one exception. She had guessed that Luke was gay, but assumed that he was just a "nice boy"; the sort who was devoted to his mother. The second vice was marital infidelity. Her fear of infidelity was not groundless. She had long known that women lusted after her handsome husband; especially some of the wives of The Charity Kings.

'Bastard!' she suddenly screamed out loud. 'Bastard!' She shouted a second time. The words echoed around her pristine kitchen. It took a couple of minutes for Jean to recover her breath and her composure. *No, there's nothing wrong with me*, she said to herself. The problem was him. He had always been sexually demanding. She found even the normal act of intercourse invariably distasteful and painful. And recently, the things he wanted to do with her. She just could not, and would not countenance. Ever.

She was driven to aquarobics by loneliness and despair. She continued to assemble her things for the lesson. Her mind was racing as she listed, checked and rechecked the items for her sports bag.

'Let's see: one final check; scissors; scissors and brushes; scissors and brushes and combs; scissors and brushes and combs and soap; scissors and brushes and combs and soap and shower gel; scissors and brushes and combs and soap and shower gel and swimming suit; scissors and brushes and combs and soap and shower gel and swimming suit and swimming hat (most important); scissors and brushes and combs and soap and shower gel and swimming suit and swimming hat (most important) and make-up bag; scissors and brushes and combs and soap and shower gel and swimming suit and swimming hat (most important) and make-up bag and talcum powder; scissors and brushes and combs and soap and shower gel and swimming suit and swimming hat (most important) and make-up bag and talcum powder and skin lotion; scissors and brushes and combs and soap and shower gel and swimming suit and swimming hat (most important) and make-up bag and talcum powder and skin lotion and perfume; scissors and brushes and combs and soap and shower gel and swimming suit and swimming hat (most important) and make-up bag and talcum powder and skin lotion and perfume and two – no, just one small towel; scissors and brushes and combs and soap and shower gel and swimming suit and swimming hat (most important) and make-up bag and talcum powder and skin lotion and perfume and two – no, just one small towel, and one large towel. Should I put the soap under the big towel? Will the shower gel be safe at the bottom? Should I put my bathing cap on the left or the right? Do I need another comb? What will I need first? Will it all go in the locker? Oh, what's this? My FLANNEL! I can't possibly go without that. I'll have to check again. Scissors and brushes and combs and soap and shower gel and swimming suit and swimming hat (most important) and make-up bag and talcum powder and skin lotion and perfume and two – no, just one small towel, and one large towel, and my flannel.'

Jean rearranged the items in her bag several times until she felt satisfied that every single item was in its best position. Each word was spoken out loud. Endless lists, never-ending questions, precision and repetition were her stock in trade. Over the years, her need for such detail had begun to overwhelm her. So much so that the mere act of packing a sports bag was for her not only mentally tiring, but physically exhausting.

Jean moved from her spotless kitchen to her equally spotless hall. She paused long enough to look at herself in the hall mirror. It was amazing how revealing a mirror could be. The mirror was merciless. She saw the plain, tired and angry face of a woman in her mid-fifties. A woman whose wardrobe consisted largely of predictable variations of a look that was really no longer fashionable: the classic, tweedy, expensive, twinset and pearls favoured by her mother's generation, available only in what both she and her mother still called 'the better kind of shop'. It was a dated style that defined Jean's very being. Jean was the template for what newspapers thought of as the silent majority; English, middle class and conservative through and through.

Yet despite her upbringing, despite her preference for relentlessly passing judgment and feeling that most people were beneath her, something was changing. The change was taking place deep inside her; something that the mirror did not yet detect; a desire of some kind. She was not self-aware enough to know where the desire came from. Or who or what had kick-started it. (But she could guess.) Nor did she know what direction it was taking her. The only thing that she was sure of was that after years of repression and self-restraint, she was resolving to bring some fun into her life.

She looked in the mirror again. Her little mouth tightened in defiance and determination. She sensed that she looked rather too pinched. She knew that she was not conventionally pretty or attractive. She had endless trouble in choosing spectacles that didn't make her look dowdy on the one hand, or tarty on the other. She never wore too much make-up, which she considered rather wasteful and common. But she did splash out every so often on her hair, and on expensive perfume. She had a certain style, and enough money to make the most of her appearance. She considered, rightly, that her hair was literally her crowning glory. She had made sure that she had a hair appointment this afternoon. Well in time for the party this evening.

Aware that the other Water Babes thought she had little or no sense of humour (which, in truth, she did not), Jean had also planned something special for this morning's last lesson. It was to be her farewell *pièce de résistance*, for which she had practised intensively. Her preparations had included using the computer, of which her husband (the Bastard) had hitherto always taken charge. He refused to believe that she was capable of doing anything that involved machines. Despite the fact that for years it was she alone who had looked after and maintained her washing machines, dishwashers, tumble driers, cookers and toasters. And the rest!

Her husband was quite wrong. Jean knew how to use a computer. But when it came to iPods, iPhones, iPads and so on, she needed extra help. Like many middle-aged and elderly people, she got help from someone much younger than herself, in the form of her neighbour's eleven-year-old granddaughter, Suzie.

Jean noticed that Suzie had one of those machines, an iPod, just like the one Luke had at the sports centre. With Suzie's help, Jean bought a new iPod exactly like Luke's. She asked Suzie to record just one tune on it. Suzie pointed out that this was a rather expensive way of recording just one song. But Jean didn't care. The song, or more precisely the tune, had been duly recorded, and the iPod carefully wrapped in tissue paper and already stowed away in a side pocket of her sports bag. With Suzie's help, Jean would no doubt make many more recordings in the future for her own enjoyment.

'For my own enjoyment, yes.' The difficulty for Jean was that enjoyment was a problem. For despite having told herself that this was to be the first day of her new, fun-loving life, Jean knew only too well that ordinary things like laughing out loud, beaming with happiness, or appreciating a good joke, let alone ever telling one, were all somehow alien to her. She knew that people thought she looked and sounded prim and priggish. She couldn't help it. She just assumed that it was her nature to be that way.

She glanced below the hall mirror and saw the photo of herself and her husband. The photo had been taken just after they had been to her husband's investiture at Buckingham

Palace. He had been honoured for his charity work with a local group called The Charity Kings. This was about twenty so-called self-made millionaires (all men) who, along with their wives and partners supported good causes. They all met regularly for social occasions and once a year for a ball. This was the highlight of Jean's social calendar.

In the photo he looked particularly striking in his formal attire, complete with top hat. Everyone agreed that, as a tall, well-built attractive man, Jean had got the better deal. He was beaming, showing that cheerful, contented, happy look that she so envied. She stood dutifully beside him, in an uncharacteristically extravagant hat, trying to look really pleased, but just managing to give the barest smile.

Jean picked up the solid silver photo frame to take a closer look at the two of them. Her head began to swim a little. Her hand trembled then began to shake uncontrollably. Suddenly she screamed and threw the photo on to the tiled floor, and stamped all over it with her heel as hard as she could.

'Bastard. Bastard. You fucking bastard!' she yelled, her tears streaming down her face. Her breathing was laboured. She found herself sobbing bitterly, almost choking with rage. 'Why did you do it, you bastard? Why? Why? Why did you just leave me like that?' She kicked the frame aside and stamped again on the broken glass in fury. She had to hold on to the hall stand to steady herself, to keep herself upright. She took a few deep breaths, and using the sleeve of her jacket, wiped the tears from her face and the saliva from her mouth.

In the immediate aftermath of her outburst, Jean slumped down onto the hall stairs, out of breath, angry with the world, but most of all briefly ashamed of and surprised at her own conduct. Stamping on a photo frame and on the photo inside it were wholly new experiences for her. As indeed were screaming, shouting, swearing, and using the sleeve of her jacket instead of her handkerchief to clean up her face. She was temporarily spent.

What her mirror – any mirror – could not fully reveal was that hers was the face of a woman whose world had recently been turned completely upside down. Her life had been shattered beyond recognition, much like the glass and photo in the frame.

To be sure, the mirror had reflected traces of disappointment in Jean's face. But no mirror could show the sadness caused by her two married sons' decision to emigrate a few years ago, one to Canada, the other to Australia. And no mirror could show the despair and confusion, then the shame and humiliation, brought about by her husband's sudden decision to abandon her. That was ten months ago. And for what she thought was the very worst of reasons: the vice of infidelity.

Jean was still unable to talk about Gordon. She suffered in what she hoped was dignified silence, too ashamed and too embarrassed to share what details there were with her mother, relatives, neighbours, or even close friends. She found it impossible to confide in the wives of The Charity Kings. She stopped going to chapel. Her faith wobbled. Everyone knew that Gordon had left her. But people, especially those at chapel, were too inhibited (or embarrassed or polite) to ask her what had happened. Terrified of saying more than she should to anyone, Jean faced things alone.

Through a series of emails and phone calls she and Gordon had already settled some practical matters. Gordon had so far seen to it that Jean would have no financial or practical worries. But Jean was unmindful of her husband's apparent generosity. She considered it guilt money. They were wealthier than she had realised and rapidly began to take an interest in her financial affairs.

Still sitting on the hall stairs, Jean woke up as if from a trance. She surveyed with dismay the broken glass and made for the cleaning cupboard. But Jean's spirit failed her. 'Bugger it. Oh Jean, control your language! I'm not going to clear up the broken glass. It can wait. I'm late enough as it is. I need to be there early.'

So, pulling herself together and drawing strength from her decision to start enjoying life, she completed her preparations for leaving the house. She was determined to finish the classes, which she had started several weeks ago. 'Maybe that was when I started this feeling about wanting to change,' she said to herself in the mirror.

She had seen the class advertised in the evening paper. The course had definitely helped in the fitness department, because as one might have expected, Jean took the exercises very seriously. Even when she was downhearted, Jean kept going. She was not the sort to give up easily. 'Onward Christian soldiers,' she regularly sang to herself. How else was she to restore her self-pride, other than by trying to impress the other Water Babes with her superior sense of duty and her diligence, both of which set her apart from the others in the group?

She made a final dash upstairs to her bedroom. She needed to check that everything was neat and tidy, and was glad that she had done so. Otherwise, with her mind still in confusion at her outburst, she might have forgotten her sturdy shopping bag-for-life. In it was an odd collection of items: a pair of high heels, a large three-foot-by-four Union Jack, and an old-fashioned bowler hat. 'To think that I might have forgotten these!' She reached for the two ostrich feathers that were stood up behind the bedroom door. They were fake, of course; nylon, except perhaps for the woolly, downy bits at the end of each barb. She had left the two feathers behind the door after her final rehearsal in front of the chevalier early this morning. They were perfect for what she wanted.

'Am I ready? Yes, I am. I can't forget my little surprise, can I? After all, it's Jean's turn to shine today, isn't it? Yes, oh yes.

My chance to show them. I know they think I'm a bit stuffy and straight-laced. And that I criticise and complain too much. But are they in for a surprise! Yes, sir! And I'm determined to enjoy my moment.'

Just to be on the safe side, she double-checked that the iPod was still in the pocket of the sports bag. It was. Next to it was the photo someone had taken of Diana and the Water Babes three weeks ago. Jean took out the photo and held it, or rather embraced it close to her chest. She cried out in a loud voice for anyone to hear: 'Oh! Thank you. Thank you. Thank you.' Tears blinded her as she left the house with all her things. She got into her car and set off in a state little short of bliss.

08.35
Luke Checks His Pride and Joy

'Well, everyone's looking forward to the party this evening.'

Salma looked up from her papers. 'Thanks. We're looking forward to it, too.'

'Sure you don't need any help; you know, with preparations and all that?'

Salma laughed. 'No thanks. Everything is "under hand" as my grandmother used to say.'

Luke knew better than to press the point or to ask yet again whether Mrs C and Salma really did not want anyone to bring even a bottle of wine to the party. 'Everything is provided,' Mrs C had declared several times, in her soothing Asian lilt. She repeated the words so often that Luke and the Water Babes began to suspect that Mrs C would even be offended if anyone brought anything to the party.

Luke moved on to his penultimate task before the lesson. This was to lay out the various flotation devices that the Water Babes would use for some of their exercises. These days, there were many such devices available. There were some for children, some for adults to sit in, some for arms and legs and so on.

Luke had at his disposal two devices which the class was already familiar with, and one new one. All were made of dense foam rubber. The first device was a pair of hand-held dumb-bells. The second device was a semicircular support often called a woggle. These two devices were often the cause of much difficulty and hilarity during the lessons. The third device was new. It was a narrow length of foam rubber. Each one looked like a stick about a metre-and-a-half long. These were called noodles. Luke laid a pair of dumb-bells, a woggle, and a noodle around the pool, one set for each person.

He moved on to his final task, checking the sound system: his pride and joy. He had organised, or rather reorganised this entirely on his own initiative. In earlier aquarobics classes, they had made do with a Heath Robinson arrangement involving a battered old cassette recorder and a useless amplification system, both of which were difficult to control and seemed to have minds of their own.

Luke's desire to improve things had coincided with his degree module on 'The Therapeutic Value of Music'. He knew that music was, or ought to be, an important feature of aquarobics classes. Yet the beneficial psychological effect of music was a feature that Di had totally neglected, much to Luke's annoyance. It seemed to him that she tolerated the old cassette recorder and the inefficient sound system precisely *because* they kept breaking down. She claimed that music got in the way of her 'instruction' as she called her work.

But Luke had persisted. At his own expense, and after checking everything with health and safety, he bought and installed powerful mini-speakers around the pool. He attached them to an iPod, which he could control from his lifeguarding chair. It was a system that was easy to turn on and off. The volume could be readily increased or decreased to suit the level of ambient noise. And once they had been recorded, tracks could be played back in shuffle mode, or individually selected to suit particular activities.

And here Luke, at first merely following his instincts, hit upon his masterstroke. This brought together his common sense, his research chapter on *Music and Movement*, his talent for using technology, and his course module on *Psychology: The Importance of Motivation*. Rather than choose all of the music himself, he had asked the course participants to nominate one or two of their own favourite tracks for inclusion on his iPod. They all jumped at the chance; even Jean, the grumpy one. The new system soon became an integral part of the lessons, whether Di liked it or not.

After checking the sound system, Luke knew that there was something else he should ask Salma. He was trying to remember what it was, but it would not come. His unremembered question hung in the air, tantalisingly out of reach.

08.40
Heppie and Shula Set Off

'I'm surprised that the other residents allow it.'
'Allow what?'
'Oh, Mum. You know very well what! Having boarders, lodgers, paying guests, whatever you want to call them. There's probably something in the lease about it.'

'Well, I don't care if there is. After all that your father did for this block: all the endless admin, the buying of the freehold, finding the best managing agents, fixing the service charges, all that trouble with the lift. And the gardens! It wasn't easy for your father, Trisha, being in charge of the residents' association. It probably helped to kill him, God rest his soul. So just let anyone try objecting. They'd get an earful from me. Anyway, I think that in fact some of residents are a bit envious.'

'Envious? Don't be ridiculous!'

'No, I mean it. At least I have some regular company. A lot of them don't.'

'And it's not as if you need the money.'

'Look, Trisha. It isn't about the money. And you know it. It's a big flat, and I don't want to move to a smaller place, not just yet anyway. But sometimes, as I said, I could do with some company. And I like having someone to look after and to share things with. And so would some of the other people in this block. I don't just mean people who are on their own, like me or poor Mr Feldman whose wife died last year. Some couples in this block, Jewish and non-Jewish alike, hardly ever see their kids from one year's end to the next; including that religious couple on the ground floor. That's a poor reward for being so religious and devout, don't you think?'

Trisha sniffed, and remained unconvinced.

'Anyway,' Heppie continued, 'it's only two students, two girls at a time, over here to improve their English for a few weeks in the summer. It's interesting to meet them and to learn about where they come from. And so far they've all been lovely girls, and really appreciative.'

'I'm not surprised. Who wouldn't appreciate staying in a big four-bedroomed flat directly overlooking the sea, in one of the most expensive blocks around, with someone to clean and cook for them all day long? And Mum, they're not even Jewish. They're...'

'Jewish? Hindu? Muslim? Atheist? What the hell does it matter, Trisha? We're all just people! So, according to you, my girls are what? Go on, say it. You're dying to say it, I can tell.'

'OK. They're *goyim*; and not just that, they're *foreign goyim*!' Trisha spat out the words as though she was talking about hostile invaders from Mars. 'And that *schwarze*, Samira or whatever she's called, could be a Muslim! A terrorist or something!' Trisha said the name Samira as though Heppie's student lodger was from an even more distant planet than Mars, rather than from Paris, where Samira was born and brought up. 'I bet she makes those *frummers* on the ground floor feel nervous,' Trisha added somewhat gratuitously.

'Shut up, Patricia. You've gone too far this time. Shut up. It's none of your business who I invite into my home. And I don't want to hear any more hysterical racist nonsense – from my own daughter, my God. Your father will be turning in his grave. We didn't bring you up to think and talk like that. So stop it. Now, anyway, what's with all this Yiddishkeit all of a sudden?'

'Don't know what you're talking about,' snapped her daughter.

'Words like *goyim* and *frummer*. As for *schwar-*' Heppie could hardly speak. 'We never taught you to speak like that.'

'It's our heritage.'

'It might have been mine, my girl. But it wasn't yours. Not until you went to bloody Manchester.'

There was an uneasy pause. These battles between Heppie Lewis and her married daughter, Trisha Solomon, were becoming a regular occurrence. Ultimately, the arguments tended to be about the same two or three topics. These were distinctly more mundane than whether or not Heppie should have tenants, or whether or not her tenants were Muslim terrorists. One of the usual topics of dispute was in fact currently uppermost in Trisha's consciousness. 'So, you're not going to change your mind?'

Her mother remained silent while she loaded the dishwasher with the last of her foreign students' breakfast things. 'Change my mind? About what?' said Heppie testily. She was perfectly aware of the contentious and mundane topic that was gnawing away at Trisha's mind.

Trisha tried again. 'So you're not going to change your mind about babysitting for us tonight?'

'Ah, so that's it! While you and Leon sod off for an evening with the Levys, leaving me to look after your kids who are old enough to look after themselves? Certainly not. I've told you already. I'm going to a party with the group from the sports centre. Your Aunt Shula's going too. We promised, and nothing will stop me. Now, out of my way, I've got to get going. It's the last class this morning.'

Trisha's frustration and fury spilled over. 'But it's Friday evening, Shabat. Isn't that important to you anymore? A fine example of a Jewish *bubbe* you are, I must say. Your own grandson takes second place to some foreign girl, while his sister has to sleep on a sofa bed in the lounge.'

'Stop before you insult me anymore, Trisha. You're being selfish and silly. I know my duties and responsibilities. I'm sure the Lord won't mind where my grandchildren sleep tonight, as long as they're safe. And I'm damn sure he won't mind if I miss one *shabbas* meal in my life.'

'Don't take *Ha Shem*'s name in vain like that.' Trisha was at her most priggish and sanctimonious.

'Anyway, why can't the kids go to the Levys with you?'

'No. We'll be talking business.'

Heppie had had enough. 'Oh, excuse me! And there was I thinking that Friday evenings were something to do with our religion!' Her sarcasm quickly morphed into genuine anger. 'You've got some nerve, my girl. You come down from Manchester, at short notice, at your convenience, with your husband and your two kids. That's fine. All I ask is that you share with two students. There's plenty of space. But you decide to kick up an almighty fuss. This isn't a hotel, you know. And on top of it all, you expect me to be your free babysitter? No way. I've got my own life to lead.'

'But the Levys are important, and could be good for Leon's business.'

'Important? The Levys? That's a laugh. Your grandfather Lewis used to tell stories about old man Levy doing the three-card trick down the Mile End Road. He always was a crook that one.'

'That's past history. The truth is that Leon–'

'Oh, Trisha, leave me out of this!' Neither woman was aware that Leon, Trisha's husband, had appeared behind them. A short, chubby man, he cut a rather forlorn figure in his brand new ready-for-the-beach outfit: white trainers with red laces, blue long-shorts, yellow and white striped top, expensive sunglasses and a green baseball cap, which he wore back to front. 'Just give it a rest. The kids can stay here and look after themselves.'

'Leon's right,' agreed Heppie. 'There's plenty of food for supper, and the girls have said they'll keep an eye on the kids. Before they left for school earlier, I asked them if they would babysit if necessary tonight. They said they'd love to. And the kids get on really well with them.'

'But–' protested Trisha.

'But nothing,' said Leon. 'This having dinner with the Levys was all your idea anyway. I only agreed to act like some creepy little *tuchus lacher* for your sake, to keep you quiet for a while. I don't really need them or their business.'

'Oh, thanks very much, Leon. That's right. Speak up for yourself why don't you? And I've never ever asked you to be an arse licker!' Trisha was near to tears, but neither her mother nor her husband felt able to offer help. They both instinctively felt that Trisha had to work through her tantrum. 'Don't be so bloody *nebbish* all the time, Leon,' Trisha complained. 'You've got no guts, no drive, no ambition. And for God's sake stop wearing that bloody ridiculous baseball cap like that. You're forty-one, not fourteen.'

Now who's taking the Lord's name in vain, thought Heppie.

Trisha was now almost completely out of breath, and her tears were turning into sobs. Her sense of defeat in the babysitting argument, together with her disappointment in her husband had finally overwhelmed her. Her disappointment had recently spread to embrace her son, who, since his bar mitzvah over a year ago had started his teenage rebel phase in earnest. Leon stepped over to offer his wife comfort, but she shrugged him off and disappeared into the dining room.

The doorbell rang three times.

'That's Shula. She gives me a lift every Friday to the swimming.' She went to the ansaphone. 'Hi Shula. Be down in a couple.' Heppie turned to Leon. 'I'll just grab my things from the bedroom and leave you to it.'

She returned with her things for the class. As she opened the front door to her flat, she turned back to Leon. 'I never thought I'd ever say anything like this, Leon, but, you know, my daughter doesn't deserve you.'

Leon just smiled wryly. 'I should have married the mother!' he joked.

He held the front door open while Heppie walked over to the lift. She pressed the call button. As she entered the lift and began her descent, Leon called after her. 'If I don't see you later, Heppie, *Shabbas Shalom*.' *Nu*, Heppie sighed to herself in the lift. *And the same to you, Leon. The same to you.*

Heppie threw her things into the back of her sister's car, and then got in the front passenger seat. 'How are things today then?' asked Shula cautiously, as she drove off.

'Oh, don't ask. In two words: im-possible. She's in one of those "you must do what I say" moods. She was never this bad even when she was a teenager. I don't know where we went wrong with her, I really don't.'

'Oh dear. That bad? You didn't tell her where this evening's party is I hope?'

'God, no. That would bring even more complaints and recriminations: "You shouldn't have sold that house"; "It was our finest asset"; "It was my inheritance". And so on.'

'What?' said Shula indignantly. 'What on earth does she mean? We sold number four years ago, just after Mum died. Trisha was only a little girl then. It wasn't her inheritance at all. It was ours, Heppie. She's living in la-la land. The big house was just yours and mine! Nobody else's.' In her anger, Shula sensed that she may have gone too far. 'I'm sorry to speak like that about your daughter.'

'No, no, you're right. But try explaining all that to her! Honestly, I don't know where she gets all that bitterness from. It all started when she went to Manchester. I've got an idea that some religious nutters up there have got to her. She's even started using bits of Yiddish, which we never taught her.'

Shula smiled. Heppie was right. There was no clue in Trisha's background that would predict her unmistakeable streak of selfishness, let alone her recent apparent fondness, originating in Manchester, for attempting to be more Jewish than Jewish.

Heppie and Shula's parents, the Golds, were not like their granddaughter Trisha at all. They were traditional Jews, but far from orthodox. They had migrated to the seaside from Bethnal Green in the mid-fifties. Their only daughter, Heppie, aged two, came with them. Mr and Mrs Gold were on the fringes of the rag trade. They were haberdashers, a word which as Heppie pointed out, people hardly knew these days.

Heppie and her parents spent the next four years of their lives in a modest seaside rented flat, long since occupied by various waves of immigrants. The Golds prospered. Heppie's father was an astute trader and her mother was an even more astute follower of trends in the clothing trade. Their first proper business, Gold Fashions , had been a great success.

Four years later, with their newly acquired cash, Heppie and her parents moved well up the housing ladder to one of the smartest streets and largest houses in town. The address was 4 Glendale Avenue, currently occupied by none other than Mrs C. It was into these relatively prosperous surroundings that the Golds' second daughter, Shula was born, a full seven years younger than Heppie. Both girls lived at home until they were married, in their early twenties.

When asked what a small family of four needed with a nine-bedroomed house, their mother used to wave her arms in the air and declaim, 'Garments, darling, we need the space for garments.' Their house was crammed full of garments of all kinds. In the 1960s the business expanded rapidly, thanks largely to the 'I'm Backing Britain' campaign, and the then supremacy of Carnaby Street. Very soon, three more branches of Gold Fashions appeared up and down the south coast.

The Jewish community in the seaside town grew apace, with even religious Jews from London moving in, taking the opportunity to share in the trend for having second holiday homes by the sea. The Golds, parents and daughters, were never themselves particularly observant. They were liberal in outlook, and many if not most of their friends were non-Jewish. And, as Mr Gold never ceased to point out, the vast majority of Gold Fashion's clients, from whom their wealth derived, were not Jewish either.

The family did, however, attend synagogue most Friday evenings or Saturday mornings, and on high days and holy days. The girls especially loved Purim and the story of Esther with its general air of jolliness. They adored making *Hamantaschen*, the sweets made in memory of the villain of the story, Haman.

And before Passover, they used to enjoy hunting through their vast house for *Chametz*, any leavened food that their father had hidden, which according to tradition had to be thrown out and burnt before Passover could begin.

But where spiritual and religious matters were concerned, the Golds were very predictable and very average. Mr Gold used to joke that if they were Christians, they would be Church of England: middle-of-the-road, attending a beautiful *shul* with stained glass windows, and not anxious to display their religion too openly to the world.

Heppie and Shula had inherited their parents' guardedness about what they called Jewish extremists. According to the Golds, these included two types. One type was Jews who were completely assimilated and wholly non-observant. The other type was orthodox Jews. The Gold girls were brought up to believe that the orthodox were obsessively religious. And worse, it was a form of religion that subjugated women. Heppie and Shula had an intense dislike of *sheitls,* the wigs worn by orthodox women. As for orthodox men, the various fur hats they wore were regarded as remnants of life in earlier centuries, and were ill thought of. They were considered unwelcome reminders of life in East European ghettos.

As adults, Heppie and Shula were mindful of Jewish dietary laws, but did not keep kosher homes. Their parents had been great fans of the prawn cocktail, and saw no reason why they, as Jews, should not provide themselves and their daughters with the culinary pleasures of their non-Jewish friends. Heppie and Shula were both of the opinion that food was there to be eaten, and had long given up separating meat and milk, avoiding seafood, and refraining from cooking the odd bit of bacon for their husbands. Both husbands had loved what they called their occasional English fry-up.

Heppie and Shula enjoyed their own 'naughty days' when they chose to leave their homes and sample non-kosher dishes, to see what they tasted like. It was as if, once free of the confines of community and domestic strictures, they could eat what they wanted, though deep in their hearts they knew that G-d must be watching.

They loved lobster, but couldn't bear the thought of preparing and cooking it. Somehow, having someone else cook the lobster made it easier for Heppie and Shula to eat it. They both realised the faulty logic, indeed the hypocrisy of such an argument, but so be it! The same was true of pork. Recently, they had both, with some trepidation, gone as far as sampling belly pork at a local restaurant. Though alarmed at first by the amount of fat on the plate, they thought that overall it was delicious. But the thought of actually cooking the stuff was still somewhat daunting, and never crossed their minds.

So it was a surprise, and hugely disappointing for Heppie to find that her daughter, since going to Manchester, had become more and more observant, and correspondingly less and less tolerant. Needless to say, Trisha kept a strictly kosher home.

'I don't know what to say, Sis,' said Shula. 'You know that Trisha used to complain to me about the name you gave her. She said it wasn't Jewish enough!'

'Hmph,' said Heppie. 'I sometimes wonder if she married poor Leon just for his surname. Solomon. Names don't come more authentic than that!'

Shula laughed out loud.

'Anyway,' continued Heppie, 'giving her an English name was just our point. We didn't want her to go through school with names like ours. Heppie, Shula. They were frankly a bit of a burden, remember?'

'Do I ever!' Shula agreed. 'Why give your child a name that

sticks out like a sore thumb? Especially in a town like this. As if life wasn't difficult enough.'

And both sisters had had their fair share of difficulties. After thirty-three years of married life, Heppie found herself alone, following the sudden death (a heart attack) of her beloved husband. And just a few months later, Shula's husband, a professional violinist, was killed in a car crash. He was on his way to his wife, who had just phoned to tell him that she had to undergo a double mastectomy. They had no children. Fortunately, both sisters had been well provided for. Now aged fifty-nine and fifty-two, they were, as the saying misleadingly has it, "comfortably off".

The moment she heard the terrible news, first about Shula and then about Shula's husband, Heppie vowed that she would take care of her little sister. This was despite the fact that Heppie herself was still in mourning for her own husband.

Throughout their lives, Heppie had always been the more practical and worldly of the two. She was on the solid side, literally as well as psychologically. She was tough, orderly, capable, and good with figures, for which she had her father to thank. She took after her father physically, inheriting his brown eyes and thick, lustrous auburn hair.

Shula had been by far the prettier of the two. She was slighter in every way, with her fair hair and beautiful green eyes, both of which came from her mother's side of the family. Shula's outlook and temperament were rather more artistic and extravert than her sister's. And no doubt because she was the younger child, Shula had been perhaps a little overprotected. It was perhaps for this reason that she carried with her an aura of innocence, bordering on naivety, which people found irresistible.

The sisters had discovered aquarobics lessons by accident, and were surprised to find that they really liked going to them.

Not that they felt that they had much in common with the other members of the class. And it was perfectly true that the Greenhill Community Sports Centre was not in the best part of town. They could easily have afforded to join a much more expensive set-up.

But the people at the sports centre as well as its location were part of the attraction. In another more expensive place nearer to where they lived, they would have probably run into too many people they knew. They would have had to answer too many questions about Shula's recovery from cancer, or about Trisha's conversion to orthodoxy. However well-meaning such questions might be, the sisters were still not adept at responding to them.

In the centre, the sisters came face to face with a broader, more assimilated world than the narrower one they normally inhabited. It was this broader world which suited them both.

'Well, thank goodness for the swimming and stuff,' said Shula.

'Takes us out of ourselves, don't you think?'

'Yes,' agreed Heppie. 'Trisha is welcome to her evening with the Levys. All they do is sit around and gossip about business, and money. And they play the "Did you know..." game all the time. You know, where everyone holds endless discussions about who is and who isn't Jewish? As if that was the only thing worth knowing about anyone. I mean, who the hell cares if Gwyneth bloody Paltrow is Jewish?'

There was a pause. Shula thought for a moment. 'Actually,' she said, quietly, 'I have it on good authority that Gwyneth Paltrow is *not* Jewish. Her father is or was, but her mother isn't, so–'

Heppie turned sharply towards Shula, and gave her an old-fashioned, highly disapproving stare, as if to say "*Et tu, Brute?*" After a pause, a sort of brief stand-off, both sisters burst out laughing. 'Hurry up,' laughed Heppie. 'We already have a reputation for being late.'

08.45
Jean and Lynne Arrive

At first Luke did not recognise Jean coming towards him. She was still in her day clothes. He was not used to seeing her in anything but her swimming togs. She was not walking so much as scuttling along, furtively, as if checking behind her to make sure that nobody was following. She was clearly in a state of some excitement. She looked secretive, like some amateur spy heading for a rendezvous with her contact.

But what really threw Luke were the large feathers Jean was carrying. She was holding on to them as if for dear life. In her other hand she was carrying a supermarket bag and an iPod. 'Oh, hello!' said Luke. 'Jean, isn't it?' he said as nonchalantly as he felt able and knowing full well who she was. He tried to speak as though someone carrying feathers into the pool was an everyday occurrence.

Too worked up to notice Salma sitting beyond Luke in the background, Jean spoke conspiratorially, nervously. 'Do you think you could do me a favour? Could you help me?' she asked, in a loud whisper. Or rather begged, it seemed to Luke.

'Well, of course. I'm always willing to help a damsel in distress,' he said reassuringly.

'The thing is, I don't want anyone to see these, especially Diana. It would spoil the surprise.' Luke presumed, only partly correctly, that it was only the feathers that Jean didn't want anyone to see.

'Oh, I agree, I couldn't agree more,' said Luke, as intriguingly as possible, catching Jean's conspiratorial tone. She was playing a game, the rules of which he did not understand one bit. Nevertheless, he pressed on. 'I do so love surprises!'

Jean pushed the feathers into Luke's arms. 'Oh, and I've got these for you too.' She gave Luke the supermarket bag, and the iPod.

'Oh, an iPod? Is the surprise for me?' asked Luke adopting as mysterious a tone as he could.

'Oh no, sorry, it isn't. Not really. Well I suppose it is, in a way.' Jean was clearly on a mission of some sort. She was practically breathless. More confused than ever, Luke stared at the iPod.

'Oh, an iPod,' he repeated. 'I'm impressed, Jean. How–?'

'Oh, it wasn't me. My neighbour's granddaughter did it all,' Jean simpered, girlishly. 'She helped me choose it. I hope it's one like yours. I told her what to record. I hope it fits your, er, machine.'

'Yes. It looks perfect. I see. And you want me to play it during the lesson today?' *What on earth is she playing at,* he wondered.

'No, no, no!' said Jean, panicking. 'Not *during* the lesson, but near the end. It's the music to go with my free expression. You see, it's my turn today. I'll need these feathers; oh, and the things in the bag too.' Jean pointed to the supermarket bag. 'Can you keep them all safe until I need them? Please.'

'Oh, of course. No problem,' said Luke, the pennies finally dropping into place. Towards the end of each session Di let each Water Babe take over her role as instructor. Standing on the side of the pool, each member of the class in turn led the others in a three - or four - minute routine which the class member had choreographed and rehearsed herself. These weekly routines had acquired the somewhat dramatic label "free expression". The rest of the class was supposed to imitate the movements of the person. That person was, so to speak, freely expressing, while at the same time acting out the part of the instructor.

No one took this part of the lesson too seriously. Free expression was intended to be part of the lesson's warming-down phase. For her free expression, Lynne, for example, had done a passable send-up of a rock chick. And for hers, Mrs C had gamely given an impression of a snake charmer. In each case, the rest of the class had tried to imitate their movements. Di and Luke found these routines distinctly gruesome, and nearly always too long. Nevertheless, Luke had insisted that free expression was good for motivation, allowing each client "to individualise and to distil her aquarobic experience", as his final research project grandiosely put it.

But to date, nobody had gone to the trouble of recording any special music for her free expression. And certainly nobody had taken her moment in the spotlight seriously enough to even consider a special costume for the occasion. *Feathers?* Luke shuddered at the thought.

'Yes, don't worry. I'll look after everything for you. Where's the recording on the iPod? So I can find the right place?'

'There's only one tune. It's right at the beginning. You won't miss it. I made sure of that. So there won't be a mistake.'

'Well. It's better to be safe than sorry, I suppose.' Luke felt vaguely disturbed, though he did not know exactly why. 'And, er, the feathers?' he asked with forced casualness, as though in passing.

'They're for my routine too. I've been practising for ages!'

Luke's heart sank. 'Oh. We are in for a surprise, aren't we!' he exclaimed with feigned delight. 'And you'll need the things in the bag too?' By now, he was feeling distinctly queasy.

'Yes! But shush. I don't want anyone to see or hear. Especially Diana,' Jean said, a finger to her lips. She looked back to check that no one was there. Especially Diana, suspected Luke.

'Oh, of course not, darling. Mum's the word,' said Luke, as he gingerly took the feathers, the iPod and the bag. 'I'll lie the feathers on the floor behind my chair in the corner, flat on the ground, so no one will see them. And I'll hang your bag behind me on my chair, next to me. I'll keep the iPod here in my shoulder bag. It will all be our little secret, just between thee and me.' Luke was mustering all the charm he could.

Summoning up the courage to utter her next words, Jean continued, 'Er, Lucy. Thank you so much. I knew I could rely on your discretion.' She asked for God's forgiveness for using a woman's name to a man.

'Of course you can.' Luke was condescending, gracious and unforgivably dishonest. 'Of course you can. Now I think I hear voices in the changing room. I think you'd better be off, before anyone gets suspicious. Especially Diana,' he mouthed conspiratorially.

Behind Luke, in the bleachers, Salma blew her nose. 'Oh!' cried Jean in alarm, turning round. 'I didn't realise you were there.' She looked disapprovingly at Salma. She was upset that Salma might have overheard some of her conversation with Luke, which indeed she had. 'I hope you won't say anything to anybody.'

Especially not to Diana, thought Salma, as if the words were already a chorus in a song. She did not respond directly. She simply smiled, saying, 'I thought that you might have seen my mother when you came in?'

Jean was caught off guard. 'Er, no. I was in a bit of a hurry. I wanted to ask Luke about something. Sorry, I didn't notice her.' *I bet you didn't notice her*, thought Salma. *You were too full of free expression, feathers, and surprises.*

There was an awkward pause. 'Anyway, time marches on,' said Luke, helpfully. As he had promised, he laid the feathers down on the floor, hung Jean's bag discreetly on the back of his chair, and deposited the iPod for safe keeping in his shoulder bag. He returned to Jean, and held her briefly by the shoulders. 'Don't you worry about a thing. You'll be wonderful. Just wonderful!'

Jean brightened up again, returning to her girly persona. She almost skipped back to the changing rooms. Before she reached them she turned round to wave to Luke. 'Remember,' she called out cheerily, vanishing into the changing rooms, 'careless talk costs lives!'

Not too young to understand what Jean's words meant, but far too young to appreciate the seriousness of their original context, Luke and Salma stared at each other, baffled. He put his finger to his head, to indicate madness, and shook his head. Salma raised her eyebrows and nodded in agreement.

'So what was all that about?' It was Di's voice. She had left the office, and was walking round the pool to where Luke was standing, near the door to the gym. 'It all seemed very cloak and dagger. She thinks she's God's gift to aquarobics, that one. Oh, thanks for putting the noodles out. They should provide a bit of fun at the end of the lesson.'

'That's ok. I think Jean must be teacher's pet,' said Luke, for want of anything else to say.

'You must be joking. Good God no, can't stand the woman.'

'Anyway, I wasn't supposed to say anything,' he said, lowering his voice to a whisper. 'It's supposed to be a secret.'

'What? God help the person who asked you to keep a secret. They might just as well have put it on the world news.'

'See those feathers?' said Luke, ignoring the jibe.

'See what feathers, where? Is this one of your not very funny jokes?'

'Those feathers there,' hissed Luke, jerking his head backwards in the general direction of his lifeguard's chair. 'There, on the floor. No, don't look now. You'll make it too obvious, girl.' Luke was aware that Lynne had just arrived in the pool area. He did not want her to suspect anything.

Di eventually caught sight of the feathers. 'Oh, it's one of your tricks. I knew it.'

'No, it isn't. Promise. Guide's honour,' said Luke, saluting in the way that he imagined Girl Guides saluted. 'They're to do with–'

He was interrupted by Lynne, who waved at him, shouting, 'Hi there, Lucy!' at the same time mwah-mwahing him from the far end of the pool nearest the changing rooms. He mwah-mwahed back.

'Hi Lynne,' he called back then quickly returned to Di. 'It's all to do with that woman's free expression later today.'

'Oh God, no. I thought we had done them all.'

'Apparently not. Anyway, just wanted to warn you. The thing is you haven't seen the feathers.'

'I haven't seen them?'

'Just believe me. Take my word for it. You haven't seen them. It's meant to be a surprise,' he hissed. He chose not to say anything about the iPod, the contents of which were also a mystery to him. Above all, he did not let on that Jean's surprise seemed to be "Especially for Diana".

Lynne had swum from the far end of the pool to where Di and Luke were standing. She trod water. 'The big day at last!'

'What excitement,' said Luke. There was no response from Di.

Lynne saw the noodles. 'Oh, what are they? Haven't seen them before.'

'They're called noodles. Don't eat them now, Di wants them for new activity at the end of the lesson.'

'Oh, right.' Lynne saw Salma in the bleachers. She swam towards the edge of the pool. 'Oh Salma, your Mum, is her arm better this week? I saw her in the changing rooms, but didn't like to ask.'

'Oh yes,' said Di. 'I should have asked. Hope it's better.'

Hell, thought Luke. *That was the question I meant to ask Salma.* 'Oh yes, how is she?' he asked Salma, looking directly at her, as if to compensate for his forgetfulness.

Salma was not at all put out. 'Oh, it's much better thanks. Much. She's fine. But thanks for asking.'

Di clapped her hands and said, 'Well, where are the others? Nearly time to get this show on the road, for the very last time.' She hoped that the relief in her voice was not too apparent.

08.55
Mrs C, Dorothy, Marsha and Meg Arrive

Jean joined Lynne in the pool but they swam past each other as if they were no more than passing ships in the night. Lynne usually wore her hair loose, but today sported a cap, to preserve her new hairdo. Jean always wore a cap, as if to keep everything under tight, disciplined control.

They were soon joined by Mrs C, slim, elegant, and unassuming in her black one-piece suit. She never wore a hat. In the changing rooms, Jean noticed that since the previous lesson, Mrs C had had her hair cut. Expensively. The combination of the black swimsuit and silver hair – she was in her mid-sixties – gave Mrs C an air of grace and superiority. She was a careful rather than a good swimmer, but clearly relished the sense of freedom and looseness that the water gave her.

Suddenly, the three women were joined by Dorothy, who bounded in as if from nowhere. The eldest of the Water Babes, in her mid-seventies, with her mannish salt and pepper bob, Dorothy was on the skinny side, but super fit. At least that was the impression she gave. But she was no swimmer. As usual, she simply ran from the changing rooms and jumped, or plopped into the water, feet first, ready to adopt her characteristic bobbing movement. Whatever the instruction, whatever the exercise, Dorothy just bobbed up and down. She occasionally varied her bobbing speed, her only concession to the different speeds and rhythms of the exercises and music, and used her arms and hands to keep her balance. She seemed always perfectly happy, joyful in fact, and as sociable as circumstances allowed within the confines of a pool.

The most remarkable thing about Dorothy was her voice, or rather the combination of her voice quality and her accent. She spoke a somewhat advanced form of received pronunciation, or what was commonly, though erroneously known as "the Queen's English" or "Oxford English". But in Dorothy's case, her accent was of an almost pre-war "King's English" variety that would not have been out of place during the early years of the BBC. Even as she dropped into the water and called out just the three words, 'Good morning everyone!' her voice carried authority and seniority. It was more than what Lynne called posh. It was a voice that harked back to another age. If it had not been for its apparent genuineness, it might have sounded ridiculous, or out of place. Laughable even. But the others simply registered it as the voice of a pleasant, probably well-off and well-educated woman, with no side to her. They all liked and respected Dorothy.

All except Jean, that is, who rated her own social standing rather higher than did other people. She found Dorothy's confidence, demeanour and voice not only intimidating, but also irritating and threatening. Jean knew that Dorothy was probably the real thing, while she – Jean – was not. Indeed, Dorothy's voice unnerved Jean as much as her constant bobbing up and down. So when, after a few bobs, Dorothy's voice boomed out to no one in particular with, 'How are we all today?' Jean did not join in the small chorus of 'Fine thanks', 'OK', 'Hello Dorothy' and so on.

'Hi Dorothy,' shouted Luke from his chair. 'Don't wear yourself out!' This was a standing joke amongst the class. The point being that the likelihood of Dorothy wearing herself out was zero. She was tireless, almost like a perpetual motion machine. Just wind her up, and watch her go.

Di began to take up her position for the start of the class. When she appeared, there was an unexpected, small round of applause from everyone, including Luke and Salma. Even Dorothy stopped bobbing for a few moments to clap her hands together, though she was not quite sure what the applause was for. Nor was Di, who in a moment of paranoia suspected that Luke had started the applause, perhaps as an ironic gesture indicating relief that this was to be Di's last lesson. But the others, especially Jean, interpreted the applause as the first in a series of well-intended farewell rituals, and her first opportunity to express her gratitude to Diana. 'I just refuse to call her Di,' was one of Jean's refrains. 'It's so vulgar.'

'Oh,' said Di, a little uncertain of how to react to the mild round of applause. 'We've got a couple more minutes before we start.' She looked round, noting that no fewer than four regulars had not yet arrived. 'And anyway, we aren't all here yet. Marsha and Meg are in the changing rooms. But the two sisters are late as usual,' she noted disapprovingly. She collected herself, and as a matter of habit, found herself saying, 'I suggest that everyone checks their water bottles, woggles, dumb-bells and things, while I get myself together.' She walked slowly to her office, already beginning to disengage herself from her usual routine.

'Aye aye, ma'am. Whatever you say, ma'am,' said Luke, saluting Di as though she were an officer in charge. He was making a final check on the volume control for the music. Di ignored him, while the others climbed out of the pool to inspect their water and flotation devices.

Marsha and Meg entered the pool area. 'Ah, here you are!' shouted Lynne. 'M and M: our terrible Siamese twins! Di said you were here.'

'Really, Lynne,' remonstrated Jean. She clearly did not want to be associated with Lynne's jokey greeting. 'It's you who are terrible. You say the most inappropriate things. Twins indeed!' Though determined to make herself popular today, Jean felt her judgmental comment would be well received. It was not. It was simply ignored.

Lynne's Siamese twins remark was comically inappropriate. Though they always arrived as a pair, Marsha and Meg were as different from each other as they could possibly be. Yet to all appearances, the two were inseparable.

Marsha was in her late twenties, tall, willowy, black, and stunning. She was certainly the only Water Babe who could wear a bikini with any degree of style and conviction. Lynne thought she was the most beautiful woman she had ever seen, and often wondered aloud why Marsha was not a model. Even Jean, with her residual lower-middle-class distaste for all things and people not English, had to admit that Marsha was something – someone – special. Luke adored her, and Di secretly envied her figure. Heppie and Shula liked her and suspected that something in Marsha's background was preventing her from realising her full potential. For in addition to everything else (she had looks, style, good nature, charm), Marsha was clearly very intelligent.

Her intelligence, thought Heppie, set her apart from most people who did her kind of job. Marsha was employed as a part-time carer. On Friday mornings, her client was Meg. Marsha and Meg could never have been sisters, let alone twins. Marsha had explained that Meg had learning difficulties, carefully using the currently fashionable and politically acceptable term.

The other Water Babes saw this label, and therefore saw Meg, in different ways. To Luke, Meg came under the categories disabled and free membership. For Di, Meg was slow. For Lynne, the term that came to mind, and that she had already used with her daughter this morning, was backward. For Jean, Meg was simple. Mrs C and Salma thought of her as mentally retarded yet disliked using the term. Heppie and Shula had been brought up to believe that such people were ESN, or educationally subnormal. Dorothy, if pushed, would simply say that Meg was unfortunate.

All or any of which descriptions should have meant that Meg, a young woman of just twenty-two, would be someone deserving sympathy. Yet, if anything, she was an object of general distaste and dislike. This was because, trumping any intellectual limitations she may have had, was her general outward appearance. Meg was the classic example of a type of woman that could be seen in any part of contemporary Britain. However, as she frequently pointed out to anyone willing to listen, Meg wasn't from *any* part of Britain. She 'belonged to' Glasgow, and was proud of it. She was five-foot four-inches tall, and grossly overweight. Her hairstyle varied from the unusual to the bizarre. At the moment it was basically blonde, short and spiky, and featuring pink and green highlights.

She thought of herself as something of a fashionista. But like so many girls and young women in the land, she was seduced by the cheapest clothes from the cheapest chain stores. She preferred their month long 'season's look' to more reliable and longer lasting garments to be found even in charity shops, which offered better value. Like many young women, Meg was especially fond of outfits that showed off her bare midriff, even in cold weather. Her most prominent features – inevitably highly visible in a swimming pool – were her thick neck, and her already pendulous breasts. Her flesh coloured bikini was far too transparent and too small for her. It seemed to please her, but horrified everyone else.

She was also, to use Lynne's memorable phrase, tattooed 'from arsehole to breakfast time.' Many of her tattoos declaimed her Scottish origins and loyalties in various forms.

These included "Glasgow belongs to me" (left shoulder), "Scotland the brave" (right shoulder), a bagpiper (left arm), a highland dancer (right arm), various thistles, and two saltires, the larger of which occupied her aforementioned midriff.

She lived on various housing and welfare benefits, and in a house designated for people in similar situations to her. Only shortage of funds had so far prevented her from engaging the services of a local tattooist, of whom there were plenty. Now that she was in England, Meg pined for an additional Scottish-patriotic tattoo that was more immediately visible, preferably on her face. Predictably, south-coast tattooists turned out to be rather more expensive than their fellow artists north of the border. So for the moment, her face had been spared.

But before her arrival in England, a Scottish tattooist had already got to Meg's hands. Each set of knuckles bore the words HATE. Luke had once (well, possibly more than once) come across the words LOVE and HATE on a man's knuckles. At the time, he had been reassured that one hand so to speak balanced out the other; the Yin and Yang of the underclass. But never had he seen HATE repeated on both hands like that. And on a woman! 'I suppose one hate is for Glasgow, and the other is for Scotland, though I can't say I've any desire to visit either,' he quipped. Heppie took a much more philosophical line. 'Who knows? Maybe one hand is for the world, and the other – is for the world?'

Most people would have to be exceptionally understanding to absorb the shock of Meg's particular combination of intellectual and physical attributes. Add to these her unfortunate tendency to treat the world – especially, it seemed, the English world – as her sworn enemy, and it would take nothing less than a saint to warm to her. Not that she was without friends, or companions, or fellow travellers. Marsha was aware that Meg moved around in a group or gang of soulmates, the sort of people most people thought of as losers, scroungers, wastrels, deadbeats and so on.

No one, including Marsha, who anyway would not have broken her client's confidentiality, knew how Meg had found her way to the south coast. Over coffee one morning, some of the class exchanged theories. Luke's theory was that she must have been sent by a particularly malevolent anti-English fairy, of the winged variety.

The others were doubtless nearer the mark in assuming that she had been duped by some truck driver. As Dorothy put it, she might have been "taken for a ride" in more sense than one. Lynne, perhaps the most worldly Water Babe of all, saw Meg's personal history in terms of some sort of internal trafficking. 'After all,' she explained to the others, 'you don't have to be from Eastern Europe to be a victim of that sort of thing. I'm from Liverpool. I should know.'

Jean found this theory impossible to accept and an unnecessary slight on her native land. 'But these things can't happen within England, surely!' she argued. The others, it turned out, were rather less sure.

Either way, Meg was very much here, and if not a shared problem, certainly something of a shared burden. Her aggressive personality – she was given to sudden outbursts of temper – was as hard to understand as her shrill voice and her impenetrable Glasgow accent. Indeed, while the others were quietly taking up their positions in the pool, ready for the class to start, Meg shrieked something that sounded like, 'Wheee! Look out, here I come,' and launched herself, bottom first, into the deep end, nearly colliding with Lynne.

Lynne turned to Marsha. 'How is she today?'

'Oh, she's fine,' answered Marsha discreetly. 'Maybe a bit nervier than usual, but she's always better after the class. The routines and so on calm her down a bit. Not having a class to come to next week is a bit of a shame, to be honest.'

'Mm, I think we're all a bit concerned about what'll happen when Di leaves.'

'OK, ladies. Are we all ready to start?' Di's voice rang out over the general hub of conversation. She stood arms akimbo, whistle at the ready. She had placed her iPhone and iPad on a shelf just to her right, and put her woggle, dumb-bells, noodle and water on the floor. She faced the water and the class dutifully lined up in front of her. She held up her noodle. 'Look, this is called a noodle. These are new today. We'll be using them at the end of the lesson.'

Di was impatient to start. 'OK, Luke?'

'Yes, ma'am.' Luke slotted his iPod into place, and made sure that he could reach the volume control easily. This was so much easier and better than before, when the class had struggled along with that battered old cassette recorder and speakers that never worked properly. He was experienced with his new sound system and sensitive enough to know when to turn the volume up or down.

'But Heppie and Shula aren't here yet,' objected Lynne.

'Well, we can't wait forever you know,' said Jean, standing nearest to Di. 'They know as well as we do that the class starts at nine. And it's already two minutes past.' Jean chastised herself inwardly, realising that this was no way to start her new easy-going life. But those sisters were impossible. They should be here on time. Behind her, Lynne mockingly and silently repeated Jean's words, giving rise to some surreptitious smiles.

'Exactly so,' said Di, ignoring Lynne's mockery, of which she had a full view. 'OK everyone. Let's start with your warm-up then. Music, Luke!' Di blew her whistle.

3. Warm Up, Arms, Legs and Water Break

09.05
WARM-UP - AN UNFORTUNATE GREETING

Di had originally considered taking her first photo of the final session right at the beginning of the class, but since Heppie and Shula had not arrived yet, she decided to wait until everyone had arrived.

Luke started his first track, but lowered the sound almost immediately, so that the instructions could be heard clearly, not that they were novel or unpredictable at this stage. The class would anyway be able to follow the movements quite easily.

'OK everyone, jogging on the spot.' Di hoped that to the class, she didn't sound as disengaged as she did to herself. She began slowly jogging, on dry land as it were. It was frankly a bit of an effort. From her position in the centre of one of the longer sides of the oblong-shaped pool, she took a dispassionate look at the Water Babes in front of her.

They had taken up their usual positions, at least for the start of proceedings. Immediately in front of her was Jean, following every move like a devoted spaniel. *There was always one in every class*, she thought. One who was anxious to please, and grimly determined to impress the teacher, as though she expected to receive a gold star for good behaviour and performance.

Behind Jean, from left to right, that is, from the deeper end to the shallower end, were Meg, Marsha, and Lynne. As recently as two years ago, Di would have found Meg at least tolerable. But the relentless routine of her job, as well as wearing her down, had made people like Meg ever harder to bear. She had always been good with the physically disabled. She had found ways of individualising their exercises and of making the most of their time in her classes. But handling people with learning difficulties was much, much harder. Slowly, she began to resent their presence in her classes. She felt that she was being given challenges that she was not able to handle well, or sympathetically. This upset her considerably. It didn't help that on top of everything else, she found Meg – her difficult and most contrary student – repulsive even to look at. She could hardly give Meg a second glance during the lessons.

Marsha and Lynne were in many ways her most receptive students. They had shown the most obvious benefits from the lessons. They had both gradually become fitter and more alert to the benefits of regular exercise. True, Marsha was already fairly fit when she first came to the class, but Lynne really had shown all round improvement. It gave Di great satisfaction to know that there was at least one person who had benefitted from her work.

Furthest away from Di was the back row of four ladies: from left to right first came Mrs C, then Dorothy, and for the moment two empty spaces for Heppie and Shula. Di had to admit that Mrs C was a sweetie. She had given Di no trouble at all, for which she was grateful. As for Dorothy, Di had long since given up trying to instill any sort of discipline into her movements. Di found it easiest to think of Dorothy as a thoroughgoing eccentric, and as far as aquarobics was concerned, a mere passenger but a cheerful, co-operative one nonetheless.

Di's feelings for the two as yet absent sisters were more guarded. She considered Shula, the younger of the two, nervy and overprotected, who did not throw herself into the exercises as much as she could have. Di found her altogether too tentative, too restrained, even bearing in mind her physical condition, about which Di was extremely sympathetic.

However, she thought that Heppie was correspondingly overconfident, bossy even, and not shy to express her opinions, positive or negative. Di suspected, rightly and wrongly, that although both sisters seemed to enjoy the classes, neither took the exercises seriously enough. Instead they preferred simply to enjoy the company, and to indulge in a weekly session of innocent gossip.

The analysis of her class was characteristic of Di, who tended to overestimate her clients' motivations for attending classes. She rather assumed that anyone who came to a fitness related class was driven by a desire to be leaner, fitter and stronger. Like herself. That was true in some cases, of course. But for most people who attended such classes, Di failed to appreciate that their motivation might be more complicated than a desire merely to lose a few pounds, let alone to improve their physiques.

It was very much to Luke's credit that, more than his manager, he appreciated that classes like those in aquarobics had psychological, social and therapeutic values in addition to their physical worth. Such values were difficult to measure precisely, but they were real enough. As he matured, and progressed through his degree course, he began to appreciate what it might be that sparked and sustained people's interest in the sports centre's activities.

He knew that while perhaps wanting some form of relatively undemanding exercise, clients might also be lonely, or bored, or simply in need of someone to see and chat to once a week. Di was vaguely aware of such motivations too, but she did not always act on her awareness.

Luke knew that Di's background and training had been physically rigorous and demanding. He suspected that she had simply transferred that ethos into her professional life. But in practice, some clients just wanted to remind themselves of their more carefree schooldays, with memories of what it felt like to be in the water. Perhaps, Luke wondered, there was a time when Di too understood such matters. He did not want to be unfair to her. But part of him considered Di to be someone from the past, whereas he considered himself to be someone of the future.

'Ok. So now bend your arms at the elbows, as if you were running. Good.' Di had to turn a blind eye to Dorothy's constant bobbing. She had given up trying to persuade Dorothy either to listen more carefully, or simply copy what the others were doing. 'Good. Feel those toes on the floor, let your heels do some of the work.'

Still jogging on the side of the pool, Di had time to have a final feel of the space to which she had given so much of her energy and time over the past four years. In the corner, to her far right, was the office she shared with Luke. The corner to her immediate right was the entrance to the changing rooms. Next to her were the shelves holding her mobile and her iPad. Underneath the shelves was her kit for the class. A few feet to her left was the door to the gym. Beyond that, in the corner, and diagonally opposite the office, was Luke's high lifeguarding chair.

'Good. You're all doing well. In time with the music now.'

At this point, Di was aware of some movement on her right. It was Heppie and Shula emerging from the changing rooms. Everyone stopped to welcome them, and on cue Luke turned the music off. This all meant an interruption to Di's warm-up session.

'Well,' declared Di. 'At last, The Merry Yiddows!'

Di's words rang out loud and clear. Whatever her intention, her words sounded like an accusation rather than a greeting; far less an amusing or witty greeting. Meg alone was too ignorant to be aware that anything untoward might have been said, and Jean felt that the sisters deserved *some* sort of telling off. But the others were caught off guard, and exhibited various degrees of embarrassment and shock.

None more so than Luke, whose reaction to Di's greeting was compounded by guilt. That was because "The Merry Yiddows" was in fact originally his label for the sisters. He had used the label in the privacy of the office. He knew as soon as he uttered the words that they were a feeble attempt at a joke. A spontaneous camp remark, by no means intended to offend in anyway, and certainly not intended for public consumption. It had been a quip too far, and Luke knew it. He had gambled on the privacy of the original conversation and on Di's discretion not to repeat the phrase, or to say who had originated it. His gamble had not paid off. The label had stuck in Di's mind, damn her, and bounced back to hit him and everyone else full in the face.

So in his heart of hearts, Luke knew that Di was not solely to blame for her unfortunate greeting. He had no idea whether Di, who was not the most educated or cultured of women, was conscious of any associations that her greeting might have. Did she know about *The Merry Widow*? Probably not. Did she know how offensive the word '*yid*' could be?

Either way, Di certainly did not understand the limits imposed by private conversations between colleagues. *Or does she know very well what she's doing,* Luke thought, paranoia invading his mind. He was petrified that in any ensuing discussion or argument, Di would defend herself by saying that she meant no harm, and that anyway, she was just repeating something that Luke had said.

Above all he was furious at her repeating something that, in other circumstances, and uttered by someone else (himself for example!), might have been amusing. Luke felt that Di had not only stolen his wit, but had tainted, even soured it.

He instantly thought of Ted. In one of their regular deep-and-meaningfuls, the older man had warned him about his acerbic streak. Luke should know that his moments of unguarded campness could lead to remarks which might be understood as outright bitchery, or worse. As Ted pointed out, there was a time and a place for everything. If Luke wanted to progress in his career – which he certainly did – then the time for vocal restraint was coming ever closer. 'Shut it, or botch it,' was Ted's terse advice.

Fortunately nothing was said, thanks largely to the heroic stoicism of the sisters themselves. They had been taught by their parents that in such moments, the wisest option was to breathe in, count to ten, and then breathe out; before anything, if anything at all, was said. Each sister took the advice, silently and with apparent grace.

Shula, ever the more sensitive of the two, simply carried on walking down the steps into the pool. Her only possible acknowledgement of Di's greeting was a slight, embarrassed lowering of the head, as she made a final adjustment to the top of her costume.

The others waited for Heppie to speak. They would not have been surprised, or blamed her, if she came out with something characteristically outspoken or combative even. She paused on the second step into the pool, and ignoring Di completely, addressed the class. 'Morning, everyone! Sorry we're late, as usual. I'm sure we're all looking forward to Di's last lesson.' If Di felt ignored or insulted by Heppie, she did not show it. Heppie and Shula took up their positions for the restart of the class.

'Why are you two always so bloody late anyway?' complained Meg.

Lynne, glad of a chance to fracture the tension, turned round to face Meg. 'Shut it, madam! And watch your language. You don't say much, but when you do–'

'But it's always the bloody same. And why do they spend so much time together?'

Marsha intervened. 'Meg. Stop. That's enough. That's none of your business. Calm down. Concentrate on the warm-up exercises.'

'Good idea. That's what we're here for, after all,' agreed Di, trying to regain everyone's attention. 'Oh, and now that we're all here, I want to take a photo. But you'll need to bunch up together a bit.'

Without talking, they did as instructed, and lined up in three rows, adopting a squashed-up version of their opening positions: Jean forming a front row of just one, with Meg, Marsha and Lynne immediately behind her, and finally, at the back, Mrs C, Dorothy, Heppie and Shula. In a show of sisterly affection, they put their arms round each other, smiling broadly for the benefit of the camera. Di was satisfied that her photo was ok, at which point she called out, 'Ready, Luke? Music!' Di blew her whistle.

The class spread out to their pre-photo positions, with everyone trying to put the past minute or two well behind them. Luke managed to find the start of the recording again, even though he was still shaking from the fear of being revealed as the *onlie begetter* of the original cause of the awkwardness.

'Ok, you know what to do by now. Just follow me: running on the spot. Good everyone. Feel those toes on the floor, let your heels touch the bottom.'

Like others in the class, Lynne desperately wanted to disassociate herself from Di's greeting. But nobody did or said anything to express their feelings. Lynne's northern directness was offended by such southern discretion and politeness. She felt that she had to do something. So she turned round to face

Heppie. She jerked her thumb behind her, to indicate that she wanted to say something about Di. She wanted to mouth the word 'bitch', but decided instead to mouth 'sorry'. Not wanting a reply, she turned back to face Di again. Having expressed her feelings to Heppie, Lynne felt much happier now. Heppie's face however betrayed no emotion. Her feelings were much harder to determine.

'That's right. Follow the rhythm of the music. Nearly done with your warm-up now.'

The music! thought Di. *Where on earth did they get it from?* She had reluctantly agreed to Luke's suggestion that each member of the Water Babes could have one or two tracks of their own choice on the iPod. But as a post-punk child of the 1970s, she had not reckoned on how varied and how dated they would be. She had underestimated the force of memory behind such choices. She found that many were of songs, singers, and groups she had never even heard of.

Take the one that Luke was using now for the warm-up. Some ancient thing called 'Somethin' Good' by a sixties' group called Herman's Hermits, for heaven's sake! Di was unaware of both the song and the singers, and did not know that in the early years of the British invasion of the American pop charts, the group had even outsold the Beatles. She was even less aware that, fifty years later, the lead singer was still touring the UK well into the twenty-first century.

Di had pestered Luke to tell her who on earth had chosen the track. But he declined to say, arguing that he had told everyone that their choices would be anonymous. He had in fact sworn everyone to secrecy, and told them that at the end of the course, they could try and match people and tunes together, and the one who got the most correct matches could keep the recording. *Some souvenir*, thought Di.

So for the moment, he was the only one who knew which person had chosen which track. And just like her, Luke could keep a secret when he wanted to. *Typical Lucy; always wanting to make a silly game out of everything*, Di thought.

It was a game that Luke hugely enjoyed. He had an extensive, almost nerdy knowledge of pop trivia stretching back into the fifties. He doubted that anyone could guess who had chosen Mr Peter Noone's very first 1963 hit for inclusion on the iPod.

With the unfortunate memory of the start of the lesson thankfully receding, and his resolution to be more careful with this witticism still holding up, Luke's usual ebullience was making a comeback. He sat up on his chair. It was the end of the warm-up, and he was happy to sing along with the final words of the recording. Some of the class knew the words too and cheerfully sang along with him.

'I walked her home and she held my hand
I knew it couldn't be just a one-night stand
So I asked to see her next week and she told me I could
I asked to see her and she told me I could
Somethin' tells me I'm into something good
Somethin' tells me I'm into somethin''

09.10
ARMS – A LITTLE ACCIDENT

After the warm-up, and when the opening song had faded and the singing had stopped, Luke paused the music. This gave everyone a moment to stretch and readjust, before the first set of exercises proper.

Lynne turned and spoke quietly to Shula, once again taking it upon herself to apologise to the sisters on behalf of the others. 'God, as if Di weren't enough, that Meg can be such a cow!' In an unusually explicit and frank response, Shula ran her finger across her throat.

Heppie for once was more forbearing. 'She doesn't know what she's saying half the time. I doubt if she would understand even if you explained things in words of one syllable. Marsha's certainly got her hands full with that one.'

'Too right,' said Lynne. 'I wouldn't be a social worker or carer or whatever they call it these days for all the tea in China.'

'Mm, to do Marsha's job, you'd need to have the patience of Job.' Lynne resumed her position in the pool, slightly puzzled. She said nothing. She assumed that Heppie must be referring to a saint. But despite her catholic upbringing Lynne could not bring a St Job to mind.

The music resumed, quietly at first so as not to drown out Di's instructions, even though Luke was sorely tempted to. Freddie Mercury this time. Luke knew that women in particular loved the words of "I Want to Break Free". The steady rock rhythm was perfectly suited to Di's arm exercises. And for those who had at one time or another seen the original hilarious video with Freddie hoovering, in housewife drag, the song was forever imprinted on their minds.

This was one of the few tracks on Luke's recording that Di really liked. She blew her whistle to summon the class together. 'Now in time with the fabulous music, work those arms! Both arms together. Not too fast.' She counted out. 'One, arms in front of your chest, elbows out. Two, arms down your sides. Not too fast. One and, two and, one and, two and. Up to chest, and down the sides. That's right. Keep those arms moving, ladies. Chest and, sides and… '

The class dutifully mirrored Di's arm movements. They liked this series of exercises, and were still fresh enough to do them well. Even Dorothy managed to suspend her addiction to bobbing for a few moments, using her arms more. However, she interpreted Di's instructions a little haphazardly. 'Dorothy!

Both arms at the same time, remember,' Di reminded her, more in hope than expectation.

'Now each arm separately, starting with the right. Punch out then bring it back. Then left, punch out, then back. Each arm in turn. Out, and, back, and. Then both arms together, punch, and, back, and...'

Di effortlessly managed to demonstrate her instructions clearly, moving her own left arm to match her spoken instruction "right", and vice versa. She had long since learned that when facing an instructor, classes followed what they saw rather than what they heard, as if watching themselves in a mirror. So although they would hear her call *'right* / left, right / left,' it was in fact her *left* arm that she moved first, then her right, and so on. But if she turned her back to the class, necessary now and again, to emphasise or to clarify a point, the situation would be different. In that case she would be facing the wall with the water and the class behind her. So when she called, 'Move your *right* arm,' she would move her own *right* arm for the class behind her to copy.

Di often wondered whether classes knew, or even cared about the many skills needed for her job. She doubted it. By now her own skills, physical, administrative or otherwise, were second nature to her, like changing gears when driving. But she no longer took any interest in improving her skills. She no longer took part in what Luke called CPD, Continuing Professional Development. After four years, no thanks. She was good enough.

'Punch, and, back, and. Think of all those men you want to sock it to, ladies.' This brought a mild cheer, and the class continued with individual variations on the theme of chest, and, sides, punch, and, back. The class was quite happy to continue in this way, until the music faded away and eventually stopped.

Di took one or two photos of Jean and Mrs C in full flight. 'Look at Jean,' Heppie said to Lynne and Shula. 'She's really giving it some wellie, like Di said!' Indeed, Jean seemed to have taken Di at her word, punching seven bells out of an imaginary man, apparently not needing any music to encourage her.

'Right,' agreed Shula. 'And even Mrs C's working at it too. Her arm or shoulder must be better this week. Look at her go. Fierce! Not like her, is it? She's usually so calm.' Di was pleased with her photos.

The class carried on, creating their own versions of the arm exercises, without the help of music.

'Oh, you know what they say,' said Shula.

'What's that?'

'Still waters run deep.'

'With Mrs C you mean?'

Shula realised that she had no idea why she had made the remark about the normally gentle Mrs C. It had just been one of her instinctive comments, which for some strange reason seemed apposite. 'No idea, Sis. It was just a thought that came to me. Forget it. Me and my big mouth.'

Lynne took advantage of the relative quiet to have a word with Heppie. 'Er, I hope you don't mind me asking. But how's Shula getting on? Hope I'm not…'

'Oh, that's OK. She's a bit wobbly now and again, but otherwise fine, thanks. She's still deciding whether or not to go for reconstruction. I know it can be a bit awkward talking to her. She blows hot and cold about being asked about how she is. But I'm sure she won't mind if you talk to her yourself sometime.'

'I suppose I'm a bit of a coward. It's just that I wouldn't want to sound interfering or anything. After all, if…' and here Lynne's voice trailed off, into an embarrassed silence.

Poor Lynne, thought Heppie. Just like so many others, when confronted with cancer: afraid to ask, afraid not to ask. Lynne was obviously nervous, or frightened. Who knew? It was such an effort trying to cope with – trying to guess at –

different people's attitudes, motives and experiences at such moments.

Some questioners were cautiously sympathetic, like Lynne. Some were just being polite. Many were more interested in telling Shula and Heppie about their own brushes with the disease, rather than wanting to know about Shula. Then there were also the plain nosey or the morbidly curious. Younger people often asked no questions at all. Perhaps because they were not old enough to imagine that the disease might eventually catch up with themselves or their loved ones.

Heppie played for time, casting about for what she hoped – given all the circumstances – was the most appropriate thing to help Lynne recover from her embarrassed silence.

'Look. We'll both be at Mrs C's party tonight. Why not talk to Shula then? She won't mind, honestly.' This suggestion was a gamble. Heppie found herself hoping against hope that she had not promised more than she, or rather Shula, could provide. 'If you like, I'll tell her that you want to have a word with her.'

Lynne didn't know exactly what to say or to feel. She settled on, 'Would you? Oh, ta very much.' Did she feel grateful? Relieved? Happy to be considered a friend? Whatever the right word or phrase might have been Heppie sensed that Lynne felt unburdened, and lighter. Heppie was glad of it. At least somebody felt a bit better!

Meanwhile, Luke was not happy at all. He was offended at the way the class had carried on with their own variations of the arm exercises. He had no objection to there being no music, but the general raggedness of the class at this point upset him. What Luke in his final research project had called an exercise routine's "unity of purpose" had temporarily broken down. That unity was a principle he had learned about and become rather attached to on his degree course. He suspected that its breakdown was simply the result of Di wanting to take some silly photos. He had no doubt that he could, and would, do better, given the chance. Suspecting that there was still another arm exercise to come, he readied himself for the next track.

Aware that she needed to regain control of the class, Di blew her whistle and called for order. 'OK ladies. Watch me; still with the arms. You'll need to spread yourselves around a bit. Watch me, before we start the music, though you've done it before. First, hold both your arms to your chest, elbows out of the water if you can. Then fling your right arm out straight, then back to your chest. Like this.' She threw her own left arm out, briefly held it rigid, and closed it up to her chest again.

'Oh right,' the class chorused. 'Yes, we know this.' And they spread themselves out a little, because they knew that this exercise required more space. Perhaps out of a sense of guilt at their recent waywardness, they quickly got into their new positions and fell into line. First they flung their right arms out straight and back again to their chests. Then their left arms straight out and back again.

'Now both arms together. Both arms out, and back again. Out, and back. Music, Luke.'

Marc Bolan and "Get It On" got everyone moving enthusiastically. Luke boogied along in his chair, never failing to be amazed that this, one of his all-time favourite songs, had been recorded twenty years before he was born! These days, at nearly thirty, he was in fact untrendy enough to subscribe to the "Rap is crap" movement. For over a minute, and with the ever reliable Marc Bolan's help, the routine's unity of purpose had well and truly returned. Luke was delighted with his choice of music.

At the back, Shula was tiring. She was nervous about overdoing things. In the middle row, Meg was flagging and was drifting into the space normally occupied by Marsha, who had temporarily moved to join Jean in the front row. Lynne, however, was energetically flinging both arms out and back again. Di signalled the end of the exercise by counting down. 'Five, four, three, two–'

It was at this point that Lynne's outstretched right arm smashed into the left side of Meg's face. 'Owww!' Meg's cry was enough to waken the dead.

'Oh, sorry. Sorry. I'm so sorry, Meg. I didn't know you were so close,' Lynne spluttered, as horrified as she was apologetic. She was aware of the force she had put into her arm movements and could only imagine the damage she may have caused.

Reeling from the blow, and hardly able to stand up, Meg covered her face with her hands. 'You fucking stupid bitch. Oh, my face!' Luke, who (like Di) was first aid trained, jumped into the water to help Meg regain her balance. But before he got to her, Marsha already had her by the shoulders.

'Meg, Meg. Take your hands away. Let me have a look.' But Meg had different ideas. She continued to thrash about, giving a very good impression of a frantic beached whale.

Lynne was distraught. She was being comforted by Heppie and Dorothy. 'Oh, Marsha, I'm so sorry. I really had no idea.'

'Really, Lynne, you should learn to be more careful,' said Jean accusingly. The others ignored the remark and its patronising, holier-than-thou tone. It had contributed nothing positive to the situation. It had succeeded only in allowing Jean to feel outwardly morally superior and blameless; when in fact, inwardly, she felt terrible. She was angry with herself. If this was the start of her campaign to change everyone's feelings towards her, she was already failing. And she knew it.

Although the incident had only taken seconds, Luke had already swum his way into the heart of the action. He tried to take charge. He held Meg by the shoulders. 'Meg, do you feel able to get out of the pool so that we can–'

Luke's intervention, especially when he touched her,

galvanised Meg into action, if it could be called that. Her body writhed about as though she were having a fit. Indeed, at that point, one or two members of the class decided in the general noise and confusion that Meg must be an epileptic of some sort.

Di took a photo. *After all*, she thought, *I'm not the lifeguard here, and we may need a record of Meg's reaction.* She ran to the office to get an ice pack for Meg's eye.

By now the music had stopped. Meg screamed and shouted at Luke. Her impenetrable Glasgow accent, together with her hysteria made it difficult to decipher what she was saying. The general tenor was clear, however. 'Get your sodding English hands off me, you bloody poof.' She was clutching her left eye. 'Don't you even touch me, you bastard!' At this point, the "Meg is an epileptic" theory died an immediate death.

Taken aback by the sheer force and volume of Meg's protestations, Luke withdrew slightly. He calculated that no one was dying or drowning, least of all Meg. But she might be injured, and until he was sure of that, he couldn't withdraw altogether.

As for the others, they couldn't work out for whom to feel most sorry. Meg, because of the injury she might have sustained; Lynne, because she was consumed with remorse at having inadvertently caused an accident; or Luke, because of the insults that Meg had hurled at him.

'Here, I've got an ice pack.' Di was terrified that any serious incident could involve her having to fill out endless official accident or complaint forms and reports. *I don't care what happens*, she thought. *I'm going home tomorrow. At least my photo might be useful as evidence.*

Only Marsha seemed to be collected enough to be decisive. 'Meg!' she shouted. 'Stop screaming and shouting like that. Calm down. Now, do as I say. Come with me out of the pool, for a minute or two. Just to check that everything's OK. You need to try this ice pack. It'll help with your eye.'

And to everyone's surprise, Meg followed Marsha out of the pool, as mild as a lamb. Marsha applied the pack. As Meg's carer, Marsha had recognised the signs of one of Meg's temper tantrums and could distinguish between those and any indication of real damage. True, the girl had been clobbered in the face. Well and truly. But Marsha knew that Meg had been in worse situations before. She had been involved in various pub brawls, and had even had a bare-knuckle fist fight with a much taller and stronger teenage boy.

'Leave her to me, Luke. I'll let you know if there's anything wrong.' Marsha's quick examination did not reveal any broken bones, or damaged nose, or splintered teeth, or obvious lasting injury of any kind. Made from tough Scottish stock, Meg had once again survived intact. Relieved, Luke returned to his chair.

'Just leave the pack there for a few minutes. You're OK. You'll be fine.'

'No thanks to that stupid cow,' said Meg, pointing at Lynne, still in the water.

Lynne swam over to Luke's lifeguarding chair, swiftly followed by Heppie. 'Oh God, Luke, I hope there's nothing wrong with her. I feel awful.'

'Put it behind you, girl. Forget it. Leave her with the ice pack. She'll soon forget that anything ever happened.'

'And how are you, Luke?' asked Heppie. She had been clear-headed enough to take in all of Meg's gratuitous insults hurled at him. She was trying to let Luke know that hers was not merely a casual question, but an indication of genuine concern for his well-being.

'Oh, *moi*?' Luke was sitting up straight on his chair, trying to pretend that he was unaffected by what had happened. 'Don't you worry about me. I'm fine. It'll take more than someone like her to topple me off my perch. But thanks for asking. Now you take care of Lynne.'

'You mustn't blame yourself. It was a little accident, that's all. And no harm done,' said Heppie, in an attempt to help Lynne recover.

It occurred to Heppie that Lynne might not be fully aware of the barrage of insults that had been hurled at Luke. After all, at the time, Lynne had been overwhelmed by guilt and fear, and although Meg's general attitude had been crystal clear, her words were barely comprehensible. Heppie knew that Lynne and Luke were close friends. So one thing was for certain: If and when Lynne did learn about Meg's insults, she could get more than a slap in the face.

'If I had to bash anyone's face, wouldn't you know it would be hers?' Heppie laughed. 'I tell you what, I bet the poor cow won't be needing any mascara tonight.'

'How do you mean?'

'Because I bet a pound to a pinch of shit that she'll have one very black eye. A real shiner.'

'Oh, in that case, perhaps I should run her up an eyepatch to go with her party dress,' suggested Heppie drily.

'Good idea. I don't think Primark sells eyepatches.' Lynne immediately felt sorry she had spoken. 'Hell. Sorry to be such a bitch. I shouldn't have said that.'

Breaking into conspiratorial laughter and with the incident now behind them, Lynne swam back to her position, and Heppie rejoined her sister.

09.20
Legs – A Refusal to Continue

'Did you ever have the feeling that it's going to be one of those days?'

Heppie laughed. 'Anyway, how's everything going? All holding up?'

'So far, so good. It's the second time I've tried this swimsuit. It's good. The top works well. As long as I don't push and pull too hard, it feels fine. No one would really notice, would they?'

'Not at all. Don't worry. Everything looks fine to me. And speaking of how you are, Lynne asked after you.' Di blew her whistle hard. *Oh, that damn whistle,* thought Heppie.

Ignoring the whistle, Shula bridled. 'I wondered what you two were gossiping about. Why doesn't she ask me herself, for God's sake? I'm the one who knows best!'

'Ready, ladies?' called Di, trying to restore order once again. Meg had rejoined the class in the pool. 'Come on now. We're running a bit late. We'll do legs now. And then you can have your water break.'

'Be fair, Shula,' Heppie protested. 'Lynne was just trying to be polite. It's difficult for some people, you know that. Anyway, I told her that she could talk to you at the party this evening.'

'Yeah, yeah. Whatever.'

There were moments, and this was one of them, when it was all too much for Shula. She had had a lifetime of being the centre of attention, and she had revelled in it. As a child, she would willingly act, sing, play the piano and dance on cue. She loved the attention, and the sound of applause, no matter how small the audience, or how modest the occasion. It had been a charmed childhood, though she didn't always appreciate it.

She was lucky in that her parents indulged her and her talents. She was never envied by her older sister, who was perfectly content to allow the younger Shula to occupy the limelight. On the contrary, Heppie, who knew that she herself had no special talent and therefore dreaded having to perform, tended to encourage her sister's willingness to show off.

But for Shula, being the openly applauded centre of attention as a child and teenager was not the same as being the whispered centre of attention as the only one in the family who had been through cancer. This was a new, unwelcome type of stardom. In her heart of hearts, she knew that sometimes, she did not handle other people's concern well. She did not know how to deal with the looks of sympathy, the tales of recovery, the drama and pain of surgery, all the talk about reconstruction, miracle drugs and the like. She was hardly any better at dealing with those people who blanked out all such topics when in her company. She was only grateful, truly grateful, that neither her parents nor her late husband had had to take the journey with her. Above all, she knew that the burden of companionship, care, and being practical had fallen on her older sister, whom she adored.

But every so often, Shula resented the dependence on Heppie. She balked at the responsibility of being as it were her sister's protectee. However, she was gradually beginning to learn how not to keep things in. She was learning to cope with her innermost feelings of isolation and occasional despair brought about by her illness. She was finally learning to talk about her problems. She was getting stronger. She was beginning to emerge from the shelter of her sister's care and was now wanting to speak for herself. She didn't know it yet, but with her sister's help, she was recovering.

'Oh, but can't we have our water break now, Di?'

'No, Lynne. This is an *exercise* class, remember?'

Hell, thought Luke. *She's pushing them too hard, and missing things out.* The next track was Handel's 'Water Music', clearly someone's witty idea of an appropriate accompaniment to the class. In fact, the rhythm was too fast for most of the exercises. And somehow the joyful, uplifting mood of the piece jarred with the sheer physical effort needed to carry out the more strenuous leg exercises coming next. So despite its title, the piece just did not work as an accompaniment to aquarobics, at least with this group of people. Nevertheless, Luke knew that if he played the track very softly, it could function perfectly well as background music.

'OK. Let's work those legs. Lift the right knee up, then down. Left knee up, then down. Right up, left down, Up, down. Let's see those knees!' The class carried on, as if marching on the spot, though rarely in time with each other. 'Good. Now as you lift your right leg, touch the knee with your left hand, like this. Then with your left knee up, touch it with your right hand, like this.'

'Oh I can never get the hang of this. I get mixed up between left and right,' said Heppie, breathing heavily.

Di urged them all on. 'Now, instead of touching the knees with your hands, use your elbows. Right knee to left elbow. Up, down. Then left knee to right elbow. Up, down. Dorothy, try and co-ordinate your knees and elbows. When your knees are up, touch them with your opposite elbow.' While the class was involved in their struggle to cope with the movements, Di managed to take a photo. 'Up with those knees, everyone,' she called out.

'If I lift my legs and knees any higher, they'll drop off.'

'At least you're fit, Marsha. Think what it's like for the rest of us!' said Lynne. 'I need longer arms, or bigger elbows or something.'

Jean wanted to say something positive, something encouraging. 'Oh, I manage fine. It's very good for co-ordination. I practise at home,' she said cheerfully.

Jean's well-intentioned intervention backfired. It was ignored. She was mortified. Lynne whispered to Marsha, 'Practise? Did you hear that? Aren't we taking all this a little bit too seriously?'

Marsha replied with mock seriousness. 'I think that deep down Jean is probably a very serious lady.'

'Mm, I could think of other words to describe her.' Marsha put her fingers to her mouth. Lynne took the hint and returned to face Di, and said no more.

'OK, ladies, legs together now. I know this is a bit more difficult, so first, watch me.' Di turned round with her back to the class, so that now they could simply copy her, or try to. She stood still. 'This is the start position. On the count of one, lift your right foot back, and touch it with your left hand.'

The class knew what was coming. 'But Di, this one's a real killer. It really hurts my thighs,' shouted Lynne to Di's back. There were murmurs of agreement, even from Jean.

'Of course it hurts! It's supposed to hurt,' Di shouted back, letting her voice bounce off the wall in front of her. 'What have I told you before? If it isn't hurting…' Di paused.

The class dutifully chorused the required response, '… it isn't working.'

The class knew exactly what to do, straining to make contact between various combinations of hands and feet, as required by the routine. 'Good, I can see you're really trying hard. Well done.'

Trying, perhaps, but not succeeding; at least not very well. They were struggling. *This is too much for them, and she knows it,* thought Luke. Any sense of regularity of movement or rhythm had long since deserted the class, not helped by the ill-suited Handel bubbling away in the background. Dorothy had all but bounced herself to the limit. Lynne, Heppie and Shula had all managed to complete one or two repetitions of the exercise, but at very different speeds. Jean had done her best to keep a steady rhythm, but was slow and careful. Only Marsha had managed to complete the exercise reasonably well. Meg ended the activity standing straight up in the water, her arms across her chest, glaring ferociously at Di. After one or two attempts at the exercise, she was refusing to move.

Marsha swam over to Meg. 'What's wrong, Meg? Come on. You could at least try.'

'Oh fuck off, Marsha, can't you? It isn't working. It isn't working. They hurt, these exercises. They're a bloody stupid waste of time. I hate them. They're doing my head in. And I hate her too. She makes it too difficult.' Meg pointed accusingly at Di. Everyone had heard her. Di stood at the side of the pool, unmoved.

'Meg. Don't talk like that. You should apologise to Di. She's only trying to help.'

'Help? She can't help me. No one can. I'm too... I'm too fucking, too fucking fat. Leave me alone. That's it. End of story.' Meg's voice reached a desperate crescendo. She had exhibited an unexpected degree of helplessness, forced out of her at a moment of crisis. Of course, she had been rude to Di and as usual her appearance and manner were against her.

On the other hand, anyone who did not feel for Meg at this point would have had a heart of stone. To see and hear a woman express such distress, and about her own body, was difficult, to say the least. Especially for a group of women who were all, to one degree or another, conscious of their own body image.

'Oh please,' said Marsha, almost pleading with Meg. 'That's no way to talk about yourself. I know you, Meg. You can do better. Don't give up on yourself like this.'

'Just sod off will you, Marsha? It's all right for you. You're thin. Just bugger off. Leave me alone. I don't need you to look after me.' She pushed Marsha away. Marsha was shaken and did not know what to do.

'It isn't your fault, Marsha. You can only do your best. She's her own worst enemy.' Platitudes, perhaps, but Lynne's words were kindly meant.

Jean's shared moment of sympathy for Meg's distress had already evaporated into thin air. She reverted to type. So what if she sounded like her mother? She did not care about what the others felt. 'She's just a spoilt brat, and doesn't deserve any help if you ask me.'

'Well, no one's asking you, thank you very much,' snapped Heppie. 'Can't you see that she's a very troubled girl? I'm not defending her. I'm just saying, well, there's got to be a reason.'

It was Shula who, to everyone's surprise, managed to calm Meg down. She swam up to Meg. 'I can't do most of the exercises either. Some can be a bit hard. Why don't you join me, at least until the water break?' And although Meg did not really believe that Shula found the exercises hard, she agreed to join her.

It was Dorothy's turn to pour oil on troubled waters. 'Let's all settle down and let's get on with the class. All this bother isn't fair on Di, is it?' Her authoritative voice had an immediate effect.

This managed to make the class feel slightly ashamed, though they weren't quite sure why. Meg suddenly decided to separate herself from Shula. She swam to and then sat on the opposite side of the pool, glaring at Di.

'Ok. Thanks, Dorothy. I think there's time to do just one more leg exercise before we break,' Di said, relieved.

No one really wanted to do another leg exercise, but went along with Di's suggestion. They were like children, trusting in the teacher's skill to help the class regain some sense of order. Handel's 'Water Music' had done its best, and had failed.

So in the awkward silence that followed, Di told the class to do running on the spot; faster and faster. She counted down to the end of the activity, 'Ten, nine, eight, seven...' leaving the class breathless. Luke was furious. *You've got this all wrong. And you know it. They need to relax, not to get all worked up again.* He had to restrain himself from interrupting the class.

Eventually Di brought the running to an end. The exercise had only lasted two minutes or so – long enough for Di to have taken a photo – but it seemed to take much, much longer.

'OK! Enjoy your water break!'

The announcement was greeted with various cries of exhausted relief. Each member of the class made her way to her water bottle, woggle, dumb-bells and noodle at the sides of the pool. Di walked briskly to her right and round towards her office, quickly followed by a grim-looking Luke.

Meg was also walking towards the office, but from the opposite direction. The two women met just outside the office door. By now they were face to face, or rather Meg's face was level with Di's neck. Neither said anything.

Suddenly Meg lifted her head up, pursed her lips and without any warning, spewed a huge mouthful of water into Di's face. Di's wet face clouded over, but otherwise did not move. 'And enjoy your water break too,' said Meg, who immediately jumped back into the pool. Di disappeared into her office, swiftly followed by Luke.

09.30
Water Break – Planning a Shopping Trip

An attempt by Marsha to apologise for Meg's behaviour was swept aside by a burst of anger from Jean. 'That was truly disgusting. Unforgivable to treat Diana like that.'

'Oh, I don't know,' said Heppie. 'I thought it had its funny side. And Di has been pushing her, well, all of us, a bit too much.'

'Nonsense. And anyway, that's no excuse for spitting in someone's face!'

'Pity Di didn't get a photo of it!'

'It's no laughing matter, Lynne. It wasn't funny. We're here to do the exercises as best we can. Meg just wasn't trying hard enough.' Jean looked towards Meg, who was floating in the water as if nothing had happened. No matter how hard she tried to improve her standing with the others, all of Jean's background got in her way. There was little she could do to restrain herself.

'It's just her confidence and self-belief,' said Marsha, not responding directly to Jean. 'It's up and down like a yo-yo. She blows hot and cold about herself.'

Heppie tried to change the topic of conversation. She held up a noodle. 'I wonder what these are for.'

Jean was first off the mark. 'Oh, they're noodles,' as if the answer were obvious. 'Diana wants us to use them at the end of the lesson.'

'Di seems to be very tense. She seems to have something on her mind.'

'Well, wouldn't you be a bit tense, Dorothy? After all, this is her last class.' Jean was elevating the last class to the status of a major tragedy for Di.

'I doubt that this being the last class worries her at all. No, it's something else that's bothering her.'

'I agree with Dorothy,' said Lynne, gulping down her water. 'But then we all have other things on our minds. Don't we? Kids, money, bills, whatever; it never stops. The thing is, to try and leave our troubles behind and just enjoy ourselves while we're here. But I agree that Di is a bit fierce with us today. And just look at her and Luke in the office. They seem to be having a real set-to.'

Most of the class tried to peer into the office.

'Could you come over here, Sis?'

'Sure.' Heppie walked a few paces down the side of the pool to join her sister.

'Would you check my *sheitl*?' They both laughed at her choice of the word.

'Is it causing you trouble?'

'Not really. But it's one of the smaller ones, and I was wondering if my swimming cap was slipping or something. Is the cap too big?'

'Here, let me see,' Heppie lifted Shula's cap a little, to see if the wig – the aforementnioned *sheitl* – underneath was causing the cap to move. 'Not as far as I can see. Does it feel OK?'

'Yes, I think so. I suppose it's just me worrying as usual.'

'Your hair's growing back nicely. So that's good news.'

'Hope so. It's certainly taken its time. Thanks. Let's join the others.'

They picked up their water bottles and walked over to the rest of the class. They joined the others and looked into the office. Though they could not hear exactly what was being said, it was clear that Luke was remonstrating with Di, and that Di was being difficult and defensive.

'I suppose she's tense because she's a bit worked up about leaving tomorrow. I know I would be about going back home after all these years.'

'Marsha's right. That's the most sensible explanation. But going home is what she wants. She's been talking about nothing else these past few weeks. In any case, it's private and none of our business. And what does any of us know about what's really going on in Di's mind? I think we all ought to calm down and drop the subject. And mind our own business.' There was general agreement with Heppie. The subject was duly dropped.

'Well, I know what's on my mind,' said Lynne. There was an expectant, nervous pause. 'Di's farewell present.' Everyone breathed a sigh of relief, glad of the opportunity to occupy the same neutral territory of a farewell gift.

'Oh yes,' was the general reaction.

'Did you get my contribution?' asked Dorothy.

'Yes, no problem, thanks. Actually, I've got everyone's contribution as agreed; everyone in our group that is, including a very generous contribution from Luke. Everyone gave me what they wanted to or could afford. The total is about sixty-five pounds.'

'That's nice,' said Mrs C.

'Hmph. Has Meg given anything?'

Lynne was becoming increasingly exasperated with Jean. 'Yes. She has. I said *everyone*, didn't I? And that's what I meant. And we also agreed that we should give one present from all of us; so no need for individual gifts or anything like that.'

'Good idea,' said Dorothy. 'Very sensible. Otherwise things can get out of hand.'

'The thing is, I'm not sure what to get her. I don't fancy making a decision all on my own. So does anyone have time to come on a little shopping trip with me this afternoon?'

Mrs C made a move to speak. But she didn't have the chance to say anything. 'No, no, no. Please Mrs C. You've got enough on with the party, thanks,' said Lynne.

Marsha offered to help. But she explained that just for this Friday, she was in charge of Meg for the whole day, so she might have to bring her along too. Lynne's heart sank at the thought of shopping with Meg. But at the same time she did not feel able to say no to the offer of help. The others guessed at Lynne's dilemma.

Shula came to the rescue. 'Oh, no need to put yourself out, Marsha. I'll come, Lynne. Count me in.'

'Me too,' said her sister, predictably. 'Anything to get me out of my flat today.'

'Oh?' said Lynne.

'Daughter problems.'

'Ah, I know what you mean!'

'We can make a little expedition of it. Have tea somewhere. Just the three of us,' proposed Heppie.

Lynne could not be more grateful, relieved, and in some strange way flattered. She was grateful to have avoided Meg's company this afternoon, though Marsha was more than welcome. She was relieved because as she had just said she did not relish the responsibility of choosing a gift on her own.

She was the sort who always volunteered to collect money and to arrange to buy cards or to wrap gifts for new babies, departing neighbours, bereaved friends and so on. But she also knew from experience of these things that there was always someone (in this group, probably Jean) who would be bound to disapprove of anything she chose on her own. Therefore spreading the responsibility for deciding what to buy between three people would make the choice easier, and for that matter more enjoyable.

Lynne was less sure about why she felt flattered by the sisters' offer to help. She knew that the sisters were Jewish, and judging by their clothes and accessories – and not by their race or religion – she suspected correctly that they were reasonably well off. Their handbags!

She also guessed that she was not the sort of person that they might normally socialise with or go out with, to the shops or anywhere else. She certainly knew that, but for aquarobics, they would not be within her usual circle of friends or acquaintances! Yet here they were, offering to help out, when they need not have bothered. Lynne felt that this offer alone justified her decision to spend some of her "Me Time" on the aquarobics class. She hoped that the sisters felt the same.

'Back on duty, ladies.' The water break had been rather longer than usual. Dorothy's announcement commanded its usual attention, as first Luke, and then Di made their way back to their places. Everyone jumped into the water and went to their usual positions.

Luke still looked grim after whatever had been said in the office. He marched rather than walked back to his chair. Di seemed a little chastened, and rather less bossy than before the break. She was taken aback by the class already lined up in the water, waiting for her next instruction. She blew her whistle, softly, almost apologetically. Everyone, Meg included, was looking at the teacher.

4. Of Dumb-bells, Woggles and Noodles

09.40
DUMB-BELLS AND ARMS – AN INTERRUPTION

'Er, sorry everyone, I should have told you, asked you, to fetch your dumb-bells with you.' Di was calmer, and the Water Babes felt correspondingly more at ease. Without a murmur, each member of the class swam back to her water bottle by the side of the pool. Then each one reached for her set of dumb-bells, and dutifully returned to her position in the water.

The dumb-bells were made of some sort of dense foam rubber. They were light enough for the ladies to hold. That is, until they had absorbed water, when they became heavier, requiring some degree of strength to work with. Effort was especially needed by the hands and wrists, but nothing too onerous.

In fact, the class liked using them because they gave each person something to concentrate on, other than specific parts of the body. It was all very well doing arm and leg exercises, but after a while, focusing on one's body parts became exhausting, and revealed the weaknesses of one's body too easily. With dumb-bells on the other hand, responsibility for a poor performance could easily be attributed not just to one's limbs, but to these external flotation devices. So it was with some relief that each class member either grabbed her set of dumb-bells or threw them to each other with a fair degree of enthusiasm.

Luke decided to play as his next track an instrumental version of "The Skye Boat Song". It always had an immediate calming effect on the class. Fortunately, the orchestra did not play the tune at a funereal pace, but at a light, airy tempo. One could well imagine the boat speeding along the waves. The lad that was born to be king would surely have been pleased at his progress.

Di's instructions were quite audible. 'Hold your dumb-bells in front of your chest, and roll them one by one forward and back. Right, left, right, left. That's good everyone. Slow down, Dorothy. You're going too fast. You'll tip your boat over!'

Some of the class were singing along. They sang with the words if they knew them, or la la'd with the melody. Marsha did not know any of the words. But from earlier sessions she knew that the tune was Scottish, so encouraged Meg to join in. 'Come on, Meg. Sing along. It's from Scotland so you should know the words.' There was no reply from Meg, who was looking distinctly sullen. 'Look. Even Mrs C knows the words.'

Mrs C made a rare contribution to the conversation. 'Yes. We used to sing this at school in India.'

'Really?' said Marsha innocently, rolling her dumb-bells forward and back as per Di's instructions.

'What do you mean, 'Even Mrs C knows the words?' Don't sound so surprised. People like Mrs C and I were properly educated. We oldies know a thing or two you know! We learned lots of traditional songs. Not like now.' Dorothy's deep voice came across a little more critically than perhaps she intended. She had for once stopped bobbing up and down and was working her dumb-bells while talking. Her little speech mortified Marsha who had meant no harm.

'Oh, I'm so sorry, Dorothy. I didn't mean to imply anything, or to offend anyone. Actually, I think my mum used to sing this when I was a kid.'

'What a pity you didn't take the chance to learn the words.'

Dorothy's follow-up remark did nothing to help Marsha feel a little less guilty about possibly having caused offence. The others could not help but hear some of the exchange between Marsha and Dorothy. But no one had made any comment. They all felt that they had to keep the peace.

'Now push your right hand and arm down and up again slowly and steadily, then the same with your left. Feel your dumb-bells resisting the pressure. Down as far as you can go, then up again.'

'Oh, Lynne, I think I might have upset Dorothy or Mrs C.'

'I heard what Dorothy said. I'm sure she didn't take offence. Or Mrs C either,' said Lynne, pushing her dumb-bell down by her side. 'They're both nice, good people. I suppose she was just taking the opportunity to speak up for older people. It's nothing personal, Marsha.'

'Oh, I hope not.'

'And I know that they really admire the work you do with Meg. Mrs C and Dorothy are old school; real ladies. I shouldn't worry. I suppose that for some of us it's a bit weird to hear older people speak out for themselves now and then. We sort of don't expect them to.' Marsha turned away unnecessarily ashamed of herself. The music came to an end. Luke decided to up the pace a little.

'Hooray!' cried Shula. 'It's Kylie!'

Luke lowered the sound to give Di the space for her next instructions. 'Hold both dumb-bells close to your chests, and twist them: To the right, and then to the left. No limp wrists now, ladies.' Di mimed limp wrists and took a quick look at Luke. Several in the class saw Di's attempt to insult Luke. He ignored her; for the moment.

This apparently simple exercise was remarkably hard on the wrists; especially when Di had them repeat the movement but with arms stretched out in front of their chests, and finally with both arms stretched outwards to the sides. There was a bit of a free-for-all as each member of the class varied her routine by twisting her wrists in each position. It was hard work, but satisfying.

Di called, 'OK, arms down to the side, and go like a train. Get those wheels moving, forwards, then backwards!' Everyone cheerfully obeyed, and chugged along.

There was a general chorus of *'Come on, baby, do the locomotion!'* Shula was getting carried away. 'Go Kylie. I love you. I love you!' Luke, who despite his enthusiasm for Ms Minogue really preferred the original version by the long forgotten Little Eva, was locomoting along in his chair. He was *sans* dumb-bells, but – no doubt to annoy Di – bearing ostentatiously limp wrists, and singing out loud to his heart's content.

Suddenly, the gym door flew open and Muscles – as the ladies called the Bosnian bodybuilder – appeared. Unseen by Di, who was busy being transported by Kylie, he crept out of the gym door into the pool area. Luke was in the corner to the bodybuilder's left, and Di to his right.

Muscles put his fingers to his mouth, signalling to the class to keep mum. It was clear that he wanted to surprise Di. For his part, Luke felt he had no choice but to sit out the unwelcome interruption. He decided to wait and see what would happen. The women had seen Muscles before and they knew him to be cheeky and disruptive. But they forgave him, because he was funny, and to most of them, gorgeous. As Luke sat in his chair, frowning, he noticed that Jane – she of the spotty face – had also emerged from the gym. She gave a little smile and shy wave to Mrs C, and then to Salma, who both waved back.

Muscles adopted his own version of a train's movement, though his train was somewhat lewder than the one that Kylie might have had in mind. Muscles lurched and swayed towards Di. When he was just about to touch her shoulder, she was suddenly aware of him behind her. She was furious. 'Oh hell, I might have known! Go away. You're interrupting!' Ignoring her, Muscles stepped deftly to the side, and began posing and flexing provocatively for the class.

They loved it, and except for Jean, took it all in good part. Jean was not totally immune to Muscles' attractions, but as usual she found it unforgivable for anyone to annoy and interrupt Diana while she was working. But at least this time, she did not actually say anything. She felt that her self-denial was an improvement on some of her earlier behaviour.

Muscles thrust his groin suggestively two or three times at the ladies and then turned round to give them a back view of his tight little buns. The class whooped and shrieked, with even Dorothy and Mrs C applauding. 'Really Mrs C, I've a good mind to tell your daughter,' laughed Heppie, as "Locomotion" finally came to a stop.

'I can see you, Mum, I can see you,' shouted Salma from the bleachers, in mock admonishment.

'And shame on you too, Dorothy,' said Shula. In reply, she playfully gave two fingers to Shula, who grinned back.

'You have to admit, he's something else.'

'Oh, he's far too short for you, Marsha,' joked Lynne. 'Give someone else a chance won't you! I must say, as a happily divorced woman, I wouldn't kick him out of bed.'

Di was trying to persuade Muscles to leave her and the class alone. 'Go away. Get back to the gym. Come on, Luke. Help me out here.'

Luke walked over to Muscles and took his arm. Even though Muscles presented himself as a toughie, he was, like a lot of muscle men, distinctly soft-centred. He was typical of his type. To Luke he was a *Muscle Mary*, all show and little substance. A good four inches taller than Muscles, Luke felt well able to take care of himself in case of trouble. 'Come on, big boy, playtime over. Can't you hear the lady? Pith off back to the gym, where you belong.' Luke spoke into the shorter man's ear.

To one or two cries of 'shame' and 'spoilsport' Muscles meekly began to follow Luke. 'Never mind. If you're looking for asylum, you can always find it at my place,' cried Lynne, somewhat tactlessly. No one laughed. Muscles knew that his luck was running out, and made his way back to the gym door. Satisfied that he was finally leaving, Luke returned to his chair.

But before he disappeared back into the gym, Meg suddenly splashed her way to Luke's corner. She remonstrated with Luke. She started frantically scooping water out of the pool at his legs and feet. 'No, no. He's lovely, gorgeous. Why can't he stay? I want him to stay. He's the best thing about this place.' Everyone, including Muscles himself, was taken aback by Meg's behaviour. Even though he could not grasp the individual meanings of Meg's words, their general sense and vehemence were unmistakable.

Jane was still at the gym door. Muscles turned to her for help. He seemed to want some explanation. 'I think she likes you, Bashir,' said Jane, carefully and clearly, for everyone to hear.

'She? Me?' He turned pale. He looked at Meg's blackening eye. Jane nodded. Horrified, frightened even, he finally fled into the gym, quickly followed by Jane.

The class stood in the water, mesmerised. The speed and sheer ferocity of Meg's intervention had caught everyone by surprise. For most of them, the interlude had simply been a game. As it had been for Muscles too, they thought. Nothing more. But Jane's explanation to him about what Meg had said suddenly rendered him less of a harmless diversion. For one thing, he had a name! Bashir! At a stroke, he became more of a real person; more ordinary.

But Meg was in tears. Marsha went to comfort her. 'Hell,' said Heppie. 'There was real feeling there. Meg's really got it bad, don't you think?'

'Difficult to tell, but it looks like it,' agreed Lynne. 'Those aren't just tears. They're sobs. Does she need another ice pack, Marsha?'

'I've asked her. She says not.' Unseen by the others, Di took a photo.

'Did you see the reaction on his face when the girl explained why Meg was shouting and screaming? It wasn't just surprise or disgust, even. He looked really afraid. He went white. Who would have thought it – a big bloke like that?'

'Well, he's not that big, Shula. But the biggest and best of men have feelings like the rest of us,' said Lynne.

Jean had reached the limits of her period of self-denial. 'You're all making too much of it; of her stupidity and his vanity.'

'You'd make a great agony aunt. Dishing out all sorts of advice to the lonely and the broken hearted.' For a moment, Jean was not sure whether Heppie was paying her some sort of compliment, or being sarcastic.

'It was all just a bit of fun,' said Marsha. 'But Meg can make a drama out of any situation.'

Shula wanted to move the focus away from Meg. 'I wonder where Di's got to. She was here a few moments ago, but she seems to have disappeared.'

'She was probably very upset,' said Jean. 'I saw her go back into her office.'

'Upset? But whatever for?'

Di had in fact gone to her office to make a prearranged phone call to her brother. She came back from the phone call looking distinctly brighter. All the bother with Meg and Muscles seemed not to have affected her. No one need have worried about her after all.

Luke, however, felt tense. Following Meg's splash attack, he set about tidying and drying his chair. Fortunately, his hi-fi gear was intact. So was Jean's bag, on the back of his chair.

But when he looked down at the floor, he cursed inwardly. *Fuck, fuck, fuck. Jean's feathers!* The artificial quills were still there, but the barbs sticking out from the central quills were soaking wet. He hoped and prayed that they were still usable. But the downy bits around the edges of the feathers were beyond repair. Far from being light and fluffy, they were heavy and clumped, drooping like dead little birds. He realised that Jean hadn't noticed yet. *Oh well*, he thought. *She'll have to improvise.*

Di was all smiles. 'Sorry about that everyone. I had to call my brother around quarter to, and I nearly forgot. Everything's fine. Just fine,' she added, gratuitously. It was as if she imagined that someone had asked her about the call. But of course, no one had.

Her spirits high, her shoulders straightened, she faced the class with a determined grin. 'Now, dumb-bells away. Woggle time, everyone!' She ignored the groans and sighs.

09.50
Woggles and Shoulders – As Easy as Riding a Bike?

'Come on everyone. Get rid of the dumb-bells. They're all over the place.' It was true. Since the interruption caused by Muscles (thinking of him as *Bashir* was going to require quite an effort) the ladies had abandoned their dumb-bells, which were now floating in different parts of the pool.

Collecting all of the dumb-bells together involved Luke holding open a large bag into which the ladies threw them, one by one. This was at best an untidy affair, partly because not everyone was an accurate thrower, and partly because Luke had to run from side to side with his bag to catch as many dumb-bells as he could. It was all rather like a TV gameshow, where prizes would be given to the person who could bag the most objects thrown at him or her. On top of which, Luke had to contend with Jean's constant attempts to help him, by retrieving any badly aimed dumb-bell and handing it to him personally, all the time tut-tutting at the general carelessness of her colleagues' throwing skills. She genuinely thought she was being helpful.

Eventually, Luke managed to collect all the dumb-bells. Each member of the class pulled a woggle into the pool or passed one to someone else. Like dumb-bells, woggles are foam flotation devices. Each one is more or less in the shape of a large letter "C". As the class had come to learn, they had a number of uses.

'Remember the first time?' said Shula. 'When we thought that the only thing we had to do was to grab the two ends and hold them in front of us? If only we'd known! We were so green. I was, anyway.'

'Well, some of us knew what they were for, actually. I looked up aquarobics on the Internet, in preparation for the course.'

Lynne turned to Shula, and in a girlish, simpering imitation of Jean, mouthed, 'in preparation for the course.' Then feeling bolder, and at the expense of being rude, she turned to Jean. 'Honestly. You talk just like the teacher's pet.'

Inwardly, Jean cringed. She remembered once again that this was supposed to be the first day of her new life. That had been the promise she had made to herself, just before she left home and set off for the lesson: Enjoyment. She really did want to enjoy life, or to try to. She *was* enjoying herself. But the class still was not warming to her. She was disappointed, even angry with herself. She consoled herself with the thought that her time for free expression near the end of the lesson was fast approaching. Then they would see a different Jean, someone who really could enjoy life. She would show them!

But she had to acknowledge to herself that until now, all they had seen and heard was the habitual prig, the prim reaper. The moral commentator destined to kill off any fun. She began to realise that her verbal spikes were not helping her case. What could she say and do to change everyone's mind? Was it even possible to change? Or were her old habits and attitudes too far ingrained? Jean began to suspect that nothing short of some minor catastrophe would be required for her to achieve what she needed most. Even though, as yet, she was not fully aware of what that was. She was not aware that she craved respect from the group. And ultimately, friendship.

Luke started a track that he had never actually played before, though it was on the list of requests. So this was a bit of an experiment. He was never too sure about the suitability of classical music for an aquarobics class. But this piece turned out to be much more familiar than he realised. It was the theme tune of a popular TV show, and was also used by some football supporters' club in the north of England.

'The Dance of the Knights' from Prokofiev's *Romeo and Juliet* turned out to be familiar enough. But as soon as it started, Luke sensed that it was gloriously inappropriate for Di's exercise. She wanted the class to stretch, relax and float. But the music worked against all those aims. With its military rhythm and its loud, warlike, rousing, brash sounds, it demanded your whole attention. It was anything but calming.

But by now, Luke was past caring. As long as he kept the volume down – which was surely not what the composer had intended – the class would do its best. But Luke made a mental note to himself: *Don't experiment with combinations of music and movement that I haven't tried out beforehand, Lucy. Don't improvise.*

Plan! No one could accuse him of not trying to learn from his mistakes.

Di blew her whistle. 'Ok everyone. Put your woggles behind your shoulders and under your armpits. That's right. Like a lifebelt, with the two ends in front of you. Then stretch, and relax. Legs out horizontal. Yes, like that. And just float. Hold the woggles steady. Stretch those legs together. Use your hands for balance. Good.' The class, including Dorothy, did as instructed. This part was relatively easy. Some of the class wobbled a bit to the left or right, but they all somehow managed to stay afloat.

'Good. Now bend your right leg at the knee, towards your chest. Then back out again, really straight. Then your left leg. Bend at the knee up to your chest. And back out straight. Now with both legs. Bend your knees, up to your chest, and back. You're doing well.'

'Oh, at last, at last, I'm doing it,' Heppie said to Shula, next to her. 'But I can't concentrate for the bloody music.'

'Me neither. I love the music. But it doesn't make me calm. It makes me want to get up and fight.'

'I think Prokofiev is magnificent.' For once, Dorothy was not bobbing up and down, but moving her knees up and down to her chest and back again, precisely as directed.

'Oh, I'm toppling over!'

Seeing that Heppie was in a spot of bother, Lynne shouted at her. 'You'll be OK. Just hang on to your woggle. Don't let go, whatever you do.'

Heppie tried, but couldn't hold on. She still had the woggle in her hand, but she had to stand in the water. She laughed. 'Thanks. You'd think I'd have learned by now. Two months ago, I thought that a woggle was just something that boy scouts wore around their necks. But now I have nightmares about these things.' She finally managed to refloat herself.

'Well done, Heppie. Now everyone: cycling. Imagine you're riding a bicycle. It really is as easy as riding a bike. Get your legs moving. This should make you move forwards. Forward everyone.'

'Forwards? So why am I going backwards?' said Lynne.

'And why am I going round and round in circles?' Marsha complained. 'Easy as riding a bike? Anyway, I can't actually ride a bike.'

'Come on, Water Babes. You can do it if you try.'

Oh no they can't, thought Luke. *Before they can do this, you have to teach them how, not just tell them and expect miracles. Teach them, Diana!*

Meg's woggle was just about big enough to encircle her back, and even to keep her afloat. She managed to do a bit of cycling. But moving forwards and backwards eluded her completely.

Until now, Dorothy was doing well. But suddenly, her woggle escaped from her grip, and floated away from her. 'Oh! A woggle! A woggle! My kingdom for a woggle!' she cried out, theatrically. The music had finally stopped and her voice sailed out above every other sound in the pool. The class was stunned. She was being more eccentric than ever.

'Ah! How nice,' said Mrs C approvingly, and loud enough for everyone to hear. 'Shakespeare!'

'Shakespeare? What the fucking hell's Shakespeare got to do with anything?' Without knowing it, Meg's sentiment evoked some sympathy. But nobody actually said anything.

'Ah. Perhaps more than you think. More than you think,' replied Dorothy, enigmatically. 'All human life is there.' She turned to Mrs C. 'Young people today, sometimes, they make me want to weep.'

10.00
Woggles and Bums – Excellence and Panic

Di blew her whistle for attention, even though the class guessed what was coming next. 'OK, everyone: woggles on bums!'

Taking advantage of being as it were on dry land, Di demonstrated what she wanted by positioning her woggle on her bum. She stuck her bum out, and placed the woggle on it, and held the two ends of the letter "C" in her hands in front of her. Then she slid the woggle from side to side, which, being out of the water, was a relatively easy task. She turned round so that the class could see her back view. It was not exactly a pretty sight. Onlookers would at least be spared the burden of seeing the class members' bums so exposed. That is, if all went well and everything took place as it should, underwater, and thus out of sight.

'Oh no, not this again. I can't keep my balance. I think my arse must be too big for my woggle.'

'No, Lynne. Think of it the other way round. Your woggle's too small for your arse. It's the woggle's fault!'

'Kind of you to say so, Heppie. But I don't think so.'

'Come on, ladies. Until we've got bums on woggles, we can't do the actual exercises.'

One or two members of the class had attempted to describe some of their activities to their non-aquarobics friends. When it came to describing what went on during the woggles and bums section of the lesson, those friends were suitably amused and amazed. Few people, in the class or out of it, could imagine the combination of hilarity, unpredictability and sheer indignity that these particular exercises could induce. Even getting into the correct position – bums on woggles – could be a struggle, let alone the exercises that followed.

It was even less likely that anyone who had not tried these particular exercises themselves would appreciate how difficult they were. No amount of earnest declarations of the sort 'Really, you can't imagine how hard it can be to sit on one of those woggles and keep your balance,' could persuade doubters that sitting on woggles (indeed perhaps aquarobics itself) was anything but a lark. At most, unbelievers thought that the idea of sitting on woggles was a bit of innocent fun and an easy alternative to real exercise, such as jogging, or even walking.

Certainly, people would have found the notion that sitting on woggles might be character building silly, and the exercises themselves utterly laughable. Yet, for all their strangeness, these would have been Luke's considered arguments in favour of the woggles-cum-bums combination. Could anyone suggest other better ways of helping the less fit among us face a challenge that at first seemed impossible, but which later became manageable? And all the while having fun. Exercising, and enjoying the company of others? And to music!

Consider Dorothy for example. In the last two or three sessions, she had learned to abandon her bobbing fetish at this point of the lesson. Instead, she had become quite adept at putting her bum in exactly the right place on her woggle. She had treated it all as an academic challenge.

She started by considering Di's instruction: 'woggles on bums'. She decided that what Di really meant was, 'Bums on woggles'. This inversion of Di's instruction was not just idle wordplay. It seemed a more logical way of expressing what was required. After all, reasoned Dorothy, one did not ask people to 'put that chair on your bum'. Instead, one asked people, in effect, to 'put your bum on that chair'. Dorothy's logic suited her tidy mind, and made the instruction easier to understand and to comply with. So for Dorothy, 'bums on woggles' it was.

Having analysed what was required, Dorothy broke down

the task of actually fulfilling the instruction into four phases. Phase 1 involved standing up in the water with a straight back, grasping her woggle with her arms slightly behind her, with the two arms of the letter "C" pointing forward. In Phase 2, she pushed the woggle down to her bottom as hard as she could, resisting upwards pressure from the water. Dorothy was not the only one who noted that Di's dry-land demonstration evaded the small matter of the water pressure issue. Then, in Phase 3, Dorothy plonked her bum in the centre of the woggle, at the same time sliding each hand from behind her back along the woggle itself to grasp the ends of the "C" in front of her. Finally, in Phase 4, she had to hold on tight while lifting her feet from the bottom of the pool, bending her knees slightly. Then, with luck, she would be floating, supported by her woggled-bum – or was it her bummed-woggle? She could not decide. Either way, it was like sitting in a narrow armchair. 'Now, I'm ready for the exercises at last,' she said aloud, to no one in particular.

'Oh, I'm not ready at all,' said Mrs C. 'I find this all a bit difficult, to be honest.'

'Me too,' said Heppie. 'I usually just pretend to do this. Di never seems to notice. I don't know how Dorothy does it. Or why she bothers for that matter.' These were questions that Dorothy herself could not have answered easily. How did she do it? Well, she did have some physical advantages, at least when compared to the well-built Heppie. Dorothy was fit and agile. Fortunately for her, she was also in possession of a small bottom. She had strong arms, and when needed, a good sense of balance.

But why did Dorothy decide to do so well, so late in each lesson? For some reason she could not explain, Dorothy knew that she had chosen this part of the lesson in which to excel. She *chose* to do better than the rest of the class, and *chose* to realise her potential. She knew that she was not the most beautiful, or the most musical, or the most athletic person in the class. But at least as far as some of these final exercises were concerned, she also knew that she was, or could be, the best. After all, she was not a fool and did not want anyone in the class to think that she was stupid. Therefore, at some point, her inane bobbing up and down, her adolescent rebellion to instruction, had to stop. Her pride in herself was at stake.

'Oh shit. I can't even sit on my woggle properly. I had it last week.'

'Yeah, that's what I heard.' Shula's lame attempt at a lewd joke was taken in good part by Lynne.

'Oh, chance would be a fine thing!'

'Well, it's quite simple really. It's just a question of balance.' Once again, Jean's attempt to be helpful fell short of its aim. No matter how hard she tried, she clearly didn't have the gift of being able to say the right thing, or in the right way. She was beginning to despair. Had her resolution this morning to begin a new life of enjoyment been a dreadful mistake? She began to think so.

She sensed that at least part of her enjoyment might be derived from desisting from her habit of making barbed, superior remarks. But she could not yet act on that sense. She did not yet appreciate that for this sense of enjoyment to happen, she might first have to disburden herself of the deep well of bitterness that sprang from deep inside her. To do her justice, that well was not entirely of her own making.

'We know it's just a question of balance,' Lynne said to Shula. 'That woman is beginning to get on my breasts.' The words came out before Lynne could stop herself. What on earth had she just said? *Breasts? To Shula of all people?* She wanted to sink into the water with embarrassment and shame. She blushed deeply. She cursed herself. What was she to do now? Apologise to Shula? Confess her colossal error to Heppie? 'Oh, Shula, I–'

'No Lynne. I know what you mean. And to be honest, she's beginning to get on my non-existent breasts too.' The ensuing half-second seemed to Lynne to last a lifetime. Then without warning, both she and Shula burst out laughing. Thinking that they were laughing at her, Jean felt worse than ever.

'Ok. Now those of you who can, with your bums on your woggles, lift your feet off the floor, but hold your knees together. Now bend your legs at the knees, like Dorothy's doing.' But no one could actually see below the surface of the water to see exactly what it was that Dorothy was doing so well. Everyone except Meg (whose bum really was too big for her woggle, or – as Heppie would have it – whose woggle was far too small for her bum) finally managed to achieve the required position. 'Now turn your right leg, the bit below the knee, clockwise. See what happens. Next music, Luke.'

Luke found the track he was looking for. He himself didn't like "The Windmills of Your Mind" very much. He found both the melody and the words intensely dreary, especially this version by Noel Harrison, who wrote the song. Still, the track had been chosen by someone for inclusion, and true to his word, Luke honoured all the requests. Also, he had to admit, the song and the exercise suited each other rather well.

'I'm turning. I'm turning. Look, Heppie. I can do it. I can really do it.' Shula was ecstatic.

'Good, ladies. Turn, a bit like the windmill in your mind.' Di took Dorothy as her model, who was turning with speed and grace. When she had turned round completely, twice, Di called, 'Now try it with your left leg: Only the bit below the knee. But this time turn your leg anticlockwise. That's great, Dorothy; excellent.' The class was managing at last to complete a passable version of the required movement. Dorothy and Marsha were doing particularly well. They were all doing so well that Di decided to take a photo. She needed to show people back home that her students could do *some* things properly.

'Yes. I'm going in the opposite direction now. And still managing to sit on my woggle,' said Shula. Meg, however, was still unable even to sit on her woggle, let alone balance, float or turn. She glared at Shula. She looked round the pool. She glared at all her classmates too. She hated them all.

From her vantage point in the centre of the pool, Meg was the first to notice that someone had lost her balance. It was Jean. She had tipped over to her left, losing her woggle in the process. Meg smiled. *Serves you right you snotty bitch. I'm not telling anyone. Drown for all I care.*

The next people to notice that Jean had tipped over were Di and the ever watchful Luke.

Much later, Jean recalled the moment she lost her balance. She also recalled not worrying about it, nor even caring. *It was like watching me in a film. At first, I didn't think I would die, but I honestly didn't mind if I did. I felt free, and calm. I seemed to tumble over once or twice and to touch the bottom of the pool with my hand. I must have come to the surface at some point, because I could see everyone doing the exercise.*

'Suddenly I remembered my own advice: "It's just a question of balance". I knew that in losing my own balance, I was paying some sort of price for my own stupidity. Poetic justice, I suppose. But then I swallowed some water. And water also went up my nose. I couldn't breathe. My lungs were really hurting. It was then that I started thrashing about, like a wild thing. I honestly didn't think that I was drowning, but I knew that I was panicking. That was the moment that I knew I had to transform myself into someone who needed help.'

When Jean had started thrashing about and panicking, the windmills had also stopped turning. Luke was in the pool in an instant, surrounded by the other members of the class, suddenly alarmed. Di was busy taking a photo. At last! For weeks Di felt that she had endured the smarmy attentions of this irritating, fawning woman. Guiltily, she relished the opportunity of finally catching this woman in her moment of humiliation.

Jean clung to Luke, as if for dear life. Even though she was panicking, spluttering and short of breath, she knew that she was not going to die. This was because, as she put it, she had not seen her whole life flash before her eyes, which – following the old wives' tale – she took as a sure sign of impending death. As she clung to Luke, Jean whispered, 'I'm so frightened. Help me. Please.'

For the first time in his life, Luke felt almost paternal. Jean was not merely holding on to him, as people had done in lifeguard training, and twice for real. She was clinging tightly to his arms and shoulders. Like a little girl. She was depending on him for more than mere physical rescue. He felt somehow responsible for more than her bodily well-being. It was a strange feeling. 'I've got you, Jean. Don't worry. Come on. Let's move away from the rest of the class. Let's get your breath back and talk.'

Di surreptitiously replaced her iPad beside her, satisfied that she had her photo and that Jean was now safe in Luke's arms. Meg was indifferent to Jean's fate. But the others desperately wanted to help her, and to offer genuine sympathy to this normally unlikeable person. Luke moved Jean to another part of the pool, still holding her. He managed to wave the others away while reassuring them that Jean would be OK. He declared that there was nothing for them to worry about. He would take care of her.

'God, I hope she's OK,' said Lynne.

'Don't we all,' agreed Heppie.

'I've got great faith in Luke. Let's just leave the two of them together for a few moments. She'll be OK.' The others took comfort from Marsha's words.

'OK everyone. Let's just settle down and relax. We can start again when Jean's recovered and ready.'

Jean eventually managed to disengage herself from Luke. She stood up in the water. 'So what's all this about being frightened?' Luke asked gently.

Jean lowered her head. 'I'm terrified that they won't like it.'

'What do you mean, they won't like it? They won't like what?'

'My routine; my free expression. It's near the end of the lesson, and I'm suddenly scared.'

Luke's instinct was to encourage, encourage, encourage. 'Ah, I understand. But you'll be fine, just fine. You've just had a tumble and a bit of a scare, probably because you're nervous about your, er, your performance. You just lost your concentration, that's all. I'm sure they'll all love your free expression. There's no need to be frightened at all.'

'You don't think so?'

'I'm absolutely sure of it.'

It took only thirty seconds for Luke to think twice about his words of encouragement and reassurance. He was suddenly afraid that his instinct had led him astray. He could have fobbed Jean off by explaining that no one took free expression too seriously. It was just a bit of fun, not worth bothering with. But this would have been too glib for Jean. It would have undermined her efforts to please. *Especially Diana.*

Or, if he had remembered in time, he could have said, 'Well, actually, your feathers are all wet and ruined, so it might be a good idea to abandon your free expression, at least for this course.'

But that might well have crushed Jean completely. After all, Diana would not be here for any future course, robbing Jean of the chance to impress her. In addition there was the small matter of whether or not the pool administrators would agree to there being another aquarobics course at all, once Diana had gone.

Jean had visibly brightened, and regained much of her composure. Luke decided to say nothing. 'Oh, you're such a nice man. You've been so kind to me. You've been so fantastic. I'm going to hold my head up high, and join the others.'

And she swam off, leaving Luke a little anxious. He left the pool. Jean joined the others. They surrounded her. She was, for the moment, an object of communal sympathy; except from Meg. But as far as Jean was concerned, Meg did not count.

10.10
Woggles and Feet – Giggles and Constipation

'Welcome back.'
'Are you OK now?'
'You gave us a bit of a fright there, you know.'

Jean was surprised by the way in which the class expressed their concern about her spill in the water. When she surfaced just after beginning to panic, she had seen everyone carrying on with their exercises as usual. She had concluded that they had not noticed she was in trouble, or worse, that they had not cared.

In some ways, she was aware that she didn't deserve their concern. All through the lesson she knew that she had been, for want of a better word, a bitch. She did not yet understand why her resolve earlier today – to encourage people to take a more positive attitude towards her – had deserted her. She was unable to appreciate that her morning ambition had lost the battle against years of the unholy trinity of her misplaced religiosity, her unwarranted feeling of social superiority and her suburban, parochial view of the world. On top of which Gordon's desertion compounded her bitterness, leaving a wound too deep, too complicated and too fresh to heal.

How could she do better? She didn't know. *Do I have to try even harder? Do I have to suffer another blow to my pride in order for people to rally round me?* Almost drowning had been bad enough. She feared there was more, much more hardship and wounded pride to come.

'OK everyone, near the end now. Feet on woggles.'

'Oh, this one is nigh on impossible,' said Heppie cheerfully to her sister. 'But let's give it a go.'

Di tried to help. 'Like I said last week, you'll all find this easier if you hold on to the edge of the pool.'

There was a general sigh of relief and agreement. While everyone was moving to a position at the edge of the pool, there were a few moments of general chit-chat. 'It's strange,' Lynne whispered to Marsha, 'but no matter how I try, I just can't warm to that woman.'

'Jean? I know what you mean. She's probably just as hard on herself as she is on us. But, well, we're not all the same. We can't be friends with everyone.'

'I don't expect everyone to be the same! Really I don't. I don't even want to be her friend. It's just me, I suppose.'

Woggles on feet; or, feet on woggles. Dorothy found this activity extremely difficult to carry out. So did the others. And anyone who has tried aquarobics and this exercise in particular would have to agree.

The idea is first to push your woggle to the bottom of the pool. This is no mean feat in itself. Woggles want to bounce back to the surface. Persuading a woggle to stay put on.the floor requires quiet and intense concentration. As Di suggested, being able to hold on to the side of a pool is useful. But it is almost impossible to hold on to the side of the pool and push your woggle downwards at the same time. This is where, theoretically, the feet come in.

'Put one foot on your woggle. Firmly. That should hold it down. Then holding on to the side for balance, put your other foot down on the woggle too.'

Like many of Di's instructions, this was easier to say than to do. Even if you succeeded in getting one foot on your woggle, your other foot had to battle against the rest of the damn thing. That is, against a piece of foam rubber that remains stubbornly almost upright, seeking the surface of the water.

The sight of the class concentrating on their downward movements, squeezing their buttocks, eyes closed tight with effort, holding on to the sides of the pool for support, was always too much for Salma and Luke. They both had to suppress their giggles. The class looked for all the world like a therapy session for constipation. Luke suspected correctly that Di was not going to miss this opportunity for a couple of photos.

Luke had chosen Slim Dusty's rendition of "Australia's most famous bush song" to accompany the ladies. It was a song that Di loathed. To her, it represented all that was dated, corny, false and inescapably masculine about the image of the typical Australian. She hated the way in which Brits in particular invariably sang this song as soon as they were aware that Australians were around. She hated the way that foreigners assumed that all Australians, including her, loved the tune and the words. She hated the way in which she was asked time and time again what the words meant. She did not know what they meant, and cared less. She hated to think that *she* was the one who had chosen the track.

But for months afterwards Salma had only to mention the strains of "Waltzing Matilda" for her and Luke to fall about in helpless laughter. There was something if not funny, then certainly idiotic about watching a group of apparently constipated women. Especially while listening to a song that despite its title was in fact neither about a dance nor a woman. It was about a man walking, carrying a bag.

Unaware that Di had been taking photos of their efforts to stand on their woggles, Jean shouted triumphantly, 'I did it. I stood on my woggle. With both feet! I hope Diana got a photo of that.' Indeed, Di had got the picture that Jean wanted.

Well, bully for you chuck, thought Lynne.

Shula was more sympathetic. 'Can you do it again, Jean?'

'Oh yes, I think I can. It's a knack. Yes, I've got it again. Look. And I'm not even hanging on to the side this time.'

'Di!' shouted Shula. 'Can you see? Jean's managed to stand on her woggle, with both feet. So can you–

'Oh yes, please take a photo of me standing on my woggle. Please Diana.'

'That's ok,' said Di. 'I've already got one.' *Silly woman.*

Mercifully, "Waltzing Matilda" came to an end. 'You ought to feel really proud of yourself, Jean.' Shula knew she was laying it on a bit thick, but it was all in a good cause. She was helping Jean recover from her panic attack. Jean could now relax and bask in temporary glory. She stepped off her woggle, allowing it to bob up to the surface.

'Yes, you can feel right proud of yourself. But remember: pride comes before a fall,' said Lynne, somewhat ungraciously. Jean's sense of pride in her achievement suddenly evaporated. Once again, her insides felt empty with dread.

'Congratulations, Jean. That was great.'

Jean found herself feeling flattered that even Marsha was taking a sympathetic interest in her. 'Thanks. I hope Diana got a good photo, that's all,' she said, in a much louder voice than she intended.

Oh, I'm sure she did. I'm sure that she's got a lot of good photos, thought Luke.

Di looked on, perfectly content. Happy even.

10.20
Noodles and Crotches – An Exercise Too Far

Normally, it was at this stage of the proceedings, before the final warm down, that each member of the class did her free expression. These were intended as a form of light relief. Members of the class accepted them as such. But for Jean, as Luke knew, her free expression was deadly serious.

He was aware that Jean had tensed up, ready for her performance. But given her upset a few minutes previously, he was not entirely sure that she would actually go ahead with her routine. He also suspected that he was being guilty of wishful thinking. The free expression sessions were at best somewhat chaotic, and none of the ladies, or Di, had kept a record of who had done what, or when. None of them had taken their moment in the sun too seriously, so no one would notice that someone had missed her opportunity to shine. But Jean would notice, thought Luke ruefully. She wanted to shine; especially for Diana. Jean, more than the others, would realise that today there was something new to soak up the time for free expression: noodles.

'OK ladies. Please give your woggles back to Luke, and take up your noodles.'

The woggles were duly returned to Luke at the end of the pool. As usual, they were thrown somewhat randomly at the big bag he held out. Then the ladies each grasped a noodle, curious to see what Di wanted to use them for.

Di stood a noodle in front of her, grasping the bottom part between her knees, so that the top part was level with her face. 'This is one thing you do with your noodle. You lie on it, on your stomach, and it helps you float. Then you just use your hands and arms in the water to propel yourself forwards.' She mimed the movement, still standing up, and used her arms, as if doing a crawl. 'Easy!'

'Mm, that might be easy for you, Di, but you've got a good sense of balance.'

'I think my noodle might be too thin to hold me up,' laughed Heppie.

'I suppose we could give it a try.' Dorothy, pencil thin, wanted to take up the challenge.

'Another thing the noodle will help you to do is this: you can lie your back on it. And use your hands to make you go forwards or back.' Di made a show of holding her noodle against her back.

The class became more critical.

'No way, José.'

'Too easy to fall off.'

'Bugger that for a lark.'

'I don't like floating or swimming on my back.'

Luke doubted that the class would be willing – or able – to use the noodles in either of the ways that Di had suggested. 'Get in the bloody water yourself and show them first,' he said under his breath.

Di was aware that the class was resisting. She had not taken into account that they were tired, and that introducing such a new element towards the end of the final class would be so risky. She could feel the prospects for some final photos fading away before her. She was losing the class.

She did not know what to do to regain everyone's attention. In a rare moment of almost panic, an idea suddenly came to her. She could not for the life of her say where the idea came from. But later, in the privacy of her own mind, she admitted to herself that probably it had suddenly emerged, unbidden, from her subconscious. Wherever it had originated, once it came to her consciousness, the idea was unstoppable.

'Well ladies, I'll show you all something that you *can* do with your noodles. Music, Luke! "Addicted to Love". It was the only request that Di had made for inclusion on Luke's iPod. She had asked for it only for this week. She had instructed him to have the track ready for the end of the lesson. 'The exercise with noodles, OK?'

Luke adored the song, in its several versions. But this original version was his favourite. He and Ted had danced to it many times in the town's two gay clubs. The clubs had big screens. They showed the original accompanying video. It was of Robert Palmer, looking in his shirt and tie less like a pop star and more like a city gent. His leonine head of hair made him look glamorous. He was backed by four identical girls, dressed all in black and wearing the same bright red lipstick. Three of them were playing, or pretending to play white guitars, while the fourth played keyboards. The video was cool, camp, sexy and immense fun.

But once the music got under way, Luke was genuinely shocked at Di's panicky choice of activity. Without warning, she inserted her noodle between her legs, right under her crotch. She posed provocatively. Foodies might have said that they saw a large cucumber, or a stick of rhubarb between Di's legs. Everyone else saw an oversized penis, which Di proceeded to fondle, to put into her mouth, and to move back and forth with her hands, miming ecstasy.

One or two of the class shrieked with surprise; for all of three seconds. Thereafter, it was only Meg who squealed with delight as she did an underwater version of Di's movements, with the top of her noodle sticking out of the water. 'I wish Muscles could see me now,' she screamed.

'Well,' shouted Di, her arms akimbo. 'What are you all waiting for? Woggles and crotches, crotches and woggles. Go! It's better than sex.'

Other than Meg, no one moved.

Can't remember that far back, thought Heppie.
She must be completely bonkers, thought Lynne.
I couldn't possibly comment, thought Shula.
I'll have to take your word for it, thought Dorothy.
Poor girl, thought Mrs C.
Then you must be really desperate, thought Marsha.
You cannot be serious, thought Salma.
Please, don't let me down Diana, thought Jean.
Dirty bitch, thought Luke.

Luke looked on, grim-faced and disapproving, unable to disguise his distaste. He knew that under normal circumstances, there needed to be only one complaint about what Di was doing and she would have had the sack. Was she making the most of her final chances to embarrass and humiliate the class? He could only hope that the ladies could work out that the responsibility for what was happening was hers, not his. He was only in charge of turning the music on and off. He was not responsible for the actual choices.

Di knew by now that only Meg was "using" her noodle. 'Are you enjoying yourself, Meg?' Di leered. It was a wholly unnecessary question, to which the answer was blindingly obvious. But Di wanted to see Meg with her mouth open, her fat face split by a grin, with a full view of her irregular, nicotine-stained teeth. Bingo! She could have taken a great photo. But a wave of temporary hostility from the class stopped her.

'OK, fun over everyone.' There was no reaction from the class. It was as if they had all resisted being bewitched by a sorceress. Luke turned the music off.

Mrs C in particular wondered whether her good nature had been exploited by Di. Had she been taken for a fool? She hoped not. If so, it was a terrible thing for a teacher to do to any student. She was suddenly relieved that this lesson would be the last with Di. She was grateful that she and her daughter would not be exposed to any more of Di's trickery. She wanted to forget the last few minutes, and just remember the good times.

Had she been challenged about her behaviour, Di would have said in all innocence that trickery was the last thing on her mind. She just wanted, after all the hard, serious work she had put in, to have a good time on this last day. But she had blown it, and she knew it. That last "exercise" had been an exercise too far.

Later, some members of the class considered whether Luke also bore some responsibility for the debacle. They decided that, given his angry glances towards Di over the last few minutes, he did not. After all, he had not even smiled when Di thrust her noodle between her legs. No. Luke was blameless. Di had been acting alone.

And, trying to recover from her mistake, she was still acting alone. 'So, with your heads towards the spectator end, where Salma is, try to lie on your noodles. Lie on your backs, and put your legs and feet on the long bit. Then just relax and float backwards, using your hands to propel yourselves to the end of the pool. Where you can, give the noodles back to Luke.'

The more assiduous members of the class, Jean, Marsha and Shula, tried to follow this new instruction. But they soon gave up. The others, Mrs C, Dorothy, Meg, Lynne and Heppie did not even bother to try to do what Di wanted. They knew that even with regular practice, this was an activity that would be extremely difficult, and potentially demeaning. Each member of the class gave her noodle to Luke. In silence.

Di had made an error of judgement; a serious error. She had temporarily lost control of her class. It was principally Dorothy who had both the experience and the intelligence to know what had gone wrong. To her, it was clear that the teacherly duties of clear guidance, preparation, demonstration, exemplification, support and checking of learning had deserted their instructor.

Why that should be so was no real mystery, at least to Dorothy. Di was leaving the country tomorrow. She was probably demob happy. *These days*, wondered Dorothy, *would anyone understand what that meant?* Either way, you did not need to be a weather forecaster to know which way the wind had finally blown. Di's final exercise idea had been a disaster.

Tired and upset, the class resumed their places and stood waiting, now without any of the flotation devices. They just wanted to get on with the final phase of the lesson, the familiar and comforting warm down.

5. Warm-Down, Free Expression and Aftermath

10.30
WARM-DOWN – DISTRESS AND A CHORUS OF SUPPORT

'OK, everyone, time for your warm down and final stretching exercises.'

Luke listened in dismay. This was in fact the group's *first* proper stretching exercise. Perhaps because she was running out of time, Di had decided to conflate stretching and warming down. But he had learned in his course that these had to be considered as two separate activities. But never mind. This would be the last time that she would mess things up. Luke knew that Di had mistimed much of the lesson. Again, perhaps because this was her final session of the course, she had crammed too much in. The leg exercises had taken up far too much time. And the noodle part of the lesson had turned out to be as vulgar as it was unnecessary.

The class could have and should have done a good deal more stretching. They should have been gradually prepared for the increased difficulty of exercises as the lesson progressed. Di had never really given any thought to the incremental build-up of her exercises, or to their relative difficulty. For someone so physical, she did not appreciate the different kinds and levels of strain that each successive set of exercises put on various parts of the body.

Each member of the class returned to her usual position.

Luke detected more than the signs of mild relief that their ordeal – for that is what this final lesson had become – would soon be over. Fortunately, everyone – including Meg – liked the warm-down exercises. So they all looked forward to a final five minutes of uninterrupted calm. It was just after 10.30, and the class was officially over. But they needed some downtime.

Luke paid particular attention to Jean. He noticed that she was a bit slow to take up her position nearest to Di. So far, Jean had given no indication that, like everyone else, she wanted to do anything but finish the class on a peaceful note. Perhaps she was tired. Her face for once was a picture of contentment, all bitterness gone from her usual expression. Her eyes were closed, and she smiled. It was as if she were in a dream.

It had become something of a tradition for this part of the lesson to be accompanied by an instrumental, piano version of "Greensleeves", which everyone liked. Luke started the track, while watching for any sign that Jean still wanted to perform, especially for Diana. He sighed. If she did want to do free expression, she was fast running out of time. But perhaps in her dreamy state, she had abandoned her plan? Luke rather hoped so.

Di blew her whistle for the very last time – or so everyone thought. 'Hands in the air, gently. Now lock your fingers together, and make slow figures of eight, out of the water, moving side to side. Rock the baby, side to side. Careful, Dorothy, you're rocking and moving too quickly. You'll kill your baby!'

The effect of making slow motion figures of eight, with eyes closed, was vaguely hypnotic. Certainly most of the class felt that this is what they had come to the class for: An opportunity, however brief, to let the stress of their lives fall away. They surrendered their minds and bodies to something other than the mental and physical tasks involved with families, jobs, chores, shopping, illness, housework, cooking and money worries.

'Remember that this final exercise has two parts. Close your eyes and just relax.' The class needed no further cues. Relieved, they did as instructed. 'For the first part, put your arms in front of you, palms outwards. Then gently lock those fingers together. Now stretch your arms out, palms outwards, away from you. That's right. Straighten those elbows and push, right out. Good. And breathe in and out, slowly.' Everyone did as required and felt better. 'Terrific. Now for the second part. Slowly raise your outstretched arms over your head. Locked palms towards the ceiling. And breathe in and out. Slowly. Raise your arms high. Let the music carry you away.'

The music was soporific. It seemed now that Jean was not the only one in a dream. The class carried on lowering and raising their outstretched arms while breathing deeply. It was a wholly satisfying activity, even for the hyperactive black-eyed Meg.

'Now up with those arms once more; right up. That's right. You can now wake up everyone! Release your fingers, and give yourself a round of applause. Well done.' The ladies came out of their trance-like state, smiling. They gave Di and themselves a soft round of applause. Right on cue, "Greensleeves" came to its gentle end. The lesson was over. 'Thanks. See you this evening.' To general cries of 'Thanks Di', 'It was great', 'See you later', Di returned to her office. She was happier than anyone that it was all over.

The first to climb out of the pool was Marsha, who stood waiting for Meg. Looking from their positions out of the pool, both Marsha and Luke could see that Jean stood stock still in the water, and seemed unable to move. But suddenly her head started twitching from side to side. She was like a little frightened bird. 'Oh Diana, Diana,' she called anxiously, breathlessly. It was like a distress signal; clear, emitted in no specific direction. Meg climbed out of the pool, but the others remained in the water.

'She's gone into her office. Didn't you see her? She can't hear you, Jean,' said Marsha, kneeling down at the side of the pool, as close to Jean as she could get. 'What's wrong?' Marsha was soon joined by Luke.

Tears were rolling down Jean's face. By now the others were aware that once again, she was in some sort of distress. They crowded round her solicitously. 'Jean?' asked Heppie, putting her arms round her for comfort. Jean shook her off, impatiently.

'Oh Luke. Luke!' Jean burst out. 'Can you please tell Diana that–'

Luke needed no further urging. He had already left his chair and was well on his way to the office. 'Don't worry. She's probably just gone for a pee or something,' he lied. 'I'll go and get her back. Give me a minute. There's plenty of time.'

'Time for what, Lucy?' said Lynne. 'It's already nearly twenty to eleven.'

'Time for my free expression, that's what!' And as Luke reached the office, Jean burst into tears.

'Oh, but I assumed we wouldn't be bothering with free expression today. So was it your turn today?' said Shula. 'I don't think any of us realised, did we, ladies?' They shrugged their shoulders and shook their heads.

'Sorry, Jean,' someone said awkwardly.

'But you've all done a free expression! I've rehearsed something. It only takes three minutes: nothing very exciting of course, but still. And I made a special recording. Luke's got it. But now that it's the end of the lesson, I suppose I won't get my chance. I don't think it's fair.'

Privately one or two of the class, mainly Lynne and Dorothy, thought that Jean was being unnecessarily immature and selfish. She had got everything out of proportion.

It fell to Heppie to propose a possible practical solution, and one that would help Jean. 'Nonsense! If it takes only three minutes, there's plenty of time, isn't there?' she said, desperately looking round for support. Some support was reluctantly offered, though not with any great enthusiasm. 'As Jean says, we've all done free expression, haven't we? Now it's Jean's turn. It's the last lesson, after all. So bugger the time.'

'I agree,' said Mrs C firmly.

'Oh no, not today; I'm knackered,' complained Meg, from the side.

In a tone that would brook any opposition, Marsha snapped at Meg. 'Get back in the pool. You're not going anywhere for five minutes.'

'Luke's gone to get Di. And if she can't make it, then you can do it just for us, Jean,' said Heppie, trying to move things along. 'I don't see anyone waiting to use the pool.'

But this only brought on a moment of panic from Jean. 'But I can't do it without Diana. It's especially for her; in return for all her hard work!'

'Oh, I see. 'Well, yes, what a kind thought', was the general response. Someone – Dorothy later claimed that it was her – shouted, 'Jean! Jean!'

And within half a minute the single voice had become a chorus. 'Jean! Jean! Jean!' The class clapped their hands with each shout. Even Salma joined in, stamping her feet in time with the chorus of support.

By the time Luke had stormed into the office, Di was about to go for a coffee. 'Don't even think about coffee! What's come over you? God, you can be a heartless bitch sometimes. Get out there and finish the class.'

'What are you talking about? It *is* finished!'

Luke was so angry that he could hardly get the words out. 'Free expression. That's what. Jean.'

'Huh? You aren't making sense.'

'I told you about the feathers and stuff, on the floor; near my chair. I *told* you they were for Jean's free expression. But you forgot. You were so keen to embarrass everyone with your bright idea about sticking those damn noodles between their legs that you didn't leave enough time for anything or anyone else.'

'For Christ's sake, is that all? Anyway, I can't stand the woman.'

Fortunately, he had not mentioned that Jean's free expression was "especially for Diana". That would have put Di off completely. Nor had he mentioned that Meg had ruined Jean's feathers, which still lay waterlogged near his chair. 'Whether you like her or not is beside the point. She's your student. You have a responsibility to her. She's out there. She must have told the others by now. She's in a real state.'

'Don't be ridiculous. She's a grown woman. She ought to be old enough to put up with a bit of disappointment now and again. That's life.'

From the pool itself, the shouts of, *'Jean! Jean!'* were now clearly audible.

'You just don't get it, do you? Of course, they're grown women. But in here they're also learners, students, teenagers, pupils, kids or whatever you want to call them. Babes. Water Babes. *Your* Water Babes, Di. You're their teacher. They just want to please you for God's sake. Don't let them down. Get out there woman, and finish your job.'

'But the time.'

'The next school group doesn't arrive til quarter past eleven. There's masses of bloody time. It'll only take two or three minutes.'

Di stood up. Without making any spoken concessions to Luke's arguments, she said, 'OK. But I'm not going anywhere without this.' She picked up her iPad, with an air of defiance.

'You can bring the whole Australian Navy for all I care.' *You wish*, thought Di as she followed Luke out of the office.

Trying his best to appear calm and nonchalant, Luke

walked out of the office, round the pool, and back to his chair. Di followed a few steps behind, disguising her annoyance. The class cheered and clapped. Luke theatrically asked for silence. 'Well, ladies, as I said: it was just a call of nature. The lady is back!' There were more cheers and applause.

Delighted and excited by the turn of events, Jean had already made her way out of the pool. She stepped lightly to retrieve her bag from Luke's chair.

'And to introduce our final free expression, over to you Di!' cried Luke enthusiastically, as if he was some latter day Master of the Revels.

10.40
Free Expression – Snatching Defeat From Victory

Di managed to enter into the spirit of things well enough to shout out, 'OK everyone. Now, by popular request, I give you Jean, and her free expression. Go Jean!' She blew her whistle for what now turned out to be the very last time.

The class cheered and clapped. Jean lost no time in asking Luke if he had the music, and to turn it on. 'OK, Jean,' he said cheerfully, not knowing what would come. 'Break a leg!' Jean looked at him, mystified. Clearly, she was not as familiar as he was with the jargon of the theatre. Nor did he really understand what the phrase actually meant. But as a theatrically switched-on gay man, he was sufficiently *au fait* with the expression to know when to say it.

Jean wanted to establish the correct joyful mood, even before she reached into her bag for her "costume". Luke slotted her iPod into his portable dock and pressed play. The class instantly recognised the big brass opening of the famous instrumental. Those trombones were unmistakable. The sound was at once atmospheric, raucous, heavily rhythmical, and highly suggestive. Four people – Di, Luke, Jean and Marsha – knew the name of the tune: "The Stripper". But Luke was the only one who knew that the recording was made by David Rose, who had composed the tune as long ago as 1957.

Everyone, including even Meg, was laughing and enjoying the unexpected fun. Prompted by Luke in his chair, they all began waving their arms in the air, side to side, in time with the music. It was as if they were all fans at a pop concert, worshipping their idols.

Jean had her back to the class. She removed her restrictive swimming hat, allowing her hair to fall loosely. This brought forth a cheer. Then she quickly reached into her bag on Luke's chair. First, she retrieved a pair of four-inch high-heeled shoes.

Thanks to all her practice, she managed to get into her shoes easily, despite her feet being wet.

More applause. Then she took out a Union Jack, which she tied around her midriff, taking care not to restrict her leg movements too much. Even from behind, the class could clearly see this for what it was: a sort of patriotic gesture. Everyone, including the "Scotland Forever" member of the group, cheered their appreciation. Dorothy surprised everyone by shouting, 'Rule Britannia,' as if Jean were Boadicea, about to rouse her troops. Finally as Jean took out and donned a bowler hat, the class was agog with anticipation and excitement. It had taken her no more than forty-five seconds to complete her carefully thought-out look.

She bent down to pick up the two feathers. This was the moment that Luke had been dreading. He carried on waving his arms, trying not to think about Jean's reaction.

Her reaction was 'Shit! Shit!' Not merely thinking the words, but saying them out loud, as she grasped the wet feathers in her hands. Fortunately, the music drowned out her curses. *Oh well. Just my luck*, she thought. *I'll just have to carry on regardless*. Her determination to impress the class, especially Diana, was undimmed.

She took one feather in each hand. She raised her arms high in the air and turned to face Diana, who was directly in front of her, a few steps away. Jean smiled broadly at her. She shook the raised, wet feathers in the air, and let the drops of water fall where they may. Provocatively putting one leg in front of the other, she stepped forward in time with the music. Di was suitably amazed. She took a photo of this normally sour-faced woman, moving towards her like an improbable variation of Gypsy Rose Lee.

In the pool, the class went wild with applause and appreciation. Several of them attempted a watery imitation of Jean's stripper walk, while holding their arms straight up and looking as seductive as possible. After all, the original aim of free expression was for the person whose turn it was to assume the role of instructor, while the others imitated her movements! Neither Di nor Luke felt that Jean was fulfilling this original aim particularly well, but who cared? Everything was ending on a genuinely happy note, and Jean seemed to be a changed woman.

Jean took up her instructor position, facing the class. 'Follow me, ladies,' she cried. With her arms now a little lower, and still in time with the music, she bumped her right hip outwards a little, and then her left hip; nothing too obvious, just enough to titillate and amuse. The class duly and willingly followed suit, bumping their hips invisibly beneath the water. Jean felt good. *At last, I am being appreciated*, she thought.

She was even laughing. She stood with her feet apart, and her feathered arms outstretched. With her arms and legs stretched out, her pose reminded Dorothy of Leonardo's *Vitruvian Man*. From that point on she could not help thinking of Jean as anything other than *Vitruvian Woman, With Feathers*. Everyone in the pool adopted a similar Leonardo-type pose, Dorothy included. They stood in the pool, legs apart, arms held out, half raised to the ceiling, holding or waving imaginary feathers.

Perhaps Jean was nearer the edge of the pool than she had realised. Or perhaps her waterlogged feathers, still held by her slightly raised, outstretched arms, were heavier than they looked. With their soaked barbs and ugly, damp clumps of artificial down around them, the feathers certainly seemed heavy to Jean.

She suddenly became painfully aware that although she had practised her moves at home many times, the feathers (along with everything else, including herself) had always been bone dry. And light. But not now; on this occasion, when it really mattered, the much practised downward movement of her arms and feathers across her body were heavier than she could have predicted, and had dramatically lowered her centre of gravity.

The first thing to fall in the water was her bowler hat. After a moment's wobble, Jean herself inevitably followed suit. She managed to straighten her body out, but only in time to ensure that she entered the water via a spectacular bellyflop. It all happened very quickly but not too quickly for Di. This time she managed to catch the scene not merely on camera, but on the iPad's video too. Luke stopped the music.

It took a few seconds for some in the class to realise that Jean's reappearance in the water might not in fact be part of her free expression routine. After all, such was the unusualness of her performance that anything might have been possible. Everything about her free expression, which so far had lasted for only two minutes, had been so uncharacteristic of Jean's behaviour. But the alarm on Luke's face, and to give her credit, on Di's face too, proved that this was yet another unplanned incident in this incident crowded lesson.

Luke jumped into the pool. Jean had already bobbed back to the surface of the water. She was naturally a bit breathless, but otherwise in control of herself. Water spewed from her mouth. As she shook her head, more water sprayed from her hair, which was now plastered over her eyes and face. She looked angrily around her. As Lynne put it later, 'Her look could have burnt a hole in the side of a rhinoceros.'

Luke and Heppie approached Jean, making various offers of help, or trying to. But that proved more difficult than expected. Jean fiercely rejected all offers of help and expressions of sympathy. She roughly brushed aside every hand or arm offered to her. Remarkably, she was still grimly holding on to the two feathers. She used them to swipe people out of her way. She made for the steps near the changing rooms. The damned Union Jack, still tied round her stomach, was heavier than ever. It was more of a hindrance than Jean could have imagined. The others cleared the way for her departure from the pool, unwilling to get in her way. They sensed that Jean needed some space and time to recover her dignity. And, hopefully, enough time to regain her recent good humour.

Jean finally reached the shallow steps near the changing rooms, and climbed slowly out of the water. She could not run, though she dearly wanted to. Her costume was too heavy. The stupid, heavy Union Jack stuck to her legs, slowing her down. To make things worse, she had lost one of her high heels in the pool. The other shoe miraculously and humiliatingly still clung on to her left foot.

Meg was laughing. Not, for once, out of spite, but because she thought it was all genuinely amusing. But the others, including Di and Luke, knew Jean well enough to know that she was not the type to see a funny side to all this. Therefore, they could not see a funny side either, not even at Jean's expense.

Everyone looked on and watched the sad, back view of Jean emerging from the pool, feathers still in hand, struggling with her soppy Union Jack, hobbling away from them on one shoe. Before she reached the changing rooms, she turned round. The class held its breath, afraid of what she might say. Barely whispering, and through gritted teeth, Jean asked whether someone could retrieve her hat and other shoe, and bring them to her cubicle.

As she left the pool area, Jean was aware of someone rapidly approaching her from behind. 'Oh Jean, I'm so sorry. Can I help? I just want you to know that I loved it. Thanks!' She tried to touch Jean.

'No, Diana. Don't touch me. You can't help. And no, don't lie. You didn't love it. How could you? I made a bloody fool of myself, as usual. It was a stupid, selfish idea.' Whereupon Jean turned her back on Di, and disappeared into the changing rooms.

10.45
Aftermath – The Changing Rooms

Di returned to the office, feeling rebuffed and hurt by Jean's rejection and by her accusation of falsehood. But she was determined not to let Jean spoil her day. Luke collected Jean's iPod from his dock, disconnected his various speakers and followed Di.

'Well, that was an unholy mess.'

'The whole thing was a stupid idea from the start. You shouldn't have persuaded me to let her do it.'

'But I couldn't predict how things would turn out, Di. So you can't blame me entirely.'

'I'm not blaming you. It was her own damn fault. And now she's upset everyone, including me.'

'So *you're* upset?'

'Of course I am. Don't insult me, Luke.'

'I'm sorry.' *I'm sorry?* Luke could not believe that he was actually apologising to Di. Perhaps Ted's advice about not being so critical and acerbic was at last having some effect. Luke could not help hoping that any change in his behaviour would be permanent rather than temporary. 'Well, perhaps you'll have a chance to make things right with Jean at the party tonight.' He did not want Di to feel any worse than she apparently did.

'Mm, perhaps so. But right now, I'm off for a coffee. On my own.' Di left the office. And that was that.

As Di made her way to the coffee shop, the class left the pool and filed into the changing rooms. Everyone felt a little uncertain about how to feel and what to do. There was a distinct air of unfinished business. Mrs C and Salma were the first to enter the changing rooms. They passed Jean, sitting slumped on a bench, her head hung down. They smiled at her sympathetically. But Jean did not see them.

Next came Meg, bounding along full of the joys of spring. She was utterly unaware of Jean's sense of defeat. 'Oh, that was great; really fantastic. I thought it was terrific! What was that tune? I loved it. Really sexy. And where did you get those feathers from?'

Jean raised her head and gave Meg a wan smile. 'Here,' she managed to say. 'You can take them.' She gave the feathers to Meg. She forced herself to add, 'Hope your eye gets better.'

'Thanks. Can I really keep the feathers? You're a pal!' She took the feathers, and went to her cubicle, genuinely delighted and grateful.

Well, thought Jean. *One person liked it, even if she is the most obnoxious, stupid girl I've ever met.* She did not consider Meg intelligent enough to be capable of sarcasm, so took Meg's praise at face value. The girl was probably not even capable of common deceit. So despite herself, Jean found herself being mildly grateful to Meg. To a person who, half an hour ago, had been the only one to ignore her plight when she tipped over into the water and could have drowned. Then, Jean had huffily concluded, Meg was unimportant. But now, without knowing it, Meg had lit a small candle of gratitude in Jean's heart.

Lynne went to her own cubicle and Shula to hers, a double cubicle that she shared with her sister.

Heppie and Marsha, however, decided to stay and to try and help Jean. Marsha was carrying Jean's bowler hat and missing shoe, retrieved from the pool. They sat on the bench, either side of Jean. She refused to face either of them and buried her face in her hands. But Heppie and Marsha were equally determined to break down the wall of anger and disappointment with which Jean had shut herself off from the class.

Heppie gently took Jean's arm and moved it away from her face. 'Can you tell us how you're feeling, Jean? Please. We only want to help.'

Jean shook her head. She started to sob. She had had enough. She covered her face again and started humming to herself, and rocking backwards and forwards. Heppie hadn't a clue what the tune was. Marsha thought she recognised it, but no more than that.

'Can I help?' It was Dorothy.

'Oh thanks,' said Heppie. 'She's obviously still very upset.'

'Can I sit next to her?' asked Dorothy.

Heppie moved aside to let Dorothy sit down.

'What's that tune she's humming?'

'Mm,' said Dorothy, nodding. 'I know it.' Dorothy put her arm around Jean, rocking back and forth with her. 'Shall you and I sing the words, Jean?'

'Please.'

Dorothy started to sing words to the tune. Jean joined in with her.

A sunbeam, a sunbeam,
Jesus wants me for a sunbeam.
A sunbeam, a sunbeam,
To shine for him each day.'

'There. Does that feel better?' asked Dorothy.

Jean nodded. Heppie took this as a good sign, realising at the same time that it was hardly surprising she did not know either the tune or the words. Jean stopped her rocking motion. *Good*, thought Heppie. Maybe Jean was beginning to let her feelings out, was releasing herself from the turmoil she was in. Dorothy still held Jean in her arms. Eventually she looked up, and spoke through her tears. 'It was all so ridiculous. I feel ashamed, and so angry with myself.'

'Ashamed? But whatever for?'

'I wanted it to be so perfect, for everyone. Especially for–' Jean could not continue. 'Those blasted feathers were soaking wet, even before I started. I shouldn't have used them.'

'But accidents just happen. There was nothing to be ashamed of, Jean! Really.'

'I'm ashamed because I thought I was good enough to impress everyone. I tried really hard. But I wasn't good enough. I'm hopeless.'

'Hopeless? No, no. When you started, you were like a real trouper,' said Marsha, touching Jean's arm. 'You were really good, believe me.'

Apart from in hospital, this was the first time that Jean had been touched by a black person. To think that Marsha was offering her comfort, and was sitting so close to her; Jean felt truly appreciative. *How things can change*, she thought.

'Shall I come and help you tidy up and get dressed?' asked Marsha. 'Then Dorothy can get changed and Heppie can go and help Shula. You need to get out of those things and take that Union Jack off before you catch your death of cold. Look. I've got your hat and your other shoe. Both a bit wet, I'm afraid. And here's your bag. Let's go and get you fixed up.'

To her surprise, Jean found herself saying yes to Marsha. She knew that she needed help, and wanted the closeness of another human being, no matter who that was. Marsha helped Jean to stand up and assisted her to her cubicle.

'Thanks, Marsha. Do you think you'll be OK on your own with her?'

'Sure. She'll be a welcome change from Meg!' laughed Marsha.

Jean and Marsha busied themselves in Jean's cubicle. Dorothy left and Heppie helped Shula pack her things and put her outdoor clothes on. Occasionally, Shula still needed reassurance that her specially constructed clothes gave her the feeling that, despite her operations, she was still a whole woman. Heppie suspected, correctly, that at some level of consciousness, her younger sister was in a state of denial about her altered identity. Heppie wanted to be around when Shula's denial of her altered self ended for good, which soon it must; the sooner the better.

'Oh, what the hell are you two doing in there? Are you lezzies or something?' Flushed with pleasure at having been given Jean's feathers, and now ready to leave, Meg felt and sounded hyper confident. 'Still farting around in there? That's why you're always late!'

Furious, Heppie stepped out of her double cubicle half dressed, and hissed, 'Do you mind? I'm helping my sister. That's what I'm doing.'

'Sister? Anyone would think she's your baby.'

Marsha shot out of Jean's cubicle to confront Meg. But before she could reach her, Lynne appeared. She took hold of Meg's shoulders and pushed her face up to Meg's. Loudly, clearly and steadily, Lynne thundered, 'Will you just shut the fuck up, or you just might get another black eye!'

Surprised by Lynne's grip and ferocity, Meg wrested herself away, and stood in a corner, sulking and pouting. 'Hurry up, Marsh. I want to go now.'

'You can just wait until I've got dressed.'

Salma coughed, to remind everyone that she and her mother were still there. 'Well, Mum and I will be off now.'

'Oh sorry,' said Lynne. 'We haven't been ignoring you. It's just that–'

'No problem. Mum and I just wanted to double check that everyone knew where to come this evening. Seven-thirty.'

'Oh yes. I've written the address down for everyone.'

'And it's on those nice invitation cards,' Heppie pointed out. 'Glendale Avenue, number four; second house up from the traffic lights, on the left.'

Salma and her mother nodded. They were both a little puzzled at Heppie's detailed knowledge not only of the address, but also of exactly which house they lived in.

'Are you still sure that we can't bring anything?'

Mrs C waved her arms. 'No, nothing,' she smiled.

'Famous Asian hospitality,' laughed Salma. She and Mrs C turned and left.

Dorothy was next to leave. 'Cheerio everyone. See you tonight.'

Lynne offered to escort Jean to the car park and to see that she was fit to drive home. But before leaving, she arranged with Heppie and Shula where and when to meet later in the afternoon, to shop for Di's farewell present.

Lynne hurried out. Jean, walking behind her, took time to turn round and wave goodbye to Heppie. Without warning she gave a girly smile and said, 'Toodle-oo!'

'She's a strange lady. Do you think she'll be OK?' asked Marsha.

'Jean? She'll be fine. I think she just wants to be friendly, but doesn't know how. She needs to change, to adapt. We all have to learn at some time or another. It's just that for some people it comes later rather than earlier. She isn't out of the woods yet, but she soon will be. You mark my words.'

'Trust Heppie. My big sister's usually right.'

Marsha gave a sigh. 'Well, yes.' She spoke quietly. 'Oh, sorry about Meg's outburst just now; it was unforgivable.' She was clearly accustomed to apologising for Meg's behaviour, but was also tired of having to do so.

'Consider it forgotten,' lied Heppie. 'As I said before; half the time she doesn't know what she's saying.'

Gratefully, Marsha chose this moment to end any further discussion about Meg. 'Well, I'm taking Meg to the medical centre after lunch. Then I expect I'll have to find something to do with her until teatime. I've got an appointment at half past four to have my hair done for tonight.'

Heppie was direct. 'Medical Centre? Meg's OK, isn't she?'

A little startled by the pointed and personal nature of the question, Marsha replied quickly, 'Oh yes. It's just that she has to have regular check ups. Blood pressure and stuff, that's all. But I think she's having some tests. For diabetes,' she added, a little indiscreetly.

'Ah.' *No surprise there* thought both sisters.

'And of course, the doctor can have a look at her eye.'

Marsha turned to leave. 'Come on, Meg. Are you ready?'

'Been ready for bloody ages,' she answered testily, glaring at the sisters.

'See you later. Good luck with the shopping,' said Marsha as she and Meg walked away.

'Talk about chalk and cheese,' murmured Shula, 'or *Beauty and the Beast*. One's as grotesque as the other is beautiful.'

'Marsha really is gorgeous, I must admit.'

'Gorgeous shoes, certainly.'

'Louboutin, do you think?'

'Probably. Or Blahnik. One or the other,' agreed Shula.

'Fake?'

'God, no.' Shula was as definite as definite could be.

Over the weeks, the sisters had taken careful note of Marsha's clothes. And accessories. They were both their mother's daughters, and could spot fashionable, well-made, *expensive* clothes a mile off. They could work out what such clothes and accessories cost as easily as if the price tags were still showing; though of course such clothes often did not actually *have* price tags. More often than not, if you had to ask how much such items cost, you probably could not afford to buy them.

'Her handbags put ours to shame even.'

'Are you thinking what I'm thinking?' asked Shula.

'Try me.'

'Not exactly everyday wear for your average part-time social worker?'

'Bingo.'

And with that display of inherited familial expertise and sisterly solidarity, the two widows, Mrs Heppie Lewis and Mrs Shula Jacobi, left the building. Their morning and their last aquarobics lesson were over.

6. Around Town in the Afternoon

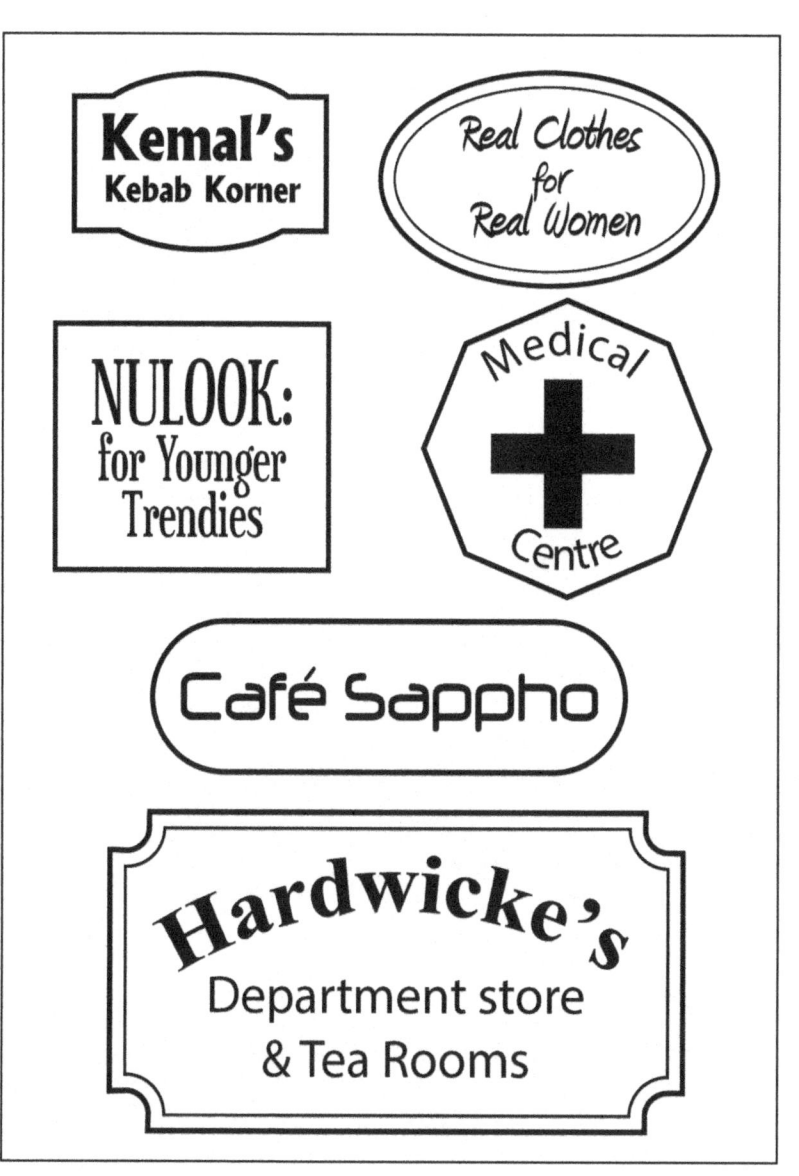

5. AROUND TOWN IN THE AFTERNOON

13.15
At Kemal's Kebab Korner – A Matter of Taste

Marsha was dreading the afternoon. Looking after Meg during the morning's lesson was bearable. But being with her for a whole day would be no fun at all. Like some of her other clients, Meg was very wilful. She had a talent for making the people around her feel embarrassed, whether they were carers, acquaintances, or even mere passers-by. She could get what she wanted by making the people around her feel awkward, by for example raising her high-pitched voice with its impenetrable accent, or by throwing a tantrum at the slightest provocation.

I'm the one who's supposed to be in charge of her, thought Marsha. *But she's the one who's boss. The truth is, I'm not senior enough or experienced enough to know how to handle her properly.* Marsha tried to look as confident as possible. But inside, she was as nervous as a mouse.

Their first challenge was to find somewhere to eat that they both liked. This was not easy. Marsha flatly refused to eat in one of the town centre's many burger bars. She tried to steer Meg into a salad bar, or somewhere healthy. But Meg would have none of it. She only had to threaten to stamp her feet to make Marsha feel unsettled.

'I want to go to KKK,' declared Meg defiantly.

'What's that? Where is it?'

'Not far. Follow me.'

Marsha felt that she had no option but to follow. There it was: Kemal's Kebab Korner, a tiny place just three streets away. Marsha's heart sank. She loathed kebabs: the taste, the grease, the smell.

'Look,' said Meg triumphantly. 'They do salads, don't they?' She pointed at the illustration of a salad outside the shop.

The idea of a Greek salad in a Turkish kebab shop struck Marsha as odd, but there it was. An image of lettuce, olives, tomato, cucumber, feta, topped with various bits of greenery. 'OK,' she said reluctantly. 'Let's go in then.'

'Hello, Scottie!' cried a blonde young man behind a revolving tower of meat, and brandishing a huge knife. 'Mm, who's your friend then?' He was talking to Meg cheerfully, but staring admiringly at Marsha. She guessed correctly that this was no Kemal, but could not quite place the Geordie accent.

'Hi Jimmie, oh, this is Marsh. I think she wants a salad, don't you, Marsh? Mine's a doner though: a big one, in a pitta, with butter inside. And a large Coke.'

'What will you have to drink, Marsh?' asked Jimmie. Personable and polite.

She would have liked a real Turkish coffee, but couldn't see one on the board behind Jimmie. So she settled for something she recognised. 'Oh, I'll just have a flat white,' she mumbled.

'Coming up. Take a seat both of you.' Jimmie and Meg evidently knew each other, and got on well. They chatted along about mutual friends and a local nightclub. Marsha envied their easy way with each other; how Jimmie simply accepted Meg for what she was; how Meg visibly relaxed in his company. *Theirs is another world*, she thought.

Their food and drink came, delivered by Jimmie himself. Meg launched noisily into her kebab. Fatty juices dribbled from the right side of her mouth. She ignored Marsha's offer of a small paper napkin, and kept on munching. Marsha felt slightly nauseous. She also felt guilty for not liking the place. Who was she to feel so superior? But she had to admit that she did.

She concentrated on her salad, declining Jimmie's offer of a whole range of partly used sauce bottles, all sticky from previous use. Meg ate and drank with amazing speed. 'Great place, isn't it? I was starving.' She downed the last of her Coke, and went to the ladies'.

Back at the table Meg braced herself. 'Oh, by the way, I've got a doctor's appointment at three.' She tried to sound casual.

'I know.'

"You can just come along. She won't care,' said Meg, airily.

'What's it about?'

'What's what about?'

Marsha took a deep breath, trying to hold on to her patience. 'Your appointment, of course. I assemed it was about a diabetes test or something'

Meg flushed with anger. 'Private.' She stared at Marsha, tight-lipped.

Once again, Marsha sensed that she was not in control. But perhaps that was as things should be. After all, her clients had rights, too. She must not forget that. She consoled herself with the thought that her own responsibilities went so far and no further. 'Well,' she said. 'We'd better pay up and get going, if we want to get to the shops.'

'OK. We pay on the way out.' They got up and Marsha paid at Jimmie's till. He grinned at Marsha, grateful for her generous tip.

'Cheers, Marsh. Come and see us again sometime.' Marsha smiled politely, while Jimmie and Meg blew kisses at each other. 'See you soon, Scottie!' he said cheerily to Meg.

'I've been thinking about your dress this evening,' said Marsha on the way out. She spoke carefully. 'I think I know a place that might have something suitable.' In other words, something that would not embarrass anyone, particularly the hostess, Mrs C; something not too tight, or too short, that would suit Meg's sallow, mottled skin, and conceal most of her tattoos. 'It's quite near here, actually.'

'Oh, no worries, I've got my eye on something,' said Meg, stepping into the street.

Marsha's heart sank.

13.45
At the Dress Shops – A Matter of Style

Marjorie ('How may I assist you?') Fairbanks had originally thought of naming her shop "16 up!". But her friends pointed out that such a name would imply an age, rather than a size. So she decided on "Real Clothes for Real Women", which she considered a little long and clumsy, but attractive and refined enough. This was after all a shop in which Marjorie did not merely "help". She "assisted".

She was currently in the throes of diversifying her business into an online store, and was finding the process more onerous than she had imagined. Still, she was adventurous, and keen to expand her customer base, thus hoping to compete with much larger companies. She had been encouraged to diversify by her friend and customer, Heppie Lewis, whose parents had owned Gold Fashions, and whose advice Marjorie valued highly. The only advice Marjorie gave her web designer and young team of advisers was never to mention the words "outsize" or "the larger woman" in their promotional materials.

She assisted people as best she could. From years of experience, she knew that her footfall clients ranged from the reluctant or embarrassed first-timers, coming to terms with the onset of middle age, to the happy band of permanently fattish sisters (of which she was one) and right through to the outrageously obese.

She assisted the mothers of the bride (and bridegroom) searching for something glamorous to wear on the big day. She assisted the women whose husbands were beginning to feel ashamed of their wives' ever enlarging waistlines. She assisted the size twenty-twos who still insisted that they could get into size sixteens.

And at lunchtimes, when the shop was officially closed, she assisted those men (be they plumbers, solicitors, teachers, labourers, doctors, truckers, priests, rugby players or whatever) who, for whatever reason, wanted to wear women's clothes for work or play. Knickers, bras and tights were always popular, and cotton frocks were coming into season. These men were not drag queens. Marjorie knew that such men often preferred to make their own fancy clothes. Nor were her male customers necessarily gay. They were just ordinary heterosexual blokes no one would look at twice. Some even came in with their wives and girlfriends.

So Marjorie was used to assisting all sorts. But even she had to admit that the couple who had just entered her shop was unusual. First, she had to decide which one of the two would need her help. This was a common problem, because women often came in pairs: one needing help, the other there to offer encouragement and advice. It was sometimes difficult to distinguish who was who, and who to address with the welcoming smile and the inevitable, 'How may I assist you?'

Inwardly, Marjorie decided that the beautiful, slim black woman with her Burberry coat was not the one directly in need of help. The other, younger one, with the dyed hair and tattoos (the black woman's neighbour, girlfriend, partner?)

was the better bet. Marjorie decided that her greeting should embrace them both.

'Hello,' said Marsha. She was feeling distinctly nervous. That was partly because she had managed to get Meg into this particular shop under false pretences. She had simply told Meg that the shop was "very nice", and had managed to get her in before she saw the name of it. Naturally, she was also afraid that once they were in the shop, Meg would throw a sulk, or worse, a full-throttled tantrum. Instead, she was merely silent.

'I'm here to help my friend find a suitable dress for a party this evening.'

'Well, shall I leave you to look around for a few minutes? Let me know if I can be of assistance.'

Marsha surveyed the wares with some dismay. Cotton frocks, wool dresses, modest trouser suits. These were not exactly Meg's style. 'Well, what do you think, Meg?' she asked nervously.

'Everything in here is too old for me,' Meg replied frostily. 'And too big. Far too big.'

'Oh, I wouldn't say that. What are you? A twenty, or twenty-two?' Marsha whispered.

'Fourteen. Or at the most sixteen,' came the sharp reply.

Body image all up the spout, thought Marsha. *I should have guessed. This is pretty hopeless.* 'Oh I see, but what about a nice kaftan? That would suit you very well, especially for this evening.'

'What's a catfan?'

'Here they are. Look. Why don't you try this one on? These dark colours would make a nice contrast with your fair skin. Something long and flowing would feel really nice.'

'No. It's like a tent. It's ugly. No.'

Marsha was desperate. She sought out Marjorie, who merely shook her head in sympathy. 'To be honest, I suspect that this isn't the right shop for her, don't you?' Marsha nodded slightly, embarrassed about possibly having wasted Marjorie's time. 'Don't worry. It happens all the time. You try to do your best for people. But... ' Marsha nodded again.

Meg walked up to them. 'This place is for big women, isn't it? Why did you bring me here? I don't want anything from here, Marsh. I know where I want to go.' And with her mercifully quiet, short protest over, Meg walked quickly out of the shop and into the street.

'Bye,' said Marsha, smiling. 'And thank you for your help. Er, your assistance, I mean,' she added awkwardly. Marjorie was not at all upset or put out. She just felt sad for both of them.

Outside, Meg felt a little less inhibited. She was angry with Marsha. She said that they had wasted up to twenty minutes, and reminded Marsha that not only did she need time to buy something to suit her "style", but also that the doctor's appointment was less than an hour away.

Before today, Marsha would have rated the chances of finding a black shop assistant with the name Chardonnay pretty remote. But here she was, right in front of her, in Nulook, a clothes shop for "the young and the young at heart". It was packed. Mostly nubile young girls, but also some not so young women who should know better, thought Marsha. The clothes were cheap, in more than one sense, and arranged on easy to reach racks, arranged roughly in order of size.

Chardonnay and Meg did not know each other, but they were rattling on as if they were old friends. Chardonnay was skinny, about twenty, and a chav. There was no other word for it: she came complete with an acquired Essex accent. But she was not stupid. She smiled at Marsha – far too well dressed for Nulook – then ignored her.

"Chard" as she was known had her target customer, Meg, weighed up instantly. Here was a size twenty or twenty-two if ever there was one, who would insist on trying on anything, so long it was a fourteen, at most a sixteen.

Meg declared that she wanted a dress for a party. 'Right, I got one or two brilliant fings for yer,' said Chard.

'What size?'

Chard knew that the things she had in mind were a sixteen. 'Dunno. But they'll suit yer well right.'

'I want a fourteen dress: short sleeves and, well, short down here.' Meg pointed vaguely downwards.

'No prob,' said Chard, completely unfazed by Meg's accent, or indeed her request. 'This colour's yours, no?' Whereupon she handed a lilac and green size fourteen lycra dress to Meg, who disappeared into a cubicle to try it on.

While Meg was in the cubicle, Chard turned to Marsha and winked. 'Don't worry. I don't think she'll even be able to get into it. When she comes out, just follow my lead. We'll get her into a sixteen, you see if we don't.'

After a couple of minutes' audible heaving and gasping, Meg emerged from the cubicle, breathless. 'So, this is OK?' she asked, barely able to stand, let alone walk.

'Oh, cool; great dress. But for movement at a party, you need something that, well, that shows your breasts a little more, and those legs.' She turned to Meg. 'What do you think?'

Appalled by what she saw, Marsha followed Chard's lead, and went along with her smart advice: *anything* to get Meg into something bigger. 'Yes, Chardonnay's right,' said Marsha, flustered. She felt that she had been outmanoeuvred by both Chardonnay and Meg. 'Yes, something that shows your breasts a little more.' Marsha could not believe what she was saying.

'Oh, that suit's me. Can't hide my titties, can I?' said Meg, in all seriousness.

While Meg had been in the cubicle, Chard had taken the opportunity to find the same dress in size sixteen, the largest size carried by Nulook. She took the dress off a rail, and deftly removed the size label. It was a trick that the manager had taught her when she started working there.

Marsha watched Chardonnay at work and was impressed. Back in the cubicle, Meg was given the larger version of the same dress she had tried on earlier. When she emerged, Chard clapped her hands and said, 'Oh yes, yes, yes. Yes to the dress! I'm sure we all agree, no?' she added, turning to Marsha.

Marsha still hated it. The lilac and green did not suit Meg's colouring at all. The low cut still exposed Meg's bosoms and tattoos unnecessarily, and the dress was still too short; with too much unnecessary beading and too many frilly, flouncy bits everywhere. And overall still too small, but better than the one before. 'Oh yes, I like it,' said Marsha, lying through her teeth.

'Me too, I've always loved dresses like this,' said Meg. 'I'll take it.'

15.00
At the Medical Centre – Thirsty Work

Then they made for the medical centre. By coincidence, both Marsha and Meg were registered there, but with different doctors; though these days, of course, patients rarely saw the same doctor twice in a row, and appointments with one's "own" doctor seemed more difficult than ever to arrange.

The centre was a relatively new building. National Health provision was located on the large hexagonal-shaped ground floor. On the first floor there were a number of smaller rooms for private consultations offering services such as physiotherapy, acupuncture, chiropody and chiropractics. The centre was a thriving, profitable business.

Marsha found the building, despite or perhaps because of its relative newness, cheerless, cold and forbidding. The nine doctors in the practice were on the whole charmless, officious, and rather full of their own self-importance. They tended to be unaware that at least some of their patients were more highly educated and richer (if that were possible!) than they were. The doctors were enthusiastically guarded by their receptionists. These were a quartet of overly made-up, blue-rinse types with startling nails. In a rare flash of humour, the doctors called them The Sisters of No Mercy.

On the practice's promotional website, the six male doctors listed the golf clubs of which they were members, while the three female doctors dutifully listed their various offspring – as well as the golf clubs of which *they* were members. Marsha was not particularly impressed. When she first registered with the practice some three years ago, she noted that, against the national trend, not one of the doctors at the centre was black, brown, yellow, or any colour other than white. *A remarkably suspicious achievement, especially these days*, thought Marsha wryly.

Meg's appointment was scheduled for 3.06 pm, and like all appointments here, was timed with military precision. Patients were typically allowed all of six minutes for their consultations. Equally typically, Meg's "regular" female doctor was not available today. But Meg was far from disappointed, especially when she realised that she was to see a young male doctor instead, whom she had not yet met.

Marsha did not feel it appropriate or necessary to join Meg for the consultation. Meg had also made it clear that she was not wanted. So when the appointment time came, she agreed to hold on to Meg's shopping, and waited in the large lobby. She leafed through one or two tattered back copies of *Country Life*. After about twelve minutes – twice the usual time allotted to each patient – Marsha became a little concerned. She need not have worried. Meg bounced out of the consultation room looking a little flushed but otherwise fine.

'Did you get your prescription renewed?'

'Yep. No problem. I'll just go into the pharmacy for a minute and collect it.'

'What did she say about diabetes, and your eye?'

'It wasn't a she. It was a he!' Meg could not hide the triumphant glint in her good eye. 'He said the diabetes was was negative. And that my eye wasn't too bad, and that it'll go down soon.'

'You'd better get one of those ice packs from the pharmacy as well.'

'OK. See you outside.'

The weather had turned. Clouds raced across the sky and it was distinctly cooler. The forecasters' promise of rain seemed about to turn into a reality. Marsha shivered, slightly miserable at the thought of having to spend the next few hours before the party with her charge. She needed to make her 4.30 hair appointment. She also fancied a cup or tea; looking after Meg was, strangely, very thirsty work. Meg emerged from the pharmacy. Despite her flimsy clothes, she seemed impervious to the change in the weather.

'Right,' said Meg. 'You can go now.'

'What?'

'You can go now. Don't you want to get ready for the party and stuff?'

'Well, yes, but it won't take me long.'

'Why don't you ring the office and tell them I'll be OK? You can pick me up at the house later.'

Meg's suggestion was just the excuse that Marsha needed. She could take advantage of the time, have her hair done, then take a long, hot bath, and also have a bit of a rest before the evening's festivities got under way.

Also, she was gasping for a cup of tea. She didn't relish the idea of taking tea at Meg's "house"; a large, smelly set of rooms occupied by a friendly, but scruffy set of unemployed and unemployable men and women. They were watched over by a grasping landlord who was taking every advantage of his tenants' state-sponsored housing allowances.

She rang the office. Her supervisor said that so long as Meg was escorted back to the house, Marsha's main duty of accompanying Meg to the swimming pool was over. What Marsha and Meg did in the evening was not her concern.

16.00
At Meg's Home – A Framed Photograph

Meg was duly escorted to her house. It reeked of tobacco smoke, gin, and cabbage. Marsha politely declined the hospitable offer of tea there. (She much preferred to make it in her own clean teapot.) She made Meg put the ice pack into the freezer, and told her to use it in about an hour. Meg declared that she 'needed a big crap', and left Marsha alone with one of her housemates, Fran.

Marsha noticed that on the mantelpiece in the sitting room there were one or two framed photographs. An odd, homely touch she thought, given young people's preference these days for digital photos. She got up to look at the biggest photo. She was surprised at what she saw. 'This is a nice picture,' she said carefully to Fran.

'Oh yes. As soon as Meg saw it on my camera, she wanted a photo done. It was taken in a club. It's Meg with a bloke called Bashir. She was very taken with him. And he was with her, at least for a couple of weeks. But it didn't work out of course. They were too different, I guess. But for a while, she was crazy about him.'

'When was the photo taken?' asked Marsha, as casually as she could manage.

'Oh, about three months ago.' Fran paused. 'I know I shouldn't tell you this,' she whispered, 'but they slept together here: three or four times in two weeks.'

'No, you shouldn't be telling me,' said Marsha. She put her finger over her lips. 'And don't tell Meg you said anything to me,' she smiled.

'No, of course not. Wouldn't dream of it.'

'Do you know if Meg has seen him since then?' Marsha felt bad, asking a question to which she knew the answer.

'No, I don't think so. Anyway, she hasn't mentioned him to me. We were all sad for her. Especially since Meg swore that he was the first, you know, the first to… She gets offers, but she's not a slag. Honest.'

Their conversation was stopped by Meg's return from the loo. Marsha's head was in a whirl. She had to get out. She hurriedly confirmed the travel arrangements for the evening. She would pick Meg up at the house at 7.15 pm in a taxi. She then fled to her hairdresser, where she had a strong cup of tea, and went home. She left Meg to explain to her flatmates how she had acquired her black eye.

15.20
At Café Sappho – Girl Talk

They chose a window table. Lynne sat with her back to the window, and Heppie and Shula took seats that allowed them to see the road outside. They each held a menu.

'Never seen so many teas and coffees.'

Indeed the list was formidable. The teas included everything from straightforward English breakfast right through to camomile, lemon, lemon grass, green, jasmine, raspberry, blackcurrant, and the distinctly exotic African redbush. The list of coffees was perhaps not so fancy, but included all the usual Americanos, flat whites, espressos, cappuccinos, lattes, macchiatos, single and double, and with or without sprinkles. The menu also had the usual array of soft drinks, water of various types and flavours, and hot chocolates.

'Yes,' agreed Shula. 'Perhaps we should get out more often, Heppie. It's like an encyclopaedia!'

'Well, I hope you like the place,' said Lynne. 'I've been here a couple of times with Luke. Apparently it's owned by two lezzie friends of his. I thought you might like it.'

'Do you mean lesbians?' whispered Shula uncertainly. 'Are you sure?' she said, looking around her, not without trepidation.

'Well, *you* certainly need to get out more,' laughed Heppie.

They had finished their search for Di's leaving present. They had wandered around window-shopping for a few minutes as the sky went darker, threatening rain. Given that the sisters did not fancy the usual Costas and Café Neros, Lynne had directed them all to Sappho's, which had opened only a few months before.

'Luke says it's pronounced "Safo's",' explained Lynne.

'Well, I must say I like it,' said Heppie. 'The modern furniture, the lighting, it all works well. And I like the way the staff are done out like old-fashioned nippies. Nice touch that.'

'Nippies?'

'Like they had in the war at Lyons Corner Houses. Before your time Lynne; and before ours, for that matter. And if this crowd is anything to go by, lesbians have come a long way from green corduroy trousers and Craven "A"!'

'What's Craven "A"?' asked Shula.

'Also before our time. Wartime cigarettes: quite strong, I think; favoured by dykes, allegedly.'

Heppie was right about the people in Sappho's being a far cry from any wartime image of lesbians. It was nearly full. The thirty or so customers included two very elderly gents, three yummy mummies with their children, several trendy teenagers, a selection of lady shoppers, and – so as not to let the side down so to speak – a pair of mutually adoring professional women dressed in near identical, expensive trouser suits.

'Excuse me. Before I decide, must go to the loo.'

'Be careful now,' giggled Lynne. She decided to take immediate advantage of Heppie's temporary departure. She summoned up her courage.

'Do you mind if I say something, Shula?'

Shula braced herself. 'No, go ahead.'

'I think you're very brave. Well, we all do.'

'All? At the pool? Do they all know then?'

'Well, nobody says anything of course. But I imagine so. All except that cretin, Meg.'

'When I had my operations, I thought it was the end of world: at the very least, the end of my world. So many women go through it. I feel for them all. The chemo and stuff was hard. I think it was that that caused the depression.'

'Is that why you decided to try aquarobics – to help with the depression? I think that's why the doctor suggested I should come.'

'Well, good for you. Yes, I suppose it was. But the main reason was Heppie. She said she would come with me and help me get my life back. Especially while I've been trying to make up my mind about what to do next.'

'How do you mean?'

'Oh, you know. What to do about more surgery: reconstruction, boob jobs and all that. But Heppie, and the Water Babes, have been the best therapy of all. Strange, people I never even knew a couple of months ago, and hardly know even now.'

Returning from the loo, Heppie could see from a distance that her sister and Lynne were deeply engaged in conversation. She correctly guessed what they were talking about, and so delayed her return until a suitable moment presented itself. She spent a few minutes looking at the artwork on the walls, all of which was for sale: the usual mix of country scenes, animal portraits, seascapes and impenetrable abstracts, together with one or two vaguely erotic sketches of the female form.

After a decent interval, Heppie returned to the table. They continued to study the menu, working their way through a bewildering selection of snacks, sandwiches, and especially cakes.

'Alfalfa sprouts? Mm, I wonder what that would be like. It would be good for our diet.'

'No thanks.'

'They do a great chocolate cake. It's called "Bohemian Rhapsody".'

The sisters protested about their being on diets, their resolutions to eat only healthy food, and their joint determination to lose weight. But catching sight of a helping of "Bohemian Rhapsody" passing by, Heppie could feel herself weakening.

'Hello. Welcome to Sappho's. Can I help you?'

'Oh, we're just deciding, thanks,' said Heppie, not looking up from her menu.

'Oh hi! Don't we know you from somewhere?' asked Shula. She was being uncharacteristically forward, which Heppie took as a good sign. 'I know. It's Jane, from the gym at the pool, isn't it?'

They all looked up. Jane grinned broadly. 'Yes, that's right. I recognised you all when you walked in.'

'You've changed your hair!' The approving observation escaped Heppie's mouth before she knew it. She regretted it immediately.

Fortunately Jane did not take offence. 'Yes. You know Mrs C? Well, she recommended her hairdresser, so I went there.'

Now was the time for compliments: 'It looks great', 'I like it short like that', 'Well done', 'Always good to have a change every so often', 'It really suits you', and the like.

'Then I went and had a facial. It's good for the spots.'

No one knew quite what to say.

'Er, I'm going to the party tonight, you see.'

This broke the conversational logjam. Genuine smiles and expressions of 'Terrific', 'See you there', 'That's great', greeted the news. At the same time, the general indecisiveness about what to order abruptly ended. Lynne ordered a cappuccino and a "Bohemian Rhapsody", without ice cream. Heppie ordered a breakfast tea, and a "Bohemian Rhapsody" with ice cream ('What's chocolate cake without ice cream?') with two plates and two forks. Shula reluctantly agreed to share Heppie's chocolate cake, and in a spirit of adventure ordered something that she had never even heard of before: African redbush tea.

Jane went to collect the order. Shula leaned in to the table and whispered, 'You don't think she's one?'

'One what?' asked Lynne.

'You know, a–'

'A lezzie? Haven't a clue, chuck. They don't carry labels.'

'Why don't you ask Jane yourself?' laughed Heppie. 'Really, Shula, you'd think that we'd led a very sheltered life!'

Shula could not be as lighthearted as her sister about such things. 'Well, perhaps we, or I, have. No, I can't ask her. She might get the wrong idea and think that I'm one!'

'Well, if she does, tell her you're spoken for.'

'Spoken for?'

Lynne gave her voice the full *basso profundo* treatment. 'By me: big, butch Lynne.'

At this point, even Shula began to see the folly and impropriety of her enquiries. All three burst out laughing.

'Heppie's idea about table linen for Di was great,' said Lynne. 'My idea of a glass vase was really stupid. I didn't think of the journey or the weight. It could have broken during the journey. I'm really glad you came with me.'

'No problem. Everyone likes Irish linen, don't they? And if she doesn't, too bad. She can always pass it on to someone else.' As usual, Heppie found the shortest, most practical route to a solution for even the most difficult of problems.

'And we can all sign the one card.'

'Yes, cards from each of us would just be silly.'

'Speaking of silly, I managed to thieve a woggle from the pool. I've joined the two ends together, and hung some corks on it. Like those hats the Ozzies wear. It took me ages. I bet she won't wear it though.'

'I wonder what'll happen to the classes now,' said Shula.

'Not sure. Luke doesn't seem to know either. I've tried pumping him, but no go.'

Jane was back with their order. They cleared a space on their table, and made room for the cups, saucers and plates. 'Is this your regular job?' asked Heppie.

'No. I'm doing a gap year before uni.'

'Don't students usually go abroad for that?'

'Not me. Can't afford it. I'm trying to save as much as I can, and get some work experience. Not this kind of work. I've just done an internship. Two months.'

'Good for you,' said Heppie. 'But I hear those internships don't pay much, if anything.'

'That's why I'm working here,' said Jane, cheerfully.

'And which uni will you go to? I think there are two here.' This was about as far as Lynne could go with this topic of conversation. But she liked Jane, and wanted to sound interested.

Jane set out their tea things then had to see to other customers. As she left their table she turned back in time to say, 'No. Oxford. Law.'

The three women had to admit to being slightly taken aback. 'Ah, clever girl; wish my daughter was more like her.'

'Amen to that!' sighed Lynne.

Enjoying tea and cake together, they gossiped a little about the class, though not with any sense of malice. They agreed that Meg was a lost cause: a sad case. They also agreed that Marsha was indeed very beautiful, and had infinite patience. Neither of the sisters mentioned their observations about Marsha's expensive accessories, for fear of prompting any indiscreet or unnecessary further queries from Lynne.

They all felt less inhibited about discussing their instructor, Di. None of them really liked or disliked her. She was something of a mystery. Especially her private life, or 'let's be frank – her love life', prompted some speculation. Lynne had asked Luke whether he knew of any boyfriends, and he said no. He was equally puzzled by Di, and like most people, drifted between half liking and half disliking his boss. Shula considered her query ('Perhaps she's a lesbian?') a particularly mature contribution to the discussion, especially bearing in mind where they were. But Lynne said no. Her source was again Luke. There was no hard evidence, one way or the other.

'I think she may be asexual,' Heppie opined, vaguely.

'What do you mean?' asked Lynne.

'Well, not sure really. I think it means someone who isn't really interested in sex either way.'

Both Shula and Lynne pooh-poohed the very idea. They both thought that even if there were people who were not interested in sex, they must have emotions, feelings, relationships. It was generally conceded that Di seemed closed off from the world, somehow. But why?

'I've got a theory,' said Lynne. 'When I got divorced, I felt really bitter about men, and wanted nothing more to do with them. I think something similar must've happened to Di; in the past, when she was in London. Some man or other disappointed her, let her down, or even betrayed her. So when she came here, she decided to cut men out. She couldn't face the hassle or the aggro all over again. Once hurt, twice shy sort of thing.' The three ladies neither knew nor even suspected that Lynne's theory was near the mark.

The person they disagreed about most was Jean. Lynne was the harshest judge. 'She's like an old maid. Nothing's good enough for her. Doesn't seem to have a good word to say about anyone; except Di of course. All that guff about practising!'

'But you joined in the chorus when we all wanted Jean to do her free expression.'

'Mm, I know, God help me. And I did feel a bit sorry for her when she took a tumble in the water. But that stripper routine was nuts; plain barmy, if you ask me.'

Shula was taking a middle ground. She hadn't quite made up her mind what she thought about Jean. Heppie, however, was a great deal more sympathetic. 'I've heard her husband left her a few months ago.'

'Hmph. Can you blame the poor bugger?'

'We don't know the full story. Perhaps we shouldn't judge. She's clearly going through some sort of trauma. I know she hits out at some of us a lot. But, well, I see her as a friendless sort of person who might be just trying to reach out.'

'Bloody funny way of showing it.'

'I know. But I suspect there's some battle going on inside her. Who knows? Anyway, I wouldn't give up on her just yet.'

Just as their conversation turned to the topic of Mrs C, Shula noticed someone out of the window, approaching the cafe.

'Isn't that Luke? Coming this way? Looking very smart, I must say.'

Lynne turned round. 'Oh yes. You're right.'

'That must be his father with him.'

'Hell no! That's not his dad, Shula! It's his boyfriend! His partner. You know, civil partner. They're planning to get married when it becomes legal,'

'Oh.' Shula blushed with embarrassment at having appeared, yet again, so naive.

Lynne explained, in a loud whisper. 'He's called Ted.' And in a more secretive whisper she added, somewhat gratuitously, 'He's nearly twenty years older than Lucy. He's great. You'll like him.'

'I'm sure I shall,' said Shula, vaguely. She turned to Heppie and whispered, 'But he's got a beard!'

'He's got a what?'

'You know, a beard!' Shula used her hand to indicate the shape of a beard.

Heppie did not have the time or the patience to work out which assumptions and prejudices lay beneath her sister's observation. (Gays don't have beards? Luke couldn't possibly fancy a man with a beard? Only "real" men have beards?) So all she could whisper in return was, 'Really, Shula. Sometimes you come out with the silliest things.'

Luke and Ted entered the cafe. 'They haven't seen us yet. Hey there! Lucy! Over here, in the window.'

The sisters were not snobs. But for once, something in them wanted to give the impression that they were not with the loud-voiced Liverpudlian waving at and calling out to two men, one of whom was evidently called Lucy. (*But which one?* wondered some of the customers.) But they *were* with her, and could not do anything about it.

15.40
At Café Sappho – Of Fire Temples and Vultures

Luke and Ted had just come into Café Sappho when Luke heard Lynne's voice. He quickly turned towards Ted, and mumbled. 'Oh, damn. Sorry, sweetheart. It's Lynne and a couple of women from the centre: the aquarobics course. I suppose we'll have to join them.'

'No worries. It'll be a welcome distraction for you. I don't mind. You lead the way.'

Luke threaded his way through the tables towards the window, careful not to let his smart Italian mackintosh touch anything. Ted, who like Luke was just over six-foot tall, but considerably heavier, had to be careful not to bump into anything or anyone. He also had to make sure that his bulky windcheater did not knock anything off one of the tables. His progress to the table was rather slower than Luke's.

Luke arrived amidst general cries of 'Hello', 'What a coincidence', 'Great to see you' and so on. Luke made his usual feeble joke about not at first recognising the women with their clothes on. Ted arrived, kissed Lynne and was duly introduced to Heppie and Shula. They had both calculated that Ted must be in his late forties or early fifties. They both also noticed that close up, Ted was visibly greying. His shock of hair, his beard, and even the hair on the fingers of his huge nicotine-stained hands all gave the impression of maturity, confidence and capability. In some ways, a good foil for Luke, the sisters thought. Pity about the smell of cigarettes though.

The people at the next table left. Their table was cleared. The three women and two men put all their outer clothes on two of the empty chairs, and commandeered the two other chairs for themselves. It was a bit of a squash, but a convivial one.

Having observed the kiss, Heppie said, 'So you know Luke and Ted quite well, Lynne?'

'Yes. I do for them. Cleaning and stuff. And Ted's babysitting my kids this evening.'

'Wish I'd known. You could have had my two grandchildren as well.'

'Not sure I could cope with four. But I'd give it a try!' The tone was friendly, amiable.

A waitress came and cleared the table. The ladies declined to order anything more. Luke ordered an Americano with cold milk. Ted wanted regular tea and a "Bohemian Rhapsody" with ice cream. He offered to get an extra fork for Luke. Luke shuddered and shook his head. 'I couldn't.' By way of an explanation, he mouthed, 'Got a bit of an upset,' patting his stomach.

Lynne immediately launched into gossip mode. 'You know Jane, that girl from the gym, works here. I think she must have gone home now. She's going to Oxford Uni.'

'Oh, really?' said Luke, clearly preoccupied with something else.

Heppie did not want the conversation to repeat the things that the three women had spoken about before. She decided to say something that she had wanted to say ever since Luke and Ted had appeared in the cafe. 'Nice threads, Luke.' She smiled, admiringly. 'The mac, and especially the suit.'

'Thanks. The mac's Italian. The suit's Paul Smith.' He turned to the restaurant, pointing at the suit. 'Paul Smith, everyone!' he mouthed. There was no response. Luke turned back to Heppie. 'An early thirtieth birthday present from hubby here.'

'Oh, very nice indeed.'

'Well,' said Ted, sounding unnecessarily defensive. 'You don't turn thirty every day, do you?'

'More's the pity,' noted Shula.

'I felt a bit stupid in that poncy London shop. Didn't want to go in, but Luke insisted. He said that if I didn't go in I wouldn't believe the price. Anyway, they took one look at me as if to say the only thing in the place that would fit me would be a tie!'

They all laughed. 'It's a thin world alright,' said Heppie.

Ted and Luke's order arrived.

'So, been anywhere or going anywhere special?' Heppie and Shula had been brought up to believe that in this life, if you didn't ask, you didn't find out.

Luke was caught out, unable to respond. He did not want to tell the truth, and nor did he want to lie outright. He blushed slightly, and in desperation turned to Ted for help, who was just about to take his first mouthful of cake.

Ted laughed. 'Oh, I just asked Luke if he wouldn't mind showing me what the suit looked like. Wanted to see what we got for the money, that's all.' He put his fork down. Luke sat back, relieved.

'In other words, mind your own bloody business!' grinned Heppie, awkwardly. 'I'm sorry, Luke. I shouldn't have asked. It was rude of me.' Luke gave one of his most gracious, forgiving, queenly smiles. Heppie thought that behind the smile, the younger man seemed decidedly nervy.

Ted was about halfway through his first real mouthful of cake and ice cream. Wanting to express an interest in Luke's partner, Shula – more or less on automatic pilot, and certainly without much thought or preparation – asked, 'So are you in the health and leisure industry too, Ted?'

Ted's cake-filled mouth hung open in amazement. Luke guffawed loudly. Lynne and Heppie covered their own mouths in repressed laughter. Feeling distinctly put out, Shula could not appreciate why her question, directed as it was at a middle-aged, overweight smoker, was in any way inappropriate.

'Oh. Priceless. Your face, hubby. Health and leisure!' The giggling continued for a full minute.

'No, I work at the local FE college. Admin. Academic registrar,' said Ted, between mouthfuls.

'Sounds very impressive.'

'So, you're all off to a party tonight?'

'Yes, at Mrs C's place. A nice Asian lady in our group,' explained Lynne. 'It's odd, isn't it? "Mrs C" is a bit formal. We call everyone else by their first names, but not her. I wonder why?'

'Don't know; probably some odd way of showing respect. Or maybe her first name is difficult to pronounce? I wonder what her surname is?' asked Heppie. 'Something like Chouwdray, or Chawla, I expect.'

'No, it's Cooper,' said Luke.

Lynne's curiosity was aroused. 'Cooper? That's a funny name for an Indian. So the husband's English! That is – if there is a husband.'

'Yes, there is. And he's as Indian as they come. I met him when she first came to register. Not a particularly nice man. Not like Mrs C, anyway. That's when he insisted that as long as Salma came along as her chaperone, it was OK for his wife to attend the lessons. Quite a concession, I think. The old fart took a bit of persuading.'

Ted shook his head, as if to speak. He was busy wiping his beard with a napkin, clearing it of the vestiges of chocolate cake and ice cream that clung to it. 'They're Parsees.'

'Come again,' said Heppie.

'Parsees, some people call them the Jews of India.'

Ted knew rather more than he wanted to know about the various members of Luke's classes. He knew for example that the current Water Babes class had two Jewish sisters in it. Luke did not tell him much more about them, claiming "client confidentiality" rather arbitrarily. ('Client confidentiality my arse,' was Ted's riposte.) Ted had also heard bits and pieces about Meg, and Jean.

Heppie and Shula bridled. One thing they both disliked was having their Jewish identity described and even identified for them by others. Orthodox Jews were bad enough. They were a constant reminder of how more liberal Jews – especially women – should behave, live and even think. But being described by non-Jews could be much worse. From personal experience, both sisters suspected that most non-Jews didn't know much more than 'Jews don't eat bacon, you know'. So they were not about to allow this man Ted – as nice as he might be – to set about describing themselves to themselves!

Remembering their dad's advice, they began counting to ten. But Heppie could not contain herself. She could only get as far as four before she said, 'And what's that supposed to mean?'

'No offence meant; none at all. I'm just quoting what other people say, especially in India. I suppose what they mean in the most general terms is that Parsees are a minority, originally from Iran, or Persia, whose lives have been characterised by exile and periods of persecution.'

'Mm, sounds about right,' said Shula, quietly.

'They were kicked out of Persia in the seventh or eighth century, I think. Most now live in or around Mumbai. They tend to be very well educated, charitable, especially to their own. Some are extremely rich.'

'There are poor Jews, you know,' protested Shula.

'Of course, I didn't say there weren't. And there are poor Parsees too.' Ted stuck to his considerable guns.

'So how did you know that the Coopers are Pars, or whatever?' asked Luke.

'Your friend Salma told me. We met her in the street and invited her in here once, remember? She liked the place. You must have been in the loo, or cruising the tables in desperation.' Ted grinned broadly. 'Am I boring you all, or shall I go on?'

He waited a moment. Everyone was too polite to stop him. He continued. 'Well, like the Jews and the Christians, and Muslims, the Parsees have just one god. Not like Hindus, who have lots.'

'One's plenty to be going on with,' said Heppie.

'They're Zoroastrians. That's the name of their religion.'

'Oh,' said Lynne excitedly. 'Like poor Freddie!' Everyone turned to look at Lynne, not expecting her to contribute to the discussion. 'Freddie Mercury! I'm a real fan,' she offered by way of explanation. 'He was one of those Zorro-whatdyermacallits. His real name was Farukh something. He wasn't born in England, you know, but in Zanzibar, I think.' Lynne's contribution was acknowledged, and Ted continued.

'Anyway, when the British were in India, they got on well with the Parsees. Largely because they didn't have lots of gods and they never had a complicated caste system like the Hindus. The caste system gave the British endless headaches about who was allowed to do what. Dealing with Parsees was so much more straightforward. There are Indian-sounding Parsee surnames like Amroliwalla. But many have surnames recalling the jobs they had during the Raj; like Engineer, Contractor, Registrar, even Fixit.'

On cue, Ted's small audience smiled.

'What about Cooper?' asked Lynne.

'It's a traditional term for a barrel maker. So old man Cooper's ancestors were probably in the trade in some way.'

'What about Parsees today?'

'Numbers declining, through intermarriage. Plus they don't allow converts.'

'Oh. Sounds familiar,' sighed Heppie.

'They worship in fire temples. When they die, the tradition used to be that they build some sort of tower, and leave their bodies for the vultures to eat.'

There was a general chorus of 'Ugh'. 'Hmm,' added Luke, 'some people carry recycling too far.'

'I knew I had a lot to be thankful for,' said Lynne, shuddering.

'But that tradition is dying out.'

There was a moment's silence, during which everyone's thoughts inevitably floated to the horrors of dying, only to be eaten by vultures.

Heppie and Shula spoke over each other.

'Shortage of vultures?'

'Health and safety?'

A further moment of quiet then the table burst into laughter, and relieved tension.

'Anyway, Ted, how come you're such a *maven* about religious customs?'

'*Maven?*'

Heppie had played a little trick on Ted. She touched her sister's knee. Here was something about their identity that clever clogs Ted did not know or understand. 'Sorry, an expert.'

'Oh, didn't you know? Before he met me, hubby was a *semenarian.*'

Before Luke's off-colour remark had time to register, Ted said, 'Well, I used to be a seminarian. We did comparative religion and stuff.'

'You studied for the priesthood?' Lynne said enthusiastically.

'Oh, you would have made a great Father. *Father Ted!*' There was more laughter at this mention of the famous TV programme.

'So what went wrong?' Heppie spoke with her customary directness.

'*Moi* happened, that's what. Ted was on the road to Brighton, where I was living at the time. Through the windscreen of his trusty old Ford he saw in the distance a great light over the town. That light was me, ladies. He just fell into my arms, and I saved him from all that religious stuff.'

The three women frowned at Luke, unhappy with Luke's dismissal of religion. Ted himself said nothing, but just shrugged his shoulders as if to signal, 'Well. What can I say?'

'Hell, look at the time! I must get to the kids' school to pick them up. It's Friday. The traffic will be heavy. Can I give anyone a lift?'

'No thanks. We're just in the multi-storey round the corner. We ought to be going as well. Shula?'

'Sure.'

'Ted and I will be here a few more minutes. We're OK, thanks Lynne. We're in the town hall car park.'

The three women collected their coats and various packets. Lynne, Ted and Luke blew farewell kisses to each other, and Ted shook hands cordially with the sisters. Outside, the temperature had dropped considerably. 'Brrr, it looks like they were right. Rain on the way.'

'Yes. Good luck with the kids. See you later.'

'Looking forward to it.'

In the car back to Shula's flat, Heppie was the first to ask the inevitable question. 'So what did you think of Teddie Bear?'

'Oh, quite nice. Apart from the stink of tobacco.'

'Mm, don't envy him having to cope with Luke full-time though. He was a bit catty this afternoon, don't you think? And sort of on edge.'

'Oh well, that's couples for you, I suppose.' They continued their journey to Shula's in silence.

Ten minutes later, Ted and Luke temporarily left the cafe. Ted wanted a smoke. He wished his young husband good luck, and watched him set off for the town hall, Room 25, before returning to the cafe for another cup of tea.

15.45
At Hardwicke's Restaurant – The Golden Rules

She was more than satisfied with her hair. And she was very glad that the little headscarf had kept it tidy, despite the wind blowing up outside. People had often commented on her hairstyle. They used to compare it with Mrs Thatcher's, which she chose to take as the greatest of compliments.

She had always thought that this was by far the best place in the whole town to take tea. Cafes and tea shops of all kinds had come and gone. There were more modern, trendier places of course. But none offered the comfort of Hardwicke's oak-panelled walls, well-upholstered seats, and beautiful white table linen with silver service. They served a more limited range of teas and coffees than the new places. But the range was tasteful, traditional, well tried. The cakes were always the same. Classic, nothing too elaborate. Strawberry meringues, Victoria sponge, custard tarts, custard creams, and her favourite, Bakewell tart. She always made a show of dithering over the menu, but in the end invariably chose her favourite. In fact, regular staff knew her as Miss Bakewell Tart, a hardly less apt name for this most proper of women. She ordered her usual tea and bakewell tart, and waited.

There was a rumour – there had been rumours for some years – that Hardwicke's was going to close. She sincerely hoped not. The staff, mostly women in their thirties and forties, wore smart, unflashy uniforms. They were unfailingly polite, and called you 'madam' and 'sir'. They didn't just say 'Are you ready to order?' or 'Welcome' or 'Hello'. They said 'Good morning, madam' or 'Good afternoon, madam'. They did not ask impertinent, insincere personal questions like 'And how are you today?' Customers were treated with what they deserved: quiet dignity.

The rumours about closure were connected with the fortunes of the present Mr Justin Hardwicke. He, by all accounts, led a somewhat dissolute life, and had accrued considerable gambling debts. Not like the original Sir Josiah Hardwicke, known for his Victorian probity and charitable interests. Apparently her grandmother knew him personally, and was among his first well-heeled customers. At Hardwicke's, one did not have 'credit', one had an 'account'. Hers was inherited from her own mother, whose loyalty to the family-owned store was unwavering. Its wares represented the epitome of good taste, and in former times (unlike now, sad to say) the customers were solid, reliable, exclusive. It was a privilege to shop there, and to be seen there. Then, customers felt like part of the oak furniture which the store used to specialise in. Again, quite different from today, when the fashion for cheap, utilitarian, modern pine furniture (*so dreadfully popular with the lower-middle and working classes*) predominated.

Coming here always reminded her of her mother, from whom she had inherited so much good sense and good taste. Her mother could remember the day, not so long ago, when the store used to have overhead wires connected to and from each department and the main cashier. The wires were operated by a pulley system. The wires made a distinctive clatter which fascinated her mother as a little girl. If you were lucky, you could still see similar systems operating in old black and white films.

Mother had a set of what she called *The Golden Rules*, which Jean to this day tried to live by. The rules went round and round in Jean's head, uncontrollable and instinctive. While she drank her tea and ate her bakewell tart, she couldn't resist testing herself. She would challenge herself to remember twelve of the rules. She mumbled quietly, so that no one would hear.

'One: Never use net curtains; they are common.

'One: Never use net curtains; they are common. Two: Rugs are always better than carpet, especially fitted carpet.

'One: Never use net curtains; they are common. Two: Rugs are always better than carpet, especially fitted carpet. Three: Always say "brassiere" and never just "bra".

'One: Never use net curtains; they are common. Two: Rugs are always better than carpet, especially fitted carpet. Three: Always say "brassiere" and never just "bra". Four: Never mix your whites with your coloureds.

'One: Never use net curtains; they are common. Two: Rugs are always better than carpet, especially fitted carpet. Three: Always say 'brassiere' and never just 'bra'. Four: Never mix your whites with your coloureds. Five: Don't talk about "serviettes", but use instead "napkins" (*or was it the other way round*?).

'One: Never use net curtains; they are common. Two: Rugs are always better than carpet, especially fitted carpet. Three: Always say "brassiere" and never just "bra". Four: Never mix your whites with your coloureds. Five: Don't talk about "serviettes", but use instead "napkins" (*or was it the other way round*?). Six: EPNS is for poor people: people in our position have solid silver.

'One: Never use net curtains; they are common. Two: Rugs are always better than carpet, especially fitted carpet. Three: Always say "brassiere" and never just "bra". Four: Never mix your whites with your coloureds. Five: Don't talk about "serviettes", but use instead "napkins" (*or was it the other way round?* Jean wondered). Six: EPNS is for poor people: people in our position only have solid silver. Seven: True gentlemen always open doors for ladies.

'One: Never use net curtains; they are common. Two: Rugs are always better than carpet, especially fitted carpet. Three: Always say "brassiere" and never just "bra". Four:

Never mix your whites with your coloureds. Five: Don't talk about "serviettes", but use instead "napkins" (*or was it the other way round?*). Six: EPNS is for poor people: people in our position only have solid silver. Seven: True gentlemen always open doors for ladies. Eight: Common people have dinner; we have lunch, or luncheon.

'One: Never use net curtains; they are common. Two: Rugs are always better than carpet, especially fitted carpet. Three: Always say "brassiere" and never just "bra". Four: Never mix your whites with your coloureds. Five: Don't talk about "serviettes", but use instead "napkins" (*or was it the other way round?*). Six: EPNS is for poor people: people in our position only have solid silver. Seven: True gentlemen always open doors for ladies. Eight: Common people have dinner; we have lunch, or luncheon. Nine: Always serve tea in the best china.

'One: Never use net curtains; they are common. Two: Rugs are always better than carpet, especially fitted carpet. Three: Always say "brassiere" and never just "bra". Four: Never mix your whites with your coloureds. Five: Don't talk about "serviettes", but use instead "napkins" (*or was it the other way round?*). Six: EPNS is for poor people: people in our position only have solid silver. Seven: True gentlemen always open doors for ladies. Eight: Common people have dinner; we have lunch, or luncheon. Nine: Always serve tea in the best china. Ten: You pour the tea first, then the milk.

'One: Never use net curtains; they are common. Two: Rugs are always better than carpet, especially fitted carpet. Three: Always say "brassiere" and never just "bra". Four: Never mix your whites with your coloureds. Five: Don't talk about "serviettes", but use instead "napkins" (*or was it the other way round?*). Six: EPNS is for poor people: people in our position only have solid silver. Seven: True gentlemen always open doors for ladies. Eight: Common people have dinner; we have lunch, or luncheon. Nine: Always serve tea in the best china. Ten: You pour the tea first, then the milk. Eleven: We do not have a lounge; we have a sitting room.

'One: Never use net curtains; they are common. Two: Rugs are always better than carpet, especially fitted carpet. Three: Always say "brassiere" and never just "bra". Four: Never mix your whites with your coloureds. Five: Don't talk about "serviettes", but use instead "napkins" (*or was it the other way round*? Jean wondered). Six: EPNS is for poor people: people in our position only have solid silver. Seven: True gentlemen always open doors for ladies. Eight: Common people have dinner: we have lunch, or luncheon. Nine: Always serve tea in the best china. Ten: You pour the tea first, then the milk. Eleven: We do not have a lounge; we have a sitting room. Twelve: You do not "pour" or "have" or "take" or even "run" a bath. You "draw" a bath.'

She went through her twelve rules as if telling a rosary; without thinking. A litany of good housekeeping practice. She murmured with hardly a pause. She gave herself eleven and a half marks, deducting a half mark for stumbling on whether, in Rule five, the correct word was 'serviette' or 'napkin'. She would need to check that. *Mm, nothing wrong with me, or my memory*, she thought.

Jean was not so self-complimentary when it came to assessing whether or not she had fulfilled her early-morning promise to soften her attitude, to make herself more popular with her fellow aquarobics students. Self-criticism of any sort was extremely difficult for someone who for years had thrived on the feeling that she was always unshakably correct – a feeling that her mother had encouraged and reinforced in her straight-laced daughter.

Diana's 'At last! The Merry Yiddows' greeting was in truth a little tasteless. But the sisters deserved criticism for being late every time. *Fortunately, I did not actually say anything*: a point in her favour she thought. She also thought that punching her arms vigorously (the bastard!) must have been well received. But why did everyone ignore her comment about practising at home? As for Meg, she did at first consider her a spoilt brat. She concluded that when she said as much, some of the others at least agreed, despite Heppie snapping at her about Meg being "troubled". And when Meg spat in Diana's face, someone had to say something in defence of Diana, didn't they?

It was the same with that stupid Muscles character: interrupting Diana like that. But this was another moment of self-congratulation, because she did not actually say anything. Well, not just then. But soon after, when Meg burst into hysterics, she could not resist telling them that they all made too much fuss about her stupidity and his vanity. 'You'd make a great agony aunt,' Heppie had said. That was unnecessary. *I was right*. It was Meg's splashing around that had ruined her feathers, she now realised.

She was sure that Luke liked her. After all, he had kept her things for free expression, and not told anyone her secret plans. And she always helped him gather everything into his bag.

But that Lynne had accused her of being the teacher's pet! Outrageous. She was enjoying herself at that point, but the class, she felt, was still not warming to her. All she wanted was to be friends with them.

She heartily wished that she had not made that remark about it all being "a question of balance". She knew that when she fell off that bloody woggle she got what she deserved. Luke had been so kind at that point; as was everyone else, apart from Meg of course. Tumbling into the water – that time – had been a near disaster. But it was a turning point. She began to feel, at last, positive about herself.

On the other hand, she could hardly bear to think about

her free expression. She had been so confident that it would work; especially for Diana. *Well, pride really does come before a fall* she reflected, ruefully.

But at the end, after that catastrophic routine (stupid costume, terrible music), why had she turned on Diana like that? First, refusing Diana's compliment and sympathy; then practically accusing her of lying. Was it because (as she now suspected) Diana did not even think of including her free expression in the class? Was it because Diana had been practically forced by Luke and by that wonderful chorus of 'Jean! Jean! Jean!' to come out of her office? *Did she not care about me at all?*

To hell with it. What does it matter? All's well that ends well, she thought, trying to inject some cheer into her mind. After all, in the changing rooms, everyone had been so kind; even Meg. So kind. Perhaps they *were* beginning to like her after all? Was it because she was changing at last? Was it because she was finally achieving her goal? She desperately hoped so.

She started to think more positively about something good: her neighbour's granddaughter, Suzie. The little girl had inducted her into the mysteries of Amazon. Jean was amazed at the range of goods on offer, and at how easy it was to open an account: a word that hitherto she had only associated with Hardwicke's. She learned how she could find things that she wanted, and to pay for them with a single click. She had always been loyal to her local high-street bookshop. But when she asked them about the book that she wanted, they hummed and hawed about it possibly being out of print, the time it would take to order, whether or not it would be an illustrated version and so on.

Well. Loyalty was one thing: efficiency and ease of purchase another. With Suzie's help, she found the title she wanted, with several illustrated versions available; all deliverable within just two or three days. And with the option of gift wrapping too! When the book arrived last week, she decided against Amazon's choice of gift wrapping (too stark, too plain), replacing it with a more appropriate, altogether more *feminine* design. All she needed now was a special card, and a mini bouquet or something similar to attach to the book. She had found just what she wanted at Hardwicke's no less, just before she came upstairs to take tea. She was thrilled, and happy.

She was about to leave. But before she got out of her chair, she sensed behind her his clammy breath, before he even spoke a word.

16.20
At Hardwicke's Restaurant – The Fancy Woman

'I'd have recognised that hair anywhere.' The voice was close, low, almost whispering. Then even closer: 'Especially, my dear, from behind.' He was taunting her. Mock seductive. Oily. Jean's throat tightened, her gorge instinctively rose, and her chest became constricted. She closed her eyes. *No. I must not be sick.*

He sat down opposite her, and ordered coffee. 'We have to talk.'

'Nothing to say.'

'Don't be silly. What do you want to do?'

She stared at him. Although he was in his late fifties, he was as handsome as ever. He had even lost a bit of weight, which, she had to admit, suited him. He had even managed, at this early part of the year, to have acquired a faint tan. Resentment flushed her mind. 'Divorce,' she said suddenly, surprising herself with her decisiveness. Yes, that was what she wanted.

'Suits me. Suits me just fine. Let's contact our solicitors and get the thing moving.' The waitress came with his coffee. 'But don't you want to know?'

'About what?'

'Well. Aren't you just a teeny bit curious?' He stirred his coffee and looked at her, almost leering at her. His sense of male superiority hovered almost visibly over the table.

'Curious?'

'About who it is?' He smiled.

'Your new lady friend, you mean? Frankly, no. I don't give a shit.'

'Oh. You don't give a shit. Bravo! Well, that's an improvement! You're learning to be foul-mouthed at last. Where's the holier-than-thou prig gone?'

'Bastard! There. Will that satisfy you? You ought to feel ashamed.'

'Me? The one who has provided for you all these years? And has been busy making financial arrangements for your future? You'll have no worries on that score, Jean. I'll see to all that.'

'Guilt money. Anyway, you seem to forget.'

'Forget what?'

'That it was Daddy's money that got you started. And some of what my grandmother left me. The rest of her bequest is still in my name, thank goodness. There was a time when you were a nobody, and you needed all the money you could lay your hands on.'

Gordon shrugged. It was true. Like many so-called self-made men who attributed their success to their own hard work, it was the support from others – financial, emotional, social – that also played its part in that success. Lots of people worked hard, very hard. But of itself, hard work was no guarantee of success.

'And speaking of money,' Jean added, feeling slightly more confident and belligerent, 'I noticed that there were several quite large withdrawals from our joint account recently.'

'Well, there's plenty to go around,' he said expansively. Which was true.

'And by large, I mean not just hundreds, but thousands; in two cases, tens of thousands.'

'Well,' Gordon said, 'You know how it is: one or two presents, a holiday. And cash gifts, to show that I'm dead serious about this relationship. We've also bought a boat, in both our names. You never wanted one, did you?'

'She must have expensive tastes, your fancy woman.'

He laughed out loud. 'Fancy woman! Haven't heard that for ages. You're such a throwback. A Victorian sourpuss. A real killjoy.'

She glared at him, knowing that his accusations were partly true. What he did not know was that she was becoming a new woman, or trying to. She was determined to succeed; to be as fully independent – and joyful – as possible. No matter what the cost to her nature, or to her upbringing. It was going to be a battle, but one that she was convinced the new Jean could win.

'I've never known a woman who could sustain an hour-long conversation about the merits or otherwise of a window-cleaning product. Good God, Jean. We were the only people I knew who had a cleaning woman for three whole days a week. What the fuck did you both find to do all day? Iron the doilies? Hoover the cistern? Lick the toilet bowls out with your own mean little tongues?'

Jean recoiled, as he demonstrated with his own tongue darting in and out. *Please. I don't want to be sick.*

Years of frustration could not be stopped. He spoke intensely, focused on his wife's despairing face, ignoring the enquiring eyes of the waitress who had just served him coffee.

'Jesus! We had a utility room big enough to open a hardware store. Crammed full with every goddamn duster, dishcloth, limescale remover, and washing-up liquid known to man. And those endless shitty mottos of yours – *Golden Rules* you called them – no doubt inherited from your pretentious, social-climbing bitch of a mother: "Net curtains are common. EPNS is for poor people. People in our position have solid silver"' His voice and manner gave an uncannily accurate rendition of his mother-in-law.

'Half the bloody country has net curtains and EPNS, Jean! Including members of my own family, as you well know. But that never stopped you from mouthing off at every touch and turn, humiliating them, and me. And anyway, who gives a fuck?'

'I only wanted to keep the house nice for you and the boys.' Her eyes glistened with incipient hot tears.

'Don't give me any crap about the boys. Why do you think they've buggered off so far away? Why do you think they never visit even at Christmas? Not to mention never asking us to spend Christmas with them?'

'No. Don't. That's cruel.'

'You did it all for yourself. Not for me or the boys: for your vanity; your so-called social position. "People in our position" indeed. As though you were something other than a middle-class, sanctimonious, tight-arsed bitch.'

Jean was afraid of what might come next. 'You've said enough. Enough.' *I can't be sick. Not here. No, not here.*

'Have I indeed? Look, I gave you a chance. I just wanted to bring a bit of fun back into our life. I should have known that a woman who did everything she could to avoid even normal sex, would turn me down. You flatly refused to open up that mealy mouth of yours for me, your husband. No wonder you refused to do what I had dreamt of for years, just one simple thing. You're not just repressed. You're just plain frigid.'

His hot, angry breath was very close to her. From somewhere, she found the strength to say, slowly and deliberately, 'I couldn't do what you wanted because I just couldn't. You are disgusting.'

He sat back. He became more settled. He spoke almost cheerily. 'Well, maybe so, but I don't understand how you can dismiss something that you've never tried.' It was as if he was talking about something strange or new on a menu. 'You never know,' he added casually, 'You might like it. I've heard that your pal Marion what's-her-name can't get enough of it. She's worn out her lucky bastard of a husband. He's even thinking of renting her out to other Charity Kings whose wives won't play ball.' He laughed loudly.

Jean did not fully hear or comprehend what he was saying. From the parts that she did understand, she didn't know whether he was telling the truth. Or was it bravado? Or just hurtful lies? All she could say was, 'I've got nothing to be ashamed of.'

'Nor have I, my dear. You just haven't grown up. It's the twenty-first century. Everyone's doing it!'

'I don't believe you.'

'Well, suit yourself. Anyway, no doubt our solicitors will be in touch with each other.'

'What if I told my solicitor why?'

'Why what?'

'Why we're having a divorce. Why I refused to indulge your, your disgusting tastes.' *I will not be sick.*

'See if I care.'

He got up and prepared to leave. 'Oh, by the way, we've, or rather I've bought a rather nice flat overlooking the sea; in both our names: views of the sea one way and the harbour the other. We're moving in together on Monday.'

Oh, I might have known: the most expensive location in the area. Only the best for the fancy woman.

'It'll provide us with a bit of financial security, like you've had for years. And you still will have. I've set up a trust fund.' He got up to leave.

'Oh, before I go, I just thought you might like to take a look at my "fancy woman".' And before Jean could turn away, he flashed a photo in front of her eyes. He bent down to whisper. 'And yes. You're right. Expensive tastes I have to admit; but hell, worth every penny. And yes, does everything I've dreamed of for years. You had your chance, and you blew it.' He laughed again. With that, Gordon left, leaving Jean to pay his bill.

The pain that Jean endured for the next two minutes far exceeded any pain that she had endured in her life so far: worse than the pain of intercourse, caused partly (though she did not know it yet) by the hardening of her pelvic floor; worse than the pain of two childbirths; worse than the pain of three kidney stones (one passed in agony, two broken by the indignity of lithotripsy); worse than the pain of grief when her father died of brain cancer; worse even than the pain and shock of her younger sister's death at only thirteen, run over in the street by a teenage drunk driver.

She fled from her chair. She had to get to a toilet. She needed to be sick. The two waitresses stood aside as her unsteady legs somehow carried her to a toilet door. She burst through and headed for the single cubicle. Thank goodness it was vacant. She slammed into the cubicle door and got to the toilet bowl. She had no time to lock the door. She had already started to vomit over her blue suit. She retched and choked on her own sick. Laced with phlegm and snot, it coursed from her mouth and nose. The remains of her tea and bakewell tart were everywhere: on her clothes, on the floor and down the side of the bowl. There was an overpowering stench of almonds and raspberry jam. The taste and dregs of both were lodged in her nostrils, mouth and teeth.

'Oh madam, can we help?' said one of the waitresses behind her. The waitress held Jean, trying to comfort her. 'We knew there was something wrong. We've seen that chap with you quite a few times. He's your husband?'

'The bastard,' Jean tried to say. Her voice was distorted by the vomit, and oddly magnified by the echoing tiles of the tiled toilet walls. She was breathing heavily, her eyes streaming with tears – even though she was not actually crying.

'Don't try to talk. Let's get you out of here. Clean you up. Hold on to my colleague. We'll go into our staffroom.'

The waitresses supported Jean as she made her way out of the toilet. As she did so, she realised with horror that it was the gents' toilet that she had gone into. This made her almost want to laugh. The two women led her to their staffroom, where they did their best to damp clean Jean's clothes, wash her face, rinse her mouth out, and help her to calm down. She managed to blow her nose free of mucus, to take some sips of water, and to say, 'Thank you. It must have been something I ate. Oh, sorry. I didn't mean to criticise your–'

'No dear. It wasn't anything you ate. It was that bloke, wasn't it? "The bastard", you called him.'

'Oh, I really disgraced myself in there, didn't I?'

'Of course not,' chorused the waitresses. 'And if it's of any help,' said the younger of the two, 'nobody but us was around in the restaurant. It's a quarter past five and we were about to close.'

'Oh, my hair. My hair! I haven't ruined it, have I? I only had it done this afternoon.'

'No, not at all. It looks very nice. You hair's fine.'

'And my handbag. On the table. Near–'

'Don't worry. We've got it. Here, look.'

'You're right, you know,' said the older waitress, with some bitterness.

Jean snuffled. 'How do you mean?'

'Bastards. Sometimes, they can all be bastards: men.'

By now, Jean had settled down a little. She felt, as she would put it, "a little more respectable". Fortunately, she had not driven to Hardwicke's. She had come by bus. But she felt unable to make the return journey on public transport. One of the waitresses had the number of a reliable firm of taxis, and volunteered to call it, using her own mobile phone.

The taxi took only four minutes to arrive at the front door of the store. The older waitress accompanied Jean in the lift to the ground floor, and to the taxi. Jean was obsessively apologetic about all the trouble she had caused, and equally effusive with her convoluted expressions of gratitude.

'No problem. No problem at all. You have a safe journey home now. Take care.'

The waitress took the lift upstairs to the tea room. It was time to clear up. 'Well,' the older one said, 'so much for little Miss Bakewell Tart. You'd think that butter wouldn't melt in her mouth. You never know, do you?'

'Too right. As my gran used to say, "Behind every face, there's a story".' The two women began to clear up the mess that Jean had left behind.

In the taxi home, Jean suddenly realised that she had not paid the bill for tea. A pot of tea and a slice of bakewell tart for her, and a coffee for him. Nor had she given the waitresses a tip, which they surely deserved. That was a poor reward for two strangers on whose kindness she had so depended. For a moment, she wanted to ask the taxi driver to turn back. But the traffic was heavy. She needed time to get ready for the party, and she needed a rest. *Sod it*, she decided. *I'll pay next time I go in. If there is a next time.*

So she sat back in the taxi, resting, and fantasising about exacting some sort of revenge on her husband. She had heard that it was a dish best served cold. She suddenly felt a chill run through her.

7. There's A Storm Coming

19.45
It's My Party!

Heppie and Shula arrived by minicab. They asked the driver to stop in the street so that they could walk up the drive and take time to look at the house. Heppie paid the fare and they both stepped out into the evening air, feeling slightly apprehensive.

It was colder and darker than they expected. They both wore overcoats against the wind. They were nervous, not sure what to expect from this return visit to their former home. When it had been their house, it was certainly as big, but somehow not so grand.

The drive was as they remembered it; a large semicircular affair, with one entrance leading up to the house, and an exit at the other end of the semicircle. Both sets of gates had been hospitably left open.

'At least we're not too late.'

'Mm.' Heppie forced back a memory of this morning's unwelcome late arrival to the lesson, and Di's "Merry Yiddows"'greeting.

'Well, what do you think?'

'This front part's a lot greener. We had only two or three trees, remember? There was a swing somewhere here. In the summer I used to sit on it, listening to you scraping on the violin, when the windows were open.'

'Hell, I'd almost forgotten her, that awful teacher. "Scales, my dear. You must practise your scales!" She was absolutely relentless. Mum and Dad, bless them, were such believers in those private music lessons. That teacher nearly killed my love of music.'

'But not completely. At least you had a good ear for music; a real talent. I never did. I was a lost cause. You were always the talented one: singing, ballet, tap dancing. You were a real little performer, even at eight or nine. Even on the violin. You made Mum and Dad so proud.'

'Oh, was I a terrible little show-off? Did I embarrass you?'

Heppie hugged her sister. 'No never. And you were never a show-off. I was just relieved that I didn't have to sing or entertain. You did me a favour. Honestly. I hated anything to do with performing in front of people.'

'Does this still feel like home to you?' Shula took in the massive two-storey house, with its three windows on either side of its imposing entrance. It seemed grander than ever.

'Not a bit. Things change. The house we moved to wasn't bigger, but it was better for us. More homely. How about you? How do you feel?'

'Oh, I'm OK. Sometimes, the early memories come back, like the music lessons. But no, this isn't home anymore. At least I don't think so. As you say, things change and move on.'

'I remember those two *goyische* boys who used to live next door at number six. The Robinsons. Nice lads. They were fun.'

'I wonder what happened to them.'

'They're probably bankers or businessmen by now, with families of their own. Or maybe pop stars? Do you remember? They knew all the songs. One of them was a great piano player. A regular little Jerry Lee Lewis. At least we all thought so. The other had a guitar. I was put on drums. I only had to bang out a rhythm, which was about my limit. And you sang so well, even though you were so little.'

From the recesses of her mind, Shula picked up a memory. She threw caution to the wind, literally, and began:

It's my party, and I'll cry if I want to
Cry if I want to, cry if I want to
You would cry too if it happened to you!

'Can't remember any more words though!'

'Oh, I can*! Prenez garde. Je vais chanter*,' Heppie said melodramatically, in her best Churchillian voice. In her tuneless alto voice, she gave the first verse a suitably teenage-tragic edge.

'Nobody knows where my Johnny has gone,
Judy left the same time.
Why was he holding her hand,
When he's supposed to be mine?'

They both sang the first line of the chorus again, with gusto.

'It's my party, and I'll cry if I want to...'

At which point they were joined by two more voices behind them.

'*Cry if I want to, cry if I want to,*
You would cry too if it happened to you!
da da da da DA!'

The four singers collapsed with laughter.

'Well I must say, you two are as camp as a row of tents! But don't call us. We'll call you.' This was from Luke. He was carrying a set of The Water Babes' CDs, which he had had made up from his iPod recording. They were all carefully placed in a small, attractive carrier bag covered with musical symbols.

'Oh, haven't heard that in years. Love it! How long have you been here then?' asked Lynne. She stood in the breeze, one hand holding on to the cork hat she had made from the woggle she had stolen from the pool. In the other hand she carried a bag with Di's present and card. She also held an umbrella.

'Only about five minutes.'

'Luke says that it's always polite to be a bit late for things. To give time for the hosts to finish preparing, blah, blah. But somehow, I don't think Mrs C will need any extra time, do you?'

'She's sure to have been ready for ages. How did you get here?'

'Ted gave us a lift, with the kids. Before they all go off for an Indian. My daughter desperately wanted to take a peek at the house, just from the road. She just doesn't get it.'

'How do you mean?'

'She can't understand that I might actually know someone who lives here, in such a posh area. And that I might actually be invited to a party here. Or that I might actually have, er–' And here Lynne stumbled.

'Have what?'

'New friends of my own. That she doesn't know. And certainly not the sort of friend who lives here.' Lynne looked down, a little uncomfortable and uncharacteristically shy.

'Ah, I see,' said Heppie, instinctively understanding that Lynne might be feeling a little out of place. 'Group hug everyone.' Lynne put the things she was carrying on to the floor, and the four hugged each other.

'Now, into the fray! Don't forget your brolly, Lynne.'

'Oh right. I think that for once, the forecasters were right. There's a storm coming.'

And after the moments of group reassurance, they walked up to the entrance, past an array of lighting designed to show the late-spring front garden to its best advantage. They stood in the big porch, in front of wooden double doors. Again, everything was brilliantly lit.

'God, I don't think I could afford the lecky even for this porch! The bill must be huge,' said Lynne, rakishly arranging the woggle hat on her head.

'Lecky?' asked Shula.

Luke translated for her. 'Electricity.'

'Oh.' As someone who never in her life had had to worry about paying utility bills, and who had not the slightest idea of what it was like to be unable to pay them, Shula felt that her simple "Oh" was the most appropriate response.

Heppie reached up to the right of the door frame, to press the bell. She immediately stood back, pulling Shula with her.

'You OK, Sis?'

'Yes. It's gone!'

'What's gone?'

'Our front door *mezuzah*. I remember the day when Dad put it up. And I remember all the others inside the house. Old Rabbi Morris was here.'

'But it isn't our house any more. Surely you didn't expect it to be still there?'

Before Heppie could say anything, the door had opened. Salma greeted Lynne and Luke, with smiles all round. Heppie and Shula hung back for a few seconds.

Heppie reached up and brushed her fingers across the empty space formerly occupied by the *mezuzah*, with its scroll of prayers and promises. It was a self-conscious gesture to her remembered past. Heppie was not a sentimental or particularly religious person. But as the memories flooded over her, she wanted to feel protected. She wanted her spirits to soar. Everything felt too ordinary.

With her sister, she entered the house, to be welcomed by Salma.

20.00
THE HALL OF MIRRORS

The two wooden doors of the porch opened up into a small lobby, at the back of which – opposite the porch doors – was another set of double wooden doors. The four arrivals giggled and jostled with each other to greet Salma. There were exchanges about the change in the weather, the delightfulness of the front garden, the beautifully lit trees, the large porch and so on. Strangely, thought Heppie, there were no kisses. Perhaps everyone was a little intimidated, embarrassed, or even shy?

They all passed through the glass doors into the large oblong-shaped hall. It was wide enough to take in the first window on either side of the porch door, and practically deep enough, and high enough thought Lynne, to accommodate all of her modest semi.

'Here, let me take your coats. Mum will be here in a minute. She's talking to Marsha and Meg.'

'So we're not the first?'

'No. And, Heppie and Shula, you'll be glad to know you're not the last!' Salma laughed.

'Well, thank goodness for small mercies,' said Shula, ruefully.

'Great hat, Lynne: corks are in this year, I see.'

'Oh, this stupid thing. Has Di arrived yet?'

'No. She rang earlier. She's going to be–'

'Oh, in that case, I'll take the hat off. But I'll hang on to it for now if you don't mind. And I'll keep this bag. It's got Di's present and card in it. We mustn't forget to sign it. But you can take the anorak, thanks.'

'Oh, and Jane's here too. She came late this afternoon, to help. Let me take your lovely mac, Luke.'

'Thanks. But I'll keep the little bag. It's got the Water Babes' CDs I made for us.'

'And your coats, ladies?' said Salma, turning to Heppie and Shula.

'Oh, let me carry those for you!'

'Such a *gentleman*,' said Salma. 'It's OK thanks. I'll just put them in the guest cloakroom. Won't be a tick.'

The guests were all a little overwhelmed by the hall; so dazzled in fact that no one had yet turned to the ritual of complimenting each other's choice of clothes. They had not even taken in the full impact of their host Salma's outfit.

The truth was that any clothes, no matter how elegant, had a lot of competition from the hall itself. Luke tried to take everything in, so that he could describe it to Ted later. Dominating everything was a huge chandelier. Though Luke was gloriously unaware of it, the chandelier was made of the finest Swarovski Strass crystal, positioned at just the correct height, its lowest point being some eight feet above the ground. It was also of classic width: the sum of the width and length of the hall. There were several matching wall lights, heightening the effects of light and luxury.

The hall contained several doors, one of which led to the cloakroom into which Salma had taken their coats. Luke assumed that other doors led to the kitchen, the dining room, and perhaps a downstairs bathroom. A wide staircase spiralled up gracefully to the first floor. There were three or four mirrors, strategically placed so that their reflections made the sparsely furnished hall seem grander than ever. A pair of glass doors led to a large sitting room.

'Not your average British Home Stores!' Luke whispered to Lynne, looking up at the chandelier. He avoided leaning on a mirror-topped table directly beneath it.

'You're just jealous,' laughed Lynne.

'You bet your sweet Fanny Adams I am. I must tell Ted to pay more attention to those *House & Garden* magazines you see at the doctor's.'

'Dream on. He'll need a better paid job too, I shouldn't wonder. Much better.'

'Oh,' said Heppie, finally recovering from the impact of the hall. 'Love the dress, Lynne. Green really suits you.'

'Yes,' everyone chorused. 'The scarf. The shoes. Lovely.'

Though not a vain woman, Lynne felt relieved. Even if they did not mean it – but why shouldn't they? – she had something to tell her uppity daughter. They had admired her second-hand green dress! She was glad that her anorak had already been taken away. She was ashamed of it, but could not afford a new coat. She came from a sensible working-class family that abhorred debt. Where possible, she refused to spend on things that she could not afford; especially things for herself. She would rather have a dodgy anorak than buy new clothes on credit. Unlike many people she knew, she held on to her dignity, rather than run the gauntlet of monthly credit card bills which she could not afford to pay.

'Heppie, you always have such style. You look great. But who's this young lady? She is so fab-u-lous. Is she really your sister?'

Luke's joshing and compliments were well meant, and well deserved. Heppie looked particularly grand tonight, her taupe blouse perfectly matching her dark skin tone. Her make-up was exquisite.

But the star sister, as Luke had so gallantly intimated, was Shula. She had decided to make a real effort. She felt like a debutante at her coming-out ball, The start of her new life. She wore a fuchsia coloured crêpe-de-Chine blouse, with as revealing a neckline as she could get away with. She wore her false bosoms, and her lustrous, deep auburn wig, with defiance and pride. A black skirt and comfortable shoes drew even more attention to her upper body.

'Fanbloodytastic,' agreed Lynne, her eyes glistening with incipient tears. 'You look lovely. What does the jewellery, the necklace mean? Is it Jewish?'

'Yes. It's a Hebrew word. It means "Chai" or "Life".' She turned to Heppie. 'Is it hanging the right way round? ' Heppie said it was perfect.

'Sorry,' said Salma, returning from the cloakroom.

'The wind's getting up a bit. I just nipped outside to check everything was OK.'

'And is everything OK?'

'Yes, I think so thanks.'

The guests now had time to admire Salma's familiar uniform of black Jaeger trouser suit, white shirt, and black high heels. But this evening, there were some additions. Diamonds. Drop earrings, and a large brooch. She looked like a modern version of an Indian maharanee. Her black eyes shone, framed by blue shadow and mascara. Her bright red lipstick lent her lips a distinctly sensuous look.

'You look sensational, as usual,' said Lynne. This led to a chorus of praise and admiration. 'Are they real?' she asked, looking at the diamonds in astonishment. 'Er, sorry to be so rude.'

'Well, I certainly hope so,' said Salma, smiling. 'They were a twenty-first birthday present from my father.'

'Beats my old man's round of drinks at the pub! That's all I got for my twenty-first.' Lynne was not at all jealous. But the difference, not in paternal generosity, but in the ability of fathers to please their daughters, did impress itself not only on Lynne's mind, but on everybody else's too.

'My friends always tell me that I have a Daddy complex. But hell, there are daddies and daddies! Wish I had one like yours!'

Everyone laughed at Luke's remark. 'Well, the diamonds suit you, Salma. A girl's best friend, as they say.' Luke was about to launch into his poor impression of Marilyn Monroe's famous song, but was fortunately cut short by Salma.

'Mm, I don't know about that. If I had to choose between these diamonds and a true best friend, I know which one I would choose.' There was a moment's thoughtful silence, as each person pondered Salma's response.

Luke was slightly miffed to be excluded from all the admiring comments about clothes. But he tried not to show it. But he felt it. He felt ever so slightly excluded. Perhaps after all it really was true that men (even gay men like himself) were from Mars, and women were from Venus. Perhaps he was wrong to come this evening? He dismissed the thought immediately. This was after all a party for Di, now his ex-boss, and he deserved to be there. But as the only 'cock' at the gathering, he felt well and truly isolated. Separate. Clearly not one of the girls, or not dressy enough to be included in the circle of 'oohs' and 'aahs'.

For no one had remarked on his outfit: perhaps because it was largely unremarkable? He didn't think so. He wore what he called his 'bluebottle' look. Light blue shirt, dark blue cashmere sweater, smart navy blue chinos, and smart, dressy red shoes: the sting in the tail, he called them.

He would have liked someone to say something complimentary about the effort he had made. But no one did. He felt peeved. And he felt angry with himself for feeling so. Yet not everything was about him, as Ted had often pointed out. So for once, he did not say anything. For once he did not draw attention to himself, or to the fact that no one had remarked on his appearance. He consoled himself with the thought that Ted would congratulate him on his restraint.

'Welcome everyone. How nice to see you.'

They all turned. It was Mrs C, standing in the doorway that led from the kitchen into the hall.

Beauty comes in many forms. And this was one of them. Mrs C was swathed in a stunning pure white sari, threaded with silver, and wearing small white slippers. With no make-up or other jewellery, and with her silver hair glistening under the lights, Mrs C put every label, every fashion house and every trend, to shame. No one said anything at first, and no one embraced or kissed her. They couldn't. She was too perfect. Compared to her, her guests felt clumsy, lumpy, out of place.

Heppie was the first to move forward. She shook Mrs C's hand. 'Thank you, Mrs C, for inviting us all to your beautiful home.'

'You're most welcome.'

This, as they say, broke the ice. Each visitor shook hands with the hostess. The atmosphere became looser, warmer and more genial.

But Lynne could not resist saying something about what, in truth, was on everyone's mind. 'Oh, that sari, Mrs C, it's just so gorgeous. You look so, er, so, well…'

Luke wanted to help his friend out. He also wanted to find a word that expressed what he genuinely felt. Without any sense of exaggeration or campness, he simply said, 'So heavenly.' Others quietly added their own chosen words. Luke and Lynne had spoken for them all, and they were relieved and grateful.

'How kind. I'm sure you could all do with a drink. Shall we go into the sitting room, and join the others?'

20.15
Old-fashioned Hospitality

Mrs C led the way through the glass doors from the hall into the sitting room. 'Oh, hello, Jane, where are Marsha and Meg?'

'I think Meg wanted a cigarette. They must be outside.'

Mrs C led everyone to the fireplace, on the right hand side of the room. There was a log-burning stove. Even though it was late spring, it was lit. It was cheerful, and welcoming.

The sitting room was large and comfortable, not unlike the lounge of a small country-house hotel, though quite without any institutional feel about it. There were several sofas and armchairs, and a baby grand. Opposite the doors through which everyone had entered the room, was a large window. On the other side of the window was a conservatory built on to the house. And beyond the conservatory was the garden, lit up for the occasion. Much to everyone's relief, the lighting in this room was much softer than in the hall. A number of table lamps and floor lamps gave the room a distinctly cosy, English feel.

'Please, do make yourselves at home.'

Even for Heppie and Shula, not unused to such lavish surroundings, making oneself at home was more easily said than done. It rather depended on one's sense of home. Still, they sat near the fire, along with the others, and chatted to Jane, who was evidently in charge of the fire.

'Drinks, Salma?'

'Yes, of course! What would everyone like?'

Salma and Jane went to the largest cupboard in the room. They somewhat theatrically opened its carved doors. It turned out to be the grandest drinks cabinet that any of the visitors had ever seen. In the upper half it had every conceivable traditional whisky, gin, rum, vodka, sherry, port, cognac and liqueur that you would find in any decent supermarket or off-licence. In the lower half, beneath a pull out serving shelf, there was a concealed fridge containing ice, a cocktail shaker, chasers, soft drinks, flavoured waters, lemons, glacé cherries and the like. Cut glasses of various sizes and shapes lined the doors.

The visitors gasped. Shula and Heppie had seen their fair share of home-installed bars – with their complicated measuring devices and their vulgar, flashy mirrored surfaces – but this was something else. Here there were no spirit measures, jiggers, or optics. The drink was simply there for the taking.

'Sorry about this,' said Salma in mock apology. 'It's my father's pride and joy. Custom made. Oak. You should have been here when Meg first saw what was in it. She practically passed out!'

'I'm not surprised,' said Luke. 'It's breathbloodytaking, excuse my French.'

'Would you like a drink, Mum?'

'Oh, not for me, thanks. I think Jane and I should go to the kitchen.' Predictably, Mrs C refused every offer of help, and then left the room with Jane.

'Mine's a G and T. Ice and two slices please, modom.'

'We've got wine in the dining room, if anyone would prefer.'

'No thanks. Not for me anyway. Ted always says that good wine is wasted on me. I wouldn't know one from another. Don't know my Liebfrauwhatsit from my Rrrrrrrioja. No. I'm a confirmed gin slut.'

'Me too, please,' said Shula. Everyone giggled at the unlikely notion that Shula might be a gin slut.

'And when you're ready, a gin and Dubonnet,' said Heppie.

Still wearing the woggle hat, Lynne got up and looked into the cabinet. She wanted to try something new, something exotic, while she had the chance – especially since she was not paying; so definitely no Baileys. She looked through various bottles. Poire Wilhelm, Triple Sec, Bénédictine, Galliano meant nothing to her. 'Oh, there'. Unsure of how to pronounce the name, she said: 'Some of that please'.

She pointed at a bottle of Crème de Menthe. 'I've seen it before, but never actually had one.'

'I know. I'll do you a grasshopper,' said Salma, unfazed. 'It's a cocktail made with this. You'll love it.'

'Oh, terrific.' Salma set to work like a professional. She dropped ice cubes, and equal amounts of cream (from the fridge), white Crème de Cacao and green Crème de Menthe into the cocktail shaker. Following a vigorous shake, the contents were poured into a chilled cocktail glass. After the briefest tasting, Lynne immediately declared herself a lifelong grasshopper fan.

'From now on, please help yourselves. Please, don't stand on ceremony or even wait to be asked.' The offer from Salma was duly acknowledged. Even so, they all thought that the invitation to help themselves to drinks might be a little *too* generous, and unlikely to happen.

Lynne sat down again, near the fire. She felt a little stupid, still wearing the silly hat, and holding on to the present and card. Fortunately Luke came to the rescue.

'Lynne, there you are. Let me put the hat and the present and stuff under the piano. I'll put these CDs there too. Do you think that'll be OK, Salma?'

'Go ahead.'

Luke went off to explore the room more fully. He intended to try every sofa and armchair in the room. He wanted to compare them for size, depth, height, and what he called "seatability".

Heppie was peering through the large window. 'Salma, do you mind if Shula and I look at the conservatory?'

'Not at all, I'll come with you. Do you want to come too, Lynne?'

'No thanks. I'll just sit here with my drink for a minute. I'll be fine.' Lynne was quite happy to be alone for a few minutes. She felt that she was in a dream. She had already seen so much to admire, so many things to talk about that she was temporarily lost for words. What was the point of words anyway? Mrs C would be well aware, without needing to be told, of how gobsmackingly beautiful her whole house was. Lynne's main thought was thank God she didn't have to clean it.

'Are you ok there?'

Lynne jumped. It was Jane, back from the kitchen. 'Oh yes thanks. How are you?'

'Fine thanks.' Jane was wearing a plain black silk blouse, black pencil skirt, smart low heels, and – unusually for a girl of her age – a pearl necklace. Lynne wondered if, like Salma's diamonds, they were real too. Lynne deduced, correctly as it turned out, that Jane was not wearing a bra. *Quite the liberated young lady*, she thought, dreading the day when her own daughter caught the no-bra bug.

Not quite sure how to proceed, Lynne settled on, 'You look great.'

Jane said nothing at first. She saw to the fire. She armed herself with a pinafore, gloves, tongs and logs. She expertly opened the stove door, refilled it with logs, and reset the ventilator lever. Then she divested herself of her togs and tools. 'Do you mind if I join you?'

'Hell no, it'll be great to have a little chat. Salma's showing Heppie and Shula the conservatory.'

'Yes. I can see them. There's a door into the conservatory to the left of the big window.'

'And Luke is trying out all the chairs in the room. Buried in a sofa somewhere I expect.'

They laughed. Both Lynne and Jane felt that their conversation was uncertain, and banal. Lynne decided to take the plunge. She wanted to learn where Jane came from. How she fitted in. What she felt. *But I mustn't be too nosey*, thought Lynne, *southerners don't like personal questions*. 'Have you been to this house before?' she asked, cautiously.

'Only once. It's a bit overwhelming, isn't it?'

'Oh God, yes.'

'I didn't know houses like this really existed, especially in my home town. Except in magazines and stuff of course.'

'So where do you live?'

Jane mentioned an estate on the edge of town. She also informed Lynne that she had a younger brother, and that her dad – a widower – was a bus driver. Her mum, a nurse, had died of cancer about five years ago. 'She was only thirty-five.'

'Oh, I'm so sorry. You and your brother were so very young. It must have been hard for you all, especially your dad.' Lynne felt drawn to Jane. Here was one person at least who seemed to come from a similar, southern version of her own background.

'These were her pearls. Not real of course. Apparently you can tell by biting on them.'

'Can you? Anyway, real or not, they're lovely. They suit you. I'm sure they're a lovely reminder.'

Jane smiled, touching the pearls for reassurance.

'He'll miss you when you go to uni, your dad.'

'He'll be OK. He and my brother get on really well. They both like football and stuff. And Oxford isn't so far away.'

'Mm. Still. It must be difficult.' Lynne considered her own situation which had been difficult enough. But she was of the view that when the chips were down, women could cope more easily than men. She decided to change the subject.

'How long have you known Mrs C and Salma?'

Jane instantly brightened. 'I met Salma first. Last year, after A levels, a number of local firms offered opportunities for work experience. Not much, just two weeks. And not paid of course. Since I was interested in the law, I was really keen on getting some experience in a solicitor's firm or whatever. That's where I met Salma. I had a great time, and she was very kind and encouraging. Then I didn't see her again for some months.'

'At the leisure centre?'

'Right. Quite by coincidence, when Mrs C joined the aquarobics. I got on well with them both, and we used to chat in the changing rooms. I felt that I could confide in Mrs C, like she was, not so much a mother, but a doctor or something? Anyway, she gave me advice on my awful spots. Really helpful.'

Lynne admired Jane's frankness, and admired too the girl's instinct not only to survive, but to improve herself. They continued chatting, mostly about the effort that Mrs C must have put into preparing the food for the party. 'Really, it would have been just as easy if we all brought along something we had bought or made ourselves. I've got this great recipe for chocolate cake–'

Jane almost burst out laughing. 'Oh, don't worry. Mrs C has a cousin who runs an Asian catering service. They've brought everything from London. They've been preparing supper, and will come back in the morning to clear up.'

Lynne was astonished. 'All the way from London? But there's only a handful of us! She needn't have gone to all that trouble or expense just for us, surely.'

Jane shrugged and smiled. 'But that's how they do things in this family. And she wants to support her cousin's business.'

Lynne was mollified a little, and glad to realise that Mrs C was not having to toil away over a hot stove. And if Mrs C wanted to spend her own money on a catering service, that was up to her.

Meanwhile, Salma was showing Shula and Heppie the conservatory. The sisters were impressed. It was, like everywhere else, beautifully and atmospherically lit. It was also well stocked with evergreens and with late spring plants and flowers. 'And I love being able to see the garden from here.' Heppie admired the illuminated rectangular pond, leading away from the conservatory. 'And look, Salma, there's Marsha and Meg, at the back there, where it's dark. Looks like they're having an argument. They must be freezing, especially Meg.'

Shula was still mesmerised by the conservatory. 'Heppie, if you turn round and look through the window back into the sitting room, there's a view straight through to the hall. It's like looking through a crystal telescope.'

This was fanciful, but – stretching a point – more or less true.

'Yes,' said Salma. 'But we didn't do it. The previous owners designed it all.'

'Quite magical,' enthused Heppie.

'Shall we join the others now?' Salma led the sisters through the door back into the sitting room.

Luke, meanwhile, had finished his exploration of the seating. He had bounced from sofa to sofa, chair to chair, enjoying the different shape of each one, and settling down for a few minutes in one of them. In his tour, he particularly admired the Persian rugs. They added to the sense of expensive but good taste, oddly contrasting with the glitzier sparkle and glamour of the hall. There were various small tables in the room. On two of these, Mrs C had even placed cigarettes and lighters. A gesture of old-fashioned (and distinctly non PC) hospitality, if ever there was one.

20.25
Elephants in the Room

The guests reassembled near the fire. They all greeted Jane, and complimented her on her outfit, especially the pearls. *Real or not, they look good on her*, thought the sisters. Heppie and Shula reported briefly on the conservatory, and Luke pointed out the chair which, in his opinion, was the best. Salma offered her guests another round of drinks and began to serve them, helped by Jane.

Everyone was aware that there was at least one elephant in the room: Di's absence. Not that anyone seemed to be too bothered. For now, they were all enjoying themselves without

Di being there. In fact, her absence rendered the atmosphere even calmer than it might otherwise have been.

But for Heppie and Shula, there was a slightly more intriguing elephant in the room: the equally absent husband and father, Mr C, or the mysterious missing Mr Cooper, as Heppie called him. The sisters had agreed to try and solve the mystery. They had agreed to ask Salma and her mother exactly the same question separately, and then to compare their answers.

First, Heppie managed to talk to Salma as she was preparing Lynne's second grasshopper. 'You said something about this cupboard being your father's pride and joy?'

Salma did no more than acknowledge Heppie's comment, and continued working the cocktail shaker up and down.

'Will we be meeting him today?' Heppie asked as nonchalantly as she could.

'I'm afraid not. He went to London three days ago to stay in our flat there. And tonight he's flying off to New York. On business, you know. He'll be gone for five days.'

'Oh, that's a shame; at least for us. We'd love to meet him.'

'Yes. Excuse me. I'll just give Lynne her drink, and then I'll just check on the food and things.'

She might as well have told me to bugger off, thought Heppie.

Salma left the room just as Mrs C was re-entering it. Within two minutes, as planned, Shula asked Mrs C exactly the same question. She was not as direct as her sister, but fortified by her second G and T, she managed to force out the question: 'Will we be meeting your husband this evening?' She gave what she hoped was her most dazzling smile.

'I'm afraid not. He's abroad on business.'

Soon, the sisters compared notes. From their memories, the two replies amounted to more or less the same. No, they would not be meeting Mr C. He was away on business.

'Did you get the feeling that they were a teeny bit defensive?' asked Shula.

'Well, yes, I suppose so. They certainly didn't elaborate at all, and, well, I also got the impression that their answers were scripted, even rehearsed. Neither of them wanted to talk about him, anyway. Strange.'

'They could just have been telling the simple truth. Perhaps we'll find out a bit more later on.'

Marsha appeared through the conservatory door at the back of the room. She looked flustered and unhappy, and was clearly in no mood to greet or be greeted, far less to be complimented on her appearance. Vivienne Westwood Gold Label, a sequin squiggle-print gown, the sisters realised at once: no accessories. She wore the dress with soaring black heels. New, about £4,000 the lot, Heppie reckoned.

'Oh hello, Marsha,' said Shula, on behalf of everyone. 'We wondered where you were. You look a bit cold. Is everything OK?'

Marsha shivered. 'It's Meg, wouldn't you know? She's in the garden, dressed in hardly anything. God knows how she stands this weather. She was already a bit squiffy when I picked her up in the taxi.'

'Looking great there,' said Heppie. She walked over to Marsha, to admire the dress.

Marsha whispered, 'I think Meg was afraid that they might be teetotal.'

Holding up her gin and Dubonnet, Heppie took Marsha's arm and whispered back: 'Mm. Far from it, thank goodness.'

'Well, I'm not taking any chances. I'm sticking to the orange squash, just in case; even though I'm not officially on duty this evening.'

'Ach, I should hope not!'

There was a noise at the far end of the room, just in front of the big window. 'Oh my God. It might still be May, but June is certainly busting out all over!' Luke almost choked on his drink.

Everyone turned to look. It was Meg, having just come in from the garden, via the conservatory. She stood, or rather swayed, at the far side of the room, painfully visible to all. She still had a black eye from this morning's incident with Lynne. She held on to an empty glass in her right hand and a cigarette stub hung from her bottom lip. Her flimsy lilac and green dress did nothing for her skin tone. It was at least two sizes too small for her and far too short to contain her flesh or disguise some of her tattoos. Her right breast was all but dropping out of the dress. She wobbled uncertainly on a pair of blue high heels, which made the frilly, flouncy bits shake all over. Marsha looked away, biting her lip in silent fury. Mrs C walked over to Meg and took her arm.

'What's that she's got on her head?' Lynne's question was the one that everyone wanted to ask, but daren't. They were all afraid of being caught between laughter and tears.

'Some sort of fascinator. Or the remains of,' said Marsha, between her teeth. 'When she got into the taxi, the bloody thing wouldn't fit in, because the roof was too low. So it got crushed or something. I don't know. Anyway, by the time we got here, it was all messed up. Unrecognisable. I tried to sort it out, but she wouldn't let me fix it.'

The shattered fascinator shook uncertainly on Meg's head. Gently, Mrs C led her towards the fire. Suddenly, Meg shouted in Mrs C's face. 'Jesus. This house is bloody brilliant!' Her cigarette butt dropped from her mouth on to the floor. She looked at the drinks cupboard. 'And mine's another Whisky Mac.' This was said to no one in particular.

First, Mrs C, then Salma moved to the drinks cabinet. 'No. Let me get it,' said Marsha quickly, silent, hot tears falling down her burning cheeks.

# 20.30
WHERE'S THE PARTY GIRL?

Marsha's offer to get the Whisky Mac was a ruse to make sure that Meg consumed as little alcohol as possible. She searched the fridge for some ginger ale, poured it into Meg's empty glass and thrust it into her hand.

'Here. Sit down and sip it slowly. Please.' She spoke with as much firmness and authority as her state of mind would allow. Marsha felt uncomfortable and miserable. Her dress was a mistake. It was too extravagant for the occasion. She was literally carrying too much fabric. Though made of the finest materials, it felt heavy and out of place, unnecessarily restricting her ease of movement. And her heels were too high. Given Meg's atrocious behaviour, she needed to be physically and mentally alert and agile, instead of which she felt clumsy and awkward. The rest of the group was not used to seeing her so upset, and they did their best to cheer her up.

'Well, Meg seems to be a little quieter now,' Lynne said reassuringly. 'Don't take it to heart, Marsha. None of it's your fault. She doesn't seem to know any better.' The others agreed, making all the sympathetic noises and gestures they could think of.

'Just try and relax,' said Salma, sitting down next to Marsha. 'Things will work out.'

The general sense of awkwardness was suddenly broken by the sound of the doorbell. Feeling a little relieved, Salma jumped to let the next guest in. It was Dorothy, whose booming, cheerful voice could be heard in the hall.

'Oh, sorry I'm late. It's ridiculous, but I only live two streets away. Oh, hello everyone,' she said, as she entered the sitting room. 'Mrs C, how nice to see you again.' They shook hands.

In her plain, beautifully tailored tweed suit, Dorothy was in no mood to engage in any superficial chatter about what everyone, including herself, was wearing. Nor did she seem to notice the surroundings, far less pass comment on them. She was, however, grateful for a drink. 'Single malt on the rocks – to keep out the cold weather,' she joked, accepting the glass from Jane.

Dorothy looked at Jane quizzically. 'I'm Jane, the girl from the gym. You saw me this morning.'

'Oh yes, of course,' laughed Dorothy, 'with our famous bodybuilder.'

'Ooh, what's he really like?' asked Lynne.

'He's bloody gorgeous.'

'Yes, you made that fairly obvious this morning, Meg,' noted Lynne disapprovingly.

'He's OK,' Jane replied noncommittally. 'Keeps himself to himself, I suppose. Works really hard at the bodybuilding.'

'Really? You surprise me. Those Muscle Marys like to work together in packs, endlessly eyeing up each other's pecs and biceps and talking supplements and steroids and stuff. No other bodybuilder uses our little gym. We don't have all the proper gear. Beats me why he comes to us.'

'He says he can't afford to go to the bigger gyms. I think he went to one of them for a while. But there was a bit of bother or some trouble. He's very touchy about the subject. He told me he's saving up to buy his own place: a gym, I mean.'

'Well, the silly sod could save a bit of money by selling that oversized motorbike of his. Have you seen him on it? Looks like a pimple on a rhinoceros. And you know what they say about those biker types: the bigger the bike, the smaller the–'

'Perhaps, but not from where we were looking this morning!' Heppie's remark cut Luke off, and raised a few smiles and nods of agreement.

Jane went round refreshing drinks. Dorothy turned to Mrs C.

'You must be very proud of your daughter.'

'Oh, I am, certainly.'

'And do you have other children?'

The unexpected directness of Dorothy's question took everyone by surprise. Heppie was particularly impressed. *Good for you, Dorothy. Maybe you'll have better luck with asking about the husband.* As for the others, the thought that Salma was anything but the only daughter, the only child, had never occurred to them.

'Oh yes. Salma has a brother. Her twin.'

Luke was thrown by the news. He had thought that Salma and he were more or less friends. But she had never mentioned her brother, far less that he was her twin. But then again, Luke had never asked.

'He lives and works in London: a consultant gynaecologist.'

'Oh, haven't your children done well!' The sentiment went around the room, in various forms.

'Thank you. His wife is lovely. And they have three little boys.'

It was as though Mrs C were unpacking a parcel, revealing one delicacy after another. The mention of grandchildren brought forth a mild torrent of comments and queries and congratulations.

'It must be wonderful to have grandkids,' said Lynne. 'I hope I do one day. Do you see them often?'

Salma was sitting in close to Luke and Heppie. 'They're a godsend, I can tell you,' she mumbled in an aside to them. 'Saved me a *lot* of bother.' Luke and Heppie thought for a moment of what Salma's words meant, or might imply.

'Well,' said Luke rather loudly. 'I'm sorry. But not every parent has the right to expect grandchildren. *C'est la vie*, as they say.'

'You are right, Luke. I know that I am one of the lucky ones. I'm proud of, and I love *both* my children. And I would love them whatever their circumstances.' Mrs C smiled at her daughter, who mouthed back, 'Thank you.' 'Jane?' continued Mrs C, 'Let's go and check the dining room.'

'It was very practical of your mother to use caterers,' said Dorothy with her usual openness.

'Oh? Yes,' said Salma, wondering how Dorothy knew.

'Your mother told me a few minutes ago.'

'Am relieved to hear it,' Heppie commented. 'Saves so much time and effort.'

Lynne was shocked at the casualness with which such things, such *expense*, was talked about. She had a brief fantasy about a Water Babes party at her own house. Surely no one would expect her to hire caterers? She had to take a few deep breaths to calm herself down.

Mrs C appeared with her latest guest: Jean.

'Oh Jean! Welcome. Sorry I wasn't there to greet you. We were all busy making too much noise!' said Salma cheerfully, her hand outstretched. Jean took her hand and gave Salma the lightest of handshakes.

Mrs C stood back. 'Jean. How pretty you look.' Jean did not know it, but she was the only person on whose appearance Mrs C had made a direct comment.

Mrs C was right. Jean wore a black brocade bolero jacket with (unusually for her) matching trousers, and a white frilly blouse. But it was not only her clothes that accounted for the pretty look. It was her face. It shone, with optimism, and with hope. She smiled, a little nervously, but it was a smile nonetheless. She was carrying a gold-coloured handbag, and held it rather like the Queen. 'Oh, thank you, Mrs C. It's sort of a new look. Well, new for me at any rate.' Then, to everyone's amazement, she gave a little twirl.

Mm. Especially for Diana? wondered Luke.

To her delight and surprise, Jean's twirl received a little round of applause. There were appreciative cries of 'Hello', 'Great to see you', 'Love the jacket', 'The trousers really suit you', 'Super blouse' and so on.

She was shaking slightly. Her smile belied the turmoil inside her. She needed to capitalise on the goodwill shown to her in the changing room after her failed attempt at free expression. She needed above all to recover from what she felt was the cruel behaviour of her husband. She needed to cauterise the wounds he had inflicted on her just a few hours ago.

'What would you like to drink, Jean?'

'Oh, I'm not sure. Er…' She suddenly turned to look at Heppie. 'What are you having, Heppie?'

Heppie was as surprised as anyone at the question. 'Me? Well, my usual party tipple: a gin and Dubonnet, actually.'

'Oh, I've never had that combination before. So I'll have the same, if you don't mind, Salma. If it's good enough for Heppie, then it's good enough for me.' She smiled again, a little more confidently this time.

A collective thought embraced the room. *Oh, things seem to be looking up for Jean.* Jean certainly hoped that they were. She needed her resolve to change to be acknowledged. She needed to have her faith in the goodness of people who were very different from herself not so much renewed, as kick-started. She was kind enough to herself to believe that she had made a good beginning this evening.

She looked round the room, and still clinging on to her gold-coloured handbag, asked as brightly as possible, 'Oh, where's the party girl?' The elephant had landed.

20.45
Supper Talk

'Here I am!' Luke said, waving his arms. It was a feeble response to Jean's question, and feebly received.

A short period of embarrassed silence was broken by Salma. 'Oh, Di! Of course. Yes. Sorry, I forgot to say. She rang about an hour ago. She's going to be a bit late. Apparently she's waiting for a call from her brother, about some important travel document or something.'

'Her brother? All the way from Australia?' said Lynne, disbelieving.

'No, the one she told us about in London. He's something to do with the Australian tourist board or whatever. Very well connected, apparently. She mentioned him this morning, remember?'

'Oh, I see.' Lynne remained unconvinced that waiting for a phone call was an adequate excuse for Di being late to her own party. 'She could have given him her mobile,' she said, critically. 'It isn't fair to keep us all waiting, especially Mrs C.'

Salma attempted to calm things down. 'Di said not to wait for supper or anything.'

There was some debate about the propriety of having to eat now, or later, when – or if – Di arrived. The room deferred to Mrs C's judgement. 'Well, in that case, may I suggest that we go into the dining room and have supper now?'

'I agree. The gorgeous smells coming from somewhere have really given me an appetite,' said Lynne. 'Plus it's way after my usual teatime.'

Mrs C and Lynne led the way into the dining room. The guests were astonished by the spread; by its size, variety, colour, exoticism and sheer generosity. Several kinds of meat dishes, vegetable dishes, breads, snacks and desserts were on offer.

'It's just a little buffet. Just take a plate and help yourselves. There are plenty of chairs.' Meg was the first to grab a plate. Jean was the last. She was furious with Diana for being late, and for some reason that she could not understand, she felt ashamed on Diana's behalf. It was almost as if Diana was letting her down.

'But there's enough to feed an army. We'll never get through this lot!'

'I'm not so sure, Lynne,' laughed Salma, looking at Meg laying into her food. 'Anyway, people can take home anything we don't eat. And Mum makes sure that anything left over goes to a good cause of some kind.' They all went round the table, complimenting Mrs C on the food.

'This looks delicious,' said Dorothy to Mrs C. 'Persian? Parsee?'

'We're Parsee actually. But a lot of our food is Persian influenced. How did you know?'

'Used to teach at Oxford. Over the years, we had quite a few students from that part of the world, including Parsees. Now which of these dishes here is specifically Parsee?'

Mrs C gave Dorothy and Heppie a tour of the table, while the others set about choosing their dishes. She pointed out the more typically Parsee dishes, including ones made of eggs. She also pointed out a chicken *dhansak*, and a lovely coconut drink of some sort. Heppie thought that the Parsee desserts shown to them, made of vermicelli and semolina, did not look too appetising. But she loved everything else.

But the guests were rather more drawn to those dishes that were more distinctly Iranian or Persian. These included lamb stuffed with rice, nuts and herbs, stewed with prunes and raisins, and dressed in pomegranate juice. A *polo* seemed to be the word for most kinds of pilaf, and the ones they tried were deemed delicious. Shula was careful to thank Mrs C for preparing a number of vegetarian dishes. Like any good hostess, Mrs C was aware that at least two of her guests might have religious dietary restrictions (which, in reality, they did not) or that others might be vegetarian proper, so to speak. Everyone, especially Dorothy, raved about the various kinds of flatbreads, all of different textures and thicknesses, and all apparently called *naan* of one sort or another.

'You know, like the naan you get in Indian restaurants. This one is called *nan-e-lavash*.'

'Oh Jane! Sorry. Didn't see you there,' said Dorothy. 'I'm impressed. So you're becoming a bit of an expert then?'

'Oh yes. Such a quick learner,' said Salma, joining in.

'Indeed she is,' beamed Mrs C.

Oh. I've been a perfect klutz! thought Heppie. She rushed over to Shula, and drew up a couple of chairs into a corner of the dining room.

'What's wrong?' asked Shula.

'Nothing,' she confided. 'It's just that I'd never have taken Mrs C for a *shidduch macher*.'

'What?'

The sisters rarely used Yiddish or Hebrew, even to each other, or with their Jewish friends. But there were exceptions: moments of great anger, or when they did not want non-Jewish friends to understand what they were saying. This was one such moment.

'A *shidduch macher*. Mrs. C,' Heppie hissed.

'Don't be ridiculous. Who on earth would she be matching?'

'Well, look behind me. But don't make it too obvious.'

'I can see Mrs C and Salma. You mean Salma? But where's the man?'

'Look again.'

'I can see only Jane.'

'Exactly,' whispered Heppie. 'Salma and Jane. Can't you see? Mrs C is trying to match them. She's very friendly towards Jane, recommending hairdressers and things. And earlier, Salma said something to me and Luke about her twin brother saving her a lot of bother, about having children and stuff. It's staring us in the face. Don't be so dim. Can't you see?'

Shula glanced at Salma and Jane again, the two of them sharing a private joke and smiling. 'Well, the two of them do seem to like each other I suppose.'

'Mrs C wants her daughter to be happy. She practically said so a few minutes ago. She's giving them her seal of approval.'

'Well, well.' Shula laughed. 'Play your cards right, Heppie, and you might get an invitation to the wedding!'

'You mark my words. Just remember where you heard it first.' Heppie felt little short of triumphant. 'I for one wish them well. Let's get back to the table.'

Everyone was still raving about the food. 'This is great,' said Marsha.

'Lovely,' agreed Jean. 'Diana's missed a real treat,' she noted, pointedly.

'Well, that's her problem. I wouldn't worry about it.'

'I've never eaten this sort of food before,' continued Jean, as if she had experienced some sort of culinary revelation, or baptism. 'I'm really enjoying it. I wonder how they learn to cook like that.'

Dorothy tutted. 'How do you think? The same way anyone learns to cook their own food,' she muttered. 'It takes centuries of tradition. Just think what you've been missing all these years, Jean.'

'I know. I admit it. I think I've led such a restricted sort of life, in many ways. My fault I suppose.'

Aware that she might have caused offence, Dorothy muttered something about everyone living a restricted life of one sort or another.

'It's all fantabulous,' said Luke, 'and just in time. I was getting really hungry. It really is too bad of Di to be so late: a bit ill-mannered if you ask me. I hope to God she turns up before too long.'

They assembled in little groups and sat down with their plates of food. Shula and Salma found themselves next to each other. 'You said the previous owners built the conservatory? It works really well. The garden was big enough to accommodate one. When Mum and Dad first–'

Shula stopped and turned away. Once again, she had spoken innocently, without thinking, just making polite conversation. She suddenly felt that she had given away a terrible secret.

'Sorry?' said Salma softly. 'You were talking about your mum and dad. And this house?'

Confession time, thought Shula. 'I have to tell you something Salma. Our parents bought this house when it was new. I was born here. I lived here for the first ten years of my life. Even though it is very different now, it holds a lot of memories.'

'Oh, you should have told us before. This must be very upsetting for you, and for Heppie, to return after all this time. We had no idea.' Salma spoke quietly, and with great sensitivity.

Heppie came over to join them. Her sixth sense told her that something delicate had been broached.

'I've told Salma about our connection with this house,' Shula said, almost apologetically.

Heppie nodded, and sat down to join them. 'I suppose it would have been very odd if we hadn't mentioned it.'

As she spoke, Salma got up to ask her mother to join them. In the next minutes, the two sisters and the mother and daughter, the original and current inhabitants of 4 Glendale Road had a good deal to talk about. There were expressions of surprise and delight about the nature of coincidence. There were explanations of how long each family had been in the house, and enquiries about previous owners, leaseholders and freeholders, renovations, structural changes, new kitchens and so on. There was much holding of hands and warm expressions of the new connections and the new friendships that the revelation had brought about. They all felt better for having talked so openly about their shared history and the possibilities for the future.

'Is this a private party or can anyone join in?'

'Oh, Luke!' said Mrs C.

Salma was the first to rally. 'Oh, not at all, we were just talking about houses and things.' She spoke loudly, so that everyone could hear and join in if they wanted to. She chose not to say anything about the conversation with Heppie and Shula. She felt it was somehow too personal and private; and possibly too painful for the sisters.

Salma's mention of houses got everyone going. The discussion was a familiar one, and so beloved of the British. Everyone contributed, even Meg, who complained about the rent in her accommodation. *A bit rich, considering she doesn't pay a penny of it herself* was the general unspoken reaction.

Favourite topics were the shortage of affordable housing, ever rising costs, the difficulties of getting a mortgage, high rents, and the wall of debt facing "young couples starting out". Other topics included the higher and higher cost of living, the outrageous bonuses that bankers gave themselves, the cost of student fees, the scary thought that interest rates might rise, the shocking increase in the number of food banks ("and not just in the north"), and the need to find more money for the National Health Service.

The conversation somehow avoided potentially sensitive issues such as immigration. No one wanted an actual argument to spoil the atmosphere of collective complaint. But subjects like rising gas and electricity bills, the unreliability of builders and electricians, and the impossibility these days of finding a good plumber (*any* plumber!) were seized on with great relish. Everyone had plenty to say. And everyone felt all the better for having said it.

21.15
The Storm Breaks

'Has everyone had enough?'
'Oh more than, thanks.'
'Full to bursting.'
'It'd be a greedy bugger who'd want more.'
'It was all splendid.'
'So may I suggest that Salma takes orders for tea and coffee, and then we all go back to the sitting room?'

Salma took orders for coffee and tea, as the others trooped back to the sitting room, arranging themselves companionably around the log-burning stove, which Jane stoked up. They had all had what Jean rather prissily described as "an adequate sufficiency". They sat and rested. The drinks duly arrived, and after-dinner sweets were circulated.

A period of welcome quiet enveloped the sitting room. One or two guests closed their eyes, and Dorothy even began to snore. 'Ooh. I could stay here forever,' said Lynne, snuggling down in her chair.

'I wonder where Meg's got to.'
'Oh, she nipped outside for a cigarette.'
'I hope not. It's pissing down!'

Marsha and Luke turned to the big window behind them. They could not see the rain, but they could hear it battering the roof of the conservatory beyond. But what they did see was even more alarming than the rain.

'Oh my God! No. No.' Marsha covered up her face and groaned loudly. This woke Dorothy, and drew everyone's attention to the window. In the conservatory, pressed against the far side of the window, was what looked like a large, wet, fat spider; a large, wet, fat, tattooed, lilac and green spider; spreadeagled against the glass. Bits of lilac and green fabric were spattered over the conservatory side of the window. Meg's badly-made dress was starting to come apart. As her body was squashed against the window, rivulets of water ran down from her hair, face, her dress, her bare left breast, her arms and legs, and her bare stomach. Some of the frilly bits had come off the dress and were either sticking to the window or simply falling off. She seemed to be screaming for help, though no one could hear anything. It was like watching a silent horror film.

In the comfort of the sitting room, the partygoers felt collectively sick. It was as if they had all witnessed some horrible crime, to which they did not know how to react.

'Oh my God. She thinks she's trapped.'

'No, Marsha. You sit down. Let me take care of it.'

'But she's–'

'No. Leave it to Heppie. She'll sort her out,' said Shula.

Closely followed by Marsha and Mrs C, Heppie opened the side door to the conservatory. The noise from the rain was deafening. Heppie shouted at Meg, and managed to drag her in from the conservatory into the sitting room.

Once inside, Meg shook herself free from Heppie, shouting and screaming indecipherable obscenities. She then began to mumble to herself, and raised her dripping arms, as if to heaven.

'What's that she's saying?' asked someone.

'I can't make it out,' said Heppie. 'Meg, what's wrong? Tell us what's wrong.'

More mumbling. Then Meg screamed. Another flash of lightning lit the sky behind her. In between the flash and its accompanying clap of thunder, Meg's voice rang out, loud enough to waken the dead: 'I'M FUCKING PREGNANT!'

Thunder shook the room. Then all the lights went out.

8. All That Glisters...

21.30
WHO'S THE FATHER? AND THE TABLE DANCER...

'Oh my God.'
'You poor thing.'
'Shit.'

Luke was the first to rally. In the lightning-lit darkness, and fighting against the sound of thunder (and remembering the humiliation Meg meted out to him during the lesson), he said, 'Well, missie, that's not the first time today you have stopped the show. Now that you've managed to get our total attention, what next?'

'Shut up, Luke. Can't you see that the girl's really in trouble?' retorted Heppie. 'Don't be so thoughtless.'

'Heppie's right. She needs help, not remarks like that,' agreed Lynne.

'Oh, excuse me for breathing,' huffed Luke.

Lynne joined Heppie and Meg, who still stood by the window, shivering and whimpering. The two older women led Meg to the fireplace, using the light from the fire and more flashes of lightning to guide them. The other women crowded around Meg, offering various shades of comfort and sympathy, from the direct warmth of Heppie's embrace to the distant coolness of Jean's gaze.

'Towels. Candles, Salma! Towels in the downstairs

bathroom and candles in the kitchen; and there's a torch in the kitchen, in the cupboard under the sink.'

Salma did not need much prompting. She ran to the kitchen (again, using lightning as her guide) and returned with candles, towels, and the precious torch. Meanwhile, Meg's wet clothes had been removed, and she was being dried by the heat of the fire, with whatever material came to hand. Towels were draped around her.

Lynne grabbed the candles from Salma, and turning to Luke said, 'Here. Make yourself useful. Use the fire or whatever to light these and dot them around.'

'I'll get some saucers from the kitchen.'

Salma returned with some saucers and her mother told her to go upstairs and fetch one of her father's bathrobes. 'They're big and should fit Meg,' she said. She also suggested that Heppie and Lynne should take Meg to the downstairs bathroom, where they could give her a quick, hot shower. Jane volunteered to accompany them with two candles.

The bizarre procession set off. Since Jane was the only one who knew which door led to the bathroom, she led the way, rather like a modern-day Florence Nightingale, though with two lamps, not just one. Lynne came next, leading a still shivering Meg by the hand. Bringing up the rear was Heppie, her hands on Meg's back, hoping to keep her upright. The storm continued, lending a distinctly gothic tone to the ghostly parade. Dorothy's semi-drunken giggly comparisons between their situation and *Northanger Abbey* fell on stony ground.

With the help of the torch and the occasional flash of lightning, Salma found the way to her father's room easily. Not that it would have been difficult even in total darkness. Both he and his room stank of cigars. After a domestic battle some years ago, it was agreed that he would smoke only in his room, which he did, frequently. Salma and her mother slept at the other end of the house, as far away from his room as possible. But at this end of the house, the acrid smell was detectable some distance away from his door.

Salma opened the door quietly, as if she were an intruder. As she entered the room, the phone extension on her father's desk rang. She picked it up at the same time as her mother picked up the main phone on the ground floor.

'Hello?' said Salma.

'It's me, Melinda from number eight.'

'Oh, hello, Melinda. It's Mrs C here. You've got me and Salma together.'

'Just wanted to tell you it's a general power cut around our area. Are you OK? Apparently the power will be back within the hour.'

'Thanks for telling us. Salma, have you got the bathrobe? A blanket will be useful as well.'

'OK. Bye Melinda. Thanks for telling us. Coming, Mum!'

Salma put the phone down and searched for one of her father's bathrobes and a spare blanket. As she walked back to the door with them, she felt something odd under her left foot. She shone the torch on the floor. She saw a little blue book which she recognised immediately: a passport. She picked it up and was horrified to realise that it was her father's. 'Oh my God!' she said aloud to herself. 'He'll need this for his trip to New York. Even he won't be able to blag his way through to his flight without this. I wonder if he's already found out that it's missing?' And the worst thought of all: *What if he's on his way back here?*

She decided that whatever happened, her mother must not know. She was afraid that if he came back this evening, all hell would break loose. Her father did not know about the party and would not approve at all. She must not panic.

She sat on the bed, feeling very anxious. She decided at once to try her father's flat, to tell him that the passport was safe, and to stay in London; anything to prevent his coming home. No answer, but she left a message. She then tried his mobile.

This time no signal. Maybe his battery was low? Maybe he was already driving back home? If he were, that was bad news. The family knew that he never used his mobile when driving, having once been caught by the police for using it while driving on the motorway. Shaking, she rang her brother's number.

'Is Dad with you?'

'No, I think he said he was going to New York or something this evening.'

'He can't. He forgot his passport. I've just found it.'

'Well, I expect he's on his way back home then. Didn't he ring you?'

'You must be joking. He wouldn't bother ringing. He would just turn up.'

'Mmm.'

'Look. Do me a favour. If he calls you or turns up, make sure he stays in London tonight. Tell him I've called about the passport. Everything's, well, just say everything's OK.'

There was a loud call from downstairs. It was Jane. 'Salma, have you got the things for Meg? Your mum's a bit worried.'

'Coming!'

Salma grabbed the passport, and hid it in her own room. Then she hurried down to the sitting room, explaining that her delay was due to the time it took to find a blanket.

Meg and her entourage had returned from the bathroom. Lynne dressed her in Mr C's capacious robe. Lynne was the only one who seemed to notice that it smelt vaguely of cigars. But since Meg herself was a smoker, Lynne decided that either she wouldn't mind or might not even notice the smell. Meg complained that the robe was too big for her. 'Beggars can't be choosers, my girl,' snapped Lynne.

'I think it would be a good idea for Meg to lie down and rest,' said Mrs C. 'But here, in this room, where we can watch over her.'

'Oh, Mrs C,' pleaded Meg. 'Please don't leave me. I'll lie

down with this blanket over me. So long as you can sit with me. Please.'

Meg's heartfelt plea hung in the surprised, silent, candlelit room. Some tried to look at Marsha. But in the darkness, her black face was hardly visible. However, her body language spoke volumes. It spoke of rejection, disappointment, even despair.

'Where's your fuse box?' Heppie was keen to do something practical. Salma explained that a neighbour had rung to say that the problem was general and should be solved within an hour.

Meg settled down with Mrs C on a settee on the far side of the room. The others huddled round the fire. They began a whispered discussion about who the father of Meg's child might be.

'My money's on Muscle Mary.'

Lynne thought that Luke might be right.

'Impossible,' snorted Jean.

'What makes you so certain, Jean?' asked Shula, surprised at Jean's sudden interruption.

Jean realised that she would have to explain or justify her reasoning. She had to say something. 'Well. Give the man some credit, some taste. I mean, she's so, well, so unattractive. And' – she hesitated – 'well, he could have any woman he wants, couldn't he?'

'What about you, Marsha? What do you think? After all, you know her best.' Salma asked her question quietly and sympathetically, even though her own mind was still in turmoil about the passport.

Marsha sighed deeply. She remembered the framed photo of Meg and Bashir. But not wanting to incriminate anyone, least of all her client, she stalled. 'Don't know. Sometimes I doubt that I understand her very well. She doesn't even understand herself.'

'But that could apply to a lot of us,' said Shula, thinking aloud.

Marsha continued stalling. She wanted to deflect attention away from Bashir, even if only for her own state of mind. 'Well, she's obviously mad about Bashir. We all saw that in the lesson this morning. At work, some people tend to think that she puts it about a bit. But others, including me, think that all her talk of boyfriends is just bravado. A colleague has seen her out clubbing, getting pissed out of her mind, like girls do these days. But he has also seen her fight off anyone who approaches her, or who tries to grope her or something. She's no pushover.' *Except where Bashir is concerned*, thought Marsha. She began to worry. Deeply.

'Oh,' said Dorothy. 'Whoever the father is, it doesn't sound too promising for Meg's future, does it? And the poor baby's of course.'

Lynne whispered somewhat tactlessly, 'Maybe she'll go for a termin–'

'Don't think so. For one thing, she's a Catholic. And she's often talked about having babies.' Marsha breathed in deeply. 'I feel rotten. I feel that I've let her down. I feel, well, responsible.'

'Not at all. Ultimately, Meg's responsible for herself. It isn't your fault, Marsha. It's just the way things go. Life can be a vale of tears sometimes.' Heppie stopped. She sensed that there was more, much more to come from the beautiful black girl from London.

'It's a nightmare. Feels like history repeating itself.'

'Meaning?'

Marsha had everyone's attention. She felt that she had nothing to lose. She felt an urgent need to tell her story, somehow protected by the candlelight. 'You see, I've got a couple of kids; same father. But we never married, and he left me; just disappeared. So…' Marsha shrugged her shoulders. 'No husband. The kids live with my mum.'

Salma put her hand up, as if to ask Marsha to pause. She

then threaded her way through the various sofas and chairs to check on Meg and her mother. They were both fast asleep, for which she was grateful.

There were various whispered questions and answers about Marsha's children, but no one asked Marsha directly why she chose not to live with her children. 'But Marsha,' said Salma, returning to her seat by the fire, 'Meg's situation is so different. There's no question of history repeating itself. She's a sort of hopeless case; whereas you've done really well for yourself; got a job and a career too.'

'Part-time social work? A career? You must be joking. Doesn't pay the bills, you know.'

'But look at you,' said Lynne, innocently. 'You've got fabulous looks, nice clothes; the lot. You must be doing something right, girl.'

'Do you think so? All I want to do is to earn money for my kids, maybe send them to private school; and to help Mum out of course.'

Is she dreaming? Private schools? thought Lynne. *On her money?*

She's in a fantasy world, thought Dorothy.

Silly girl, thought Jean.

There must be something else she hasn't told us, thought Shula.

Just keep quiet, Heppie thought. *We'll find out more soon enough.*

'I can imagine what you might be thinking. "Where does she think she will find money to do all that? How can she afford all that as well as the clothes and shoes and stuff? She must be crazy to want to send her kids to private school".'

The atmosphere in the darkened, candlelit sitting room was tense. Jane tried to distract herself by suddenly deciding to refuel the wood-burning stove, which she did noisily, as if her life depended on it. Marsha waited until Jane sat down again. 'You see,' she said slowly and carefully, 'the truth is–'

'Oh good, I feel a confession coming on!'

'Oh for God's sake, shut up Luke. Can't you see how difficult this is for Marsha? Don't be so cruel. Button it!' The women all turned on Luke, who did not understand how his remark – his prediction – could generate such hostility. Lynne's words were so reminiscent of the advice given to him by Ted. Button it. Or lose it. Acknowledging the strength of everyone's feelings, Luke offered Marsha an apology.

But confession was the right word, thought Marsha. She was fed up with pretending. She wanted to cleanse herself of unnecessary deceit. The quiet of the darkened room encouraged her. 'Oh that's OK. Well, as I was saying, the truth is, I've got another job.'

No, she can't be! thought Lynne, despairingly.

She shouldn't be telling us, thought Dorothy.

I knew it, thought Jean, with satisfaction. *She's a whore.*

Poor woman, thought Shula.

Just keep quiet, Heppie told herself again.

'I'm a table dancer.'

The silence that followed Marsha's statement was as complex as only some silences can be. It was made up of several different layers, including incomprehension, shock, embarrassment, curiosity, disgust and sheer ignorance.

'I'm lost. Someone will have to explain this to me,' said Dorothy. 'Who or what is a table dancer?'

'It's sort of halfway between pole dancing and lap dancing,' explained Marsha.

'Oh?' said Dorothy, who was no wiser.

'Pole dancing is where people, usually girls, use poles to dance around. It's now established as a form of exercise and they even teach it in schools. It's very athletic really, and involves moves called climbs, spins and even upside-down movement.'

'But there are girlie clubs where girls do it to entertain

men, showing off their bits and pieces,' explained Lynne slowly, unable to conceal her disapproval.

'Ugh. Disgusting,' sniffed Jean.

'And lap dancing is much more, well, sexy and erotic. Where, Lynne's right, girls entertain men by dancing either very near them or even on their laps. But with table dancing, which is what I do, there's no actual physical contact with clients –'

'Hmph. As if.' Luke was typically sardonic.

'But in our place that's true!' protested Marsha. 'We have a public entertainment licence that forbids direct contact between girls and clients. And our owner really sticks to the rule. He calls it "the One Foot Rule".'

'How do feet come into this?' enquired Dorothy, who felt that she was on a very steep learning curve.

'"Foot" as in twelve inches. No client is ever allowed to be within twelve inches of the girls, and vice versa of course.'

Luke could not contain himself. 'Well, I don't know about you, ladies, but in my experience of men, twelve inches, or thirty centimetres in new money, is more than enough to keep a girl safe. And if there are any exceptions, I'm more than open to offers.'

Despite the air of tension, there was a slight ripple of laughter, broken by Shula. 'Well, so much for women's liberation, feminism and all that.'

'It's not that simple. I'm in charge of my own life. It's my choice, my decision to do what I do. Most of the punters are decent enough. I'm now in charge of recruiting new girls. We take care of them well. Some really need the money, you know. Some of the punters can be quite understanding, and generous.'

'Appalling.'

Heppie remonstrated. 'Who are we to criticise, Jean? Especially those of us who have probably never had to worry about money. I had well-off parents and have always had a good, well-paid job. Other women, no doubt like you, have had husbands to take care of things. I freely admit that I haven't a clue how most people live, or manage to survive. And as far as feminism is concerned, the arguments are more complicated than you might think, Shula,' added Heppie with unusual fierceness.

Salma agreed. 'Heppie's right. It isn't fair to judge people without knowing the circumstances. After all, it could be argued that if some men are bloody stupid enough to pay money for whatever goes on in those places, some women should be clever enough to take it.'

'I would never stoop so low.'

The idea of Jean working in such a place, stooping or not, brought a wry smile to the others.

'The thing is, I can't afford to be too precious. It's just a job, to get me what I want: Money; for me and my kids.'

'I don't want to criticise, honestly. But your kids can't wear your clothes, Marsha.'

'Oh those. I realised that you and Shula had noticed. Some I get cheap from some model friends of mine.'

'I'd always assumed that at one time you were a model; living a glitzy, glamorous life. But, well, apparently not.'

'Sorry to disappoint you, Lynne. My life is far from glamorous. And as far as my clothes are concerned, some of them, I admit, are gifts from clients. But I sell on most of the clothes; eBay. They're just another source of cash.'

'Speaking as a lawyer, I would only say that it could be dangerous working in a place like that. Apart from which, there are other, more, well, personal dangers to consider.'

Marsha went on the offensive. 'I can assure you, Salma, that where I work is definitely not a knocking shop! The owner doesn't tolerate rowdy stag parties and stuff. It's a well-run place, where men and even some women go to have fun and relax. We look after the girls well. Some of them are students; Jane's age.'

'You're talking about The Pink Snake on the ring road?' asked Jane.

'Yes.'

'One or two of my college friends have worked there. They said it was OK. Easy money, once they got over the embarrassment. They said the owner is a hoot. And it's true. He doesn't allow the clients to mess with the girls. Of course, I don't know if some make dates with girls outside hours, so to speak.'

'Well, what goes on outside the club is not my business.'

'So you must be Miss Mallow?' asked Jane, smiling.

Now it was Marsha's turn to be genuinely embarrassed. 'Yes, I'm afraid that my professional name is Miss Marsha Mallow.'

'Oh, priceless. I bet that draws them in,' laughed Luke.

Shula wanted to examine other issues. 'Maybe some of the punters are generous as you put it. But perhaps in your case it's because, apart from being attractive, you're also black?' She spoke the words hesitantly.

'Partly I suppose. Yes, I will admit that being one of the very few black girls in this town can be, well, a plus I suppose. Perhaps I am exploiting my colour. That does trouble me.'

'As well as exploiting your femininity.'

'And even exploiting men,' added Heppie, a suggestion which was met with general derision. But she had spoken without any sense of moral outrage and without consciously making any overt political point.

Lynne took Marsha's hand. 'I think you've been very brave telling us all about this.'

With the exception of Jean, the others murmured their agreement. 'Yes,' said Dorothy. 'It's been really helpful. These are complex issues.'

'But', cautioned Lynne, 'I hope you keep to the rule about not seeing any of the punters outside the club. I wouldn't want you to get mixed up with any of that sort.'

'Well. It's difficult. I do run into people now and again. In a town of this size it's sort of inevitable I suppose. But a lot of the punters are out-of-towners. Anyway, thanks everyone for listening. It's great to have understanding friends,' said Marsha, staring straight at Jean.

'Well,' said Heppie. 'This all started out with Marsha feeling bad about Meg.'

There was a collective moan of recollection. 'Oh, some party this is turning out to be,' said Marsha.

'What's a party without arguments, tears, revelations and intimate confessions?' laughed Heppie.

'And this party doesn't even have its main guest,' added Shula.

'Think of it as not simply a party for Di,' said Lynne. 'It's also for us, the real Water Babes. After all, Di's only the instructor. In the lessons, she doesn't even get herself wet, does she?' There was general laughter and murmurs of agreement; except from Jean.

'I know it's a bit dark in here, but how about another round of drinks?' asked Salma.

'I could murder a cup of tea,' said Dorothy, hopefully.

'And I would kill for a coffee.'

These suggestions were met with a surge of enthusiasm. At which point, the electricity company obliged with a surge of its own. Just as suddenly as they went out, the lights came back on. There was a cheer, followed by a round of applause, and a sense of relief.

22.00
The Name Game – And the Blue Stocking

Everyone took a few seconds to adjust themselves to the light and to the fading sound of the storm.

Mrs C and Meg woke from their slumbers, and the others – at last relieved by the need to do something other than talk in whispers – found various jobs with which to occupy themselves. Jane attacked the dwindling fire with unusual ferocity. Salma, still trying to suppress her fears about her father's possible arrival, took orders for tea and coffee. Accompanied by Lynne, she then set off for the kitchen. Heppie, Shula and Jean tidied up the dining room, in readiness for the caterers' return in the morning. Dorothy took charge of extinguishing candles, and Luke found himself energetically plumping up various cushions, and drawing curtains. Only Marsha, somewhat exhausted by her "confession" (she could think of no other word to describe the telling of her story) remained where she was, recovering her composure.

The party-goers reassembled around the fire, enjoying their teas and coffees.

'Di still hasn't arrived then?'

'No, Mum. And it's already after ten. Maybe she won't even turn up?'

'Well,' sighed Luke. 'Against my better judgement, I tried ringing her about half an hour ago, but no answer. I left a message.'

'Oh, perhaps she didn't want to come while the storm was on; and it was so dark of course.'

'Mm,' said Luke, doubtfully.

'Oh, but I know what we can do. We can all sign the card for her, just in case,' suggested Lynne.

Luke went to retrieve the package from under the piano and took out the card. They all dutifully signed it. The card was quite big but fairly ordinary – definitely no kangaroos or suggestive messages. Lynne simply wrote "With best wishes for your future". Other than Jean, who added a lone "Thank you for everything" to her signature, everyone signed with their first names only.

'Shula is such a lovely name. I know only one other Shula: that horsey character in *The Archers*.'

'Oh yes. I've often wondered what the name means,' said Jane.

'Oh, it's short for Shulamit. It's an old Hebrew or Arabic name. It's in the Bible. Doesn't suit me really; it means "Peaceful" or "Tranquil", and I'm anything but,' laughed Shula. She was dreading what might come next. And, of course, come it did.

'And Heppie?' asked Lynne. 'That must be short for something too.'

'Oh no. My bloody name. It's been the bane of my life. No, I'm not telling you. It's just so awful and so stupid. Don't know what my parents were thinking of.'

There was a little giggly chorus of, 'Heppie, Heppie, Heppie.'

'No. Wild horses wouldn't drag it out of me.'

'Go on,' said Shula. 'I'm sure that no one would tell, would you girls?'

Luke took it upon himself to reply on behalf of "the girls". 'No, never, it'll be our secret,' he smirked.

Dorothy spoke up. 'I imagine it's originally Russian; also originally from the Bible, no?'

'Oh, don't pretend you don't know, Dorothy. Pretence doesn't suit your educated mind,' noted Heppie, a trifle acerbically.

Luke would not let go. 'Well, don't leave us all in suspenders girl, spill!'

'Hep-si-bah,' announced Heppie, slowly, relishing the pain of explanation.

'Hell,' said Lynne, at her most tactless. 'You poor thing. No wonder you shortened it to Heppie. What sort of name is that then?'

'Yeah, Hepsibah. It's exactly as Dorothy said. It means "My delight is in her". I'll have you know that in the Bible she was a queen.' This time, Heppie spoke with a certain amount of defiant pride.

'Oh sorry, your Majesty,' laughed Lynne, amidst general good-natured merriment.

'Actually I think I was named after some great aunt or other, from Russia. And there was Yehudi Menuhin's sister, the famous violinist. She was also called Hepsibah. So I was in good company really. But of course no one at school appreciated such niceties. They used to call me "Bah Bah"; as in "Bah Bah Black Sheep". Oh God. I hated my name then. Kids can be so cruel, can't they? But in a way, having such an unusual name toughened me up. So I've got my parents to thank for that I suppose.'

Shula sensed that her sister had had enough. She turned the conversation in a slightly different direction. 'I imagine Parsee names have meanings too?' she said to Salma.

'Yes, they do,' said Salma, blushing.

'Salma's name means "sweetheart",' said Jane, with a little more enthusiasm than she had intended.

'Oh, I see,' said Shula, embarrassed. 'Yes.' *So Heppie was right*, she thought. The sisters smiled at each other, knowingly.

'We were just saying this afternoon that we don't know your first name, Mrs C,' said Lynne, half innocently. The others waited, almost with bated breath. 'I hope you aren't offended when we call you just "Mrs C". It just sounds a bit formal.'

Mrs C steeled herself. 'Oh no, not at all. It's just that my name is rather difficult to pronounce. It's "Fe-resh-the".' Several members of the group tried it, claiming, with some justification, that the name was not too difficult for them to pronounce.

'And does it have a special meaning?' asked Heppie, still smarting from having had to reveal her own first name to all and sundry.

Mrs C said nothing. Her daughter spoke up. '"Angel". It means "angel".'

'Ah, how perfect,' said Luke. 'Just right. Most English names are boring, I think. I know that Luke wrote one of the Gospels. But I don't think it has any special meaning.'

'"Light giving",' said Dorothy. 'But that's from the original Greek. Very few people know that now.'

'But you know it, of course,' said Luke. 'Our Dorothy seems to know everything, doesn't she?'

'So what about "Dorothy" then?' asked Heppie, not expecting the name to have any significance attached to it.

'"God's gift",' sighed Dorothy. 'And if you can believe that, you can believe anything,' she added with a note of despair. 'But talking of how cruel kids can be, I was never called "Dorothy" at school.'

'That's funny. I was always called Dorothy.' Luke's attempted joke came and went, unnoticed.

At this point, Dorothy began to feel that she needed to tell them all something about herself. She needed to respond to and to contribute to the "confessional" rhythm of the evening. She was becoming increasingly unhappy about her burgeoning reputation of being a Miss Clever Clogs. She did not feel the need to apologise for her educational background. At the same time, she decided that she had nothing to lose by *explaining* one or two things. She felt that such an explanation would make it easier for her to fit in, and therefore easier for the group to accept her more fully, as a far less knowledgeable and extraordinary person than they assumed her to be.

She gritted her teeth and began. 'Dotty. Potty Dotty. Snotty Dotty. Swotty Dotty. And that was at a posh girls' private school, where everyone was supposed to be ladylike and polite. Some hope! My surname is Duncan. So I was also called DD, Dunk and so on. I never had a brother or sister, a close friend, let alone a boyfriend, to my name. Not even a father. He died when I was ten. My life was ruled by my bloody mother.'

'Oh, that sounds a bit harsh on her.'

'Not at all. In fact, I'm being kind to her. At school, the other girls used to talk about rock and roll, jazz, clothes and stuff. But it all passed me by. It was all a closed book to me. Mother wouldn't allow what she called "trivial nonsense" . I was very bright, you see. She made me study, study, study all the time. She didn't want me to associate with other girls.'

'Perhaps she was just ambitious for you?'

'Ambitious? She was that, I suppose, and very determined. But nasty with it. Once I bought a pop record, in 1964 or '65 it was. When my mother found it, she stamped on it and threw it out.'

There was a general chorus of sympathy. 'But didn't you rebel?', 'Most of us did at some time or other', 'Teenage angst and all that'.

'No, I didn't. "Teenagers" came along two or three years later. So I didn't really know how to complain. Anyway, there was a family tradition to uphold. My grandfather and father had both gone to Oxford, and my mother was determined I should go there too. Which I did. But I didn't just go. I ended up staying there: a glittering career in an ivory tower. Forty years in the same damn place. Just to please my mother. Some glitter!'

'You said something earlier to me about teaching at Oxford,' said Mrs C. 'But some people, especially women, would have given their right arm to be as clever and successful as you were.'

'I'll be going up next October,' said Jane, quietly. 'Law.'

'Oh? To Oxford?' said Dorothy quickly, backtracking. 'And I'm sure you'll have a good time there. Just try not to get trapped into staying, like I did. My "reward" was that I became a bit of an expert, which, of course, pleased my mother.'

'An expert on what?' asked Heppie.

Stony faced, Dorothy replied with, 'The Punic Wars. People still quote my publications, apparently.'

'What a scream. The Pubic Wars!'

Someone giggled at what she assumed was Luke's deliberate mishearing. Jane, however, took Luke's error rather more seriously. 'No, Luke: The *Punic* Wars. Ancient Rome and Carthage,' she corrected, sniffily. Turning to Dorothy, she then said, 'Are you by any chance *Professor* Dorothy Duncan?'

'Guilty, my dear. I was a bluestocking, a word you hardly hear anymore. The genuine article.'

'Oh wow, everybody. Dorothy is really famous! She's an historian. And a few years ago, you wrote a book on feminism, isn't that right, Dorothy? *Feminism Is For Men, Too*. Fantastic, I loved it.'

'Lord. I think Ted's read that. He said it was really good. Did you really write that book?'

Before Dorothy could reply, Lynne blurted out, 'Oh, all that bra-burning nonsense. Not for me.'

'If I may say so,' said Dorothy calmly, slipping back easily into tutor mode, 'feminism has moved on since those days. And stories of burning bras were much exaggerated. Feminism in its third or fourth phase, and–'

'I know, I know,' insisted Lynne, brushing aside Dorothy's words. 'But honestly, I think that sometimes we women push men aside too easily. Remember the two blokes who came to the first two lessons? We weren't very friendly to them, were we? We sort of ignored them, as if they didn't belong. So they left. Personally, I thought it was a pity, myself.'

'I remember them,' said Shula. 'Perhaps it was the name we gave ourselves.'

'Mm. The Water Babes is sort of sexist, isn't it? It wasn't our finest hour, perhaps,' suggested Heppie. 'Discrimination is discrimination, after all.'

Dorothy was offended by all this talk of women exerting pressure over men. 'But in the end, those men made their own decision.'

'Men still have a lot to learn,' said Salma, quite forcefully. It became clear that no one wanted to pursue any further arguments about feminism, especially not with Dorothy in the room, and with fans of hers, such as Jane and Salma.

'So you retired from Oxford?' said Heppie, hoping to bring the conversation closer to more mundane and less controversial topics.

'Yes, but in the end rather earlier than I wanted to. My father was long since dead as I said before. My mother became very ill about ten years ago. I wasn't particularly in love with Oxford, but I certainly didn't want to come back here. But I felt I had to. So I decided, unwillingly, to come home.' She spoke with undisguised bitterness.

'But wasn't that the right thing to do? She was your mum, when all is said and done.'

'For some people perhaps it would be the right thing to do, but not for me. I became my mother's dogsbody. She had all the money in the world, but refused to hire nurses or go into a private nursing home. She made my life hell, as she always had done.'

In the awkward silence that followed, everyone tried to think of something useful to say. Shula broke the silence. 'What happened to your mum?'

'She died about eighteen months ago. Best thing she ever did.' Dorothy sat and stared into space.

The group was shocked at Dorothy's apparent hard-heartedness. 'But Dorothy, as Shula said, she was your mother. You did your duty as a daughter. That must give you some comfort?'

'No, Heppie. I didn't want comfort. All I wanted was a life: a normal life, a life of my own. My life was sacrificed for the sake of my parents' ambitions, especially my mother's.'

'But as you said about the men who left the Water Babes, you must have made your own decisions too.'

'Ah. Touché,' said Dorothy, blushing.

'Things are never that one-sided. So at some time or other you must have had a free choice to live life on your own terms,' persisted Heppie. 'You can't blame your mother for everything. None of us can.'

'I know. But I felt trapped; boxed in. Hemmed in by guilt and fear I suppose. Can you imagine? Me, of all people – supposedly an upstanding feminist, an independent thinker and all that – unable to choose my own life. It's all so ironic, so stupid.' She exhaled deeply, and slumped down in her chair.

Lynne felt unable to follow the ins and outs of Dorothy's thought processes. But she was curious enough to want to know the answers to simpler questions. 'If you don't mind my asking, Dorothy, was there ever, well, you know–'

'A man? No, never. Never. I just didn't know what to say to men. I mean on a personal level. Professionally there was no problem of course. Most of the men I met in my working life were platonic friends, bores, or jealous of my reputation. And before anyone asks, there was no woman in my life either. I know that some people assumed I was a lesbian. But I'm not. Or at least I don't think so. Anyway, it's never happened.'

'How do you mean?'

'You know: romance; sex; all that. Love. The moon in June. Never happened. It feels that I've lived my whole life without either giving or receiving love.'

'Oh,' said Marsha. 'How sad. But it takes two to tango, as they say. Maybe for some reason or other you just didn't or couldn't read the signs.'

'Some form of emotional blackspot you mean? I just can't say.'

'The opposite of someone like Meg,' suggested Marsha, feeling a little reckless. 'She reads signs that aren't actually there, and thinks that men are crazy about her when in fact they're not. Other people can't read signs when they *are* there. They don't, or can't, see or notice people who might be fond of them, or even just, well, interested.' From the approving reactions to her words, Marsha inferred that her explanation of Dorothy's situation had passed muster, at least for the moment.

'You make me sound as if I were autistic, or had Asperger's or something!'

Marsha stared back at Dorothy. 'No. It was just a thought, that's all.'

'I just don't know why things turned out the way they did. But what I do know is that for whatever reason I have missed out on things that are usually considered important, even necessary in life.'

'Like friendship?' asked Mrs C, quietly.

'No, not really. It's something deeper. I once heard a song. It had a slow, vaguely oriental melody. The words included something like *"the greatest thing you'll ever learn, is just to love–"*

'Ah, "Nature Boy",' said Heppie. 'Yes. It was one of our parents' favourites. It's about "a strange enchanted boy".'

'And you know, those words are so true,' said Luke.

'Can you remember the words, Shula?'

Shula could not remember the words, but she could recall the tune, which she hummed for everyone, with the words that Dorothy remembered: "The greatest thing you'll ever earn it just to love, and be loved, in return".

Shula stopped. She was only too aware that unlike Dorothy, she and her sister and no doubt others in the room, had experienced what, according to the song, was the greatest thing.

'Yeah,' said Lynne. 'Beautiful words. I suppose it happens to a lot of us, at least for some of the time; and for the really lucky, for longer.'

'Well, whatever it is, it passed me by. Like rock and roll and jazz all those years ago. I seemed to be left to float alone, adrift. They say no man is an island. I'm not so sure. Sometimes I think we're each of us in our own way like a lonely island.'

'But there's no need to be alone, Dorothy.'

'No?'

'Look around you,' said Mrs C, indicating the circle of faces. Dorothy looked at the faces. First, Meg, dressed in Mr C's robe, pale, sullen, and unusually silent; then Jean, equally silent, looking uncharacteristically reflective, detached; then Luke and Lynne, holding hands, smiling at her; then Salma and Jane, radiating some sort of inner peace. She also saw Heppie and Shula, who God knows had had more than their fair share of problems, but had nevertheless survived. As indeed had Marsha. Finally she saw Mrs C, a model of graciousness and calm.

'Yes, thank you, all of you. After my mother died, I just had no idea what to do, where to go. I was finally free; free but frightened.

'Of course I tried all the usual clubs and group activities: painting, walking, reading, even the University of the Third Age. But nothing seemed to work, or to give me any real satisfaction or genuine interest. Everything I tried seemed to be something I could already do, and do quite well. At least that's what I thought.

'Then by chance, I saw an advert about the leisure centre. Aquarobics. Here was something I *couldn't* do! That I didn't know about. I wasn't sure what I expected to find when I joined the Water Babes. But I was in luck. I found you all.'

While Meg and Mrs C remained seated, each person in turn hugged Dorothy. Who could tell what Dorothy really thought about their various expressions of friendship, sympathy, and warmth? But they were sure she felt something.

The doorbell rang. The sound provoked cries of 'At last', 'About time!', 'She's here'. Jane got up and went to the front door.

With closed eyes, and shaking from top to toe, Salma tried to block out the thought that the caller was her father. She hoped and prayed that her guests were right, and that the caller was Di.

9. Complicated Lives

22.30
The Music Quiz and Gifts

When Jane came into the room with Di following somewhat sheepishly behind, everyone cheered, and Salma was able to breathe a sigh of relief.

Di was met with a range of greetings, each appropriate in its own way.

'Well, hello party girl.'

'Hi there, stranger.'

'We were beginning to think you'd never come.'

'Did you find the house easily enough?'

'How did you get here?'

Di smiled wanly but said little in reply, other than saying that a friend had given her a lift, and that they had found the house very easily thank you. *At least she seems to be showing some sense of having let everyone down*, thought Luke. *She doesn't seem to be her usual confident self.*

Heppie whispered to Shula that she hoped that Di would at least have the good grace to apologise to Mrs C for being so late. To offend the normal rules of hospitality so brazenly was, for someone like Heppie, tantamount to sin itself.

'Welcome,' said Mrs C, rising from her seat to shake Di's hand, and showing not a trace of annoyance. 'I'm so glad you could make it. You must be very busy at the moment.'

Mm, thought Luke, *typical of Mrs C to provide her late guest with a smooth exit from a social difficulty*. And on cue, Di seized on Mrs C's graciousness as a welcome opportunity to explain her lateness, or, as some of the others would have put it, to make her excuses.

'Oh yes, we had so much to do; so many last minute things to arrange. And that storm! The time just flew by. Hello everyone.' She spoke breathlessly, nervously.

No actual apology then. Heppie and Shula were shocked. They were also thrown by Di's appearance. She had clearly made little effort to dress up. Of course, no one would have expected smart clothes so near to her departure. But she could at least have worn cleaner jeans, a tidier shirt and newer trainers. They noticed that she even had the string around her neck, on which she wore her whistle, now mercifully hidden behind her shirt. Her hair was a mess. The sisters were not alone in concluding that Di had not even bothered to shower. She was edgy, distracted.

And although the sisters, along with everyone else, dimly registered the "we" in Di's words, it was only Luke who consciously wondered to whom the "we" might refer. Perhaps the friend who had given her a lift? Or had she had help from neighbours, or friends, or a particular friend? Luke did not doubt that Di had had plenty to do. But he was far less sure that she would have trusted anyone other than herself to pack or to tie up the loose ends of her time in the UK.

Salma took on the role of hostess. 'Come here, Di, and sit by the fire. Can Jane get you a drink? Would anyone else like a top-up?'

With Di's eventual arrival, a mini tsunami of relief had blown through the room. And with it a sudden need for the hard stuff had materialised. Excited by the prospect of Di's company, Jean threw all caution to the wind and asked for a large, *very* large, Bailey's. Dorothy and Lynne decided that they wanted a fortifying whisky. Heppie and Shula opted for brandy, their tipple of last resort. Salma and Jane chose the sweet liqueur route, Cointreau, as did Marsha. She would not allow the newly pregnant Meg to have any alcohol, which made Meg angry. But she had to settle for a soft drink. Luke and Di were partners in moderation. They asked for white wine. Mrs C went for abstinence, "to keep Meg company".

The extra round of drinks seemed to work wonders. While Jane busied herself handing them out, everyone seemed to relax, and finally to recover something of a party spirit.

Di in particular began at last to rise to the occasion, answering their various questions. The Water Babes learned that yes, she had enjoyed her stay in the UK, not so much in London, but certainly here on the south coast; that she had finally managed to pack everything, and would send her overweight baggage by ship; that she was leaving tomorrow late morning and staying with her brother overnight; that he would drive her to the airport for her flight on Sunday evening; that she was travelling home in some style – business class! *Hmm*, thought Luke. *All those private lessons must have paid well.* Her arrival would be a total surprise to her parents and that she didn't yet know exactly what she would be doing when she got home. But she had vague plans to start a business of some sort.

Everyone wished her well for the future. She even managed a little laugh and a confident smile. 'Oh, I'll be OK. Don't worry!'

'Oh! Time for presents!' said Lynne. Luke jumped to attention and retrieved their packets from beneath the piano. 'First we got you this cork hat. Look. I made it from a woggle.'

Di had a moment to decide. She could either put the stupid hat on the floor beside her – that is, time to acknowledge the gift but then to ignore it – or, she could go along with the party mood and wear it for the rest of the evening. She looked at Lynne, recognised the effort that had gone into making the hat, and chose to wear it. *Good girl*, thought Dorothy. Everyone cheered and clapped, even Jean, who found the sight of Di with her woggle contraption embarrassing and even a little humiliating.

'And we got this card for you, to wish you well.' Di opened her card, and was glad to see how tasteful it was. *Thank goodness*, she thought. No kangaroos or billabongs. 'We've all signed it.'

Di found herself oddly touched. The corks on her hat wobbled as she read each signature.

'Naughty of me I know,' said Jean coquettishly. 'I wrote a special little thank you message for you,' she continued, pointing out her signature and the only message on the card. Luke rolled his eyes in despair. The others were silent, watchful.

'Oh thank you, Jean,' said Di, looking up at Jean, causing the corks to wobble about again. She considered her next words very carefully. 'And may I say what a nice jacket you're wearing, Jean.' Most of those present appreciated the effort it must have taken for Di to express her unusually generous and flattering comment. It was another acknowledgement: this time of the effort that Jean had made.

For her part, Jean simply said, 'Oh, thank you. It's nothing really.' No mention this time of her "new look". She turned away in an attempt to prevent tears. She was both in heaven, and in agony.

Lynne broke the awkward silence. 'And we all clubbed together to buy this for you. We thought it would be easy for you to pack.'

'Oh. How kind. Isn't the wrapping paper spectacular?' said Di. 'Can I open it now?' Everyone chorused yes, of course.

Di opened the box of Irish linen. She was appreciative and grateful, and untied the various bows to take a close look. 'It's beautiful. Beautiful. I know just where that will go in my new place.' Luke was surprised at Di's reaction to the linen. She was like a new bride, planning the domestic details of a new home. 'I shall treasure this always,' she continued. Luke couldn't believe his ears. He thought she might cry. But she didn't.

Lynne was thrilled, and blew a kiss at Heppie, whose idea the linen had been. 'Luke. The music. Now!'

'Oh yes,' said Luke. 'Of course. And this is something I've worked on. It's a CD of the music all of you chose for the lessons. There's a copy for Di, and for everyone.' He reached into his small carrier bag and retrieved the CDs. They were called *The Water Babes 2014.* He had designed and printed a suitably blue, watery cover with the title emblazoned across it. And on the back was a full list of the songs and music played in the order that they had heard it in this morning's lesson. He gave the first CD to Di.

She was delighted with it. 'Oh, fantastic. Did you do all this yourself, Luke?'

'Yes, I did everything except choose the songs of course. You did. I mean you all did. At least I think all of you did. Some chose more than one. Here you go.' He took great pleasure in handing out a CD to each Water Babe, including Salma and Jane who, strictly speaking, were not members of the aquarobics group and who had not chosen any of the tracks. Everyone was delighted, receiving their souvenirs with various cries of 'Terrific', 'What a great thing to have', 'You must be very clever to have done all this Luke', and so on.

'I wonder who chose "Waltzing Matilda"?' said Lynne. 'Quite a clever choice.' Di winced inwardly at the mention of her least favourite track on the CD.

'I bet I know who chose "Locomotion",' said Heppie, smiling at her sister. Someone started singing the song.

'Oh, you're not allowed to guess yet, Heppie. I promised everyone that all the choices would be a secret. Until tonight that is. Time to play "Lucy's Music Game"! Each person takes one of these sheets.'

Whereupon, with some excitement, Luke handed each person a printed chart. It was headed "The Water Babes Music Game". Beneath the title were the rules.

> *How to play: Study the list of songs and music. Then match each track with the Water Babe you think chose it. A bottle of bubbly for the person who gets most correct matches!*

'Oh, no prizes for guessing who chose "The Stripper" then,' murmured Lynne.

'Shush,' remonstrated Luke. 'Before you speak, everyone has to go down the list silently and make their choices first then we can swap lists and mark them.'

This was met with a wall of protest. 'Sod that for a bag of chips,' as Lynne indelicately put it. Everyone argued against Luke, saying that it would be more fun to discuss the tracks and matches openly. After all, this wasn't *Mastermind*, was it?

'Well yes, I admit it. And a fat lot of good it did me.'

'What do you admit?' asked Dorothy, puzzled.

'That it was me who chose "The Stripper",' said Jean, grimly. She brightened. 'But I chose two more tracks though.' This caused the others to scan Luke's list with a more determined curiosity. 'But,' said Jean loudly, interrupting their searches, 'I want to make a special, and I think particularly appropriate presentation to Diana. So put down your sheets of paper please.'

This sudden assertiveness on Jean's part worked. The others stopped chattering and doing the quiz, and like a class of small schoolchildren faced with a defiant teacher, gave Jean their full attention. Jean reached for her handbag, and took out a prettily wrapped parcel, which she ceremoniously handed to an embarrassed Di, still wearing her woggle.

'What's she playing at?' muttered Lynne to Shula.

'This is my special gift to you, Diana.'

Marsha was furious. 'We were supposed to make do with one present from all of us, weren't we? She's never satisfied that woman.' Luke was equally incensed. Not just because Jean was violating the agreement not to give individual presents, but because at a stroke, Jean had shifted the centre of attention away from himself and his quiz on to her.

Embarrassed, Di opened Jean's special gift. It was a book; a novel. Di glanced at the title and put the book face down on her lap. 'Oh. Thanks Jean. Is it about, well, us?' She felt at a loss, uncertain as to what to say or to do.

'Well,' simpered Jean, blithely unaware of the general atmosphere in the room. 'Not exactly, but I can see what you mean,' she noted almost condescendingly, as if talking to an illiterate schoolgirl.

By this time, everyone was desperate to know what the book was called, and why it was so special. Most people in the room had no ideas at all about what it might be. It was only Dorothy who had the wit to compose in her head an instant list of possible titles, which included *The Well of Loneliness*, *The Group*, and *Oranges Are Not the Only Fruit*. At the same time, Dorothy doubted very much that Jean was either as self-aware or as well-read as those possibilities might imply.

Mrs C came to the rescue. 'May I?' she asked Di quietly, offering to take a look at the book.

'Oh sure, go ahead,' said Di. She thrust the book into Mrs C's hands, almost as if it were a bomb.

Mrs C seemed to be searching for the right words. 'Oh, how nice.' And echoing Jean's note of condescension to Di, she added, 'Yes, I can see why Jean might have thought it appropriate; in the circumstances.'

'Come on Mrs C. Don't leave us in suspenders,' ventured Luke.

'It isn't *The Water Babes*. It's *The Water Babies*,' she announced, emphasising the words *babes* and *babies*. 'It's a

Victorian novel by Charles Kingsley. It was popular when I was a child. I expect Dorothy and Jean read it at school too?' She appealed to them for help.

Dorothy nodded her head slightly, but Jean was more expansive. 'Yes. I read it at Sunday school. It's all about this little chimney sweep called Tom who drowns and turns into a water baby. He has all kinds of adventures. I love the character called Mrs Doasyouwouldbedoneby. Anyway, Tom finally helps his old master to repent for his sins. Tom is rewarded by being turned back into human form, when he invents all sorts of things like steam engines.' Jean smiled broadly, proud of her precis.

If a room could ever be described as nonplussed, then it would be this one. Various comments on Jean's choice of gift were attempted. At best they were half-hearted mini compliments: 'Oh yes, how nice', 'Ah, I see' and 'Interesting', were hardly encouraging to potential readers. At worst they veered towards the impolite: 'So?', 'I never read old novels anyway' and 'What's all that got to do with Di?' were typical.

Mrs C said nothing. But she was secretly relieved that Dorothy spoke up, expressing views with which, secretly, she sympathised. Looking straight at Jean, Dorothy said: 'Well, the title is an amusing coincidence I suppose. And it's true that the book does speak up against child labour and poverty. But I personally don't like it. It's very preachy and prejudiced. Sorry. But that's just what I think.'

The party spirit had well and truly evaporated. Jean felt deflated. The others lapsed into silence. Luke felt that the chances of reviving his music quiz were zero. Anyway, he was tired of trying to keep things moving along, of helping to make everyone feel happy.

'Oh, I nearly forgot,' said Di suddenly, retrieving her iPad from her small shopping bag. 'You've all given me some great presents and surprises this evening. So here are some presents from me to you! I'll send them all to Luke when I get home.'

'Ooh,' shouted Meg, who had not spoken for some time. 'Great. The photos! Let's have a look.'

'There aren't many; only about a dozen or so. It shouldn't take long.'

It didn't take long at all to see the sort of photos that Di had taken. The first, of the whole group in the pool, lined up in front of Di, went down well, and was met with cries of approval and satisfaction. Most of the others were met with a wall of frosty silence, which Di, in her excitement and voluble commentary, mistook for praise. 'There you are, Meg. It looks like you're having some sort of fit!' She laughed. Meg sulked, and was even more shocked by the photo which showed her sobbing about Muscles' dismissal from the pool.

One photo – with woggles – showed the class, especially Marsha and Dorothy doing well. That one certainly made people happy. Two or three people were amused by the photo of the class leaning against the side of the pool, struggling to push their woggles under their feet, thus looking as if they were engaged in mass constipation. But overall, the Water Babes found Di's photos underwhelming and disappointing. Irritating.

This was especially so for Jean, who was heartbroken to find that no fewer than three of the photos showed her at her worst. The first was taken when she was panicking in the water. The second showed her in her stripper's outfit striding sexily towards Di. And worst of all, the third photo, taken a few moments later, caught the moment at which she had tumbled over into the pool. 'Isn't that great?' said Di. And as if to add insult to injury, she added, 'I got that on video too!'

To her credit, Jean bore her humiliation with fortitude. At least she had provided Di with some amusement. But the others, including even Meg, were troubled by what they took to be Di's malign intent to make them look silly and awkward. As Salma said to Heppie: 'Well, if that's what she thinks of you all, she should have buggered off to Australia well before now.'

'Well, Di. Thanks. I look forward to receiving the photos when you get home. In fact, I can't wait to see what I'll do with them.'

Luke's sarcasm pleased everyone. Except for Di, who seemed preoccupied with thoughts of her own. So Luke's sarcasm completely bypassed the person to whom it was directed.

23.00
A Girl's Best Friend

'Thanks everyone. You've given me so many presents and surprises tonight. Now for a surprise of my own!' There was some shuffling and uneasy coughing. It was getting late. Meg and Shula felt that they couldn't take much more. But along with Dorothy, they didn't know how to end things politely and graciously.

With the others, they watched in horror as Di reached into her shirt top and began to extricate the string which held her whistle.

'Oh God no,' cried Lynne. 'Not another blast on that bloody whistle. Please.' Her cry of despair was echoed by all present, even by Mrs C who did not like to insult her chief guest, but who nonetheless secretly wanted her to go home.

'Oh no, you can forget my whistle. That wouldn't be any surprise at all.' She extricated the string from her shirt front. 'But what about this for a *real* surprise?' In the two seconds before pandemonium broke loose, Luke had to concede that this was Di's *coup de gr*âce, delivered not thirty minutes after her late arrival. Yes, it was Di's evening. A ring was all it took.

Meg set everything off by letting out a loud, hysterical scream of excitement. This was quickly followed by a volley of questions, most of them directed at Di, but a few asked by the Water Babes to each other: 'When did this happen?', 'Are they real?', 'I wonder how much it cost', 'Who is he?', 'Is he Australian?', 'Do we know him?', 'When's the date?', 'Is it real?', 'Is it as expensive as it looks?', 'When did it happen?', 'Where did you meet?', 'How did she manage to keep this secret?'.

As for Di herself, she just had one question. 'Has anyone got a pair of scissors so I can cut the string and show you all?' Several handbags were opened. Salma rushed off to the kitchen.

In Salma's short absence, the group remembered their manners and realised that the appropriate thing to do on such an occasion was not to bombard the new fiancée with questions, but to congratulate her and to wish her and her soon-to-be husband well; which they did, though with varying degrees of enthusiasm and sincerity, ranging from Lynne at the top of the scale, down to Jean, at the bottom. She was happy for Di, but her happiness was tinged with a veil of sadness. The reasons for the sadness were not clear to her, though they were obvious to some of the others.

Luke stood aside from the general clamour. This was the sort of occasion on which he realised that at least in some respects, he was a normal male. As a child, he and his dad had watched in wonder at his mother's addiction to the hatch, match and dispatch pages of the local paper. She had a habit of reading aloud entries about every name she recognised, even of people they did not know personally. Night after night his mother regaled them with the births, marriages and deaths of local celebrities, of unknown neighbours, of distant relations he and his dad, despite his mother's insistence, had never heard of.

Slowly, Luke began to develop his hidden (he hoped) streak of misogyny. Of particular fascination to his mother and to her female friends was the column devoted to engagements and forthcoming marriages. He began to think that no matter how badly treated women might be by their menfolk (via infidelity, adultery, violence, rape and so on) all was forgotten in the thrill of an engagement, or the announcement of an imminent wedding. So it was in this room. At least three women, Lynne, Marsha, and Meg had good reasons to question the benefits of a close association with a man. But here they were, all gaga about a show-off diamond ring.

Salma rushed back from the kitchen. She joined the circle of women, as if preparing for a seance. She cut the string, and was the first to hold the ring and to pass it round for all to admire. It brought forth predictable exclamations of admiration.

Though she was no jewellery expert, Heppie knew enough about diamonds to know that part of their value lay in the magic "4Cs": cut, clarity, colour and carat weight. All superb, she decided.

Mrs C impressed everyone by her knowledge. 'Ah yes, wonderful. Cushion cut, with side stones even. You're a very lucky girl, Di.' She was not alone in entertaining vulgar thoughts: who did Di know who could afford such a thing?

'I know. And this is the box it came in.'

'Hell's bells! I should have seen the name on the inside of the ring,' said Heppie.

'Robin egg blue! Tiffany Blue,' gasped Salma, duly impressed. Di had certainly done very well for herself.

'Did you choose it together?' asked Marsha.

'Well, yes, we did. We both wanted the best. And fortunately, he could afford it,' lifting her eyes towards heaven.

'Well, it's certainly nobody I know then,' Lynne laughed.

'Since this is a sort of celebration, I wonder if this is a moment for champagne?' asked Salma.

Opinion was divided. Heppie, Shula, Dorothy and Mrs C all declined. 'Champagne would really tip me over,' said Shula. 'I've still got some brandy. I'll certainly toast the occasion in that if you don't mind.' The rest took up Salma's suggestion. She and Jane rushed around to find glasses and a bottle of chilled Dom Pérignon.

'But coming back to the main mystery, I don't suppose we're going to meet him are we? Or get to know anything more about Mr Gorgeous?' Marsha looked Di straight in the eye, not very hopeful of a favourable response to her challenge.

'Oh, I don't see why not,' said Di with fake casualness, and ostentatiously inserting the diamond on to her ring finger. This caused yet another burst of chatter. 'When?', 'Where?', 'How do you mean?', 'Are you serious?'.

'Sure I'm serious. I'm not teasing. Honestly.'

Not much, you crafty bitch, thought Luke.

'So shall I open the bubbly now, or wait a bit? Until, er, he arrives?' asked Salma, not sure if that was an appropriate question.

Before anyone could answer, the doorbell rang. Everyone, including Luke, held their breath. Marsha and Meg found themselves clutching each other in suspense. Expectant looks were exchanged. Salma was terrified that it was her father. *But he would hardly be likely to press his own doorbell*, she thought. She gripped the unopened bottle of champagne in her left hand and held it tight against her chest.

'Oh,' said Di, affecting nonchalance. 'I expect that's him now.'

Jane moved into the hall to open the front door. *I think I've had a bit too much to drink*, she thought. Everybody was watching her from the sitting room. Her legs were shaking so much that she could barely walk.

23.15
Thurprithe, Thurprithe!

Jane opened the front door. Her first shock was that she could hardly see anyone, because the person at the door was dressed in black, head to toe. Black leather. Quite menacing, especially since the apparition was so unexpected. On automatic pilot, Jane simply said, 'Oh, please, come in.'

And as soon as the person stepped into the hall, still wearing a black helmet, Jane got her second shock. She was so taken aback that she had to lean on to the table in the middle of the hall to support her. The new arrival briefly acknowledged Jane, and then mimed a sort of 'Where do I go now?' gesture, though without divesting itself of any gear at all. Feeling distinctly faint, Jane pointed to the double doors to the sitting room.

Even before the newcomer opened the sitting room doors, Luke knew who it was. He would have recognised those immense thighs and that booted waddle anywhere. He could not believe that Di and the man had been so secretive, so deceitful.

Di stood up, beaming. 'Here he is!' she grinned. *Like a farmer introducing her prize bull*, thought Marsha. It took barely a second for the others to realise who it was. He raised the visor on his helmet.

'Thurprithe thurprithe! Yeth. It'th me!'

There was a general intake of breath, followed immediately by the sound of sobbing, from Meg. She clung closer to Marsha, who tried to offer what small comfort she could. 'Shush Meg. Don't, please.'

'Oh, I had a premonition. I knew it would be you,' said Lynne, wise after the event.

'Don't be ridiculous. How could you?' protested Heppie. Her low opinion of Lynne's perspicacity was shared by others.

'Bollocks, Lynne,' countered Marsha. 'You're just trying to be clever. I bet you're as shocked as anyone,' she insisted, looking at Jean, who sat white-faced, frozen like a statue.

Jane came into the room from the hall. Briefly, she was the object of everyone's attention. 'I didn't know anything, Salma. Honestly, nothing at all,' she said to everyone. Indeed, she did not.

'Welcome, and congratulations on your engagement,' said Mrs C, in an attempt to pick up the pieces of a difficult situation.

'Thankth,' said Muscles, aka Bashir, grinning from ear to ear. He removed his helmet.

The tension relaxed slightly, giving way to a predictable series of questions, though not from Meg, who was still sobbing, or from Jean, still frozen in her chair. 'When did he pop the question, Di?' (A few months ago.) 'So when's the big day?' (Oh, sometime next year.) 'Are you both going to Australia?' (Yeth. I'm tho ekthited.) 'What are you going to do when you get back?' (Bash's got a great job lined up; as manager of our new business, a gym. And there'll be a pool of course. He's had a lot of help from his cousin, who's some sort of landowner in Bosnia.) 'Was it easy to get a visa and stuff?' (Di'th brother helped.) 'What are you going to do with your bike, Bashir?' (He's already got someone in London to buy it from him. Got a good price.)

But the questions on the minds of the more financially literate of the group, the majority in fact, were never asked. Even so. *How the hell could both of you, let alone either of you, afford all this? The fare? The new business? Not to mention that bloody ring!*

Instead of asking that and similar questions, Heppie filled the pause in the conversation with appropriately anodyne remarks. 'Well. The linen we bought will be extra useful in your new home. If we'd known, we could have bought you a proper *wedding* gift,' she said pointedly. A small, though faint chorus of support echoed the sentiment. 'And we could have had a proper engagement and farewell do,' she said brightly. This suggestion however was met with silence.

'Oh, look at the time. We should be leaving,' announced Di. 'You ready, Bash?'

No one argued with Di's announcement. Not even the hostess. She could not bring herself to say the usual polite delaying tactics. So there was no 'Really?', 'Are you sure?', 'A coffee perhaps?', or anything remotely similar. Like everyone else, Mrs C was relieved that Di and 'Bash' were leaving. Though no one could say so out loud, they all secretly wanted to have a gossipy post-mortem on events of the last hour or so. On top of which, most were desperate for a reviving cup of coffee.

Bashir donned his helmet. Di went into the hall, and put her various presents on the table and then put her coat on. She reassured everyone that her helmet was outside, with the bike. Their eventual exit was a somewhat rushed affair. Di grabbed her presents and kissed three or four people, promising to write when she got back to Melbourne. Bashir had already gone to start the bike. Luke stepped forward from the melee in the hall and practically pushed Di outside. Then, to cries of 'Bye', 'Good luck', and 'Thanks for everything', the couple drove off into the night.

'Oh,' said Jane looking at the hall table. 'Di's forgotten her book.'

'Hell, don't let Jean see it. She'll be devastated,' Heppie said anxiously, turning to Luke for help.

'Don't worry. Thank God she's still in the sitting room, struck dumb or something. I'll make sure she doesn't see it,' said Luke. He proceeded to hide the book in his coat in the cloakroom.

They returned to the sitting room, one by one.

"Bash' indeed!'

'I'd like to bash her, the little madam.'

'Not so little. Did you notice? She's at least two inches taller than he is; and a bit older, of course.'

'Something doesn't add up, I'm sure of it. Perhaps that cousin of his is a black marketeer or something.'

'They say there's no accounting for taste.'

'Their own business? I bet that her brother's got something to do with all this. He's the Mr Fixit, I bet.'

'Anyone for coffee?'

God yes, was the general response. Jane started to stoke up the fire yet again, while Salma and Lynne went to the kitchen and prepared coffee for everyone. Except Jean. She had broken her silence at last, whispering hoarsely that she would prefer tea.

By the time drinks had arrived, the tension in the room had eased, giving way to a collective sense of unquenched curiosity and mystery.

'That's better,' said Heppie, sipping her coffee. Carefully she turned to Jean, sitting next to her. 'And you, Jean? Is your tea OK? How are you doing?'

Jean responded unexpectedly with a broad, genuine smile. She put down her tea, and covered her mouth. And began to chuckle. The chuckle became louder and louder.

23.30
PEOPLE AND THEIR SECRETS

As Jean's chuckling developed into outright laughter, everyone became alarmed. After all, in the few weeks that they had known Jean, no one had seen her really smile, let alone seen or heard any sign of joy from her. But now, she was developing a good old-fashioned belly laugh, one which was rapidly turning into what looked like hysteria.

'Has anyone got a spare hanky? Her eyes are watering.' Jean leant forward then threw herself immediately backwards, coughing and laughing at the same time.

'Here. Out of the way, Heppie,' said Dorothy. 'I've seen this sort of thing before with undergraduates; highly strung, especially at exam time.'

'Oh, what to do?' said Salma, who, along with nearly everyone in the room, crowded round Jean's chair, as she began to choke with exhaustion, only to start up again: laughing, choking, breathing heavily, eyes watering.

'Stand back!'

They were all stunned at the speed and force of Dorothy's slap. It immediately started an argument.

'No, Dorothy! That's wrong,' screamed Jane.

'Leave her alone. She knows what she's doing.' This was from Luke.

'You've hurt her,' wept Shula.

'The old remedies are the best. That's what my mum would have done,' said Marsha.

'Poor Jean,' said Heppie.

'Serves her right. The silly cow. It's stopped her anyway.' Meg, now fully recovered from her sobbing fit, almost spat the words out.

'But it was nothing less than common assault,' protested Salma.

Common assault Dorothy's slap may have been, but it seemed to work. Gradually, Jean began to settle down. She could now recover her breath, wipe away her tears, and massage her face to relieve the pain of the slap. She was offered and drank more tea, and her throat began to ease. She was not angry with Dorothy. In fact, she was still smiling. 'Sorry about that,' she said quickly. 'God, I must look a real mess!' Everyone assured her that she looked fine; which of course was far from the truth.

'It has been a difficult evening for all of us,' began Heppie, slowly. She was about tell Jean that they all appreciated how very difficult Di's engagement announcement must have been for her. Fortunately, however, Jean's broad, soothing smile prevented Heppie from making a difficult situation even worse.

'Oh,' said Jean brightly. 'It's true that I've had my ups and downs this evening. But actually, I feel absolutely fine. I feel great in fact; like a load has been lifted from my mind.'

Mrs C congratulated Jean. 'Good for you,' she said. A sentiment they all echoed.

'Yes,' said Jean, beaming. 'I can see more clearly now. I expect she will eventually see more clearly too.'

'She? See what more clearly?' asked Shula.

'Diana. When she learns that her darling Bashir was being well and truly "bashed" himself.'

'What do you mean 'bashed'?' asked Salma.

'Oh, did I say "bashed"? My mistake. Sorry, I meant *fucked*,' Jean said calmly.

Heppie dropped her cup. Everyone did a double take, as if checking their hearing.

'What?' asked Heppie, for once all at sea.

'Fucked,' repeated Jean. 'What do you think it means?'

'You cannot be serious, Jean!' boomed Dorothy.

'Oh, I've never been so serious in my life.'

'And, if we may ask, bashed, fucked or whatever you want to call it by who?'

'By whom, Lynne, by whom.'

'For God's sake stop being the know-all teacher, Dorothy. There's a time and a place for everything.' Dorothy ignored Heppie's remark, and joined the rest, waiting for Jean.

'I can't put it any more clearly. Let me try again.' Jean gave a cough before continuing slowly, giving more or less equal weight to each syllable. Her tone was frankly vicious. 'For the past few months, Bashir, your favourite Bosnian, has been taking it up the arse from my soon to be ex-husband, Gordon.' A tone of sheer venom overtook her. 'I believe that taking it up the arse is generally known as being fucked, or more correctly I suppose, as being *buggered*. Excuse my directness, Mrs C.' Apart from a slight tremble around the mouth, Jean regained her composure slowly, like a snake settling down.

'Oh, I think I've had more than I can bear this evening,' said Shula. Meg began to whimper. The others were too open-mouthed to speak.

'Luke!' shouted Lynne.

'What?'

'Is this true?'

'Is what true?'

'You know. That Jean's husband has been shagging Muscles.'

'How the holy fuck should I know?' Luke replied, completely mystified by Lynne's accusatory tone.

'Maybe you've seen them in the clubs or something? And aren't you people supposed to have some sort of radar, where you can automatically sense that someone is–'

'Whoa. Stop there! I'm sorry to disappoint you all ladies.' Luke was indignant. 'My gaydar, which I suppose is what you are referring to, must have run out of batteries. I haven't been out and about for months. Anyway, I'm happily settled with Ted, as you well know, Lynne.'

Lynne was like a dog with a bone. 'But I thought you might have heard or even seen something.'

'Contrary to what you might think, I'm not one of those queens that likes to gossip. And I haven't had the time. I've been too busy studying and things. If you must know, I've never seen or heard anything about Muscles, and I haven't a clue what Jean's husband looks like.'

Jean reached for her handbag. She had a fairly recent photo of herself and her husband, taken at a reception for The Charity Kings. 'This is him. That is, if you want to see. His name's Gordon.' Despite everything that Luke had said, she was as anxious as Lynne to hear what Luke might have to report.

'Gordon?' Luke was silent for a second or two. It was the silence of possible recognition. He looked at the photo. There was no disguising the fact that Luke recognised Gordon from the photo: recognition; confirmation. He tried to think what he would say next. 'Ah yes. Never met him personally. He appeared on the scene about three years ago. But as I said, I wouldn't know whether he's been around since then. People called him Flash.'

Lynne spoke, hardly concealing a note of triumph. 'See, so now we know something at least.'

'Flash?' asked Salma. 'Was he conceited or something?'

'*Flash Gordon*! No guesses as to where that name came from,' said Heppie, smiling.

'Who was Flash Gordon?' asked Jane. The older members of the group just shook their heads.

'Actually, Salma's right. He was conceited, and vain. Always drank whisky when the rest of us settled for beer or wine. Drove a Porsche apparently. He was always flashing his money around.'

'Evidently not the only thing he was flashing around,' said Jean tightly.

'Some people also called him Bighead. Big head, if you see what I mean.' It took a few seconds for Luke's meaning to sink in. Imaginations were running wild. 'But as I said, not that I ever had the pleasure.' Luke sat back, lips pursed. Salma and Jane could not help grinning. Luke turned to them and spoke through the side of his mouth. 'Apparently his thing is absolutely gi-bloody-normous. Muscles certainly must have earned his keep!' At this Salma and Jane could not prevent themselves from giggling.

The other women were angry with Luke. This was not the time for private jokes. They felt that a joke of any kind could be at Jean's expense. She had suffered enough. 'Sorry, Jean,' said Mrs C. 'They weren't laughing at or about you,' she said, looking at Salma disapprovingly.

'But coming back to the main point, did you ever see or hear anything about Gordon and Muscle boy?'

'Never. And that's the truth, Jean.'

'So Jean, how can you be sure that the two of them were, er, an item?'

'Because I saw my husband this afternoon in Hardwicke's restaurant. That's when I found out that he was fucking Bashir. He showed me a photo of the two of them, arm in arm, in some fancy boatyard. They've bought a boat together. Or rather Gordon bought it and the silly sod put it in both their names. He even did the same with a flat.' Jean did not have the courage to say where the flat was, or how much it must be worth. 'And Gordon, the stupid bugger, thinks that they're moving in together on Monday.'

'So,' said Heppie. 'We now know where the money for the ring and everything came from.'

'And that's not all. He made several withdrawals, big ones, from one of our accounts. I assume that money went to Bashir too.'

Ah, that would explain the Harley, thought Luke.

'Hmm. Quite the little gold digger,' said Marsha. There were several nods of agreement.

Probably not the only one, thought Heppie.

'I've just had a thought,' said Dorothy. 'Shouldn't someone tell Di?'

'Tell her what?'

'That she's running off engaged to a crook – a bisexual one at that!'

'No. As Lynne would say, sod that for a bag of chips. Let her find out in her own time. The fool deserves all she gets.'

They were all astonished by the complete turnaround of Jean's feelings. *Hell hath no fury indeed*, thought Heppie. *I think I'd be bitter too, in the circumstances.*

'Anyway,' continued Jean bitterly. 'How do I know if Diana wasn't in it from the beginning? She could have been a deceitful crook, like him?'

'You mean she *planned* all this, and knew about Bashir getting all that money from Gordon?' Salma asked, amazed.

'As I said, how would I know? Or anyone else? She was certainly secretive, as you all know.'

'What do you think, Luke? You know her best,' said Marsha.

Luke weighed his words as carefully as he could. Uncharacteristically serious, he tried to be fair and just. He played for time. 'Do I think that Di actually helped Muscles to squeeze money out of Gordon? Or that she knew where the money was coming from? I don't have the highest opinion of Di, God knows. But no, I can't think she would be capable of something so devious, and so dishonest. Really. I don't see her as a thief. And she certainly wouldn't knowingly take up with a man who's both a thief and another bloke's bum boy. I mean someone who was regularly being fucked by Gordon or anyone else for that matter. I think she really believed that Bashir's money came from his cousin in Bosnia. And of course she had some of her own, not to mention any help she got from her brother. No, I think she was completely taken in by Bashir. She was humongously naive; big time.'

'But how could she be so stupid?' demanded Heppie.

'Because she's desperate. She so wants to show her parents that she can be as successful as her brother. He's got a great job, a wife and two kids. I've seen the photos. She once told me that she's always been in a sort of competition with him, and that he's the parents' favourite. So when a man comes along who is reasonably presentable, ambitious and apparently loaded, she jumped at the chance. Probably her last. So no, I don't think, to be honest, that she's the real villain here. The real villain is that bastard Muscles.'

The room reflected on Luke's interpretation. 'The truth is, we'll never really know what happened. But Luke's explanation certainly fits what we do know,' said Dorothy. 'Who knows? Perhaps even Bashir was more sinned against than sinning?'

'What the hell does that mean?' snapped Lynne.

'Surely you aren't making excuses for him, Dorothy? For that creep,' protested Marsha.

'He isn't a creep. He's gorgeous,' whimpered Meg, half asleep, still being held by Marsha.

'No. No excuses. But you have to think of it from his point of view as well.'

'Do we indeed?' said Shula, with heavy sarcasm.

Dorothy persisted. 'Look. He was a refugee, asylum seeker or whatever from Bosnia. God knows what he must have seen and suffered over there. Perhaps he was in Sarajevo. It was a slaughterhouse. He probably trusts nobody. Not even here in England. He was stuck. And he was bisexual, even gay. He wanted to get out, no matter what the cost. He would see Di as a one-way ticket to a better life. Would it be so surprising that he would use everyone and everything to his own advantage? Once he's settled in Australia, he'll probably dump Di. And so it goes on. It wouldn't be a defence in a court of law. But still.'

'Let's hope for her sake, that Di isn't pregnant,' muttered Lynne.

Her remark made the sleepy Meg sob again. 'Come on, sleepy head. Let's get you tidied up a bit. Then we should be going home.' Marsha led Meg to the downstairs bathroom.

The others were silent for at least a minute. Heppie sighed deeply. 'What complicated lives we lead; people and their secrets. As Dorothy says, we'll probably never know the full story.'

Salma, with her back to the glass door leading to the hall, was gradually aware that Lynne and Dorothy were staring at something behind her. She turned round to look, just as her mother stood up and made for the door. Salma's spirits, already quite low, plummeted even further. As if the evening had not been chaotic enough.

10. Going Forward

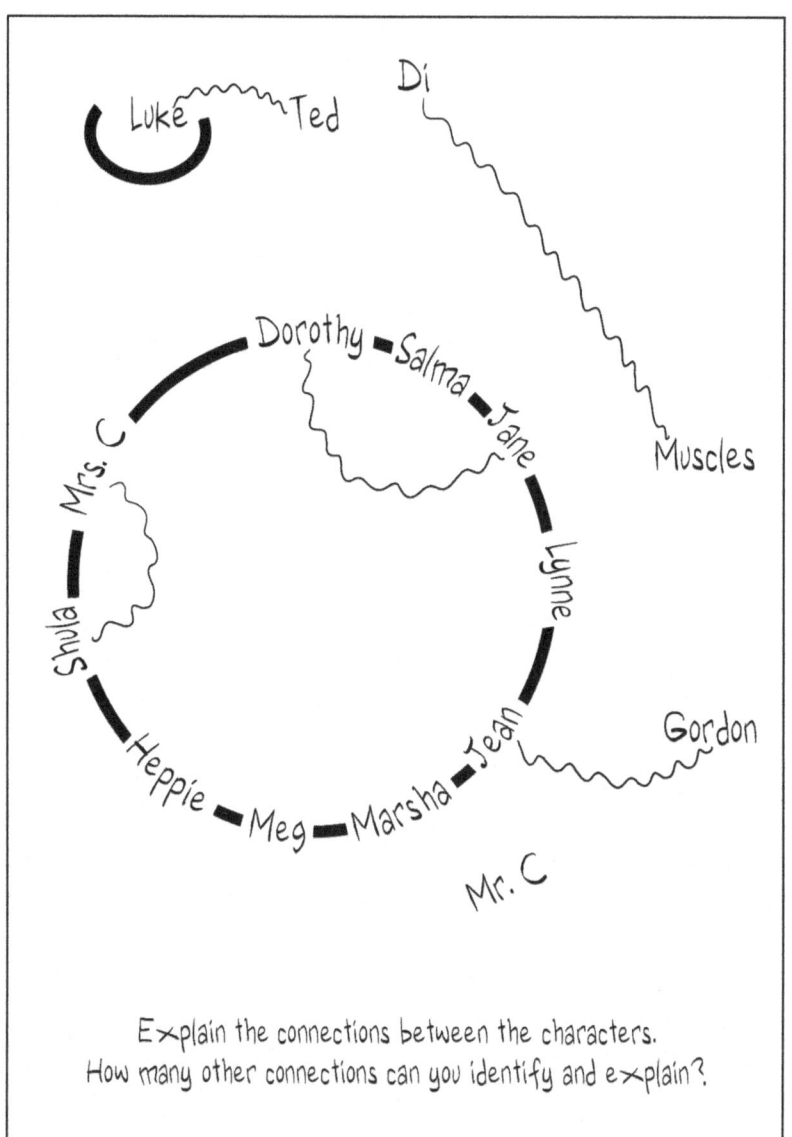

Explain the connections between the characters.
How many other connections can you identify and explain?

23.55
The Man of the House

Now everyone turned round, so that they could see into the hall.

Mrs C greeted the man whom the guests assumed, correctly, was her husband. They guessed that he was in his late sixties. Small, balding, slightly overweight but impeccably dressed.

Mrs C went up to him and took his coat and put it away in the cloakroom. Heppie noticed that there was no other physical contact between them. In the few seconds that Mrs C was out of sight, her husband looked through the door into the sitting room and saw his wife's guests. There was no reaction from him. He casually took out a medium-sized cigar and lit it, blowing a small cloud of smoke into the hall air.

Behind him, unseen, Marsha appeared briefly from the downstairs loo, where she had been getting Meg ready for their departure. Looking somewhat alarmed, Marsha quickly closed the loo door, quickly locking herself and Meg in.

Mrs C returned to her husband's side, and led him into the sitting room. 'This is my husband everyone,' she said graciously.

For some reason, everyone had stood up when he had entered the room, as if he were some mediaeval mogul emperor. Jean found herself giving a small involuntary curtsey, though she hardly knew why. There was a general round of 'Hello', 'Pleased to meet you', 'We were just about to leave actually', 'Nice to see you' and so on.

Mr C waved his cigar hand in the air, in a successful attempt to calm everyone down. 'Hello ladies,' he said, studiously ignoring Luke. 'You are most welcome to my house.' A small, stocky man, he managed to exude an air of ownership (it was after all, his house), authority, and male superiority. He inhaled and then exhaled more cigar smoke, this time via impressive nose jets. 'Please, everyone, do sit down.' He remained standing.

Heppie was in one of her if-you-don't-ask-you-won't-find-out moods. 'Your wife and Salma have been wonderful hostesses.' Mr C just nodded his head very slightly. Heppie pressed on. 'Salma said that you were planning to go to New York this evening?'

'I've been ringing you all evening I was trying to let you know that I found your passport in your room, but couldn't find you. I was hoping you'd ring home, so that I could have brought it to you at the airport or sent it by taxi or something.'

'You were in my room?'

No thanks for finding the passport. No reaction to the suggestions about getting to the airport; nothing, except for the hostile question about Salma being in his room; in his territory. In an instant, the temperature in the room seemed to have dropped several degrees.

'That was my fault. I told Salma to go up and fetch one of your bathrobes.'

'One of my bathrobes?'

'Yes, there was a storm here earlier, and someone got very wet, so we needed something to dry her out.' Salma looked round desperately for Meg.

'Oh,' said Dorothy, sailing to the rescue. 'I think they must still be drying out and changing, getting ready to leave.'

'And I must leave you ladies to get on with your gathering.'

The guests protested. They must get going; babysitters to relieve; taxis to call; 'Goodness, is it midnight?' They had had a great time.

Mr C waved his cigar dismissively. 'No, no. The night is young. You must stay for a final drink. I insist. Salma.'

'Yes, of course.'

'Fereshthe, can you come upstairs and help me unpack for a moment? Then you can come back to your guests.'

'I'll come too and give you your passport. Jane can get the drinks.'

'Oh yes, of course. No problem.'

Mr C turned to leave the sitting room. Before he left, he looked at Luke, as if noticing him for the first time. 'Ah, don't I know you from somewhere?'

Luke suspected that Mr C knew perfectly well where and when they had met. 'Yes, when you came to register your wife for the aquarobics class at the leisure centre. You agreed that she could come so long as Salma came along as a chaperone.'

Mr C all but sneered. 'And you were the only man here tonight?'

Luke said nothing.

'I suppose you must have been the entertainment then!' Mr C laughed and shook his head in mock despair, as he once again snorted a smelly nose jet. Into Luke's face. The remark and its accompanying gestures were interpreted correctly by the others as a combination insult. They sympathised with Luke, whose eyes blazed with hostility and contempt.

As his wife and daughter followed Mr C out of the sitting room and upstairs, their guests were in little doubt about their feelings for the man of the house.

00.05
Twist and Shout

From the secrecy of the downstairs bathroom, Marsha could hear Mr and Mrs C and Salma climb the stairs. She could even smell the smoke from the cigar, as Mr C passed within inches of the locked door. She calculated that she must have been in the bathroom for at least ten minutes, during which time Meg, fortunately, sat quietly.

They were just about to emerge when Meg pulled Marsha close to her. She sniffled. 'It was Bash.'

'What do you mean?' said Meg, fearing the worst.

'Who got me pregnant. I know that sometimes you don't think much of me, Marsh.'

'Go on.'

'But I swear on the Bible that it was Bash. He was the first, the only one; three months ago, when we met at a club. I took him to my place. But after two weeks, he dropped me.' Meg's head drooped. She was exhausted, quite beyond tears. 'And then he turned up at those stupid lessons. We were as surprised as each other. And that's the honest truth, Marsh.'

Marsha was immediately aware of the implications of Meg's ordeal. She had told no one at her house that she had met Bashir again at the pool. She must have been in agony. Rejected, and mortified. Marsha was overcome by Meg's suffering. She held Meg closely for a few moments and whispered: 'Hold on Meg. We'll get over this. You and me; together. I believe you. Just promise me for now that you won't tell any of the others here. Please.' Meg desperately needed to hear that someone *believed* her. In Marsha's arms, she nodded her head to indicate that she would keep the promise.

Marsha's mind could barely cope with Bashir's hypocrisy, duplicity, and promiscuity. By now it was certain that in the past few moments, he was simultaneously having affairs with Di, Meg, and Gordon. And God knows who else along the way. She did not have the words to curse him enough.

When Marsha deemed it safe to emerge from the bathroom, they both quickly crossed the hall to the sitting room.

'We wondered what had happened to you both. Are you alright, Meg?' asked Heppie. 'Come and sit next to me.'

'Er, have I missed anything?' Marsha asked cautiously.

'Hell, you certainly did,' said Lynne. Between them, the others related what had happened when Mr C had been in the room. They reported on the "aura of hostility he seemed to surround himself with" (Shula), his "fucking male superiority" (Lynne), his apparent "bossiness" (Dorothy), "the awful smell of his revolting cigar" (Jean), and his "unforgiveable rudeness to Luke" (Heppie). Jane stared into space, pale and tense. Luke looked as if he were about to explode.

'Oh,' said Marsha, looking and sounding mildly surprised. 'Really?'

Yes, really, they all said.

'So what do we all do now?' asked Dorothy.

'I suggest we wait until Mrs C and Salma come down. We can hardly leave without saying goodbye properly, can we? Let's have that other drink. I'd like just water, if you don't mind Jane.'

Heppie's plan met with general approval. Jane and Lynne saw to what everyone hoped was a final round of drinks. It was getting rather late, after all. Marsha was torn between wanting to get Meg home on the one hand but not wanting to leave while Mrs C and Salma were upstairs. That would risk causing offence. So, she decided, reluctantly, to stay.

In the silence that followed, Lynne and Heppie decided to check on their families. They compared notes.

'Gemma, my daughter, answered. She said that the evening had gone really well, which frankly was a bit of a surprise. Gemma can be a bit awkward when she wants to be. Ted took them for an Indian, which they all enjoyed. When they got home, Jason settled down to watch one of his favourite cartoons. And Ted decided to teach Gemma how to waltz! For a big chap, he's a great dancer, and apparently she loved it. I'm pleased, because I've always thought that being able to dance is a good thing, especially for young people these days, who don't seem to know any of the old dances. Gemma was really glad, because she feels that she can now do something that her pals at school can't. Jason has fallen asleep now on the settee, and Ted has just gone out for a smoke. Well deserved I should think. Anyway, I told her that Luke and I should be home soon. How did your call go?'

'My son-in-law answered. He and my daughter had gone to a friend's house for supper, and my two tenants looked after the kids. My daughter is a worrier, and of course she couldn't resist calling the kids while she was out. But everything was fine. The kids got on with my tenants, two girls, really well apparently. They played games and stuff, and didn't watch telly at all. So success all round I think. Thank goodness. My son-in-law said to stay as long as I wanted. He'll stay up and wait for my taxi, after I've dropped Shula at her house.'

They joined the others. Jane had put Luke's CD on low. There was some humming along, and recollections of the morning's eventful lesson at the pool.

Jane took Luke aside. 'Luke, Mrs C and Salma have been gone for over ten minutes now. I'm a bit worried.'

Jane looked unusually drawn. 'Yes, I can tell you are. Do you think they're OK?'

'Oh, I'm sure that they are, but–'

Luke could hear that Jane sounded overconfident. He guessed that she wanted to ask him something. 'You want me to go up and check?'

'Oh, would you please?' She looked relieved. 'Er, after all, it is getting a bit late for everyone.'

'Sure, no problem; upstairs is it?'

'Yes. Mr C's room's easy to find. Turn right at the top of the stairs. It's the last door at the end of the corridor, on the left.'

'No problem. I suggest you join the others, and just relax. I'm sure everything's fine.'

Luke climbed the stairs, determinedly humming "The Skye Boat Song" as he went. At the top of the stairs he turned right. He only had to follow his sense of smell. The trail of cigar scent became stronger and stronger as he went down the corridor, until he reached the door to Mr C's room, where the scent became something of a stink.

Even before he leant to the door to hear what was going on, he heard Salma cry out. 'No. No. You can't!'

'Shut your damn mouth. This is between—'

Luke needed to hear no more. He burst into the room. He saw a family scene which reminded him of an old-fashioned illustration in a Victorian or Edwardian novel. To his left was Salma, her fist in her face, looking tearful and horrified, pleading with her father. To the right was her mother, kneeling on the floor, looking up at her husband, also pleading with him, and grimacing in pain. Her sari was spread around her. Mr C stood over his wife menacingly, his left hand grasping, or rather squeezing his wife's right shoulder.

'Let her go. NOW!'

'Bugger off. This has nothing to do with you. This is family business. This is my house, and she, both of them have been using it for some sort of silly party.' Mr C held on to his wife's shoulder.

Luke took two steps forward and squared up to Mr C. Much the taller of the two, Luke grabbed hold of the older man's hair with his left hand and pulled his head back. Mr

C's grip on his wife's shoulder loosened. Luke pushed his clenched right fist into his adversary's face. 'If you so much as touch her again, I swear I'll knock your fucking head off. I've had enough of you for one night.'

Salma rushed round and helped her mother stand up. Mrs C seemed to have sustained no lasting injury, though her shoulder may well have been bruised. 'Go into another room and try to recover a bit. I'll see you downstairs in a few minutes. I won't let on to the others.' The two women did as Luke instructed, and fled the room.

Mr C, his shoulders slumped in defeat, sat on the side of the bed.

'You have no right to—'

'Don't talk to me about rights. Don't talk to me about anything at all. You're a bloody disgrace.'

'But she's my wife, and—'

Later, Luke could not remember the details of what happened next. The truth was he lost his temper. He stood to his full height, and pushed Mr C back on to the bed, pinning him down with his left arm. 'I told you to shut the fuck up.'

Luke found himself grasping Mr C's testicles. 'And this is just between you and me,' hissed Luke into Mr C's anguished face. Luke pulled and twisted violently, ignoring the other man's cries of astonishment, protest and pain. Mr C shouted, but Luke shoved a pillow on his face and mouth. Luke was pulled and twisted harder and further, until neither man could bear it any more.

It was over. One man was left crouching on the bed, in a foetal position, attempting to hold back sobs of pain and humiliation. The other man was standing up, taking deep breaths and rapidly recovering his composure. Then he left the room feeling happier than he had felt all evening.

00.25
DISSEMBLING

Luke returned to the sitting room. He did not give Jane, or anyone, a chance to ask him how things were upstairs, or where he had been for the past few minutes. He simply breezed in, announcing that all was well, and that Mrs C and Salma would be down any minute now.

Fortunately for Luke, he was right: determined not to display any sign of anxiety or stress, Mrs C and Salma swept into the sitting room behind their protector and saviour. Slightly flushed and breathless, they greeted everyone as cheerfully as they were able, explaining their delay by saying that they had just been for "a little wash and brush-up". The room seemed to brighten up a little, even though no one was really deceived by the dissembling and bravura performances on show. Clearly, something *had* happened upstairs. But for the moment, no one dared to enquire further.

For the next few minutes, the CD continued to play quietly in the background, and a welcome sense of peace descended on the room. Each person was content to be lost in his or her own thoughts.

00.35
CONFRONTING MR CHOWDHRY

She doubted that anyone had noticed her leaving the sitting room. Well, not so much leaving, she had to admit, but sneaking out. Like the others, she was very tired. But she was determined to get to the bottom of things, even if it caused a confrontation.

She crept towards the stairs. Leaning on the right-hand wall for support, she went up step by step. *Anyone would think I'm a burglar or something*, she thought, carefully lifting her dress so that she did not trip over it and make a noise. Any noise would spoil the surprise; for she had no doubt. Yes, it would be more than a surprise: a shock; a revelation, on this, a night of revelations.

With each step, her own part in this whole business became clearer to her. Yes. She had to take some responsibility for her own actions. She was fully aware that she was no St Theresa. But she was not totally wicked either. Was she? She hoped and prayed not. She had been foolish, even selfish. But not wicked, surely.

It must be this way. That smell! As she mounted the last step and turned right, the tide of self-analysis, which was in danger of morphing to a sea of self-loathing, suddenly began to ebb. *No*, she thought. *It takes two to tango. I'm not going to shoulder all the blame*. Her ankles stiffened, her legs gained strength, and her back straightened. She reached the last door on the left. *This is it. He must be in here*. She opened the door quietly, stepped silently into his room then closed the door behind her.

The room was quite dark. More so in fact than the corridor she had just left. It took a while for her eyes to adjust. There was only one small lamp on, on the far side of the room. He was sitting there, at his desk, with his back to her. He seemed to be slumping forward, uncharacteristically subdued. 'So, Mr Chowdhry.' There was no response. She spoke again, this time more loudly. 'So, Mr Chowdhry.'

His back straightened. He winced. He resumed his bent position, and swivelled slowly round in his chair. He could barely sit straight, but tried to look up and to focus on the door. It was so dark that he could not see her at all clearly. She took a few steps forward. To her surprise, she saw that he had been weeping. He seemed to be in some pain, and was clutching his groin area.

'Is that you, Marsha?' he whispered.

'Yes, it is. Mr Kamal bloody Chowdhry, or whatever your name is.'

He wept openly. 'Kamal is my first name. You know now that I'm not a Chowdhry.' He wiped his face. 'I can't understand. Why are you here?' He was in despair.

'I'm here because your *wife* invited me. Your *wife*,' Marsha added bitterly. 'Who could have guessed that she and I would be in the same group at the leisure centre? Some coincidence eh?'

Slowly, he was able to raise his eyes and to look Marsha directly in the face, through his tears. 'Yes. I was going to explain.'

'Explain? Don't lie. You've been lying through your teeth all along, haven't you?'

'I wanted to tell you the truth. But–'

'No. The truth isn't in you, you bastard. You've been deceiving me all along. All that rubbish about coming down from your home in London for regular short business trips here. The evenings spent at the club, the nights spent in my flat, or in some second-rate hotel. It was all a front, wasn't it?'

Kamal Cooper hung his head low, unable to speak.

'I'm not stupid you know. All the girls know that most of the men at the club must be married. It's written all over your faces. We just let you get on with it; part of the game. But even I never suspected that the man I was seeing was married to someone local, someone here, right in front of my nose! To a wonderful, kind woman like Mrs C, who never did anyone any harm. And Salma: to treat your own daughter like that. It's terrible.'

His eyes flashed defiantly. 'She's no daughter of mine.'
'What?'
'All the education and advantages in the world, and nothing to show for it. She's a bloody freak: won't wear dresses. Never had a boyfriend. As I said, no daughter of mine.'
'You're so stupid and cruel. She's a successful, respected woman. More than anyone like me could ever hope to be. You don't know how lucky you are; a lovely wife and daughter. God knows what they'd think if they knew the truth about you.'
'Maybe they do,' he said miserably. He looked up. 'I don't know and I don't care. Maybe one of them also knows about you: the dresses, the presents, the shoes; all for you Marsha.'
'That's the trouble in this town. There are too many men with too much money to spare and not enough to spend it on.'
'Except on people like you.'
Marsha was furious. She spat on him. 'You little shit. Don't you talk about "people like me" in that way. And don't you dare drag me into being responsible for this mess! God knows I've never asked you for a thing. It was never for me, Kamal, and you know it. It was always for you. So that you could carry on your life the way you wanted it to be; to suit you, and no one else. As for the presents, as you call them, for me they're just a means to an end. And if you didn't know that, you're even more stupid than I thought.'
'But you said you liked me, Marsha. I thought that there was something between us. Something special.' He slipped down from the chair, knelt on the floor in his dressing gown, and held on to one of Marsha's shoes. She became alarmed. The possibility that he was fond of her (or perhaps more than fond) had of course occurred to her. But she had dismissed the thought immediately. She was not prepared to admit that at one time she had feelings for him, or thought she had. After all, she would never accept gifts of any sort from a man she

did not have *some* feeling for. She was not that cynical, or that greedy.

Marsha thought hard for a moment. She was used to examining her own motives. And on such occasions, she did not always like what she saw. But, defending herself, she knew what kept her going. She knew what her priorities were, and she had always stuck to them; feelings or no feelings.

'Get up, Kamal. Don't be ridiculous. You're living in a fantasy world.'

He tried to stand up, but could not. She saw that he was in pain, and needed help. He held on to her and eventually sat back on the chair. He winced again, and bent forwards.

'What's wrong with you?' she said. 'Has something happened to cause this? Do you need a doctor?'

For a moment, Kamal thought of telling her what Luke had done to him. But that would simply raise more questions which he dared not face. 'No, no. I just sprained myself reaching for my dressing gown. That's all. I'm OK.'

'Well, it's all over.'

'What do you mean?'

'You and me, Kamal: all over.'

'Can't we just–?'

'No.'

'Please. Don't say anything to my wife, or Salma.'

'I don't think that's my job.'

'No, I don't suppose it is.'

'So, Mr Chowdhry, I've got an end of party to go to.' With that, Marsha turned and walked slowly to the door. She left the room, opening and closing the door as quietly as she had done when she entered the room.

00.45
Coincidence and Connection

Marsha was convinced that just before she confronted Kamal, the corridor outside his room was well lit. But now it was quite dark. *Someone must have turned the light off*, she thought. 'Hell,' she said softly to herself. 'I hope to God nobody heard.'

Had Mrs C been outside the door while she and Kamal were talking? Had Salma been there? She had no way of knowing, of being certain. She made her way slowly towards the top of the stairs, which were lit from the hall below. *No*, she decided. *Someone must have turned off the light in the upstairs corridor from the bottom of the stairs, in the hall.* The thought that anyone had heard the confrontation between herself and Kamal was too fanciful, too horrible to contemplate. She tried to erase the thought from her mind.

Marsha paused at the top of the stairs. She heard cheerful sounds coming from the kitchen, and was amused to realise that two people were making cocoa for everyone. *Cocoa! Only in England*, she thought. She heard Luke say, 'I'll make one for Marsha just in case; when she's finished in the bathroom or whatever. Don't forget the sugar.'

Marsha hid in the upstairs corridor until the kitchen sounds died down. Then she ran down the stairs and across the hall into the dining room, from where (confounding her expectations), she could tell that the party seemed to have revived somewhat. She could not hear exactly who was speaking, but she certainly heard the chorus of 'Really?', 'You're kidding!', 'No!'. She tidied herself as best she could, and made her way into the sitting room. If anyone had missed her, no one said so. They were too animated and preoccupied.

Lynne was particularly excited. 'Oh, hi Marsh. Did you know? Shula and Heppie lived in this house when it was first built. Shula was actually *born* here, right here. Now, how's that for a coincidence! Oh, and here's some cocoa for you.'

It took a while for Marsha to readjust to the new tempo of the party and to the topic of conversation. 'Oh, thanks. No. I didn't know. Unless Shula or Heppie mentioned it, and I, er, forgot?' She was temporarily nonplussed.

'No, we didn't say anything to anyone, except to Mrs C and Salma of course. We didn't want to, well, take over the party, and we thought it best if Mrs C mentioned it, if anyone.' Heppie sensed that her explanation for not mentioning the "coincidence" was distinctly feeble. By not mentioning the coincidence herself, she had only wanted to be discreet.

'In fact, it was big mouth me who blurted it out,' laughed Salma.

'Coincidences are strange, aren't they?' said Jane. 'For instance I had no idea that both Dorothy and I would both have a link to Oxford, or that I would meet an actual professor this evening, let alone the author of a book.'

Mrs C spoke next, quietly. 'Well, yes. Personally, I'm not sure there's such a thing as coincidence, or fate, or destiny or whatever you want to call it.'

'No?' said Luke. 'But there has to be something that explains these things, don't you think? Some coincidences are almost, well, creepy.'

'I remember once being on a train with my dad. There were two other blokes in the same carriage. Somehow, I can't remember, the topic of kidney stones came up. It turned out, amazingly, that my dad and these two other blokes had all had stones. It was a coincidence, I suppose. Anyway, once they got talking, you would have thought that these men had known each other all their lives. They were a sort of club, comparing notes and things: three completely different people. My dad was a Liverpool docker, the others were a posh bloke from down south, and a black guy from Manchester way. But they had this kidney-stone connection. It was, well, like a reunion.' Lynne paused,

'It's not quite like that with people who have had cancer. But I see what you mean,' said Shula.

'Yes,' said Mrs C. 'I think it's all about connections between people. We're all connected with each other in different wys.'

'Like with the internet, I suppose.'

'Not really, Marsha' said Mrs C. 'In fact, I think that the internet often gives us the illusion of being connected. Those connections are often superficial. No, I am thinkng about deeper, *personal* connections.'

'Hmph, like me and that Muscles.' There was a deep sigh from Meg

'Oh don't, Meg. Not again,' said Marsha.

'The connection between me and him was real enough.' Jean sipped her cocoa.

There followed an awkward silence. No one could think of anything helpful to say. Jean smiled, and continued. 'Muscles and me, as you all know, were both well and truly screwed by the same person: Flash Gordon.' A wave of sympathetic murmuring directed itself at Jean. Marsha and Meg kept quiet.

I don't feel any connection to anyone in this room, thought Luke. *But on second thoughts*, he reflected, stealing a glance at Salma and Jane, *perhaps I'm wrong*.

'I'm not saying that we are necessarily aware of the connections between ourselves and other people,' said Mrs C. She looked around the room. 'In fact, I suspect that most of the time, we just don't know what links there are between people. Finding out the truth might be very painful. Perhaps human beings have a knack of avoiding knowing about some connections. Knowing the whole truth can cause too much pain.'

Christ, she knows about me and Kamal, thought Marsha. *She must do. Or does she? Either way, she's not saying.* Marsha suddenly had a mental image of herself sitting in a large field, blowing on a dandelion. She knows me. She knows me not. She knows me. She knows me not. On and on.

'Do you think we can ever change? And perhaps alter some of these connections?' asked Jean suddenly.

'How do you mean?'

'Well, like me. I know that I am often too critical, too serious. It can make me, well, unpopular.'

'No, no, Jean. You're amongst friends here,' said Lynne, regretting some of her critical comments about Jean during the morning's lesson.

'I think that's because of my childhood. All that religious talk; it has a terrible influence, you know. Bigger than I thought. Sometimes, I feel as though I want to undo whole sections of my life and start again.'

'Well, we're Jewish as you know,' said Heppie. 'I think it's impossible to change that. And childhood stays with us. But bits of us can and do change, don't you think? Growing up, marriage, having a child, it's all bound to have an effect of some sort. I don't know whether you can change your nature, what you were born with, though.'

Luke's mind turned back to his days of being "forced out". He recalled that his mother had mentioned that he should go to a psychiatrist, to "cure" him of his homosexuality. 'Right. My stupid mother thought there was a cure for being gay, as though it were some sort of disease, which it most definitely is not. It's part of my nature.'

'But perhaps there are other things that do change us, or parts of us. Like school, or family circumstances, or money, or—'

'Go on Jane,' Shula said.

'Or death.'

'Ah, indeed,' said Dorothy, deep in thought.

Jane continued. 'So what I mean is these things can cause big changes; especially regarding these connections. They must be different according to different phases of our life.'

'Did anyone see that play called *Six Degrees of Separation*?' It was Dorothy, rousing herself, clearly preparing for a mini-lecture.

'Do you remember, Shula? We didn't see a play, but we saw a film with the same name. Oh, over twenty years ago. Something about Sidney Poitier? To be honest, I couldn't follow all of it. But I remember we liked it.'

'I didn't know there was a film. Anyway, the idea in the play is this: any individual in the world can be "connected", to use Mrs C's word, to any other individual through a chain of no more than five people. I think the original theory came from Hungary or somewhere, in the twenties.'

'Come again? How does this work in practice?' asked Heppie.

'There were lots of attempts to explain the theory mathematically, which frankly, I can't follow.'

'Oh. Then there is something that the professor doesn't know about?'

Dorothy ignored Luke's interruption.

'But later an American guy in the sixties demonstrated the theory. He lived in the Midwest.

'First, he made several packages all addressed to the same person somewhere in another part of the States. The address included the person's occupation. Then he gave one package each to a number of different people, chosen at random. None of them knew anything about the man the package was addressed to. Next, they were asked to send the package on to someone they knew; someone who was most likely to know the addressee, perhaps because of the name, the profession, or the address. Each person in the chain was asked to do the same: to send the parcel on to a friend most likely to know something about the addressee.'

Dorothy paused. Like any good teacher, she was trying to check that everyone had understood so far.

'So? What happened?'

'Well, the guy who did the experiment assumed that it would take up to a hundred links in the chain before the package reached its destination; when in fact it arrived after only half a dozen links. He was amazed. Any two individuals could indeed be connected by only a handful of others.'

'Mm, interesting. But how does this affect a group like us?' asked Heppie.

'I see it as an extension of Mrs C's idea about connections, applied not just to a small group like us, but to the world at large.'

'But as you say, we're just a small group,' sniffed Jean. 'And we're hardly typical, after all.'

'Who's to say who or what's typical these days?' protested Heppie. 'Just because we're women, well, most of us, and just because we happen to go to the same leisure centre in the same town doesn't make us freaks. We shouldn't put ourselves down. We're people, just like anyone else. We're typical enough. True, we don't *represent* anyone, we're just us. We are our own story. Well, I've said my piece.'

Everyone was taken aback by the force with which Heppie spoke.

'I don't think we're really a story,' countered Jean. 'If we were, one of us would be the hero, or the heroine: the centre. Someone like Diana, perhaps,' she whispered faintly.

'But Jean, Di isn't, or wasn't actually a Water Babe,' Lynne pointed out, not quite sure of the point she was making. 'She couldn't, or shouldn't be the main character in the 'Water Babes' story.' Lynne used her fingers to indicate inverted commas around the words Water Babes.

'I don't see why not. I don't see why any of us here couldn't be the main character actually. It's just a matter of one's point of view.'

God forbid that Jean should be the main character in any story, thought Luke. *If anyone, I would choose Mrs C to be the heroine in their story. She seems to be the only sane one around here. She touches everyone.*

'Oh,' said Dorothy. 'All this talk about stories and characters is just a distraction. They're just fiction. But this isn't fiction. This is real life!'

No one had an answer to that.

01.00
Somethin' Good

'Well, it's been quite an evening!' said Heppie, standing up.

And that was it: a signal that the party was over, and not just for Heppie and Shula, who also stood up. Everyone saw the signal, heard it and felt it.

'We won't solve the problems of the world, will we?' laughed Lynne.

'We can but try though.'

'Maybe you can, Dorothy,' said Jean. 'But not tonight, please.' This was said humorously, which, given the ups and downs of the evening, boded well for Jean's spirits. Her remark was met with a general chorus of 'Agreed', 'Well said', 'Too right'. She herself balanced the weight of her many disappointments against the weight of the group's support and encouragement, and her new found popularity. Now, at last, the scales came down firmly on the side of the group.

Therefore, on the side of what she rightly took to be her new found popularity.

Everyone made their way into the hall. Salma and Jane retrieved coats from the cloakroom, and Mrs C graciously accepted individual and collective thanks for hosting the party. Of all the guests, Meg was the most effusive and indecorous. She gave Mrs C a sloppy kiss, declaring that this was the nicest house she had ever been in. And could she bring her friends next time?

Various phone calls were made to taxi firms. Dorothy said that she would walk home, and that she would be perfectly safe. But Luke and Lynne insisted on taking her with them in their taxi. Taxis were also ordered for Jean, for Meg and Marsha and for Heppie and Shula. Jane was to stay overnight at Mrs C's house.

Luke went outside to look out for the taxis. In the hall, the women found themselves gathering round the glass-topped table under the chandelier. Someone called out, 'Group hug, everyone!'

There were enough of them to form a complete circle around the table. They stood together, each one with her arms clasped around her neighbours' shoulders. A sense of strong, silent solidarity rippled round the circle. Slowly, the circle began to sway left and right. A voice began to la la the tune of a song. Surprisingly, some thought, it was Dorothy; grim-faced, determined, erect, singing into the middle distance. The others picked up the tune, and one by one, joined in. Quiet and nervy at first, the la la sounds grew slowly in volume and confidence.

To Dorothy's left were Salma and Jane, smiling at each other. Then came Lynne, singing more loudly than the others, assuming the role of cheerleader. Next to her was Jean, soft voiced, her head held down, looking at her shoes. To her left was Marsha, at first slow to join in, and struggling to refrain from biting her bottom lip; then the newly pregnant Meg, swaying more than most, her breasts half exposed by her skimpy dress. She tilted her head back and focused on the ceiling, as if unaware of everyone else. Finally, came Heppie, Shula and Mrs C. With her right arm, Heppie was valiantly holding on to Meg, who seemed to get heavier by the minute. With her left arm Heppie supported her beloved younger sister. Shula had decided, while singing, to examine everyone in the circle one by one, almost as if she were counting them off and memorising their names. When she turned to her left, Shula noticed that as she put her arm round her neighbour's shoulder, she winced. So Shula held her lightly, tenderly. She also saw that the chandelier had picked out the silver threads of her sari. Mrs C was bathed in light.

Dorothy (again, to most people's surprise) then broke into the words of the tune. She seemed to know them very well. The others who knew the words, or even just some of them, joined in when they could, their voices fiercely defiant; and going forward:

'I walked her home and she held my hand
I knew it couldn't be just a one-night stand
So I asked to see her next week and she told me I could
I asked to see her and she told me I could
Somethin' tells me I'm into somethin' good
Somethin' tells me I'm into somethin' good.'

Epilogue

LUKE

Ted and I eventually got home at about quarter past two this morning.

At something like quarter past one I went outside to wait for the taxis. I felt a bit alone, cut off from the rest of them. It was frankly a bit chilly. Then, would you believe, I heard them all singing inside; that Herman's Hermits' song. I looked through one of the windows. There they all were in a circle, shoulder to shoulder, and swaying a bit. Without me. Again. Evidently not one of the 'group', I couldn't help but feel excluded once more. Ah well, they seemed happy enough, and clearly didn't miss me.

Eventually they stopped singing, just as the first taxi was arriving. They all piled out of the house, hugging and kissing each other, though this time I was included in the general goodbyes. There were tears, exchanges of addresses, emails, phone numbers and the like. I couldn't help wondering what Bully Boy upstairs was thinking.

Above all, they wanted to know what would happen to the lessons, now that Di had left. Of course, I was dying to tell them that I had applied for and had already been interviewed in the afternoon for Di's post. I know that Lynne and the sisters had seen me all dressed up in Café Sappho, but I don't think they suspected it was for an interview.

But I couldn't say anything until I had heard the result of the interview! Also, Ted had sworn me to secrecy, or 'confidentiality' as he called it, in case everything fell apart. He was right in thinking that I would be terribly disappointed if I didn't get the job, but he didn't actually say that in so many words. Also, I didn't want to raise any false hopes of my own. And although I wanted to tell the Water Babes that if I was successful, I would make sure that the classes continued in one form or another, it would have been wrong to raise their hopes too. So I said nothing. And felt strangely proud of myself.

There were three candidates in all. The other two were from out of town. I'm not sure. I get nervous about interviews, so I couldn't really tell if it had gone well or not. Ted and I had done some practice runs, which were really, really useful. We role-played in turn, sometimes me taking the part of interviewee and sometimes the other way round. It was just a matter of practising questions and answers, most of which were predictable I suppose.

What mattered more was getting me to act and behave in an appropriate way: Not too much hand flapping; not too many campy quips and that sort of thing. I found all the rehearsals with Ted helped me to see myself as others might see me. And believe it or not, I began to understand myself more. So in the end, I felt calm and composed during the interview. I felt normal! The biggest problem was this weird older woman on the panel, who wouldn't stop grinning at me.

Anyway, Lynne and I dropped Dorothy at her house, which turned out to be a huge Victorian mansion probably worth millions. We got to Lynne's place, and then Ted brought me home.

I told him what happened between me and Mr C. (I assured Ted that I had left no visible marks on the man.) I knew that the situation could not end there, and that Mrs C or Salma would have to call the police, if they hadn't already done so. I was pretty sure that they were safe for the night. But Ted and I have decided to go round later today, and have it out with Salma at least.

Ted lit a cigarette and got us both drinks. I then started to tell him about the other things that happened during the evening. He was either a bit bored, or at least preoccupied. I suppose that as usual, I was gabbling a bit. After all, there was a lot to talk about!

Then he sat beside me on the couch and said, 'Listen to me, laddie. I've got some news for you as well.' Whenever he called me "laddie" I knew it was something serious. Important. My first thoughts were for my father. Was something wrong with Dad? 'No, nothing like that. Now, I know these things are supposed to be confidential. But the thing is this. You got the job!'

'What?'

'Congratulations! You're the new manager of the Greenhill Community Sports Centre, or Sports and Leisure Centre, whatever they call it.'

After all the hard work, the study, the hopes and dreams, I couldn't believe it. 'You mean I'm the new Di?'

'I certainly hope not. You're not the new anyone else. You're the new you. The new Luke.'

'How on earth do you know? Are you sure?'

It seems that Ted had a senior colleague whose wife was on the interviewing committee. She was the older woman on the panel. The one who wouldn't stop grinning at me! Against all the rules and regulations, the wife had persuaded her husband to ring Ted at about nine o'clock. She was even listening in on another extension, chipping in now and then.

Apparently she and her husband have two granddaughters in one of my kiddies' groups. She had heard about me from them, ages ago, and they raved about me! So she was definitely on my side, and wouldn't entertain the idea of giving the job to anyone else.

A happy coincidence if ever there was one. Or as Mrs C would say, "a happy connection".

Also counting in my favour was that I was local (no problem with the hassle of moving expenses), and that I didn't need Di's flat, which the council could now sell. Above all, they were impressed by my degree. The other applicants only had diplomas of some kind.

The references were good too. There was one from my tutor, who praised my capacity for hard work and tenacity! Then one from my bank manager about solvency and stuff. The third reference was from Di of course. I had to have one from her, and I was slightly dreading what it said. I hadn't told her much about my application, largely because she was preoccupied with other things. But it seems that she really spoke up for me, and even recommended me for the job! 'It was, all in all, a good package,' said Ted. 'And apparently you interviewed really well. Very calm and measured. I'm really proud of you, laddie.' He held me close.

'But why didn't you ring me when you got the news?' Which was beginning to sink in.

Ted sat down. There was a long silence. 'Why do you think?'

My mind searched for possible reasons. 'Ah, because you think I would have told the people at the party, don't you?'

'Yes. I know what you can be like. Sorry.' He paused. 'And would you have told them?'

I thought hard about the answer. My former, show-off self might well have said something. But over the past few months, I had grown up a bit. I could feel it inside me. Call it age, maturity, increased self-awareness, discretion or whatever, I was changing. I think that getting the job marked the completion of the change. For the moment at least, and for the foreseeable future, I was where I wanted to be. So few people are that lucky.

'If you can believe it, no, I wouldn't have told them. Two reasons. First, it would have been unfair to pull focus on me during the party. The party wasn't for me, and it wasn't in my house. In fact, sometimes I felt a bit like an outsider.'

'And the second reason?'

'Well, confidentiality of course!'

Ted breathed an almighty sense of relief.

'But that woman on the panel didn't seem to think much of confidentiality, did she? Or her husband for that matter. He shouldn't have rung you really, should he?'

'Dead right.' He shook his head in mock despair. 'So much for confidentiality, especially in provincial town halls!' Ted laughed. 'But just because others don't stick to the rules, it doesn't mean that you shouldn't. So don't say anything to anyone until the letter comes from the town hall. It should be here on Tuesday.' He game me a big, warm, reassuring bear hug. 'You promise?'

'I promise.'

And it is a promise I intend to keep. I can't wait to tell the Water Babes. But only after the letter of appointment arrives.

Acknowledgements

I would like to thank Ann Arscott and Sally Green, for reading and commenting on early drafts of Chapters 1 and 2; Carole White for her technical help and support; and Lindy Lifford, for explaining the mysteries of women's dress sizes. Also thanks to Bournemouth Borough Council, whose aquarobics classes gave me the original idea for a group through which the ideas in the novel could be expressed, though I must stress that there are no connections between the aquarobics groups I attended and the fictional group in the novel. Finally, many thanks to the team at Troubador/Matador for their kindness and efficiency.

Permissions

The author is grateful to Alfred Music Publishing for permission to reproduce lyrics from "It's My Party!", and to sony/atv for permission to reproduce lyrics from "I'm into Somethin' Good" and "Loco-Motion".

'I'm Into Something Good' Words and Music by Gerry Goffin and Carole King © 1964, Reproduced by permission of Screen Gems EMI Music Inc/ EMI Music Publishing Ltd, London W1F 9LD

'The Loco-Motion' Words and Music by Gerry Goffin and Carole King © 1962, Reproduced by permission of Screen Gems EMI Music Inc/ EMI Music Publishing Ltd, London W1F 9LD

'It's my Party' © 1963 lyrics reproduced by permission of the Alfred Music Publishing Company, PO Box 10003, Van Nuys. California 91410

All efforts have been made to contact Golden World Music Publishing who hold the rights to "Nature Boy", but have proved unsuccessful.

Appendix 1

Luke's Music Quiz

Look at the chart on the next page.

Match the music from the lesson with the characters who you think chose it! Give reasons for your answers.

Compare your choices with one reader's answers on page 342.

Remember! Characters may have chosen more than one song. Choose from Di, Dorothy, Heppie, Jean, Luke, Lynne, Marsha, Meg, Mrs C and Shula.

Which TWO characters did NOT choose any song?

Note: All the recordings can be found on YouTube.
   Please see Appendix 2

During the lesson	Music	Chosen by
Ch 3 09.05 p18	I'm into Somethin' Good - Herman's Hermits	
Ch 3 09.10 p20	I Want to Break Free - Freddie Mercury	
Ch3 09.10 p30	Get It On - Marc Bolan	
Ch3 09.20 p44	Handel's Water Music - Handel	
Ch4 09.40 p2	The Skye Boat Song Traditional	
Ch4 09.40 p7	Locomotion - Kylie Minogue	
Ch4 09.50 p22	The Dance of the Knights - Prokofiev	
Ch4 10.00 p37	The Windmills of Your Mind - Noel Harrison	
Ch4 10.10 p50	Waltzing Matilda - Slim Dusty	
Ch 5 10.20 p59	Addicted to Love - Robert Palmer	
Ch5 10.30 p3	Greensleeves - Arranger: David Neveu	
Ch 5 10.40 p17	The Stripper - David Rose and his Orchestra	

The two characters that did not choose any music were…

During the lesson	Music	Chosen by
Ch 3 09.05 p18	I'm into Somethin' Good - Herman's Hermits	Dorothy
Ch 3 09.10 p20	I Want to Break Free - Freddie Mercury	Lynne
Ch3 09.10 p30	Get It On - Marc Bolan	Luke
Ch3 09.20 p44	Handel's Water Music - Handel	Jean
Ch4 09.40 p2	The Skye Boat Song Traditional	Mrs C
Ch4 09.40 p7	Locomotion - Kylie Minogue	Shula
Ch4 09.50 p22	The Dance of the Knights - Prokofiev	Dorothy
Ch4 10.00 p37	The Windmills of Your Mind - Noel Harrison	Heppie
Ch4 10.10 p50	Waltzing Matilda - Slim Dusty	Jean
Ch 5 10.20 p59	Addicted to Love - Robert Palmer	Di
Ch5 10.30 p3	Greensleeves - Arranger: David Neveu	Mrs C
Ch 5 10.40 p17	The Stripper - David Rose and his Orchestra	Jean

I think the two characters who did not choose any music were Marsha and Meg. Susie Jones

Appendix 2

The Music and YouTube

All the music in *The Water Babes* can be seen and / or heard on YouTube. Please use the following references:

Ch 3: 09.05 Warm Up – An Unfortunate Greeting
(I'm into) Somethin' Good
Peter Noone
https://www.youtube.com/watch?v=pvBTMoVNVcI

Ch 3: 09.10 Arms – A Little Accident
I Want To Break Free
Freddie Mercury
https://www.youtube.com/watch?v=kEKVLjXO2Fk

Get It On
Marc Bolan
https://www.youtube.com/watch?v=XspsJACj8WY

Ch3: 09.20 Legs – A Refusal to Continue
Water Music
Handel (Orchestre Paul Kuentz)
https://www.youtube.com/watch?v=2tVmjN1y0Ek

Ch4: 09.40 Dumb-bells and Arms – An Interruption
The Skye Boat Song, instrumental
Traditional (Arr Allan Ferguson)
https://www.youtube.com/watch?v=vrCNEDOla0M

Locomotion
Kylie Minogue
https://www.youtube.com/watch?v=4xiHfuyGVkE

Ch4: 09.50 Woggles and Shoulders –
As Easy as Riding a Bike?
The Dance of the Knights
Prokofiev (City of Prague Philharmonic Orchestra)
https://www.youtube.com/watch?v=vGnuVerNLSA

Ch4: 10.00 Woggles and Bums – Excellence and Panic
The Windmills of your Mind
Noel Harrison
https://www.youtube.com/watch?v=WEhS9Y9HYjU

Ch4: 10.10 Woggles and Feet – Giggles and Constipation
Waltzing Matilda
Slim Dusty
https://www.youtube.com/watch?v=CwvazMc5EfE

Ch4: 10.20 Noodles and Crotches – An Exercise Too Far.
Addicted to Love
Robert Palmer
https://www.youtube.com/watch?v=XcATvu5f9vE

Ch5: 10.30 Warm-down – Distress and a Chorus of Support
Greensleeves, instrumental
Arranger: David Nevue
https://www.youtube.com/watch?v=P5ItNxpwChE

Ch5: 10.40 Free Expression – Snatching Defeat From
The Stripper
David Rose and his Orchestra
www.youtube.com/watch?v=5bLX06yR3wYVictory

Ch7: 19.45 It's My Party!
It's My Party
Lesley Gore
https://www.youtube.com/watch?v=XsYJyVEUaC4

Ch8: 22.00 The Name Game and the Blue-stocking
Nature Boy
Nat King Cole
https://www.youtube.com/watch?v=Iq0XJCJ1Srw

Ch10: 01.00 Somethin' Good
(I'm into) Somethin' Good
Peter Noone
https://www.youtube.com/watch?v=pvBTMoVNVcI